THE REVENGE OF RITA MARSH

THE
REVENGE
OF RITA
MARSH

NILESHA CHAUVET

faber

First published in the UK in 2024
by Faber & Faber Ltd
The Bindery, 51 Hatton Garden
London EC1N 8HN

Typeset by Faber & Faber Ltd
Printed and bound in the UK by CPI Group (UK) Ltd, Croydon CR0 4YY

A CIP record for this book
is available from the British Library

ISBN 978-0-751-38210-1

2 4 6 8 10 9 7 5 3 1

(Not) for the children.

We are our choices.

Anonymous

PROLOGUE

It's difficult to think of that night. I can't do so without seeing the moon full, the lunacy of it eclipsing my mind. I still hear the sound of stone knocking against skull, the crunch of twigs under my soles. The high pitch of owls in the trees that somehow foretold the ending of this story. Even now, I feel him leaning onto me, offloading his weight, *begging* me to carry him further into the dark, where he also seeks answers. That one night defines my entire life. No matter how much I try to move on, there can never be anything else.

He was lying in the woods for over three weeks before they eventually found him. The police combed the earth for ten days with two Beagles and a Labrador, to help sniff out the evidence. Local volunteers from the Horsham area, mainly rich retirees, ex-bankers, a few well-known businessmen and women, laid out tea and digestive biscuits on folding trestle tables. Their presence provided hands-on assistance when police services are already so limited.

Of course, it didn't have to end like this. Had he just done what I asked him to, it would have been different. What people don't realise is that all this time he was lying there, a part of me was lying with him too. I turn it over in my mind, asking why, despite our conversations, he chose to make things more difficult.

I tell them, in no uncertain terms, it was not deliberate. Nor was it premeditated. It was simply a result of a line crossed. But that line, as I know now, is as thin as a spider's web, though it gives the impression that it is unbreakable.

It's complicated, this notion of justice, of trial and retribution. Even now, I cannot quite fathom the morbid fascination, the social commentary, the conflation of events – mine and his, deliberately misconstrued by the press to make *me* look like the criminal. I replay that night in my mind. I tell myself, what happened was *justified*. I am a woman too. I had to protect myself.

I suppose it's inevitable that hunters eventually get hunted down, that they too must pay for the crime for which they hold others to account. In an uprising, the best reason to act is to achieve an outcome so much greater than yourself. But when the system fails you so terribly, what choice do we have but to take matters into our own hands?

I never intended any of the things they accuse me of, however. We do not always choose what we become, nor whom we love. Neither do we choose how things turn out. Sometimes things happen, things beyond our control. Perhaps you'll see for yourself in my story.

I

I've moved through life, these past five years, barely remembering my own name. I've been living as Holly for five weeks. But there have been others, too. Some of them as young as seven, others, anywhere up to fifteen.

The scent of coffee drifts in from a Starbucks on the corner of New Globe Walk, overlooking the pier. I've parked my Ford Transit behind the wooden O of Shakespeare's Globe. This is the only spot I can find without a double yellow line on the edge of London's South Bank. I'm following this dirty trail to the end, to its rightful conclusion.

Last night, I was in South Kensington, next door to the tube, leaning against a lamp post beside a steaming falafel stand. The night before, in Willesden Green, loitering about a corridor in a dilapidated council estate. A week before that, in High Barnet, skirting the edge of a sports field in the rain.

Each week is different. My life is in a permanent state of stand-by. I'm ready to press play at the last minute, but sometimes, like this week, we're called out three times. Other times, just once. It's always the same, regardless. Everything runs like clockwork.

The Friday air is sweet and warm. The sky is tinged with a smear of burnt orange. The city streets of Southwark are swept cleaner than where I live in the leafy suburbs of Harrow-on-the-Hill, with its crooked cobbled lanes and posh public boys' school; where you'd think the rich kids are protected from the horrors of predators, but sadly, not so.

I rest my elbows on the steering wheel. I bend my head to avoid being conspicuous. On the passenger seat to my left is the file I've collated of the back-and-forth in the forum, printed and bound in chronological order. Photos and videos are downloaded onto a USB stick. It's taken five weeks to gather up this evidence, but it could all be for nothing unless the police do their job properly. It's hard not to blame them for the state we find ourselves in, though I try, really, I try. Inaction is killing us all inside.

I'm tired, so very tired. A heaviness soaks into my skin. But I know the tiredness is only temporary. That eventually, when it's all over and done with, I'll feel euphoric.

There's a rumble of a car engine behind me. I glance up at the wing mirror and see a Toyota Sedan, with blacked-out windows, pulling up. It has a dent just beneath the left headlight, which, in the warm haze of sunlight, appears like a giant blister. It's Spider, short and stocky, with long black hair and a criss-cross tattoo like a collar around his neck. He's in the driver's seat wearing dark glasses, sporting his favourite combat jacket. His jaw is freakishly square, he's chomping on gum.

Spike sits beside him, a black cap pulled down low over his face. I can barely make out his familiar hooked nose and ginger goatee, but I know it's him by the way he hunches to the side, as if the weight in his body is unevenly spread. On nights like these, we move together as a three, like a pack of wolves at dusk, going only by our street names. We've carefully prepared for our sting, united by a strong, primal urge to protect the innocent. Spider torn by the pain of his own childhood, interrupted. Spike still searching for answers.

The engine switches off. Spike bends forward, as if fiddling with the car radio. Just then, my phone vibrates.

This is it. Let's go get him!

The headlights blink and Spider nods. It's my cue to get out of the van. I wedge the file under my arm. The door thuds behind me. I head towards a wooden bench overlooking Bankside Pier and sit down, scanning the rippling water. A river bus passes, leaving foamy streaks on the surface. The sun disappears behind a cloud. I shiver in the cool breeze as the sky begins to darken. I'm frantically checking my phone, thumbing through the last messages I've received, or rather Holly has received, from Zia_123.

I can't wait to see you, baby.
It's gonna be so much YUM! xxxx
I waited all day for you. I book a room for us.
Don't tell anyone! ♥

These are from Zia Ahmed, and each time, his messages are the same. But there are hundreds of men just like him, posting comments within only a few minutes of me uploading a new profile picture. This time, I did what I always do to prepare. I sat back, waiting for him to take the bait, careful not to coerce him. I chose my words carefully. But now I'm tested and tortured, every time, by the necessary levels of patience required. You wouldn't believe how many of them there are out there. How little time it takes for a man to flash his penis to a child.

It's 8 p.m. A bell tolls in Southwark Cathedral. I run things over in my mind, to be certain I've got everything with me. That I've left nothing out that might give the police an excuse to call out the integrity of what we're doing. I dial the number for DCI Lawson. He picks up after the first ring.

'We're here,' I say. 'Zia's on his way. I suggest you come now, if you want to be a part of this.'

I hear Lawson sigh on the other end of the line, a muffle as he calls out to someone in the background. There are footsteps behind him, the crackle of a car radio.

'Don't do anything stupid, Rita. Hold him there until we show up. I hope your evidence is solid. If not, it'll be you who's in trouble.'

My throat constricts, but I reassure myself that it doesn't matter what he thinks. Our intention to help is genuine, backed by a legitimate citizen-led initiative that is very much needed.

I glance into the distance and see a stick figure walking towards the bridge, tall, wearing a hoodie with a white stripe down each arm. He looks left and right, then all around him. As he nears, I see his hood is up, strings pulled taut at the neck. His joggers are thin like drainpipes. He moves to the concrete edge and pulls out a phone from his pocket. I look down. Before me, a message appears:

Are you close, baby? I am excited!! I cannot hold it.

I dial Zia's number; I need to be certain I've got the right man. When I hear the phone ring, and see Zia place the phone to his ear, I hang up. I thumb a message:

I don't have much battery left. But just letting you know – I'm on my way!

From the corner of my eye, I see Spike and Spider walking, keeping close to the wall of the Moonlight café. I pick up speed, walking towards Zia, and as I do, Spike and Spider follow straight behind me; closing in.

As I near, Zia is still there, staring down at his phone. He doesn't notice me, creeping up behind him – easy does it now. I start to run. Spike and Spider are running too. I try to catch my breath at the same time, I don't want to alarm him. I can't afford to mess things up at this crucial moment.

I press REC.

'Hello, mate. It's Zia_123, isn't it? But your real name is Zia

Ahmed?' I slow down. 'You're here to meet Holly, is that right? Holly who's *twelve* . . .'

Zia looks up. He scans behind him, then looks back at me. His face is blank, his eyes large and bulging. He has a moustache, thin and fuzzy. It makes him look young, like he might only be eighteen. He's old enough to know better, however. He knows exactly what he's doing.

'You've asked her to meet you here, so that you can take her to a hotel, to have *sex* with her, isn't that right, Zia? You've booked a room in the Travelodge. You've been sending her explicit messages, photos, videos of yourself, for the past five weeks . . .'

My words are rushed, I remind myself to slow down. The sentences must be clear and audible if they are to count.

Zia doesn't answer. What can he possibly say? He steps back, shaking his head and hands. I see he's about to run, but I know he won't get far. Spike and Spider have him surrounded. Their eyes are fixed on him like prey.

Zia staggers back, falling to his knees. He's unable to stop shaking.

I shout from above him, staring down at his crown. His hood slips off his head, falling in folds around his neck.

'You're here to meet Holly with the intention of having sex, aren't you? You realise that's child abuse? Holly is *underage*. She's a *minor*.'

'No, no!'

Here we go again.

It's always the same with these men. First comes the denial, then the lies, the regret. Most often there is an apology, but rarely is there repentance.

Zia slaps his hands against his head. His fingers tug at his hair. 'You are making a mistake. I only here for talking, for *friend-ship*.' He pinches the lobes of his ears, like I'm supposed to believe him – to forgive him, even. His face is broken, cheeks scarlet, hands pressed over his chest.

Spider bends, grabbing hold of Zia's wrists, wrenching them behind his back. 'You're under a citizen's arrest, mate. You ain't going anywhere.'

'Please stop! You are hurting me. This is no right. You are making big mistake.' Zia is hunched. His voice is shrill. Spike digs his elbow into Zia's back, and Zia lets out a groan.

'Woah, easy!' I gesture for them to be gentle. I don't want it to appear that we were too heavy-handed on the video. I know from experience how this could backfire, inciting criticism of our methods from social commentators.

'I have a file here,' I say, thrusting it into the air. 'All your messages are logged. There's no point denying what you did. We have everything you ever wrote in this file. Do you understand what I'm saying?'

He understands, finally he understands. Zia closes his eyes and shakes his head, covering his face. I'm hoping that we're building, finally, to an admission of his guilt.

'Are you denying you ever contacted Holly?'

I must ask, see. There's a risk that people might think we're deliberately confusing him when English is not his first language.

Zia rocks back and forth.

'You knew she was twelve, didn't you? Surely you *knew*,' I say.

'No! I think she is being eighteen, I no realise. Please, sister!' Zia stares at me, his face strewn with tears. His bottom lip trembles. 'You are like me, I can see. I will do anything you are asking.'

I look away – he's taken me by surprise. It's unexpected since that's not how I see myself, nor how the world sees me. My heart pounds inside my chest. A part of me wants to listen to him more – because it's the first time anyone like *him* has said this. But I know I can't allow myself to be distracted. The only thing that matters is that he's guilty.

Spider wrenches Zia's arm a little harder. 'Filthy pervert,' he spits.

Zia's head falls and he stares at the ground, at my shadow shape-shifting and eclipsing him.

'You knew exactly what you were doing.' Spider again.

Spike hawks up phlegm, spitting onto the pavement beside Zia's feet. He wipes his mouth onto his sleeve, hissing, clenching and unclenching his fists.

Zia breaks down, and for a second I think of his family, of their dreams of immigrant opportunity. But then I remember clearly, like I always remember, at this precise moment, what happened to me. What happens, daily, all over this city and beyond, to innocent children.

'You really fucked things up, do you hear me?' My voice breaks.

'I am *begging* you, sister. *Please* . . . letting me go. I am innocent.'

I step back. My legs feel strangely numb. I'm overcome with an overwhelming urge to punch him.

Zia flings himself forward, pressing his hands onto my feet, begging me for forgiveness.

'Sister, sister . . .'

I kick his hands off me. 'Stop it. Just stop it! This is real life, not a Bollywood movie!' The camera's still rolling, my hand is shaking.

I turn and see Spike run towards the police car as it pulls up. Spider stays close to me, so close I can hear him breathing. By now, it's dark. I see only headlights. Spider grabs Zia's collar. 'Get up, you idiot,' he says. 'Get up now!'

'I said, go easy!' I yell. This time it's real, not just for the video.

Spider is taken aback. He gives me a stormy glare.

Zia still presses his hands onto my feet. I feel him wrapping his fingers around my ankles, as if to stop himself from falling.

'You brought this on yourself,' I say to Zia. 'No one made you do it. You would have carried out a crime against a child,

9

and that's rape. Don't you get it? She was twelve, for fuck's sake. What were you thinking?'

There's too much shrill in my voice, too much of *me* being recorded.

'Say something,' I say, urgently. '*Why* did you do it?'

Spider pulls Zia up. By now, Zia is so dazed, so emotional, he can barely keep upright.

DCI Lawson runs towards me. I hear his footsteps, then see him emerge from the dark into the glow of the street lamps. His white polo shirt is buttoned tight at the neck, his face is flushed pink, bald head filmed in sweat. There are three other police officers behind him. Lawson averts his eyes as he approaches, snatching the file from me.

'Nice to see you too,' I breathe.

He grunts. 'This is completely unacceptable,' he says. 'Switch it off. I don't want to see that video on the internet.'

But I'm still filming, holding the camera straight.

Licking his fingers, Lawson leafs through pages of chat history. 'So, what do you have here?'

I avoid filming Lawson's face. The last thing I want is for this film to be about the police when *we've* done all the hard work to get us here.

'It's a file of evidence we've gathered, to help you lot out,' I say. 'I'm filming just in case we need it.'

'Well, I don't,' he snorts, flicking pages, his eyes widening. 'Is the so-called "evidence" you've gathered all here? Nothing missing?'

'Nothing missing.'

'I do hope so, for your sake. And just to be clear, I'm not condoning any of this, so I hope it carries some substance.' He snarls, scraping his teeth against his top lip. Lawson's attitude, right there, is the reason I refuse to work more closely with the police. Other groups have caved in, collaborating with them earlier in the process, succumbing to the pressure. But not us, not Raven Justice. We don't need the police involved in our business, tying us up in red tape, asking too many questions. This is the point we hand over – no sooner.

I clear my throat.

'This is Zia Ahmed. Works in IT at a company called Print Works on Copperfield Street. Recorded residential address: in the file, close to Southwark Station. He's been sending Holly, aged twelve, explicit messages for five weeks. Asked her to meet him here to have, in his own words, a *sex meeting* with her.'

I begin the briefing, official and thorough, just how we believe things should be done. They ought to be grateful. I challenge the police to shoot holes in our methods.

Lawson nods, scanning the pages. He stops, his eyes resting on something in the file. Spike and Spider still have Zia surrounded.

Zia is standing, his hands clamped over his head. 'I do nothing wrong,' he pleads.

'Stop denying it,' snaps Spider. 'We've got everything logged. You knew you were messaging a girl, underage. She told you she was twelve.'

'To be fair, she told you several times,' I say. 'Within the first three lines of your exchange.'

'I guess her age was just a minor detail though, wasn't it, mate?' Spike interjects. 'Or is *young* how you prefer them?'

Lawson slams the file shut.

I whisper to Lawson. 'You can see why things sometimes get heated. He's understandably angry.'

'I've heard enough.' Lawson faces me, his nostrils flaring. The other three policemen stand attentively behind him. 'We'll take over from here. Please put that down.'

I roll my eyes, because every time, this is what he does.

'I mean it. I advise you not to post that video online or you are in danger of jeopardising our investigation.'

There's a crackle in the air – the sound of a police radio. One of the policemen behind Lawson is speaking.

'Fine, I won't post it,' I reply, but something about it feels like a lie. 'I'm filming so that you have a record. So that you *know*, we're being *professional*. I'm fed up with you lot accusing us of being trouble-makers.'

Given Lawson's superiority, I grow convinced that it's worth upsetting the police by posting the video.

He grunts. 'Well, just make sure that's all you're doing.'

In a different light, I might say Lawson had a friendly face, certainly one you could reason with. But not like this. In the dark he appears like an angry wolf, scavenging for food. I can't understand why he seems intent on sabotaging our efforts. It's obvious how much the police need us.

'Just a reminder,' I say, 'we've helped you out here. Given you everything you need so you can make an arrest. I think you'll find it's obvious he's a paedophile. The public won't need much convincing.'

I lower my hand. I'm still recording. I think of the editing needed, but this video is a good one. Bound to attract considerable attention.

'We're the ones trained to do the job properly,' he says. 'Please don't forget it. *We* are the professionals. You're just a bunch of aggravated amateurs. What you don't seem to realise is that you're interfering with the proper administration of justice, with your online presence and camera phone.'

My face burns.

Lawson turns to Zia.

'Zia Ahmed, I'm arresting you on suspicion of grooming a minor, with the intent of carrying out a sexual offence. You do not have to say anything, but it may harm your defence if you do not mention, when questioned, something which you later rely on in court.'

Zia covers his face with his hands, and I hear him call, 'Astagh-firullah, Astaghfirullah,' again and again.

Finally, repentance.

'You're welcome,' I say to Lawson, as the handcuffs lock.

I step back, my job is done. I stand to the side, watching the rest of the scene play out like something in a TV crime series, still filming with one hand on my phone. I pull a loose cigarette from my pocket, and then a lighter to light it up. I watch Lawson saying something to Zia, Spider and Spike standing beside him.

Zia is led away by two officers and Lawson scowls at me, as if *I'm* the criminal here, not Zia. Then he walks away.

I'm filming the pavement, my scuffed trainers. I let the camera roll, only semi-conscious of what I'm doing. I feel my body shake as I think of Zia, as I hear him calling, 'Astaghfirullah, Astagh-firullah,' again and again. I shudder when I think of Lawson, intent on tripping me up, even though I've said – to his *superiors* – that I want nothing more than to work together, peacefully, to help solve this societal problem.

Lawson leads Zia towards the police car. I nod at Spider, our usual departure sign. His long hair blows in the wind. He pats Spike on the back, as Spike limps on ahead with his cap pulled down, hiding from the world and this moment. Spider looks down, his hands wedged into his pockets.

Lawson pushes Zia's head down into the back of the police car, and I hold my phone up again, stretching out my arm, intent on filming this last, satisfying shot. I press the red button to stop recording and drop my arm. By the time I look up, Spider and Spike have gone. I make my way up the hill, towards my van, and I message them in our WhatsApp group.

Intense, but worth it.

I approach the driver's door, and a message fires back in our group from Spike.

Great job. Another one of those scumbags gone. He deserves everything that's coming to him!!

Before long, that familiar feeling arrives like a wave, a slow creep of satisfaction that I did something I ought to be proud of. I saved a child, and in so doing, I reclaimed a small but important part of myself.

In the van, I throw my cigarette butt out of the window and lean back in my seat. I play back the video on my phone, winding myself up thinking of Lawson: how he's quick to criticise what we do, when everyone knows the police can't keep up with the scale of the problem we have escalating in London. They're likely devising a plan to take us out. I wouldn't put it past them. They want to prove we can't be of proper service. It's just like the police to do that.

My face burns.

I clip the beginning and the end of the film, cutting out Lawson and the pavement shots so that it makes for smoother viewing. There's a shot of Zia's face – nice and clear, that makes me smile inside. The public deserve to know about these perverts. Spider and Spike won't mind. I decide I'm going to post the video.

I open the Film2Go app and add in the titles: *Paedophile caught meeting 12-year-old girl for sex!*

With the network signal as bad as it is, the clip takes a couple of minutes to upload onto Facebook. I'm waiting, file buffering. I see Zia's face in my mind again, I can't erase that image of him, the one of him falling to his knees; touching my feet. I hear him crying, begging for me to save him. I swallow hard. I know I must suppress all emotion, but it still gets to me, really it does. You'd have to be twisted not to feel any compassion. There's any number of reasons why he would do something like this. Maybe he was abused himself. He'll no doubt claim he's suffering from a mental illness. They always do, when trying to absolve themselves of taking any responsibility. But some of them *are* victims. I know, too, that he is a son, a brother – maybe even some poor kid's father. But had we given him a chance, he would have committed a crime. The worst kind: the kind there is no coming back from.

Thanks to us, he's been caught. Thanks to us, he's been arrested. It makes no difference to me that he's Asian like me. He's been handed over to the authorities to receive justice, via the laws that govern this country, however imperfectly. We prepared a case and saved the police valuable time, whether or not they appreciate it. Yet right now, I don't feel satisfied. I know it's likely that Child Protection will release him. They'll say we acted too quickly – too recklessly. They'll look for tell-tale signs of our mistakes; look for whether we *coerced* him. And if by some miracle he does get convicted, chances are, the penalty will be too lenient. Zia will be back on the streets, free to re-offend, hunting for his next child victim.

That's why we post videos, Lawson. That's why we do this.

My stomach grows tight. I stare down at my screen. A green tick appears to confirm the video is uploaded.

Everyone knows the problem has grown worse over the years, with thousands of men using or viewing child abuse online each year. It's gotten so out of hand that even the police are beginning to adopt our practices. But they can't do it themselves – they need us. We're more grass roots, more in touch. We can move faster than they can.

Whatever – their politics matters not one jot to me. We're here for the ones who cannot protect themselves. The children are the only ones that mean something. What we do, we do for them. Because on every street corner, in every shopping mall, in a playing field or school near you, I hear them.

As the final stroke of sunlight fades in the sky, I turn my key in the ignition and pull out onto the road. I drive for miles in a straight line, as the dark blur of the city, tinselled in lights, grows distant behind me. After several hours of aimless driving, I accelerate onto the A40 towards Watford.

The low hum of the engine is soothing. A stale taste in my mouth signals morning. I'd love to say my job is done, but the truth is, it's only the beginning.

I bite my lip to stay awake. I tell myself again and again: I'll get them in the end, I always do. I'll hunt them down, one by one. I'll make sure they're off our roads for good. I know who they are, I know where they live. But they will never really know me.

My name is Rita Marsh now, not Rita Patel.

And I am unstoppable.

2

But the following morning is an anti-climax. At home in Raven Court, I'm washing dishes in my narrow coffin-like kitchen, jutting a hip against the edge of the sink. I stare out of the window, teary with condensation. By now, it's a fresh and glorious Saturday morning, one of those you would serenade with a hymn: birds singing, sunflowers dancing, bold and wholly resplendent. My eyes sting with tiredness, but the night still flows through me.

In the distance, I hear coughing and I feel a pull in the pit of my stomach, just knowing that it's down to me to make sure that my remaining two residents are taken care of.

This is my life, an elaborate juggling act. There's not much room for forward planning as I desperately hold things together as best as I can, though I live in fear that, at any given moment, it will all fall apart.

I empty the tub of water in the sink, pulling out the plug, watching the water drain. My stomach twinges as it all comes up again. It's playing on my mind, that sight of Zia last night, bending to touch my feet. His pleading for me to release him. *The audacity of it.*

I don't want to check my messages. Nor do I want to read comments under the video I posted on Facebook. In the cold light of day, I regret I ever posted it. I should have held back, done what the police asked. Now, I've just gone and proved their point. I've subjected myself to backlash.

I look around me, wondering how long it will take to rearrange the furniture.

I need to keep myself occupied.

After letting go of all our staff in March because of mounting costs, I know it's down to me to keep everything afloat, even though my heart's not in it anymore.

Focus.

Breathing.

Find something to do and immerse yourself, fully.

I've been reading books by Dr Geeta Goswami, a psychotherapist, but I'm not sure whether it's helping.

To distract myself, I move to the table where my laptop stands and begin to check the copy I recently rewrote for our website. I move my cursor over the text.

At Raven Court, we are acutely aware of the anxieties that moving a loved one into care can bring. We support each care transition sensitively, with compassion and understanding. Here, you can be confident in our expertise on the issues facing elderly members of our community, such as depression, loneliness, and isolation. We don't judge those families who can no longer cope with caring for their elders. We pride ourselves on the services we offer and promise to take good care of them.

It was something Mum and Dad talked about when they first bought the place twenty-five years ago to try and make a go of things. Not judging, simply caring for elderly residents.

I hear coughing again. I know it's Margaret. She could do with a little extra help. I feel ashamed not thinking of her sooner, thinking only of myself.

I rush into the kitchen to fix a bowl of soup. I break a piece of bread from a baguette delivered fresh from the local bakery, and I walk up the stairs.

I glance up at a framed photo of my parents on the landing. It's a shot of them on their wedding day, hanging on the cracked wall to my left. My mother with her wispy blonde hair, the shawl of her red sequinned sari swept over her shoulder. My father with his philandering eyes, his shock of black hair, carries the air of a moody Heathcliff. Both sides of the family – Indian and white, stand awkwardly in the background. I stare at my father's face once more, squarely in the eyes. Then I look away, determined not to let him ruin my day.

When my parents died, almost seventeen years ago when I was eighteen, I worked my hands until they were sore. Something about that very thought feels Asian. It's the only trait I'm willing to accept, since ordinarily, I despise being labelled.

I walk along the corridor, carefully carrying a tray.

Immerse yourself in what you're doing. Pay attention to the smallest of details.

But then I see Zia's face again, I can't seem to block him out. I feel his hands pressing down onto my feet. I'm aware he sees me as one of his own, that he expects forgiveness because he believes we have a shared ancestral history. His assumption tugs at the part of me I prefer to keep hidden, that Asian side of my father's line that I've deliberately blocked out, convincing myself, when I look in the mirror, that somehow I am different.

I walk along the corridor to Margaret's room.

Focus on the moment. Do not succumb to distraction.

This place is tired, shabby and neglected – Mum and Dad would be livid at the state of it. It's nothing like the polished, prim Victorian property they once made cosy and intimate, home to a full house of lively residents. But it's not my fault. I can't do it all. I can't unleash the potential in this business when I'm cleaning the streets. I never wanted to run this place to begin with. But it gives me an income, at least. I'm grateful to have a business. Whilst the decor might be dated, everything patterned and velvet like something out of the sixties, it's safe and clean. Raven Court is one of the most affordable care homes in Harrow, set back from the main road in a private patch of green, nestled behind a cluster of giant oak and cedar trees.

As I enter the bedroom, I see Margaret lying there, still and peaceful, her skin soft and grey. Her lids are half-closed – she's drifting in between worlds. The slit of her mouth is open just enough for me to hear her breathing. Her lips are cracked, crusted with salt, and form an oval shape.

I pat Margaret on the arm, she grunts and jerks forward, spluttering as if she's spitting out medicine.

'How are you feeling, dear? I thought you might like a little soup, freshly made.'

I place her tray on the table next to her bed. Her blanket is messy, so I go about rearranging it. She opens her eyes and tries to get up, but then she relaxes again.

'Would you like me to help you up?' I peer into her eyes, as she stares up at the ceiling. 'Do tell me what you need, anything you like. I'm here for you, Margaret.'

She drops her head to the side, staring at me. Recognition descends and she smiles, but only briefly, then she's gone again.

I fumble inside my pocket for an ophthalmoscope. I open her droopy lids, shining a light on her pupils.

When Margaret first arrived, her son, Mark, dropped her off like she was a bit of dry cleaning. His wife waited for him in the car. She was freshly tanned from a recent trip to the salon, honking the horn between applying thick coats of lipstick. That was eight years ago. In that time, Margaret and I have spent hours in conversation. She's told me stories about the Second World War. How she met Bill, her late husband, in a bar, falling in love at first sight. How he cradled her in his arms for five hours when she miscarried their first child.

I move closer. 'Perhaps you'd like me to read something to you,' I whisper.

Margaret's hand slips and I replace it onto the bed. I walk to the bookshelf beside the door, scanning the shelves for a volume of poetry. I run my fingers along the spines and pull out a book: *Poems for Life*. I open it up on a random page. Leaning a shoulder against the wall, I begin to read.

Life is one long breath,
blown on the coldest day . . .

I manage just one line before she begins shouting.

'Leave me alone! Get out, just get out of here!'

I stand up straight, staring at her, part of me resigned to another one of her episodes.

Margaret is strangely propped upright in bed, her blue cellular blanket is messy after I've only just rearranged it. Her back rests against a pillow, her face a network of angry lines and creases. Her eyes are wide open, so full of tears, and she coughs. Before I can do anything, she throws her bowl. I jump back, slamming my back against the wall. Her bowl hits the edge of a table and smashes, as if in slow motion, to the side of me.

'Get out, you stupid woman. I don't want to hear your poetry, do you hear?'

My legs are strangely anchored to the floor as I try to take in her words.

'Get out I said!'

My eyes fill up and my lips tremble. Her dementia is acute now, and I know none of this is her fault. She doesn't know what she's doing. But still, her words are hurtful.

I bend to pick up the broken pieces of her bowl. The carpet is sodden with soup. Margaret is still muttering something; coughing, spluttering, turning her head into her pillow. I place the pieces on the tray.

'I'm sorry, Margaret. I just wanted to do something nice—' but by now, her shoulders are juddering.

'Go!' Her voice is muffled.

I close the door behind me as I leave, intent on giving her a little privacy. I walk down the stairs, sliding one hand along the banister for support, carrying the tray in the other. I try not to listen to the sound of her crying, nor focus on my erratic breathing. I place Margaret's tray on the kitchen counter, then settle down at the wooden table.

How long can it continue, this double life? This over-extension of myself, this predatory prowl that others might call *obsessive*? Because right now, I don't seem to be doing either of them particularly well.

I pull my laptop out of its felt cover.

It's all grown too much. There's no way I can deny it. The hunting is intense, high-risk, relentless. I'm aware there's only so much I can do. Each day, the problem is growing worse. What I need now is a peaceful night, a bit of time to think. If I'm honest with myself, perhaps even to relinquish the heavy weight of this responsibility. But what kind of world would this be if we all gave up? That would be too easy; that would be like failing.

I begin to search aimlessly . . . then I search for something specific: a chatroom. Just something to occupy me through the night, whilst my mind continues its incessant pendulum-swinging.

Sunday morning is gorgeous and I'm feeling better rested. I drive to Costco Cash & Carry, that supersized one in Wembley, just behind the football stadium. I need to keep myself loaded with chores like restocking the kitchen larder – that's all I keep thinking about. I don't want to dwell on the video I posted, because now I've received some new messages on Teen Chat and Playground. It's the two social sites I frequent most often.

This time, I've uploaded a Snapchat-filtered photo of a girl with long hair and a cute button nose. She's surrounded by a kaleidoscope of butterflies. I call her Nisha Mistry and she is a wonderful creation. Curled up on a bed, next to a sunset-coloured Corgi, she's pouting for a selfie, just like young girls do when they see older, more popular girls doing the same. She's wearing yellow shorts and a T-shirt, and I'm sure, just by the way Nisha is seated, that image of her will reel them in. Sure enough, it takes only two minutes.

Hello sweetie. How old are u?
WOW! You look lovely in yellow. A real sunshine!
You're so well developed. Has anyone ever told you that?
13? You look more like 18! Lol!

The rest of the responses are so vile, I immediately want to delete them. But next come the photos, each one of them a reminder of why I spend my nights hunting. In this job of round-the-clock social engagement, with messages back and forth, you see photos and videos you'd rather not see and can never *unsee* once you've clicked on them. The filth is enraging.

I stare down at my hands, pale and worn, hard and veiny.

There comes a point when it all becomes too much.

Caught in the middle of perversion is a feeling so familiar, it's almost normal.

I catch a glimpse of my face in the wing mirror.

I'm too white to be Indian, too Indian to be fully white. You'd think these days it's good to be an inbetweener, that it's an advantage to sit on the fence, to be free to pick a side. But that's not how it works, because often you're left alone, undecided.

What I am is a mishmash of cultures that can bend and flex to suit different worlds, and because of that, I am useful. But deep down, when the lights are dimmed, when the noise settles, I'm aware just how confused I feel.

In Costco, I snake my trolley in and out of the aisles, but at the same time, I'm deleting messages hurtling against the light of the blue background on my phone. Moving to aisle 25 lined with freezers, I regain a sense of calm, as the cold air cuts into my face.

I would really love to meet you. How about Wednesday?

In the back pocket of my jeans, already too tight around my waist, my second phone – my personal one – vibrates. I pull it out, and I see there's a new WhatsApp message from Raven Justice.

10.19 Spider:
Earth to flamin' Raven. Where are you?? Call us urgently.
That video you posted! This one blowing up badly!!

I stand there for a second, trying to comprehend what they mean. But then a link to a news article appears:

www.standard.co.uk/zia-ahmed

I'm moving, pushing my trolley – literally holding my breath. I click on the link as I park myself against a wall, next to jars of low-price pickles and pitted olives.

The signal in-store is so bad, my phone keeps buffering. I watch everyone around me with their families, busy bees with their shopping baskets. I edge further along the window, in search of better reception.

Finally, the article appears:

18 August 2019
STING VIDEO GOES VIRAL
Alleged paedophile jumps into Thames after Raven Justice confrontation.

In a face-off on Friday, controversial vigilante group lured Zia Ahmed, aged 32, into a honey-trap with fake profile, logging online sex chat with 12-year old girl.

Raven Justice filmed his police arrest and posted the sting video on Facebook where it received thousands of likes. Ahmed took his own life in the early hours of Saturday morning after being released by the Metropolitan Police on grounds of insufficient evidence. His jump was captured on CCTV. Following his death, the police have confirmed they are not looking for any further suspects in connection to the incident.

Ahmed moved to the UK from Pakistan with his parents in 2004 with hopes of a better life. He studied Business Management at London Metropolitan University and later worked in IT at a printing company in Southwark. His phone was found on the edge of the bridge from the spot where it is believed he jumped. The last recorded message was to his mother, declaring his love and innocence.

A relative of Zia who wishes to remain anonymous said: 'I can't believe what's happened. Zia was a good boy with a bright future. Whatever he was accused of, we are certain it is a mistake. He was targeted by this group without a fair trial and that is not right. The shame led him to take his own life and the family are suffering badly. We will never recover from this loss. We ask the public to please respect our privacy.'

Raven Justice is a covert group of vigilantes who prefer to remain anonymous. The group is believed to be organised by a woman and two male accomplices. In the last five years, their efforts have led to 25 arrests but only two convictions. Following Zia's suicide, there is mounting pressure for them to reveal their identity. The Association of Chief Police Officers says the group's tactics have grown increasingly hostile in recent weeks. 'We do not condone their activities because their interference corrupts vital evidence, but we are trying to find

ways of working together, peacefully and constructively, with
vigilante groups. It's part of a longer-term strategy.'
  Spokespersons for Raven Justice declined to comment.
Do you know the people behind Raven Justice? Contact us
with any information: news@standard.co.uk.

I'm shaking so hard I don't realise there's a woman beside me,
talking.

'Excuse me,' she says curtly, 'could you move your trolley?
You're blocking the walkway.'

I stare at her for too long.

It can't be. It just can't be true. He can't have killed himself.

The woman stares at me, as if waiting for me to apologise. She
moves her trolley past me with a little girl in dungarees skipping
at her side and shakes her narrow head.

'*Honestly.* Some people. No sense of urgency.'

10.23 Spider:
This is the last thing we need. That scumbag is dead and now
we're being blamed for it!

I turn right and see a 'payment' sign, but the queue to the tills
is so long I don't think I'll ever get out of the store quick enough.
All I can think about is the article, how we try to do a good thing,
to stand up for what we believe in, but then one mistake makes it
blow up and somehow, we have another problem to deal with. I
didn't want him dead, though. None of us wanted that.

I click on Facebook, scanning the comments beneath the video
clip of Zia.

Paedo! Sick bastards like that need locking up!

Go, go Raven Justice! Sure as hell the police aren't moving fast
enough.

But there is another post too, from Mary_100.

Why OUT him like that? Why not just go through the courts?? How do WE know for sure he did anything??!

Yeah. I agree. Roughing him up like that was bang out of order.

The latest comment:

Are you happy, Raven Justice? That poor man is DEAD!!

I pay up as fast as I can, but my hands are shaking so much I can barely hold onto my wallet.
What if I got it wrong?
What if Zia was innocent?
For a second, my mind scrambles from overload, but I manage to breathe, to retrace steps in my mind. I distinctly remember dialling the number sent to Holly in the chat – and it was Zia, *Zia*, that answered.

Next thing I know I'm in my van, slumped at the wheel, counting likes and scrolling through endless messages. I bite my lip so hard it starts to bleed. On one phone:

I love you so much, Nisha. You are so beautiful

On another:

Ruislip Lido – BE THERE – 1hr.

I start the engine, about to press my foot down. This is a sign, surely, that it's over. I need to get out. There can be no more indecision.

Through the windscreen, I stare up into the sky, watching clouds gather. I see the arch of Wembley Stadium stretch across the horizon like a steel rainbow and I wonder, even though I've driven past it so many times, what it must feel like to sit under it, staring up into the dark as the roof closes.

3

I wait for Spider by the reservoir – he says he's coming alone. Spike is too shaken to leave the house. He's busy seeking legal counsel.

I watch the rush of dirty water lick the edge of the sand and I bend to pick up a stone, skimming it across the water. I imagine what it might be like to visit the lido with a loved one, to enjoy a summer picnic, watching geese waddle by. I wonder what it must be like to live a *normal* life. Now, *normal* feels so foreign to me. A flock of ducks splash about, raising a squall as they flap their wings. I pick up and throw another stone. It only just misses them.

I shouldn't have posted that video. It's the one time I should have listened to the police. The damage is irreversible and it's all my fault but there is nothing I can do to change it.

Behind me, footsteps crunch into the sand, that familiar sound of thick trainers. A warm breeze sweeps over my face, and I hear leaves rustling.

Spider stops a few steps away from me. His long black hair is loose and messy, tendrils blow on either side of his head. He nods towards a wooden bench next to the fake beach and we walk together towards it in silence.

I take a seat, watching the rise and fall of his chest. I wait for him to say something, but his voice is shaky.

'Where you been, Raven?' He avoids my eye, remains standing. 'We're in a right mess. We need to protect ourselves.'

'I'm sorry. It's all my fault. Lawson said not to post the video, but he wound me up so badly.'

He sighs, tapping a cigarette on his packet, lighting one up with the schwick of his lighter.

'Well, it's what we do. It's why we're effective. Five hundred thousand followers and growing. But this last job has blown up badly. Some of the comments from our own fans . . .'

Spider shakes his head. He raises a foot onto the wooden seat next to me to better balance himself.

'It's exactly what the police want – to deter us,' I say. 'They'll use it to apply pressure.'

'Yeah, everyone is talking about it. Zia's all over the news. The police are *blaming us*, can you believe it? What a cheek. No one understands that we were there to do good.'

I pinch the skin on my hands. Maybe this is the moment to tell him, we can't go on as we are. I, for one, have had enough.

'We're not responsible for that scumbag dying,' he says, sucking hard on his cigarette. He breathes out smoke, slowly. 'Zia killed himself. We never pushed him. But still, there's the video.'

'I'm worried they will use that to threaten us. Either shut us down or get us to work *their* way – and *with* them.'

'Well, we won't do it,' spits Spider. 'That's what we agreed.'

'But pressure is mounting,' I say. 'It's only a matter of time before they put in place formal regulations. Maybe we need to reassess things.'

He grunts. 'It's like you're getting cold feet, Raven. You're getting all scared, when all along, we knew the risks we were taking.'

'I'm sorry,' I say, digging my hand into my pocket.

'I say we just fuck 'em,' he says, after a while, lighting up another cigarette when the other one expires. 'We'll do the handover because that has to happen with the police. But we can keep surveillance and sting activities separate. Worked fine all this time, didn't it? We don't need to co-operate with them. Those other groups are weak for giving into the pressure.'

'I agree.' But I say it with an ulterior motive. For the first time,

I feel bad that I'm letting down my own brothers. 'I say we *do* nothing. We *say* nothing. It will probably die down, anyway. But this is a moment, you know? We need to reassess our future.' There's a shrill in my voice. My heart beats faster.

Spider is silent, like he's thinking.

'I never said I wanted out.' He turns, glaring at me long and hard. 'Is that what you're thinking?'

'This story is big. There is no way we'll survive it,' I say with my head down.

Spider takes another drag on his cigarette, and I ask him how Spike is. He does not answer, but stares into the sand, kicking at a dried worm with the stub of his toe.

'Well, look how that turned out,' says Spider. 'You can't be serious.'

'I am.'

'Jesus, Raven. Have you lost your mind? Five years of hard work and you talk as if it's nothing.'

'They want us shut down,' I say. 'Don't you see? It's only a matter of time. They know we won't ever work the way they want us to. And I don't want to do anything different.'

'But maybe we bring more people in,' says Spider, 'rather than packing it all in. If the problem is getting worse . . . we should *grow* this.'

I consider his statement and feel a slow panic rising inside me. It's the same feeling I have whenever things get too much, like things are growing and sprawling out of me like poison ivy.

'We need better protection,' he says, 'like, proper security and filming equipment. You said so yourself, the problem is getting worse, the police can't cope, so we need to get ahead of it.'

'We're not like those other groups,' I say. 'It's always been the three of us. I would rather we didn't do it than join the others.'

Spider throws down his cigarette, stamping his foot onto it. 'But if we expand, we could keep our independence. There are groups all over the country. We could join them. Form a coalition.'

I scoff and Spider glowers at me. 'If you're wanting out just say it, right? Don't mess us about because our whole lives are invested.'

I almost choke – it's like a wet sponge is lodged in my throat. I resent the way he suggests that I haven't given up my life too. Like I've not invested myself sufficiently in the movement. I was the one that started it.

'Go fuck yourself,' I snap. It's all I can think to say.

Spider throws his head back and laughs. 'So, I guess we ain't good enough for you now, eh? One sting goes wrong in five years and suddenly you want out.'

'I never said that. But, *yes,* that is what I want.' For the first time, I am sure. That is my decision. Finally, I've blurted it out.

But Spider says: 'Fuck you, Raven. A bit of trouble and then, *kraa kraa,* Raven flies. What about the children, eh? How can you think of just yourself?'

He flaps his arms making idiotic squawking sounds, and finally I get up and walk away, Spider's voice trailing. There are children playing behind me, a dog barking, a baby crying. I wipe a sleeve across my eyes, and I tell myself it's over; there's no way I'm ever looking back. I'll find another way of doing good because I *can.* I am Rita Marsh today, but tomorrow, I can easily be someone else.

4

I'm parked outside a private clinic in Ealing, in a posh, residential house. Beside the front door, to the left of the brass knocker, a small plaque reads: *Dr Geeta Goswami, Psychotherapist.*

It isn't too intimidating here – despite a statue of a lion baring its teeth, pouncing in mid-air, positioned right by the front window. In the front garden, an olive tree emerges from the gravel in somewhat Biblical fashion. I can't help but wonder if it's deliberate, this middle-class understatedness. Nothing on the outside of this clinic alludes to the number of books its owner has sold. Nor the column she writes weekly in the *Women's Digest*, Geeta's Corner, that's got everybody discussing their personal problems.

Geeta has been in demand ever since her book, *What's Wrong with Me?*, came out. I realise it's the same question I've been asking myself, repeatedly, ever since Zia killed himself a week ago. Each time I think of him, I am conflicted. On the one hand I know I have made the right decision, that it can't go on, this juggling act of a life, because in saving others, I've lost something of myself. Hunting has become too dangerous. But then on the other hand, I think of the children. I'm plagued with guilt. In the night I wake up in cold sweats, tossing and turning for hours.

My appointment is at three and I'm petrified at the prospect of trying to untangle the past five years. Even though I've talked to Geeta in my thoughts, had numerous private conversations in my mind, told her what I experience – overwhelm, foreboding, anxiety – I don't know where to start. Each time, I've heard her warm, melodic voice, her strong Delhi accent, assuring me that such thoughts and feelings, given the circumstances of my life, the changing world in which we find ourselves, are *entirely* to be expected.

But now, here I am, about to talk to Geeta in real life.

I switch off the engine and walk up the front path, chequered in black and white stone. As I take a deep breath and ring the doorbell, I tell myself, once again, I'm doing the right thing. I need to *do* this, or – if left any longer – I risk doing something else stupid.

An old lady answers. She's wearing a sensible white blouse, a dainty row of pearls. She greets me with eyes that seem to say, *'you're here – well done'*, and ushers me into the living room.

'Have a seat, Rita. I'll take you up to see my daughter in just a few minutes.'

She rearranges the magazines on the side table.

'Would you like some tea while you're waiting? Maybe some water?'

Just being in that front room, with its scent of lavender unfurling from an oil burner, walls dotted with black-and-white Hollywood photos, I want to start bawling.

'Water would be lovely,' I croak.

I glance up at the bookshelf, stuffed with books on poetry and modern art, while I wait to be called.

Inside Dr Goswami's office lies a row of hand-carved elephants, bespeckled with mirrors, that look like they're taking a long, leisurely walk along the back shelf. I sit down onto a stiff leather chair, biting my tongue, suddenly hungry and craving chocolate.

'Oh wow,' I say, as my eyes fill up. 'I'm sorry. I wasn't expecting this at all. Ever since I got here, I feel . . . weepy.'

My body trembles and I look around, as if there's someone else in the room responsible for my reaction.

'It's perfectly normal,' says Geeta, kindly.

She hands me a scented tissue and I thank her, dabbing my eyes.

'Take your time.'

'I'm sorry, I don't know what's happening, or why I'm crying,' I say, hurriedly. 'I feel so stupid. This is not what I'm usually like, at all.'

She leans back into her chair, waiting for me to compose myself. After a while, she tells me a little bit about her background.

'I was born in India,' she says, placing a finger on the edge of her glasses. 'But now I'm a permanent resident in the UK. I love London and what I do. I love to help people. Would you like me to help you, Rita?' She leans forward, peering at me.

I nod like an eager child.

'Tell me a little about yourself,' she says.

I tell her about Raven Court, about my parents and their car crash. I figure it's probably best to start there.

'I see. I'm very sorry to hear that. It must have been difficult.'

I take a sip of water. 'I'm over it,' I say.

'Are you?'

'Truly.'

Her brow creases, and she scribbles something on her pad.

I notice the room smells of instant coffee and buttered toast. I lean back further into my chair, making myself comfortable.

I stretch out my legs to help me relax, taking in the bare breasted figures of the Gustav Klimt prints on the wall. There's one I can't seem to take my eyes off, just beside the bookshelf. It's a close-up of a woman crying golden tears. It hangs next to another print of a woman naked in the embrace of another nude female. Something inside me prickles.

Geeta looks up, following my eye to the wall. She is concentrated as she goes on. 'I'd like to manage your expectations of what these sessions are and what you might get out of them. Essentially, they provide a safe space for you to process unconscious emotions, so you can probe more deeply into things.'

I nod, my body seizing. My chest tightens.

'That is how we begin to shift things,' she says, 'through inner enquiry. That is how we can experience a transformation, by re-arranging thoughts and emotions, patterns of behaviour. There is no expectation of outcomes, however. No pressure at all. So, tell me, Rita. What is it you do in your spare time?'

I hesitate.

I hunt paedophiles, Geeta. They're everywhere, did you know that? It wouldn't surprise me if there's one not far from here, perhaps even a few doors down . . .

'I don't really have any spare time, Doctor. Do you? This is London. I'm terribly busy looking after the elderly as part of my day job. But now, I'm determined to make provisions to change things somewhat.'

She's silent, as if waiting for the space between us to swell and to contract.

'That's good,' she says. 'It's a very good start.'

'Over the years, I seem to have filled my life with so many things,' I say after a few minutes. 'So much of it is important, *has* been important, but now I can't seem to prioritise, or distinguish those things that are just for me. I don't know who I am or even what I want anymore.'

She nods, like she understands, and I wonder, then, how many more women like me sit in this chair, saying something similar.

'And how does that make you feel?'

'Lost,' I say. 'Right now, I'd say I'm in a dark place. I don't know if I will ever find myself again.'

Geeta falls silent.

'Was there ever a time when you *did* feel like yourself?' she asks. 'When you were not lost. Is that something you can remember?'

It is an insightful question, but I don't know the answer. Instead, I grow aware of how my fingers begin to tingle, how my shoulders ache. 'I can't say that I can, specifically. I don't know how in touch with myself I really am.'

'How does your body feel?'

'I've had a few problems,' I say.

'Oh?'

'I menstruated late, growing up. When everyone started their periods at school . . . I was still waiting for mine.'

'At what age did it arrive?'

'Seventeen.'

'And now? Are you regulating normally?'

I look down. 'Sometimes. It's not something I necessarily pay too much attention to.'

Geeta is thinking, then writing something down on her pad which I realise I find most irritating; that noise of her pen scratching against the paper makes my teeth feel funny.

'So, is this what we do, just talk?' I ask. 'Nothing like regression or muscle relaxation. Mindfulness?'

Geeta smiles, like I'm quoting a line from her book, going out of my way to pay her a compliment.

'We talk, yes,' she says. 'Do you like talking?'

'Depends.'

'Depends on what?'

'On what we talk about.'

'What do you like to talk about?'

For fuck's sake.

'Anything,' I say. 'I can talk about anything. It's one of my strengths. When you do what I do for a living, you need to know how to communicate.'

'I see. And what do you do for a living?'

I think to myself, this session is costing me £175 an hour and I'm *a-mazed* by how much I'm being fleeced.

'Don't give me the official description, but tell me of its meaning,' she says.

'I don't know how to answer that,' I say. 'Is there something we can *do*?'

'Do?'

'You know, like those exercises you mention in your book.'

'You've read my book,' she says. She smiles.

'I have and it's just that I think I would respond better to doing something rather than talking about it. I've done enough talking, and it's not helping.'

'I see.'

I want to leave just then. I consider cutting my losses and getting the hell out of there.

'Maybe you can give me some tablets,' I say.

'Oh?'

'I'm getting spots. Look.'

I show her a rash on my arm.

She peers at it, and I notice her face contorting a little.

'But you sleep well, yes – or do you have trouble sleeping as well?'

'It's not great at the moment.' I take a deep breath, curling my toes in my trainers. 'I do the counting exercise you talk about in your book. And when I feel overwhelmed, I focus on key details, like you say, to slow down my thoughts.'

'Very good.' More scribbles. 'It's better you visit your GP for that rash. Show her what you showed me and have it examined properly. I'm afraid I'm not qualified to prescribe treatment for it. As for sleeping, it's best to find alternatives before resorting to tablets.'

'Look, I'm not being funny, but I think maybe this is not working.'

She smiles, knowingly, like she knows better than me, better than everyone else, about my own life story. 'Why do you say that, Rita? We've only just begun.'

'I'm feeling a bit . . . restless and bothered . . . just sitting here. It's not you – please don't think it's *you*. It's probably me. I'm not cut out for this.'

38

'We need time. You've started a process. You need to give yourself permission to feel . . . different emotions,' she says.

She can see I'm not impressed.

'What is it you feel you should be doing?' she asks.

'Something constructive.'

'Like?'

'Like . . . being there for others when they can't stand up for themselves. Something like that.'

'I see. Interesting. And what if you didn't speak for others, and you just spent a few days in quiet contemplation, connecting with yourself. How would that make you feel?'

'I'd get irritated,' I say.

Geeta looks up at the clock and I see that an hour has passed – which is just as well. I have no idea how the hour ended so quickly, but I'm relieved the session is over with.

'You've done a great deal of work just now,' says Geeta, in a school counsellor kind of way. I guess it was not intended to patronise, but it was patronising all the same. 'How do you feel about it?'

I shrug my shoulders. 'Numb, I suppose.'

'Numb is a perfectly valid response. It does not require interrogation. Are you committed to your growth and inner enquiry? If you are, we can really *do* something together.'

I stare at her, blankly.

'It does require some work, Rita. I will not pretend that it is anything but hard work. You need to be ready and wanting it for yourself, which I think you are – or at least, I hope so.'

She smiles, and to me – for the first time, she appears radically different to how she appears in her book or in online interviews. Perhaps I haven't given therapy a chance, but there's a strange smell to it, like spoilt milk.

I realise I've blocked out thoughts of Zia from my mind for a whole hour, but now his face returns, pressing itself onto my brain with greater ferocity. I squeeze my eyes closed. I try to focus on the blurry kaleidoscope of colours behind my lids. But Zia is still there. I see him clearly, I feel him close to me.

'Do what works for you, Rita. If it's breathing and mindfulness that works, continue with that until our next session. Just don't be hard on yourself. I can see you're wanting to be present for others, to rescue even. But maybe now is the time to concentrate on yourself.'

'Is it effective, longer-term?' I ask.

'Is what effective?'

'The breathing.'

'Sure it is. But it depends entirely on where the breath originates.'

I stand to gather my things, and in the corridor, I wait for Geeta to finish talking to her mum in low whispers. I'm unable to make out precisely what they're saying. I scan the walls, my eyes drifting across the health and safety certificates on display. I see a noticeboard, plastered with leaflets on various national and local support services available.

Relate. You are not alone. Come and talk to us. 0300 003 2324.

But I don't want to talk anymore. I'm not sure what it is that I want. I just know I don't want this. What I want – and need, is time to think about what to do next, to sort out my life and to catch up on all the time I've lost, if that's even possible. I want to forget the lifestyle of late nights and online roaming. I know I can never tell Geeta the truth about what I did – what I still think about daily. She wouldn't understand. No one ever does.

As I descend the stairs from the clinic, my feet sinking into the carpet, I realise how heavy and stirred I am. Just one session, and I feel worse than when I started.

I pay up at the desk in cash when Geeta's mum opens a logbook. She hands me a hand-written receipt, her eyes flashing with the anticipation of booking me for another session.

'When would you like your next one?' she asks.

I shake my head. 'I'll call you.'

I get out of there as quickly as I can, past the olive tree, the lion, and I turn the key to the engine of my van, determined never to set foot in that place again.

And yet the next day, I am strangely sensitive, like I might burst into tears at any minute. But with so much to do in Raven Court, I cannot allow myself to spend time dwelling on it.

I'm in Derek's room. He's seated on a plastic chair beside his bed wearing only a towel wrapped around his waist. His back is hunched, and he glances up, his eyes cloudy, breathing raspy. I know he won't stay still like that for too long. He's calm for now at least, and that is a welcome relief for a Tuesday morning.

I wring my cloth over the sink, feeling my palms burn, and I listen to the sound of the water trickling; I find it strangely soothing. I unfold the damp cloth and turn to Derek. 'There we go, all nice and ready . . .'

I move closer to him, pulling on a pair of plastic gloves.

'I'm going to start with your face, then your neck and shoulders. When you're comfortable, I'll move down below. Would that be okay with you?'

I fold the towel into quarters.

It might not appear like there's much left of Derek, just sagging folds of skin, but he has some spark in him. Most days, I can barely keep him quiet. Behind his eyes there's a flicker, sometimes a flame; the story of his life plays out, over and over again.

'I'm using lavender-scented soap. You like lavender, don't you Derek? It was the first thing you asked me when you checked yourself in, eight years ago. Do you remember? You asked me whether I grew any lavender in the garden.'

Today, Derek's face hangs heavy, and even though the day is warm, the skin on his arms is pricked like chicken skin.

'I don't want you to catch a chill. I'm getting this over and done with quickly, I promise.'

Derek mumbles something as I move closer to him, bringing my face up close to his.

'What is it, Derek? Thinking about home on the dairy farm in Yorkshire? A dry shampoo would be good. Or, if you sit by the sink, I'll happily wash your hair with water. Which would you prefer?'

I wipe his hands to relax him. But Derek flinches so I step back, not wanting to alarm him.

'. . . I hear the old girl barking. I tell ya she's barking outside my window. Ain't nowt wrong with the marmalade . . .'

I glide the cloth over his shoulders, brushing long strokes down his arms. I soap the cloth once more, then move it down, along his chest.

'There's lavender on this towel. Can you smell it? It's ever so fragrant. Here I come, I'll be gentle. I'll clean carefully . . .'

Next, I apply the dry shampoo, the silver strands of his hair running between my fingers.

'There's nothing to worry about, Derek. It's me, Rita Marsh. You remember me, don't you? Rita from Raven Court. Just wiping you down. You'll be fresh and sweet-smelling in no time.'

He mumbles something, rocking back and forth in his chair. I can barely make out the words. Something about horses and hares.

I'm out. I'm finally free. Free to do whatever I want and to begin a new journey.

Derek stares up at the yellow stains on the ceiling, as if deciphering a hidden sign in the water marks.

He reaches out his hand and gently strokes my hair as I clean him down below. I think to myself, if I ever sold this place, these are the moments I would miss most. Just he and I, talking alone.

'Rita Marsh . . .'

I flinch, as if someone saying my name out loud – my new name – is somehow alien to me. 'That's me,' I say. 'I'm here. Not exactly going anywhere.'

I stand, then move towards the sink. I peel off my gloves, carefully washing my hands.

'Why you always on yer own?'

I don't know how to answer him. I help him up onto his feet, assisting in dressing him in fresh pyjamas. I ease him gently into his bed and replace the covers.

The sound of applause from a sitcom emanates from the TV. Standing by the edge of his bed, I consider Derek's question, like I'm pondering Eastern philosophy.

'I don't know why I'm always alone, Derek. I like my own company, I guess. Or maybe I don't know how to let others get close to me.'

I stare at Derek; his eyes appear brighter. They're flickering. 'Where did the others go?' he asks.

'The other care workers?'

'Aye,' he mumbles.

'I had to let them go. Not many of you left so there was no point in keeping them on.'

He's lost in thought again. 'When's my missus coming round?'

I smile, rubbing Derek's arm. 'Anne loves you very much. How could she possibly not love you?'

I see the loose flesh around his neck tremble as he swallows. His eyes glaze over.

'I don't like being on my own,' he says. 'It's horrible. Why am I on my own?'

I squeeze his hand.

'I'm here whenever you want, Derek. I'm not always the best company, mind.'

He looks down like he might be remembering something.

'Get out of here, Rita,' he says.

'I'm sorry?'

'You should get yerself out. Go see some interesting places.'

'I'd love to get away,' I say. 'I'd love to do something different.'

He closes his eyes, his chest rising and falling, and I stand there for a while watching his breathing settle into a slow, steady rhythm. I switch off the TV and pull the strings to the side of the window to lower the blinds. My footsteps are heavy as I close the door.

5

The dim light on my laptop flickers as my finger swipes over the silver trackpad. I scroll over the messages I've received, or rather Nisha has received, overnight. I try not to read them as I hit delete. When I hover over a particular word, or see something grotesque I'd rather not see, I hit the keyboard more forcefully.

My head is a tangle of wires as I remind myself the hunting is over. I don't need any of this. But I also know that I might need to hold a little evidence back, should the police hold me responsible for Zia's suicide. It's only a matter of time before they call me in, ask me what the hell I was playing at by posting the video on Facebook. They'll most likely use that as a bargaining tool. It's just like them to do that, to use his death to their advantage; to miss the bigger picture and focus only on the details. But I know they can't prosecute me. At best, they might accuse me of undermining a proper administration of justice. I'm not taking any chances, however.

After an hour or so, I feel restless, so I open another tab in my browser. I log onto Facebook to see what other – *normal* – millennials are doing.

Sarah Peters pops up. An old friend from school – big tits, concord nose. At least that's what they called her back then. I see she's posted something on her timeline that looks vaguely interesting.

Happy Birthday to ME! I'm 35 today and feeling so grateful for my family.

I sometimes bump into Sarah in Tesco. Fortunately, it doesn't happen too often. That smug, homemade bread sense of happiness is too much for me to stomach.

I click on the list of my other 'friends' and see Michaela Woods, her painfully tight perm. She works in medical PR, has a laugh that boomerangs off the walls. I first met her in the pub one time in 2009, and later, she sent me a friend request.

Weather is so fine, I'm drinking wine!

I can only assume that, after making a point of telling me she's teetotal for health reasons, something sent Michaela into retrograde.

Next, I search for someone I know, someone closer. There aren't many friends to choose from, but there's Javid Kureishi. Pretty boy Javid who I've known since starting high school in 1995. We've kept in touch ever since. Back then, Javid was a loner like me. Moved down to London from a shabby house in Leicester. One of those Pakistani kids with pushy parents, intent on getting him married off at sixteen. Javid is tall and lanky with large almond eyes, his face perfectly angular, well suited to the cast of a Bollywood movie. At school, he used to sport one of those black biker jackets, which he wore with stiff, skinny trousers, his face slapped with teenage angst and insecurity. We hung out a lot during those school years. Like two lost souls conjoined by our unspoken differences, just getting through the temporal inconvenience of childhood before properly starting our real lives. Fast forward twenty-four years, Javid is a successful defence lawyer. Things turned out well for him. Our friendship has grown into the kind that is, were we both not otherwise inclined, a lot like an open marriage. We've rolled in and out of each other's lives, seen each other grow from awkward teen into mortgage-paying adult. But we can go a while without keeping in touch; only now, I realise it's been six months.

Met the love of my life! I am the happiest I've ever been!

I blink twice, as I take in his news.

I click onto his profile page and begin trawling through his historical status updates.

1 August: Lol! Look what I just found, clearing out my garage!

I stare down at the photo. *Brentwood High Yearbook, 2000.*

4 July: Kebabs for dinner. Loving this spread!
13 June: This Pride month I'm standing up and speaking out.
2 May: Prosecco in Bar Hemingway, Paris Ritz. Living the life!

There it is again, that twinge in my stomach.

There's nothing else posted about this 'love of my life' – no comments underneath. But I notice the post has 94 likes.

I slam my laptop shut, aggrieved to be excluded from such important developments. I'm aware I haven't spoken to Javid in ages and that it's *my* fault, not his. I realise then how much I miss him. *Have I really been that distant?*

My mouth feels dry. It hurts to swallow. All I keep thinking is, how could I have let things slip so badly? Whilst I've been hunting at night, everyone else has been getting on with living a full life. I wish, in moments like these, that I could start all over again. Maybe set up a business *I* would enjoy, perhaps something simple, less headache, like running a small café or coffee shop where I'd sell fancy mini cakes and flavoured croissants.

I grab my phone and relax back onto the sofa. I wonder whether I should text him, but then I think, it's been too long. I should call him, instead.

I rehearse a few things I might say to Javid in my head, just to overcome the awkwardness that is bound to be there. I dial his number.

Javid, how are you? I know I haven't called you in so long.
No, really? Has it been six months? Gosh, I'm so sorry.
I had no idea. In my defence, there are so many elderly members in our community who really must take precedence.
Oh, wait. Did I tell you? I hunted men at night. Note the past tense, since one of them killed himself. I can assure you, he was guilty. He wanted to have sex with a twelve-year-old girl. Would you believe it? Now I'm frightened that the police will turn up on my doorstep.
By the way, did I mention? I was hunting for five years! You'd be proud of me – you really would. Me – getting to know law enforcement! We can compare Post-it notes. Do you fancy coming over? I can order us a pepperoni pizza.

The phone rings twice before going to voicemail.

I hang up and throw my phone onto the sofa. Within seconds, it vibrates. I move to the window before I answer it. There's a crackle on the line, I feel my head rush. I can't recall the last time I had a normal conversation.

'Where have you been?' It's Javid.

Typical lawyer, going straight for the jugular.

'Javid! It's been a while, hasn't it? How are you? I was just calling to check in.'

Javid is quiet, like he's thinking about what to say next.

'Are you there?' I ask.

'I'm here,' he says. 'Rita, you sound a bit weird.'

I'm not sure how to respond. I am hopelessly unprepared for his inevitable inquisition.

'I'm fine. Just tired,' I say. 'Had lots of work on.'

'What have you been up to? Where are you now?'

48

'I'm at Raven Court. I was just calling to see how you are, that's all. Do you fancy coming over?'

He's silent again. 'Look. Before you start,' he says, 'I know what this is . . . I've been meaning to tell you . . . Please don't be angry.'

'Tell me what?'

'Promise you won't get mad? I know how you get upset when I don't tell you things.'

'Go on.'

'I met someone.'

I try my best to sound surprised. 'Well, that's good, isn't it? It's about time you did. I was starting to get worried!'

'Presumably that's why you're calling? You saw my post? Look, I would have told you sooner, but you never answer any of my calls.'

I don't remember any calls.

'I know what you're going to say . . . but this one . . . it's *different*.'

I don't know what to say. A part of me is grateful that Javid is talking about himself, just like he always does. It helps to take my mind off the lost cause that is myself.

'I'm happy for you, Javid. Really, I am. Come over and tell me all about it.'

He hesitates. 'Yeah. Alright, I will,' he says, defiantly. 'It would be good to see you, like you said.'

Later that evening, Javid arrives on my doorstep with a bottle of wine. He's carrying a white carrier bag containing what looks like takeaway. I open the door. His hair is floppy, and he carries the air of someone who's just returned from a run. He looks remarkably relaxed for someone who deals with petty criminals inside a courtroom.

He walks shiftily into the living room, a hand wedged into his pocket, looking around the place like he doesn't recognise the four walls. It's as if the last twenty-four years we've been friends and hung out here never happened.

'Give over. It's not been that long,' I say, every part of me tense. I've been a terrible friend – terrible.

Javid places the bag down on the dining table and rubs his hands. 'You're hopeless,' he says. 'It's been six months. It's a good job I've been too busy to see you, anyway. Still, at least you *know* you're hopeless. You have some humility and self-awareness, which is something.'

He takes a seat as I walk into the kitchen to grab two plates. I purse my lips, preparing for the worst of it. If I'm lucky, he might only give me a short lecture on the virtues of friendship, but then again, that is not Javid. Javid likes to rub my nose in it.

'I'm glad you came,' I holler, as I slam cupboards closed. I try to make out that things are normal. 'I've missed you. Life is crazy busy. I'm sorry. I should have explained . . .'

I hear Javid grunt and, when I get back into the living room, I find him scrolling through his phone. He places it back in his pocket.

I watch, plates still in hand, as he opens the plastic bag, peering inside. He sniffs at the food and my stomach growls. He's brought Chinese and it smells heavenly.

'I forgot how thoughtful you can be. If nothing else, I've missed you bringing me some takeaway.'

Javid laughs as he grabs the plates, placing them on the table. He unfolds the foiled corners of each carton. I open one up, biting noisily into a prawn cracker.

'So, what is it that's been taking up all your time?' he asks.

'Just this place, really.' I clench my left fist as I talk.

He scoffs.

'I think you owe me an apology before you pronounce judgement. About your Facebook posts . . . Strange way for friends to find out information.'

'Not that strange,' he says. 'That is the purpose of social media.'

'Very funny,' I say. I smile, a beaming smile just for him, but he's not amused. I'm aware our unspoken game of one-upmanship might go on for a bit. 'Beer?'

Javid nods. I rush to fetch him some out of the fridge. When I return, he pops a cracker into his mouth. 'I met someone,' he says, munching. 'But it's early days. I'm just seeing how it goes.'

There's something in me that doesn't sit comfortably. It's a feeling of having your best friend potentially leave you. It hits home just how much I've abandoned my normal life. That could be me, in a relationship, doing something normal.

'I'm happy for you,' I say. Because I truly am. Javid deserves to be happy. He is a good person.

'I'm worried about you, Rita.' Javid unhooks the top of a beer bottle. 'I don't hear from you for *months*. Then you send me odd text messages in the middle of the night, but you're never around when I call you back.'

'What text messages?'

I don't recall any text messages.

Javid pulls out his phone and begins reading my messages out loud.

How has it come to this, Javid?
After all these years... what is it all about?
Life is not how we thought it would turn out.
So much evil on the streets!

It's strange hearing him read my words out loud. They sound alien, like they've been composed by someone else.

'Most likely, I had one too many. You try running this place. You'd know what it's like if you did.'

Javid jabs his fork into a mound of noodles and turns it clock-wise. He shoves a forkful into his mouth, chomping over his plate. 'I get it,' he says.

'Do you?'

I stare at the bottle of wine on the table. I avoid opening it. I know that if I have a glass, I won't be able to stop. I move from the dining table to the sofa, to make myself more comfortable. My back rests against a cushion, and we stay in silence for a while. Finishing his beer, Javid comes over with his plate, taking a seat on the armchair opposite. I'm lost in my own world, thinking about Spider and Spike. How it is that we've spent five years hunting together and that it's ended – just like that. It all seems too tragic. I watch Javid eating, checking his phone. When I look up, I see his plate is wiped clean – cleaner than when it came out of the dishwasher.

'Jesus, Javid.'

'I was hungry.'

'I can see that.'

He blushes, finally relaxing.

'So . . . Tell me everything.'

'Matthew is lovely . . . I met him at a party . . . We were intro-duced, and we hit it off immediately.'

Something inside me warms. 'And? Anything else?'

'Well,' says Javid, grabbing another beer and gulping it down. He flops on the armchair with a spring roll. 'He's a solicitor. Mainly property, family, wills, probate.'

'I see. In your legal field, then. How convenient.'

Javid laughs.

'Like I said, I wanted to tell you, but you weren't around. You're *never* around, that's the problem . . . You were like that at school. Always disappearing – skulking in the school corridor.'

I shove another cracker in my mouth. 'Thank you for the reminder.'

'So? What have you been up to, Rita Marsh?'

'Nothing much,' I mumble.

'Come on. Spit it out. You've been very elusive.'

I can't understand why he is asking me so many questions. 'I had a lot on, running this place. People coming in and out. I can barely keep up with it.'

'How many of them are left?'

'Two.'

'Doesn't sound like a lot.'

'Keeps me busy, though. I call in the staff when I need to.'

'But what is the long-term plan?'

Javid nibbles on the end of his spring roll, staring at me, like he's mulling something over.

'I'm trying to figure that out,' I say.

He pauses for a moment. 'Look, Rita. I know it's not for me to say, but this place . . . keeping yourself indoors all day long – it's not healthy. It's good you're thinking about your future because I do wonder whether this business is even sustainable.'

I feel my defences rise like iron gates.

'Please don't start, Javid. You're not an expert on how to live my life. You've no idea what you're talking about.'

Javid places his beer beside his armchair and sighs. He leans forward, holding out his hand. 'I'm just saying that because I care. Come here, you big teddy bear.'

'Don't,' I snap.

'Hey! What's the problem? I'm just being affectionate. I know you like to think you're a superhero, but we're all vulnerable.'

I want so badly to silence him, to tell him what I've been up to, the various identities I've created. I want to tell him that I've walked away from hunting, which he knows nothing about. He might be in law, but I've been there, on the streets, doing the real job of upholding justice, confronting the worst kind of criminals.

'Just listen to you,' I say. I clang my fork on my plate. 'One new relationship and suddenly you're an authority on the subject. I'm tired. I'm running around all day. I'm on my feet. When evening comes, I just want to flake out. Do you understand what I'm saying?'

He stares at me. He's about to say something, but then his phone vibrates. He grabs it, flicking open his messages.

He is emotionless.

'I'm working on some big plans,' I say. 'Just in case you're wondering.'

'Oh?' he mumbles, staring down at his phone, wholly distracted.

'I'm thinking about selling up. Doing something different, like opening a café somewhere quiet, outside of London.'

'Mmm. That right?' But Javid isn't really listening.

'That him? Is that Matthew, Mr Lover Lover?'

Javid laughs.

'No, I'm just in this group for the Brentwood High reunion.'

I sit bolt upright, then get up and walk towards him. I peer down at his phone with curiosity.

'What are you doing in there? You didn't even like school.'

Javid sighs. 'Yeah, but they've organised it.'

'*They?*'

'Martina White, remember her?'

I can't say that I do, but the name sounds vaguely familiar.

'I have to turn up, don't I?' says Javid, glancing up. 'I need to rub their faces in it. Just look how I turned out. Pretty spectacular, I'd say.'

I laugh, slapping him on the back. 'You've such a big head, do you know that? Count me out.'

'Come on, Rita, it will be fun. I'll add you to the group,' he says. 'I'll send you a link.'

'Forget it.'

I begin clearing away the dishes from the table.

'You're doing an amazing job. Look, you even run your own business. I'll add you to the group. Reconnecting with old friends will be good for you.'

'Fuck off,' I call. 'I wipe old people's arses.'

'It's a *noble* profession,' he says, pulling out my phone, which is sticking out of the back pocket of my jeans.

'What are you doing?' I turn, lunging forward to grab it back. But Javid is too quick and moves away. He is thumbing on my keypad. I forgot he knows my PIN. 'Granted you could do with something else in your life. But I know you like to keep it simple. There you go, invitation to the group accepted.'

I want to hit him. *Why did I not change my PIN?* I've wanted to hit Javid for twenty-odd years. But instead, I throw a noodle at him, which lands, hanging over his ear.

'Rita. Stop it. You're a child. See? Back to school you go.'

'What the hell is that supposed to mean?' I pop another cracker into my mouth, then attempt to walk away but Javid grabs my arm.

'Come out. Let's have some fun. We can get drunk, maybe smoke some weed.' His eyes shimmer and for a moment I want to tell him everything that's happened. I know that out of everyone, he would stand by me, no matter what, that this is what true friendship is, and nothing else.

'C'mon. Let's have a laugh. We haven't had a laugh in *so long*,' he says.

And that's when it happens, that's when I think of her. The one who still lingers like a shadow, appearing occasionally in my memories of childhood. With all this mention of a reunion, I allow myself to think of her – just this once. I rise above the pain, the dread of walking away from the last five years. I wonder what she's doing now. I dare to picture her, with her long hair tumbling in waves, skin soft and pale . . .

Would she be there at the reunion? What would I say to her if she was?

I feel myself melting. But then my phone pings, and I immediately grab it off Javid.

I stare down at the screen. I watch it ping again. It's Lawson. I feel my heart racing.

'Who is that?' asks Javid.

'No one,' I say, swiping the messages away. 'Just someone about a booking.'

Javid lets out a groan. 'See? Always busy. That's the problem with you, Rita. You're just no fun. But you *are* coming to the reunion, right?'

I nod, without even realising it.

'Well, that's a relief,' says Javid. 'Because for a second, I thought I might have to tickle you into submission.'

The cemetery is dead quiet. Around me, graves are laid out like pieces on a chess board, headstones curtained by tall, scraggly grass. To an outsider looking in, a cemetery might appear like an odd choice to meet up, first thing in the morning. But I know this place well. I come here often. I figure Lawson won't come down quite so hard if we talk in front of my parents.

I hear the traffic from the busy main road leading to the Hanger Lane gyratory, winding cars around the enormous roundabout like thread around a bobbin. I take out a cigarette and light up, sucking hard on the filter.

Behind me, I hear footsteps. I don't bother to look up. Before I know it, Lawson's standing beside me, staring out into the distance. He nods, and I nod back. He's wearing light baggy jeans and a brilliant white T-shirt.

'You let me down, Rita,' he says.

That's Lawson for you. No preamble – nothing like that.

'I was wrong to post the video,' I say. 'I'm sorry, really, I am. If I had known what would happen in advance, I never would have done it.'

Lawson scoffs. I feel him watching me from the corner of his eye.

'It's disappointing, really disappointing,' he says. 'But then I can't say I'm surprised. You did exactly what I and everyone else in the police department expected.'

I bite my tongue and feel my mouth water.

'If I'm honest, I've wondered why I've been so lenient,' he continues. 'I should have shut you down like everyone said, as soon as you lot started. It's obvious groups like yours struggle to exercise restraint. You don't seem to understand how your methods are a hindrance to achieving the outcome we all want, that is, paedophiles being locked up.'

I swallow hard. 'It was you, to be honest. *You* wound me up.'

Lawson laughs. 'I see. All my fault now, is it? I made you do it. Helped you type out the headline, made you upload the video straight after we arrested him. How you could possibly think I would condone it *after* I gave you a clear warning is beyond me.' He throws me a sideways glance, then stares at the ground. 'I have been your biggest advocate.'

'Maybe you didn't mean to come across all high and mighty, but you did. I thought *you* – the police – needed reminding that *we* don't need you. *You* need us.'

Lawson tips his weight onto his toes. He clenches his jaw and reflects far into the distance.

'Videos like that do more harm than good. It jeopardises legitimate procedures and it can have devastating consequences,' he says. 'What happened to Zia is too appalling to even contemplate. It's why so many, high up, questioned involvement with you. Whether you like it or not, those you confront are entitled to a fair trial. You need to get your head around that.

Sure, we've worked with other groups in the past, but there have always been strict rules about co-operation. The fact that you've ignored our instructions undermines your own integrity. You've broken our trust – my trust. It means now I have to work harder to justify any support moving forward.'

'Justify?'

'Zia is dead, Rita.'

'I'm sorry,' I say, because deep down I am. 'I messed up. But what doesn't change is that Zia was a bad guy. The evidence was all there. I gave it to you, remember? I lost my temper, that's all. I know I should have controlled it. But what we do as civilian groups is invaluable. Don't let one mistake warp your entire opinion.'

Lawson thrusts his hands into his pockets.

'We provide a valuable contribution,' I say. 'Don't ever forget it.'

'And don't you forget that you need police advocates like me onside to deliver a conviction.'

Something inside me sinks. It is true: justice for us hinges on successful convictions.

'Seems you're incapable of being objective. Or you don't understand what you've gotten yourself into. Zia's death is the very reason *why* the police opposes your existence. You lot seem to think it's okay to do things according to your own standards. Anyone would think you've written the law yourselves, the way you all carry on.'

Lawson is being deliberately difficult, I think, overly critical.

'Appreciate the wisdom, but as far as I recall, we were there, helping *you* lot out. Our very existence highlights the fact that the police are not doing enough. Certainly our followers say so. You can complain about lack of resources, a lack of government investment. But either way, you need us. Whether you agree to our existence or not, you need us – to prove a point. If nothing else, to make a case for more budget. You *need* us to help sort out this problem which you're unable to deal with yourselves.'

Lawson scoffs.

'You're welcome,' I say.

'He left behind a wife; did you know that?' Lawson fires me a look, grinding his teeth. 'Zia had a three-month-old baby girl. His entire family have been shamed. Lord only knows how they will live with the pain.'

Something in my throat catches. I feel small, very small, just then.

'Perhaps he should have thought of that before trying to meet a twelve-year-old girl for sex. Or was that just to fill time until his own daughter was good and ready?'

Lawson looks at me, stunned.

'Jesus, Rita.' He pulls out a handkerchief from his pocket, folding it in half, wiping his brow. 'What a thing to say.'

Lawson stares at me, his eyes dark and serious.

I rub my forehead, feeling the pressure of his glare. This is not good. None of this is good. Of course, I could tell him I'm quitting Raven Justice, but I don't want him to think he's won. Besides, I'm not even sure what good it would do. The way this is going, it would not exonerate me from Zia's death. The police will need to pin this on someone eventually. The public are bound to ask questions. The support we have, the fans, the followers, which is so important, could be gone in an instant.

'Look, I don't disagree that your intention is well-meaning. I respect the work you've done over the years, gathering evidence, helping us, unofficially, with leads and enquiries. And all that on top of running a business.'

My ears prick up. I'm surprised at the change of tone in his voice.

'But there's got to be some sensitivity to the possible consequences.'

I swallow hard.

'Now, I do believe that, defined in the right way, some good might come from us working together . . .'

He pauses, as if waiting for a reaction, but I don't dare give him the satisfaction.

'I would be willing to explore what that might look like,' he says. 'But there must be changes – and some rules established.'

I feel my body tense. I stare at the grass, brushing gently against the gravestones.

'Maybe you could assist with investigation, evidence gathering . . . The alternative, should you disagree, of course, is not good,' he says. 'Zia's death will need explaining. Someone needs to be held accountable.'

Lawson's phone vibrates in his back pocket. I watch as he pulls it out, reading something on his screen. He switches it off and slips it back into his pocket. I'm grateful for the distraction, if only for just a minute.

It's a dilemma, all this. Of course, I saw it coming. The police have been approaching other groups and some of them have caved in. But this never appealed to Raven Justice. I would sooner pack it all in than declare an allegiance to ineffective coppers like Lawson. I can see now what Lawson is doing. He's using Zia's death as a means of dangling a carrot.

'I don't know what you're getting at,' I say.

'Oh, I think you do. You're smart, Rita. Really smart. We could do with someone smart, helping out with police efforts.'

'I'm sorry?'

'You need to make a choice,' says Lawson, turning to me. 'You can't carry on as you are. Follow strict protocols, and you can do some good. Go it alone, and most likely, you'll end up in trouble with the law yourself.'

'How convenient,' I say.

'Intelligent, surely.'

'And what about the others? They will never agree to this.'

'They are less useful to us, I'm afraid. We know who the ring-leader is. It's brains we want. Although we'd want you to keep an eye on them. Keep us informed of any separate activities.'

I feel bad for my street brothers, but I know what Lawson says is true. Brute force never wins over brains, and both men are known to be a little, well, impulsive. I was, and always have been, the mastermind of the group.

'Send us the leads,' says Lawson, 'plus all the evidence, and we can do the sting together. Bring us in earlier, during the entrapment stage, so that we can guide efforts better.'

I scoff. 'You mean play fiddle to your tune.'

'That's not how I would phrase it,' he says.

'Right you are.'

'So, you'll consider it?'

I think of Zia. I think of all the trouble I'm in. I need to say something to get Lawson off my case.

'I need to think about it.'

'How long?'

Already, he's running out of patience.

'I don't know. This is all a bit . . . overwhelming.'

Lawson looks up into the sky, then glances down at the gravestones, his eyes scanning over my parents' names. He presses his lips together. 'Look, I'm sorry. I do understand this must be difficult.'

I nod, kicking a stone with my toe. 'It's fine,' I say.

'When you suggested we meet here, I thought it was strange, but I didn't realise—'

'I said, it's *fine.*'

After a while he asks, 'Did they ever find the driver responsible?'

'The police you mean?' I scoff. 'Don't get me started.'

'That's hardly fair, and you know it.'

With his voice warmer, his shoulders relaxed, Lawson suggests I let him know where I stand in a couple of weeks, if that is at all possible.

I nod, feeling utterly deflated.

He follows my gaze as my eyes settle on a woman placing flowers upon a gravestone. She rolls out a mat and sits down, her head held in her hands. She rocks back and forth, and I close my eyes.

'I appreciate the time you're giving me,' I say.

'No problem. I want things to work out just as much as you do. I want paedophiles locked up, and our children kept safe. But there is a way to do things.'

'And just to be clear, if I agree to do this, you'll protect me from any blame concerning Zia's death? You'll ensure that nothing is pinned on me – now or in the future?'

I'm sure I see Lawson's eyes glitter with victory just then, an inner smugness washing over his face, which he tries so hard not to revel in. 'You've earnt this favour. I can strongly consider keeping your name out of it – particularly should the family want a further investigation. But there will be no more concessions like it afterwards.'

'And the other two? You'll leave them alone as well?'

'You are our primary focus, Rita.' Lawson smirks.

'We'll need to define exactly how we work,' I say, 'that is, if I co-operate. I can't do the hours I'm doing now. Something's got to give.'

Lawson raises his eyebrows.

'I mean it. I want my name – and Raven Justice – kept out of the press. I need cover from this shit storm.'

Lawson chews his tongue, then after a while, he nods. 'It's a deal.'

RIP. I stare down at my parents' graves and throw down my cigarette.

*

62

That night, as I lie in bed watching branches sketch moonlit shadows on my bedroom wall, I wonder how long it will take for me to feel like myself again. I'm proud of myself for getting out of hunting. I have no intention of working with the police. Why would I strike a deal when I've committed to living my life differently? I feel much calmer knowing I've been granted cover. But I also know I can't keep Lawson dangling.

I stare into the darkness and disappear into my mind. I recall a vision of my younger self walking through the school corridor towards the library, carrying a heavy rucksack, the weight of it hurting my back. I push through double doors, approaching the student lockers. I pull out a ribbon tied around my neck: it's my key. I remember how Dad insisted I wear it because I had already lost several.

I unlock the door and suddenly jump back, slamming against the wall; I hear a crashing sound. From the top of the stairs, voices roar with laughter. I glance up and see a crowd of sagging faces over the banister. On one side, Indian girls, on the other, only white. There is a dead mouse inside my locker with a block of rotten cheese. The stench is so bad, I pull the sleeve of my jumper and cover my mouth to stop myself gagging.

The laughter grows louder in my head. Then comes a chorus of jeers.

Stupid dyke. Fucking mix-breed.

A hand presses down on my shoulder and suddenly I feel myself calming. It's Javid, telling me to ignore them. I could be anyone I wanted to be – I could choose where I belonged. What did it matter that I did not fit neatly into their categories? That's what made life more interesting.

As my awareness returns to the bedroom, my body feels old and tired.

I want to rediscover who I really am; I want to feel like myself again.

6

In a hair salon, the following week, I sit like a stiff board in my swivel chair, staring at myself in the mirror. I run my fingers through my hair, my scalp still warm from a basin wash.

The salon is in a dodgy backstreet on the outskirts of South Harrow, nestled amongst vaping huts, South Indian grocery stores and dry-spice curry houses. Before long, a tall, lanky hairdresser with the name Tracy pinned to her chest, stands behind me. She's wearing a stylist's apron that hangs over her hips with big, square pockets.

'I take it Sandra's washed your hair?'

She smiles, and I notice red lipstick staining her front teeth.

I nod, not sure what to expect. I know only that I need a new look, to help me forget about the past five years of my existence.

'In that case, let's get you sorted.' Tracy runs her pale fingers down my scalp and my spine tingles. 'Quick dry and then we'll start. Would you like a cup of tea while you're waiting?'

My shoulders fall. 'That would be nice,' I say.

I haven't been in a salon for so long, I wonder how my hair might turn out. Whether I can ever be desirable. I notice how dry my skin is, tinged with grey, but there it is, that feeling I have forgotten. A flutter of excitement that perhaps I'm starting life all over again.

I bend to grab my phone from my bag on the floor, and I send a message to the Raven Justice WhatsApp group:

We should talk about things. Shame to end it like this. I want to see you both. No matter what happens, friends for life! xx

Tracy returns with a mug of tea, placing it beside a tub of hair-brushes soaking in pink liquid. She pulls on a pair of plastic gloves.

'So, what we doing to you, then?'

I stare at my reflection. 'A cut, maybe? Something with a bit more style. I just want to look nice. I've hated the way I look ever since I was a child.'

Tracy tilts her head as she stares at me.

'Poor thing, to be feeling like that. I think you've got lovely eyes; do you see? So deep and blue, and so powerful.'

I feel something warm as I take in her words. I'm not bad-looking, after all. I have good bone structure.

'I think we all have something we don't like about ourselves.' Tracy smiles. 'Those blue eyes are gorgeous. Which side of the family are they from?'

'That would be my mum,' I say. 'I didn't get much from my dad except a headache. His eyes were brown.' Tracy laughs and I smile to myself.

I stare down at my phone in my lap. Spider is typing.

'We could do a colour,' she says, 'perhaps a dirty blonde?' She wipes her hands on a towel hanging on the trolley beside her. 'If there's someone special in your life, we could surprise him.'

I consider her comment – her assumption about me. I straight-en up, reaching forward to bring my mug to my lips. I smile faint-ly as I blow over the top.

Tracy trots off to retrieve a stash of magazines from the table, beside the cash register. When she returns, she kicks a clump of red hair to the side and places the magazines on the ledge, just in front of me.

'How about you look through those for a bit of inspiration? I need to rinse Nora's hair.' She nods to the woman on my right, who looks up, her eyebrows rising in a shared moment of silence between us. 'While I do, have a think about what you really want.'

'I don't know what I want, that's the problem.' My phone vibrates as two messages appear:

11.39 Spider
Not much worth sayin, Raven.

11.40 Spike
Dunno know how U can live with Urself!!

I catch a whiff of Nora's Chanel perfume as she sashays towards the basins.

I suppose it's only normal that when we decide to move on, there are some we must leave behind when we do. But it pains me to think I may never see Spike and Spider again. We've been so close, with so many shared experiences.

I bite my lip to stop my eyes filling.

I want to ignore Raven Justice – I want to think about something else. I open the Brentwood High Reunion group and begin scrolling through the 914 messages that appear.

How many going? I counted 50, right?

Damn! I'm so excited to see you lot. A high school reunion!! XX

More like 70. LOL!

I click on the group icon, a picture of coloured balloons and streamers. Class of 2002, it says. I scroll down the list of participants. It's hard to tell who's who. Not everyone has uploaded a profile photo – all I see are their phone numbers. Of course, there's Javid. A close-up selfie of him pouting in front of an antique mirror. Naturally, he is the exception.

I return to the chat and run down it.

Have you guys heard??? Thumbs up if so!

Sshhh! Let's not talk about it here.

It's not like anyone is going to overhear us!

We can talk properly in school because we SHOULD, ok?

I don't know what they're all talking about.

I go back through the list of names, but I still can't quite place them.

For a moment I wonder if she's there among them, but I can't find her.

I check to see whether Javid has made any comments, but there's nothing. I fire him a text:

That WhatsApp group is just weird! What the hell have you got me into?

After a minute, he sends a message back: a cry-laughing emoji.

I see Tracy rubbing a towel over Nora's head from the corner of my eye and I switch off my phone, disconnecting myself from the prospect of having to rekindle childhood memories I would rather forget.

Tracy returns. She sees I haven't bothered to look through the magazines.

'You're clear on what you want, then?'

I nod, even though I've not given my hair a single thought. 'Let's go for blonde, the full works. Make me look like a different person.'

Tracy stands behind me, grinning like I've just made her day. Nora stands, brushing the hair off the arms of her sweater.

'What's your name, love? I like to know the names of all my clients. To think I forgot to ask,' says Tracy.

My mouth is dry, but I feel myself warming. When I stare at myself in the mirror, I notice my eyes are shining. 'I'm Rita Marsh,' I say.

Tracy winks. 'Well then, Rita Marsh. When I'm done with you, you're going to look like a different person.'

After seventeen years, Brentwood High School in the grey wash of Kenton is still a dump. The brick building is old and tired and looks like it might fall in the slightest wind. The rooftop is both square and sloping in odd places. And then there's that smell that all schools seem to have, no matter how many times the floors are mopped: that stale odour of adolescence baked into the walls that stays with you for years and years afterwards.

I'm standing in the playground, just a few steps away from the main entrance. The weather is warm. I'm scanning the grounds for Javid – I wish he'd hurry up. I pull out my phone from my handbag and see he's texted me:

SO SORRY! Running late from work. Meeting overran. Be there as soon as I can. Xxx

I close my eyes and take a deep breath. For a moment, I regret I ever allowed Javid's infectious optimism to get the better of me. Entering a high school reunion on my own is not something I'd signed up for. I start to doubt whether being here is even a good idea, but I walk into the school building, following a crowd in front. I know, deep down, that doing something hard like this, something new, is probably good for me.

I continue down the corridor and turn into the main assembly hall. A young girl wearing a yellow summer dress and a red checked apron approaches me. She greets me with a stiff smile and a cold glass of Pimm's. I notice the silver necklace around her neck, bells and horseshoe charms resting on her collar bone. I think of Derek in the Yorkshire fields. I hope that he and Margaret will be alright with the nightshift cover I put in place. I gulp down my drink, wiping my mouth with the back of my hand. The young girl watches me, dumbfounded.

The school hall is so much smaller than I remember it, seated in assembly all those years ago. The faded blue paint is peeling. The velvet curtains adorning the barricaded window appear dusty. The wooden floor appears new; a bright tan colour, freshly polished. I glance down at the painted white lines, remembering the squeaking sound my plimsolls made in PE as they rubbed against the floor in a hopeless game of badminton, aged thirteen.

There are a few people around me standing in clusters, in light and friendly conversation.

I catch my reflection in the window, and I run my fingers through my hair. I'm wearing a pair of smart beige trousers and a plain white T-shirt, and I think I look good. No matter what happens tonight, at least I came through. I mentally toast myself as I raise a cup to my mouth.

The hall starts filling with guests, and I scan a few of their faces. I'm hoping Javid might walk in at any moment, to save me from this lonely experience. As a few minutes pass, I begin to recognise some of them. There's Alina Petrov with the bob, Asif Khan in a tracksuit, Martina White in dungarees with a slight hunch – and oh, dear God, Peggy Lim, dressed up and teetering in seven-inch peep-toe heels. Jason what's-his-name is there too, his swagger in denim a picture of male cockiness, just as I remember it was in school. Sanjay Patel, probably the most 'successful' out of the lot of them, walks in ever so smoothly, in a cream linen suit.

Just then, much to my dread, I am accosted, slapped in the face with the overpowering notes of floral perfume.

'Rita Patel, is that you?' I turn around, affronted that someone dares to use my old name. It sounds so alien, it may as well be an insult.

'Only I *swear* it is. It *is* you!'

Melissa Reynolds. No getting away from it. Chest puffed out, pink lips pouting. She's wearing enough hair extensions, pinned to her scalp, to swallow her neck and face whole.

I look down into my glass, then at the over-sized buckles on my sandals.

'Nice to see you.'

Melissa grins. 'You look so . . . *different.* Actually really good. Miles different from how I remember you at school. Did you cut your hair short?'

We stand facing one another for several moments. I feel like I'm in a house of warped mirrors. Melissa can't stop staring at me. Her eyes crawl all over my face and then drop momentarily, running along the lines of my T-shirt.

I never liked Melissa back then. I'm sure I don't like her now. I'm not convinced that people like her ever change. As if remembering something too, pleasured by a memory she's certain I'd rather forget, her smile widens, growing ever more sinister.

'So strange, isn't it? Us all meeting up like this.'

I nod, taking deep breaths, counting in my head.

'Have you connected with anyone from school?' I ask.

'A few faces. Glad it's just us and no teachers. What about you? What are you doing now?'

I tell her about Raven Court, half-expecting her to get bored. But she nods, as if genuinely interested.

'Care homes are so important,' she says. 'We need them. I would even go so far as to say we are screwed without them.' She bites her lip. 'I work in marketing. High-end hair and make-up brands.'

I nod.

She cranes her neck over my head and her eyes widen as they settle on old friends. 'No way! Can you believe it?' she squeals. 'There's Stephanie and Peggy!'

Before I know it, Melissa has gone. I take in the names and feel my stomach knot. Relief washes over me when Sanjay breezes onto the stage with a glowing smile. He taps on the spongy head of the microphone. Hush and stillness falls, as he carefully unfolds a piece of paper.

Behind him there's a banner with a shot of our year photo. The Brentwood crest, a cubit arm entwined by a wreath of laurels, in the top right corner. Underneath it says '*Rise up*', the high school motto.

'It's amazing to see you all here,' he says. 'I'm surprised you all showed up.'

Susurrations of laughter.

I place my empty glass down on the table and lean against the wall. I can't help but notice a group in the corner, huddled and whispering, ignoring the rest of us.

'I think if we had known all those years ago how our lives might turn out, our experience here would have been different . . .'

My phone vibrates from inside my bag, nestled under my arm, but I ignore it.

I hear sounds of shuffling feet. Bodies rearranging and being seated. I rest my eyes on a chair in the front row close to the exit. I notice they're out of Pimm's, so I pour myself a glass of white wine and take it with me as I sit down.

I cross and uncross my legs, unable to get comfortable. All I keep thinking about is what my life has become after leaving school. Non-descript. A parallel universe. If only I had known then what I know now; all the things I would be involved in, the difficult choices I'd have to make. The plates I'd be juggling. I don't know how I feel about it. Only that it's time I made different choices.

'It's good to remind ourselves of our roots, of lost friend-ships . . . of where it all started,' Sanjay says.

I lift my handbag from the floor, wanting, for some reason, to record the moment. I want to listen to it later. As a reminder of how far I've come. I do that, sometimes: I record stuff. I did that on various jobs, preparing for a sting. Old habits die hard. Those past five years of hunting really meant something. But as I pull out my phone, staring down at my screen, I can't help but read the WhatsApp messages hurtling in.

Are we meeting up after school LOL? I want to know the latest!

Anyone who fancies coming to mine afterwards is welcome – just like the good 'ole days!

We should talk about it though. It affects so many of us who knew him.

I don't know what they're talking about. I scroll through the names in the participants' list.

Alina Petrov
Martina White
Tahir Ali
Javid Kureishi

I'm about to stand up, to get myself another glass of wine, to disappear into the washrooms like I did all those years ago when I needed to hide, but I hear my name being called. I freeze. At first, I think it must be some sort of mistake.

I switch off my phone and throw it into my bag. But as I look up, Javid is standing over me. He's clean-shaven, hair swept back. He's wearing a blue tailored suit that gives him the air of having just walked out of a high-powered boardroom meeting.

'Woah! Look at you, Rita. You look amazing!' he whispers.

I stare down, touching my hair, which is now damp with sweat. 'You made it then.'

'I did,' he says. 'Sorry for being late. *Love* the blonde look. Listen, when Sanjay has finished speaking, we're all going up on stage. Each of us just needs to say a few words before we kick-start the mixing and mingling.'

'I'm sorry?'

'Relax, Rita. Not all of us recognise each other. We thought it would be a nice idea – so everyone can see us. You're first up. Don't say I didn't warn you.'

I lean back into my seat; I feel my head rush.

'Relax! Everyone is doing it,' he says. 'You don't need a speech or anything like that. Just introduce yourself – say a few words. Keep it light.'

I watch Sanjay walk to the edge of the stage and I feel sick in my stomach.

'Are you serious?' I say. 'Count me out.' I'm shaking my head, but Javid is not listening.

He returns, laughing and slapping my back. 'Don't be dramatic. We figured it was easier. It was purely a coincidence that your name was first.'

'We? What do you mean, coincidence?

'Me and Sanjay.' Javid turns his head and watches Sanjay. Then he moves closer to me. 'God, just look at him. He turned out beautiful.'

He pulls back, rests his hand on my shoulder. 'You'll be fine. Seriously. You of all people have nothing to be ashamed of. Besides, it will be confidence-boosting.'

Sanjay talks into the microphone once more. 'We thought it would be a good idea for you all to come up, one by one, and introduce yourselves. Just to kick-start the evening. Of course, some of you know each other, but we've all changed, haven't we? To avoid a kerfuffle, we've drawn names out of a hat, so the order is totally random.'

'I don't want to do it,' I say to Javid. 'I'm fine to stay here.'

'Too late,' he says.

'Rita Marsh,' says Sanjay.

'What?' I look around me, panicking.

'Rita, just go. If you go up first, everyone else will follow.'

Before I even know what's happening, Javid is coaxing me up onto the stage, handing me the microphone in front of *everyone.*

He winks, then bends to whisper in my ear. 'You show them, yes? I think you're amazing, Rita. If nothing else, you look brilliant.'

I'm standing in the middle of the stage, staring out into the hall.

I look around me, silently, pleading for someone to help. A wash of familiar faces transports me to the year of 1995 at the start of high school. I want to elbow Javid hard in the ribs, but when I turn, I see he's leaving the stage. He turns, then gives me the thumbs-up. I stare down into the microphone, realising this is Javid's 'tough-love' brotherly way of forcing me to be present.

'I don't know what to say. I haven't prepared anything.'

I'm mumbling, my knees trembling. I anchor myself to the floor, to steady myself. 'I'm Rita Marsh. Not sure whether you remember me. I used to be called Rita Patel. But I changed my name, for . . . um . . . personal reasons. Marsh is my mother's maiden name.'

There are nods in the audience, as if some of them do remember me. Some smiles, too, which is somehow reassuring.

'I'm told spontaneity is a good thing,' I say.

More nods, a few coughs.

'So, after I left school, I uh . . . got into the care home business. My mum and dad bought one – before they died. I inherited it. It was doing quite well. That's what I've been doing ever since.'

I'm not sure whether to continue, but I do, trying to avoid Javid, whose eyes I don't want to meet. *I'm going to kill him.*

'I guess that's what makes you a success, right? Choosing something to do and sticking with it. Standing up for what you believe in. School didn't teach me that, however. I had to figure that out by myself. So yeah, can't say that being back here is at all appealing.'

There are mumbles and a little laughter in the audience. An awkward silence follows soon afterwards.

Sanjay is seated in the front row, his face rounder than I remember it. He stares at me, his eyes intense and piercing, but he's smiling, stiffly, as if he's a little embarrassed for me. Stephanie, Melissa and Peggy are whispering and giggling in the corner.

My mouth keeps moving; I can't seem to stop myself. It's clearly the nerves, the adrenalin, taking over.

'We all lead different lives now. Some of us, more than one. That's how busy we've become.'

My cheeks are on fire. I feel the electricity inside me flying. I don't know what comes over me, but I keep scanning the audience, watching everyone's faces. For a second, I hope, I pray, she will walk in . . . There's only one girl who would find this funny, who could get me to laugh about it afterwards.

'A teacher once gave me some good advice,' I say, 'advice that I've clung onto ever since. It's that you don't need to be seen or to be liked. The only thing that matters is that you *do* something.'

I notice Peggy on the edge of her seat, her eyes as round as traffic lights. Javid is standing just below the stage. I can see him turning, trying to meet my eye. He mouths something which looks like he's saying, *are you alright?*

'But what do teachers know? Most of them talk shit. If you want a decent education, go find it in the real world you're living in.'

Silence.

'And one more thing. I don't know why anyone thinks re-unions are a good idea. Maybe it's to make them feel better when they discover everyone else is seriously fucked-up as well.'

More silence.

'Okay, so . . . that's enough from me. Public speaking is not really my thing. Have fun – don't think I'll be joining in.'

I half-walk half-run off stage as the next person steps up. Javid grabs me by the elbow as I make my way to the exit.

'Rita. You are funny! How many have you had?' But before his grip tightens any further, I shrug him off and move to the back. I grab another glass of wine and leave the hall, the doors swinging like the bar doors on the set of a cheap Spaghetti Western. All this happens in a matter of seconds, and I thank God it's over.

I pull my phone out from my bag and check my messages. There's one from Javid.

Wait for me. I'll come find you. Hope you're not driving! x

But there are other messages from the WhatsApp group too.

LOL!!!! Now THAT's how we do it!

Seriously guys . . . there's been a development. Check it out!

Messages keep hurtling in. After the ones about me, they move on to discuss something different. It's about a teacher and my body shivers.

Did you hear about it?

I heard it from my cousin who knows the girl in question!

I scroll down the messages but there's no further word. I press my bag to my chest and walk down the corridor before Javid catches up.

The corridor is dark, and narrower than I remember it. It's like walking into a tunnel. At the end, a slip of silver light from a LED playground lamp glows. I climb the stairs, gripping the banister, wandering through the corridor. I press my face against the glass doors of the classrooms. I try out the handles, but they are all locked.

It's hot upstairs; I feel my T-shirt sticking to my back. I stop by classroom eleven and instinctively, I turn the handle to the door. I'm half-expecting it to be locked, but the door opens.

I remember this room: a former English classroom.

Inside, a strange smell of wet sawdust hits me, and I walk towards the window, staring out into the playground.

The sky is darkening and I get the distinct impression that it might rain. Sure enough, after a few minutes of me standing there, I hear a roll of thunder in the distance.

Through the window, I see dark dots of a few guests from the reunion run from the edge of the football field towards the common room at the back.

I want to leave before I get soaked. I exit the classroom and hurry down the stairs, rushing towards the back door. But before I can escape, I hear my name being called.

'Rita. Where are you going?'

I turn quickly. It's Javid.

'Jesus! You scared me,' I say. Javid stands before me, smiling. I can smell his Paco Rabanne aftershave and the detergent reeking from his shirt.

'I don't feel comfortable, Javid. I need to leave. You stitched me up and I'm pissed off about it.'

'What? But, *why*? C'mon. Don't be ridiculous. It's no big deal. Besides, the reunion has only just started. You will not believe some of the people I've bumped into. Remember Jason and Martina?'

I shake my head.

'People have changed. They're not like they were at school. They're not all dickheads.'

'I just don't feel great,' I say.

'What's the matter? Are you upset about going on stage or is it something else? A dodgy curry?'

Before I say anything else, Javid rushes to embrace me and I find myself holding him, resting my hand on the smooth of his back, taking in the citrusy notes and lavender smell of him.

In that moment, I want to tell him everything, because I know he really cares.

'I'm proud of you. Sorry if you felt a bit exposed. But you needed to do it, to put yourself out there a bit.'

'Fine,' I say. 'But I'm feeling run down. I don't want to ruin your evening. I just need to leave. I'll feel better after a good night's rest.'

'Want some air? Come, let's go outside.'

Javid grabs my hand and we run across the playground, just like we did when we were young, carefree – free from it all. I find myself smiling, reluctantly, and then, seeing Javid run like a lunatic, I begin laughing. We veer towards the left to the school gates. Javid stops suddenly and so do I. Breathless, we move to the main entrance, standing under a shelter.

'Rita—'

'Please. I am not drunk, if that's what you're asking. Those glasses were tiny.'

Javid laughs. 'It's not that. All I was going to say is . . . have you heard?'

He stares at me, his eyes piercing. Slowly, he pulls out his phone. 'There's a story making the rounds. You'll never believe it.'

'What story?' I start to panic, and I feel something in my stomach pull. I think to myself, this is it. I've been found out. I'll have to explain myself to Javid and worse still, everyone else.

I grab hold of his phone, but I soon realise, the story has nothing to do with me. It is far worse than I could possibly imagine.

The Harrow Times, Thursday 29 August 2019
Pervert Author Accused of Affair with Underage Pupil

Michael Stellans, a former North London teacher turned author, is accused of having sex with an underage student. Michael Stellans, aged 51, is accused of having an affair with a student when she was 15. It is alleged the affair took place in 2005 when Stellans was 38, employed as an English teacher at Lady Magdalen Girls' School in South Harrow. The woman, now 29, wishes to remain anonymous. She contacted police after watching Forbidden *on Netflix.*

'It was too close to home. I was 15 at the time we dated, and I believed he loved me,' she said in a statement. 'Now I realise how wrong it was. Men like that can't expect to get away with it. He brainwashed me.' Michael Stellans was arrested, but then released on grounds of insufficient evidence.

Forbidden *ranks at No. 1 on Netflix this week. It follows the story of Martin Dabussier, a French teacher who begins an illegal affair with brilliant student, Natalie Peters, aged 15. Unable to cope with the pressure, Natalie takes her own life.*

Stellans, whose latest book, The Shattering, *is released in March 2020, recently secured a six-figure advance for his next three books. He became a teacher in 1994 aged 27 after studying English Literature at Exeter University.*

Michael Stellans was unavailable for comment.

Seeing his name in print after all these years unsettles my stomach. I can hardly believe what I'm reading, nor comprehend what it means. Only that I always knew, on some level, this man was creepy, that something about him, which I couldn't quite place, was a bit off. This article is both shocking and confirmatory of a profound instinct from childhood. My mind stirs, as memories of him dislodge.

I see him so clearly; straight-backed like a long-distance runner with the smooth air of a lone-ranger woodsman. His pale chalky skin, his hair bleach-blonde and spiky. I remember the way he talked with his posh public-school voice. Of course, I've seen him in the papers a bit over the years, but I make a point to ignore him.

'Bad, isn't it?' Javid snatches his phone from my hand and switches it off, placing it in his pocket. 'Who would have thought it? That disgusting pervert. I remember him. Never liked him. Always thought there was something not quite right about that teacher.'

My hands are shaking. Javid is chewing gum. The sound of it is so loud, it feels like a pounding in my eardrums.

'So much of it about,' says Javid. 'No wonder people are taking it into their own hands. Did you hear about that guy—'

'I've got to go,' I say. I want so badly to get out of there. I need to get home, to search the internet for every single story I can find about this case.

'Are you sure? They're going to serve food. If your stomach hurts, eat salad. Hell, just have the dessert. The party's only just getting started.'

'I'm not hungry,' I say, as I walk away. 'I'm sorry. I need to go. Call you later.'

'Rita – no! Please stay!'

'No, Javid.'

'Well, that's just too bad. I'll just have to tell everyone how badly you turned out.'

'Goodbye, Javid.'

'Shall I tell them you have diarrhoea?' he calls, his voice trailing.

I'm heading out of the school gate. I pull out my keys, trying to steady myself, but by now, I'm feeling pretty spaced out. I walk up the road towards my van as the warm breeze blows more forcefully. I feel the drizzle of rain falling harder.

How could I have missed that?

Count: one, two, three . . . Breathe, nice and easy.

I move behind a giant oak tree, hiding behind its knobbly trunk, and I stare into the bark reading the initials of childhood loves. I'm fumbling around in my handbag, ignoring my vibrating phone, desperately searching for cigarettes when I hear my name being called.

At first, I'm not sure if I'm daydreaming, but then I hear it again.

I squint, unable to see who it is. I just about make out the outline of a car and something moving in the distance. I walk towards it and as I approach, I see that the car is a red Fiat Spider and is so polished, rain drips down the bonnet like diamonds.

The driver's door swings open.

My heart beats faster as a woman glides out.

'Hi,' she says. The glint of her gold necklace catches my eye. 'I was wondering whether you'd be here.'

She stares at me awkwardly, her hand sweeping across her fringe, eyes scanning the road around her. When she meets my gaze, it is distant and searching, slowly slipping into familiarity; that sensation of knowing that people often need a little time to process her presence. Her face is tanned and gaunt, with a touch too much make-up on. But she has lost none of her elegance. She stands tall, watching me.

'Leila?' I smile, something in my throat constricts. Inside, I am both terrified and rejoicing.

She reaches out her arms and moves towards me, pulling me close. I feel her ribs, the deep groove in her back. We stand like that for a while as my eyes close, as I sink into the flesh of her.

When she pulls away, she gives me a strange look, almost an accusatory glance. I feel tense, even though I *know* she can't possibly know anything of my life, of what I am doing now, nor what I have been doing, all these years.

'It's so strange to be back here,' she says.

I stare at Leila, unable to speak.

'And now you're blonde.' She laughs, relaxing. 'I never saw that coming.'

Leila says it feels strange to be returning to school after so long. That although she was told about the reunion, she doesn't feel comfortable going inside. 'Reunions are never a good idea,' she says. I see her lips moving, but I'm not sure I'm listening. She stares at me for some time, running her eyes over my face, remembering me, just as I'm remembering her.

'It's good to see you, Rita. It's been a long time.'

She has stopped talking, and stares at me, her eyes clear and round, so full of concern.

'What is it?' she says. 'Why are you looking at me like that? Is there something wrong?'

I cover my mouth and look down. 'Nothing's wrong. I'm so sorry. You must think I'm incredibly rude. I'm just a bit shocked – I wasn't expecting to see you, that's all.'

Leila nods.

'How have you been?' I ask, wanting to draw attention away from myself, from how stupid I must appear.

She sighs. 'I've had better days.' Her voice is a touch deeper; more hardened. She glances at the school gate. 'Too many bad memories in there. How was it for you?'

'How was what?'

'The reunion.'

I shrug my shoulders and Leila smiles, like she understands perfectly well.

'What are you doing now? Want to go somewhere?'

I swallow hard; a voice inside my head urges me to remember to be cautious.

'If we stay out here, we'll probably get soaked,' she says.

Remember: Leila was not always a nice person. She could be selfish, self-absorbed. She said hurtful things with little emotional intelligence. But the greater part of me dares to be spontaneous, to go with my heart, my feelings, because we're no longer children. We've moved on. Things are different now, surely.

I hardly notice the rain as I process that she's here.

So, while two voices battle it out, one was always going to win. Though I can't possibly know it yet, the hinges of the door to our younger selves tremble, and my decision to go with her locks me in. But there is nothing that can stop me, because even after all these years, no matter what's happened between us, I would follow her to wherever she wanted.

7

I follow Leila in my van as she slips through B-roads, past rows of terraced houses and pavements dotted with black wheelie bins.

It occurs to me that perhaps someone somewhere is throwing me a line. That as one door closes, another opens – and maybe, it's for a good reason. I don't understand what it means to be reunited with a former friend, one with whom the connection is so deep, it's easy to forget my own significance. But right now, I'm delighted. I could do with a friend to help me cope with those things in the past I would rather forget, to help me build back my own confidence.

But I know nothing of how Leila's life has changed, nor who she is now. Her hopes and fears, where she directs her feelings. In my van, still waiting for the traffic light to turn green, I firm my grip on the steering wheel, and wonder if there's anyone special she's seeing. I listen to a radio bulletin announcing blackouts over the weekend. I press my foot down on the gas when the light finally changes, concluding that not much can change between two friends who were close. Seventeen years gone, yet here I still am, tailing Leila in our grown-up vehicles. There's a strange hold she has over me, even after all this time. I feel a rush of excitement. I think of all the conversations we've missed. I think of how special I feel, just being in her orbit.

Leila pulls into a side road, in front of the Pyramid, a Lebanese shisha lounge on the corner of Salmon Street. Blacked out windows, scarlet awning, a neon sign. I park up just behind her car, and we meet at the door. Leila removes her sunglasses.

We're greeted by the slippery smiles of three oily men. Tight black T-shirts, rippling arms and Arabic tattoos. They each stare at Leila and then, perplexed, at me, as if unable to comprehend how two such different women, one graceful, the other graceless, could enjoy the same company.

I trail behind Leila as she leads me to the back, walking towards a purple sofa with scattered pillows, puffed up like pitta bread. Leila flops onto the sofa, kicking the sandals off her feet.

'I'm hungry,' she says. 'What do you fancy eating?'

I take a seat opposite her, my body feeling sluggish and over-sized. I'm trying desperately not to meet her eyes. My hands are clammy, my inner thighs sweating. So much about her feels different, yet I know the girl I once knew is still in there, somewhere.

On the speakers above me, they're playing classical Turkish music. Bright, expressive, alive, and full of feeling. Leila tugs out the blue-ribbon tie in her ponytail. Under the light of the Eastern lanterns, she appears as a lioness. Her cheeks seem airbrushed. Her shoulders slight, her arms so slender they look like they could easily break. I notice her collar bone protruding as she slips off her cardigan. For a second, she seems vulnerable, as she runs a lacquered nail over her bottom lip, every one of her careful movements disarming the men around her. Eventually, one of them inches closer. Leila looks up, then nods. He immediately grabs hold of the menus.

Assi, as his name tag reveals, flashes his brilliant white teeth. He smells fresh, like chopped parsley and mint.

Leila doesn't bother to look up – she's too busy scanning the menu. She waves him off like he's a terrible bore and asks him to return in just a few minutes.

I don't know what I'm doing here. It's as if no time has passed between us, and yet here I am – a wholly different person – trying to make sense of it all.

'Have you kept in touch with anyone from school?' I ask, wanting to know whether it was just me she had ruthlessly cut out of her life, whether there was anyone whom she deemed worthy to remain in her inner circle. Memories return to me: how she discarded me like a used dishcloth whenever she felt I'd served what she considered to be my function. How she wasn't always kind – often making snide comments about my hair and terrible dress sense.

'Can't say that I have,' she says.

'And your work? What is it you now do for a living?' I ask.

She smiles awkwardly. 'I'm a researcher for a TV production company; trying to figure out how I might get myself in front of the camera.'

She leans back, brushing the velvet seat with her palm. 'You know, I meant to keep in touch. It's just . . . things moved on so fast after we broke up from school. I threw myself into a new life at university – thought I'd go to Durham, but then I had to go through clearing. Got in to study English Literature at London Metropolitan University. It wasn't my first choice, but at least I got a degree. After that, a one-year postgrad course in journalism, endless hours of interning . . .'

'You did well,' I say. 'At least you ended up doing what you really wanted.'

Leila smiles and my chest aches. It never occurred to me that I might be able to follow my own dreams, however ill-defined they were. Mum and Dad had made up their mind that I would take over Raven Court. There was never any debate involved.

'Sometimes, I think about you,' she says. She says it so suddenly, it takes me aback. 'I think of that night and of our friendship. I don't believe I ever thanked you,' she says.

'Thanked me?'

She searches my face; her eyes tell me she's being genuine. 'We were young. We were exploring. It was perfectly natural. I'm glad I shared that with you. A moment of pleasure and innocence.'

I remember how her body felt next to mine, soft and gentle; skin so clear you could sometimes see her blue veins through it.

'I'm grateful too,' I say, my throat scratchy. 'It was a long time ago and we were just children.' Inside me, a tide recedes, then the water rushes forth with greater ferocity.

We order mint teas and settle on salad and some vine leaves to start. We agree to share a 'mixed grill for two' as a main, which requires us to lean over a single plate. This is mainly Leila's idea.

'I understand you had your reasons for not keeping in touch,' I say. The mint tea arrives in glass tulips, and I stare down at the leaves swimming around. 'I'm not offended.' I want to tackle the difficult subject head-on. 'It was just strange the way it ended, that's all. It made me think I did something wrong. I often think about it. But I guess we all needed to move on.'

Leila stares down at her hands, then lifts the steaming glass to her lips.

'Not much changed for me after school,' I say, not wishing to create any awkwardness. 'I decided against going to university. Dad got his way. I hung around, helping out in the care home and then . . . well, it became permanent.'

'Raven Court?'

I nod.

'I heard about the accident,' Leila says, after a moment. 'I can't tell you how sorry I was to hear about it. Rahul told me – my brother, remember him? It's just so tragic. I could hardly believe it.'

My body feels strangely numb. I've grown accustomed to displays of condolence and sympathy but somehow hearing her say it, hearing the words escape her soft lips, makes me feel emotional.

'It was a long time ago,' I say. 'I'm over it.'

'Well,' says Leila, crossing her legs, shaking her head, 'I think it's great that, *technically,* you're in charge of your own business. That's surely an achievement.'

I purse my lips. Achievement isn't necessarily what I would call it. A pain? Yes. Bleeding me dry and not making me any money? That too. A business of my parents' choosing and not my own, that's what it was and still is. It's hard not to feel resentful. 'Mainly the home takes care of itself,' I say.

The salads arrive on round plates, adorned with pomegranate seeds, blistered with tomatoes. The portions are so small I could easily devour them both myself.

Leila pecks at her food like a bird, jabbing her fork into a cucumber. I pull out my phone, staring down at the WhatsApp messages.

Can't say I'm surprised. He was always a wierdo!

What a perv. There were rumors about him, remember?

Do you think he did it on purpose? So he had something to write about?

Jeez. That's f*ck*d up if so.

Has anyone seen a recent pic of him? OMG! He is GROSS!!

There is a message from Javid too:

I'm still here… finding it a bit boring now tbh! Totally understand if you're not comfortable. Hope you feel better. Let's talk later with a takeaway? On second thoughts, maybe that isn't such a good idea. A few people here suggest Dioralyte. Apparently, works wonders.

'I don't suppose you've heard about Stellans,' I whisper. 'There's been a story about him in the news. Have you seen it?'

Leila places her fork down and stares at me blankly.

'Some people in our year were discussing it at the reunion,' I say.

I tell Leila what I know, and I watch her grow pale. After a few moments, as if catching herself out, she stares out of the window. She turns suddenly, to say something, opening then closing her mouth, but then thinks better of it. She glances down at her plate. I feel I ought to wait for her to say something first.

Leila pops a tomato into her mouth. 'His books are starting to sell. So, of course, they need something to talk about.'

'You can't seriously believe that,' I say. 'I never liked the guy, and I don't think he was selling much.'

'He's talented.' She points at me with her fork, her eyes piercing my skin. 'You normally see through such things. I'm surprised you believe it.' She stands up, grabbing her handbag, placing the strap onto her shoulder. 'Besides, you know how some girls are . . . making stuff up. Just give me a second, okay? I need the loo.'

I'm surprised by her reaction and call the waiter over as soon as Leila turns her back. I ask him for a glass of water. If money were no option – if I wasn't driving home – I would surely order alcohol. But I realise they don't sell any here, anyway.

The ice rattles around my glass as I drink. I pull out my phone and thumb Javid a text message. It's to get him off my case, though if he could see me now, he'd be delighted I was rekindling old friendships.

Very funny, Javid. Anyway, all good here. Things are a bit busy for me over the next few days. I'll text you a date later. Do you remember Leila? She turned up!

When Leila returns, her eyes are wider and glassier than before. They're darting about the place like she's nervous. I watch as she lifts her serviette and dabs her nose. She tries to compose herself, but she's acting a little *adjusted.*

At first, I think it's me. But then . . . I know that look. I've seen it so many times on others. Girls sniffing a little something in the toilet, just to help them get through the day. But I don't want to pass judgement, nor make out I've noticed.

89

'I'm surrounded by journalists at work,' says Leila. 'I know what they're like. Always making stuff up. Did you know? Only two weeks ago, it was the one-year anniversary of the death of Aretha Franklin. But the legend that is *Aretha* receives only marginal coverage.'

'I don't follow you,' I say. Because really, I don't. I don't know what she's implying.

'The *media*, Rita. They're all so fickle.'

'Are you suggesting that Aretha Franklin deserves more column inches than a story about grooming?'

Leila winces. *Grooming.* 'Whatever that girl is saying, we can't know her true motivation. That's all I'm saying.'

'I see.'

I realise that Leila must have Googled the story and has most likely read it in the toilets.

'Leila,' I say. Just her name rolling off my tongue makes me reminisce. Leila, the one who lit up my childhood, and gave me a reason to live. 'You *can't* be serious.'

A few seconds of silence pass, seconds that feel like they contain the eternity of childhood. I hear a wailing siren, which, for a moment, I think is going off in my head, but turns out to be coming from inside the restaurant.

Leila freezes, unsure what to do. She flags down the waiter and asks him if the alarm is a real one or merely a drill.

The three brothers scramble from the back into action, jumping over the counters, waving a tea cloth in the air, but all I keep thinking about is how passionately Leila made her point about Stellans.

Assi approaches, terribly apologetic, his brow beading in sweat. He ushers us out. 'Just five minutes, then everything normal,' he says. He waves his hands about, and one conveniently finds its way onto the curve of Leila's back.

We both grab our bags and make our way to the door. I feel

myself growing increasingly vexed as I'm hanging about like a spare part in the courtyard at the front of the restaurant.

Under the red awning, Leila stands beside the outdoor lamps, her face tinged soft pink. I watch her pull out a cigarette, her hands unsteady. 'I'm assuming you don't smoke?' she mumbles. The cigarette wobbles between her lips.

I shrug my shoulders. 'Been known to.'

Leila tilts her head back, drawing the smoke fully into her lungs, then exhaling with a long, drawn-out breath. She hands me a cigarette and I lean forward as she flicks her lighter.

Just then, Assi comes running out of the lounge, his face sparkling.

'So sorry about this,' he pleads. 'We cannot stop the alarm. Fire Brigade is coming. But please come back. I am so sorry for this situation, really, I am. Everything you eat today is free of charge.'

Leila and I turn to one another. She grunts, throwing her cigarette onto the ground, stubbing it out with her toe. '*Honestly.*'

'Well, I guess that was a short meeting.' I laugh, but inside my stomach sinks. There's so much left unsaid between us.

'We should meet up again. Continue the conversation in my flat,' she says. 'I want to show you something. And we need time to talk properly.' She pulls out a piece of paper from her handbag, rummaging for a pen.

'Shall we just swap numbers on our phones?' I ask.

'I prefer paper,' she says.

She presses the paper onto my back, scribbling down her number and address. 'Sunday for dinner around eight. Does that work for you?' She hands the paper back to me.

I stare down at her address. A flat in Kensal Rise.

'I'm free,' I say, trying not to sound too enthusiastic.

'Great,' she says, squeezing my arm. 'Look, Rita, I know you mean well, but about earlier, about Mr Stellans, there's probably a lot to the story you don't know.'

I nod, thinking that I know more than she does. I know men like Stellans. I know exactly what they're like. But I clench my jaw because I know I have put all that behind me. I'm a bigger and better person; more reasoned, more *responsible*. There's no way I'm going back there again, allowing myself to downward spiral.

Leila turns to walk away, but then she stops. 'By the way. . . It's best you don't park your van outside my flat; the neighbours will really hate that. There's plenty of space down the road. Maybe text me thirty minutes before you arrive, and I'll order an Indian.'

I stand there waiting for something further, waiting for her to tell me that, on second thoughts, I'm right about Stellans. How could she have missed the signs? But, just like that, she disappears.

It's Saturday morning. I draw the velvet curtains back in Raven Court, allowing the warm sunlight to drench me, to soak into the marrow of my bones. I close my eyes, and when I open them again, my eyes settle onto the horizon, observed through tall French windows.

I think of Lawson, of how I've been keeping him waiting; making him believe I'm still working for the police so that he protects me from any backlash over Zia. I think of Raven Justice, of all the hard work I put in, building a group to rid the streets of men like Stellans, when all along, there was a paedophile on my very own doorstep. It's hard not to get angry.

Leila is still there in my mind, that sight of her face, her skin pulled taut like a drum, her necklace glistening around her neck. I can see her, taste her, the delicate sweep of her clavicle, silky smooth like warm treacle.

I walk into the kitchen, considering what to prepare for breakfast. I settle on something special for Margaret and Derek, like scrambled eggs and smoked salmon. But there it is again, that dreaded feeling returns. I stare down into the sink, clearing away last night's dishes.

Did I forget? I must never forget. A young man committed suicide and a teacher who taught me, and countless other children too – one whom parents trusted – turned out to be a paedophile. How could I not have known, or at least understood, what must have been so blatantly obvious?

It's a test, all this, to see if I'll return to my old life, slip back into the thrill of hunting – it must be. I hold firm that I've made the right decision to get out. I cannot undo all that now.

After breakfast, I clear the dishes, stacking plates into the cupboards, tossing spoons into the cutlery drawer. I wipe down the counters and I dry my hands on a dishcloth. I glance at the rota pinned to the noticeboard.

I am too busy, and I need help; I know that. A story like this requires thorough investigation. I figure I can't just sit back and do nothing. I must make myself useful. Do a little harmless research. If one girl has stepped forward to accuse Stellans, most likely there are others, too. Others too afraid to come forward to reveal what he did to them because of what it might do to their family.

I untie the apron from my waist and take a seat at the kitchen table. I lift the screen of my laptop and type the name, Michael Stellans, into Google. There's a metal taste in my mouth as I watch the search results appear. At the top, the story in the *Harrow Times*, which I've already read one too many times, and can't bring myself to read again. But there are other references, too: his author biography on Wikipedia, a list of books he's written for Heron. I read a quotation of his, here and there, on various author websites. I wonder then whether his books contain clues, whether there are hidden perversions embedded in the layers of their prose. I visit Amazon and type his name into the search field. Stellans' books appear in a scrollable carousel at the top and I click through them:

Little Boy Blue
Infidels
Dead Ends
Into the Darkness

His forthcoming, *The Shattering*, due for release in March 2020.

I click on his author headshot.

Michael Stellans is seated beside a curtained window with a crooked smile and folded arms. My stomach turns just looking at him.

Upstairs, I hear footsteps and I glance up at the clock. I should really take Margaret and Derek into the garden for some fresh air, so I haul myself up.

In the garden, Margaret sits in her wheelchair with a blanket over her knees. She stares out into the distance and seems content, watching the leaves rustle in the trees. I can tell by the way she closes her eyes and breathes that she's enjoying herself. A breeze passes and her eyes flicker. Next to her, Derek struggles to stand up from his wheelchair, so I run towards him, and lend him my shoulder to lean on. I pass him his stick and off he hobbles, in the direction of the pink hydrangeas.

I take a seat on a wooden bench donated by the two remaining sons of former resident Betty Clarins. I have one eye on Margaret, now dozing peacefully in her chair, the other on Derek. I watch him stretch his arms out, his back trembling, dragging his stick alongside him in the grass. I drink in the sounds of nature. I find myself drifting, thinking of Leila. Thinking how my life might have turned out had we stayed in touch all these years.

The sun sends flecks of light onto the stone slabs where Margaret has begun snoring. Her head tilts to the side and I'm aware I need to take her upstairs, or risk her hurting her neck. Derek reluctantly complies when I call him in. I help him up from his knees from where he's been observing insects by the old out-house that is currently unused. Once inside, he shuffles behind me as we walk together into the narrow lift, me pushing Margaret. In the lift, he looks up at the ceiling, at the flickering light. Moving up to the first floor, he glances down at the wheelchair.

'Is she sleeping, my Anne?'

I place my hand onto his. 'Anne loves you very much,' I say.

Derek stares at me, his face fallen. Eventually, I settle them both back into their rooms, then enter my own. I need to catch my breath, to gather my thoughts.

In my bedroom, the stale smell of morning and dust hits me in the face. I move to the window to open it, then turn to my cupboard. I don't keep many mementoes from school, never felt the need. But I do have a few things I cherish.

I open my cupboard, and I pull down a box from the top shelf. I lift the lid and smile, examining the fragments of the notes Leila and I exchanged in class alongside a few brown envelopes. Inside one of the envelopes, I discover a lock of hair that belongs to Leila which I forgot I had. I stole it after we once visited the hairdresser as teens. I remember how much I loved stroking it in private.

I open another envelope and leaf through some old photos. There's one of me and Leila seated on the grass. Another, one of those official photos of our entire school year, lined up in the main assembly hall. Leila appears lost as she looks away from the camera.

There's another photo, too. One where Leila's seated on a stone step outside the art block – her shoes muddy at the tips, her skirt tucked under her knees. It must have been taken in the first few weeks of her starting at Brentwood High. I notice her shoes again, the ones I remember she wore on her first day. They were not the usual kind, shiny and black with a pasta bow on top. Hers were plimsolls: the kind you wore for indoor PE. I remember thinking how strange it was that she was wearing them. Ugly things they were. I thought she might have made more of an effort. At least *tried* to avoid getting her head kicked in.

Leila arrived at Brentwood High in late January, 1998. On her first day, she walked into the classroom like she'd spent the morning in the park playing on the swings. The weave in her plaits was loose. Dried leaves and twigs were stuck to her tights at the back of her knees. I remember holding my breath, wondering how this would play out, whether the others would pounce on her as soon as the bell rang. But she was oblivious – cocky, even. Mrs Smith introduced her as having just moved down from Glasgow, quick to caution that we should all be *nice* to her, that we ought to remember how nervous *we* were on the first day of school. Scotland was as distinct and foreign as San Marino. It was clear to me, from the very first moment I saw her, that Leila was different.

Leila sat down at an empty table at the back of class, calmly laying out her things. She glanced at me once, and I remember smiling back. When the bell rang at the end of class, I followed her, hoping we might get to talk. That she would see me and accept me as a friend. I followed her, noting that she was walking in the wrong direction for Chemistry.

Down the main corridor, Leila stopped occasionally, leaning against the wall, waiting for the other kids to pass. She opened her bag and pulled out a map, holding it this way and that. I remember the first thing I said to her as I approached.

'You look lost. We've got Chemistry next. Want me to walk you?'

She relaxed in my presence.

'Oh, thanks. I was worried I'd be late. I don't even know where I'm going!'

I cleared the walkway for her, shoving the smaller kids to the side. 'I'm Rita Patel, by the way.'

She stopped suddenly. 'No way. Are you Indian? You don't look Indian at all.'

'My dad is Indian,' I said. 'But my mum is white.'

'Oh.' She smiled knowingly. 'I get it.'

I asked her how long she'd been in London. She told me she had moved down at the weekend. This was her first full week in a new town, so it was understandable that she was disorientated.

As we walked across the playground, she began firing questions at me: is the food any good in the canteen? Can girls wear something different for PE, like a skirt, instead of jogging bottoms? How did your parents get together? Was everyone okay about their marriage or was it a big drama?

She did not ask me any questions about myself, except those ones about my parents. I remember how grateful I was for that.

Outside Chemistry, we trailed at the back of the line. I told her that we should let the others go into class first. When the coast was clear, we took our seats at the back.

'Have you been at the school since the start?' she asked, peeling off her rucksack.

I nodded. 'Don't worry, you'll soon settle in. Just stick close to me,' I said.

At the end of school, we walked home together. She said her first day had gone better than expected. Around us, the late afternoon sky was darkening.

She was quiet as we turned the corner to her house, her hands fidgeting in her pockets. Here, the tired brick houses were much smaller compared to the mansions on the main road. I noticed a pile of black rubbish bags, a soiled mattress in one corner.

'Do you want to come in?' she asked. I could see how awkward she felt, but I was too busy wondering whether the door of her parents' home marked the end of us both hanging out that day.

I looked up, staring at the views of Greenwood Estate at the back of the house, known to be notorious for drugs and crime and God-only-knew what else. I was willing to take my chances.

'Sure,' I said.

I heard a woman singing in a high-pitched voice, like you hear the women do in Bollywood movies.

Leila rolled her eyes. 'My mum,' she said. '*So* embarrassing.'

I waited in the hallway as Leila entered the matchbox-like kitchen. Through the glass door, I could see her mother wearing a peach-coloured sari splashed with ferns. She was leaning over the cooker, stirring a steaming curry pot. I stared at the mango-patterned wallpaper in the hallway, thinking how nice it must be to have your mum at home waiting for you with a home-cooked meal instead of a cold plate of clingfilmed ham in the fridge. I wondered what it might be like if things were reversed: if my mum had been Indian and my dad had been white. Whether that way round, they would have argued as much.

Leila was mumbling something. All I could make out was her saying something like, *just for a bit. Please Mum! She's got no one at home.* But when I think about it now, I might have been mistaken.

Leila's mum opened the kitchen door.

'So, you are Reeta,' she said, staring at me like I was a strange specimen. 'I am Sushmita.' Her eyes were large, just like Leila's, and lined with black kohl. Her eyelids appeared heavy. Her speaking voice was a lot deeper than her singing one.

'Are you hungry, dahrling?' she asked.

Before I could answer, she held out a plate with a hot chapati, dripping in ghee.

I stared down at the plate and thanked her, for some unknown reason, by bowing. Leila burst out laughing and pulled me upstairs.

'Come on. My idiot brother is not back yet so we've got the place to ourselves.'

In Leila's room, I stared down at the pile of clothes on the floor, her dressing table scattered with cosmetics, hairbrushes and coloured ties. I noticed a pile of magazines and several titles of poetry. Keats, Larkin, Yeats. There were some other far eastern titles as well, mostly Chinese translations; titles I'd never even heard of.

'You like poetry?' I asked. It was a stupid question. She was so different from the other Indian girls I'd met.

'Sure.'

I told her I loved poetry too, which of course was technically true. Rap was a form of poetry, I told her. 'Do you listen to Eminem? He's going to be big.'

She told me a few things about her life in Glasgow, how her parents had moved into a shoe-box house as immigrants before she was born, after leaving Uganda. Moving to the UK had been a dream for them. Leila said she felt lucky to be born and raised in Scotland. But London had always been their target destination. So much was riding on them making it here.

'Basically, my dad said things will be better in London for me and my brother, now that Blair's Prime Minister. He says he can make more money as an accountant. That this is a golden age for Great Britain.'

I stared down at the carpet and noticed a small stain in the pile. 'Well, I think it's really brave.'

We heard rustling downstairs in the hallway. 'Rahul's home,' she said. 'You'll probably hate him.' Leila got up to lock her bedroom door. 'If he asks you too many questions, just ignore him.' The footsteps outside stopped momentarily and we both giggled. Eventually, we heard the door to the bedroom next to us slam shut.

In whispers, I told Leila about my parents too. How they met in the DIY store, B&Q, when my mum was on the cash tills and my dad was purchasing lightbulbs and paintbrushes. He was doing up the house he shared with his first wife. I told her how he then married Mum – which he never should have done, because Dad took ages to get a divorce. How the families on both sides constantly argued. Leila listened, and occasionally nodded. She never asked me any difficult questions like the other girls did. She just placed her arm around me, gently squeezing my shoulders. I could have told her anything in that moment. She was so accepting.

I'm back in the present moment, and I lie back onto my bed on my side, fanning the photos in a spread so I can take a good look at them again. Laid out like that, I want to find a deeper meaning in them. The reason why Leila acted so funny sometimes. I scan through my address book on the side table, noting the name of the agency providing emergency staff cover. I feel an overwhelming urge to get myself organised – because if there was any doubt before, I now want to be certain concerning the truth about Stellans. I grab my mobile only to discover that Leila has sent me a text:

Can't wait to see you tomorrow! xxx

For a second, my breath catches.

8

That Sunday evening at her flat in Kensal Rise, Leila is wearing a grey summer dress with a drawstring at the waist. The dress is nothing special, just a casual thing to lounge in, and yet I must try not to stare too hard, nor follow the lines of her as she wanders into her open-plan kitchen, overlooking the lounge and dining area. She's opening cupboards, pulling out plates haphazardly, loading them up with garlic olives, cheese, and dry roasted peanuts. I watch her from the living room through a hatch in the wall. She has her hair swept up into a high ponytail and every time she turns, her gold-leaf earrings jangle.

But Leila is jittery, every movement of hers performed and strained. As I look around me, I'm surprised how dark and small her flat is, how lonely it feels. Scattered pieces of her world are everywhere: notebooks, takeaway flyers, piles of newspapers. Her laptop sits on a side table beside dirty mugs, marked with pink lipstick. Leila tells me she's researching for a new TV series which is why there's a pile of new gadget magazines on the settee. But I also note the row of wine bottles snaking along the edge of the wall, all the way to the start of the kitchen.

This flat appears to belong to a woman who has, in some senses, given up. Someone who doesn't care what people think, but far from being liberated, it reveals how conflicted she is.

I wonder if I should tell Leila about my hunting paedophiles to justify my reaction to the story of Stellans. Perhaps it will settle her to know that my life is messy too. But I don't want him to take over the conversation again. All I really want is to talk about *us*, this meeting – how we move things forward. I want an opportunity to level things, to know what is going on inside her head. Why she behaved the way she did all those years ago. Surely she remembers how some days we were close, some days we were strangely distant. She must understand that it would leave me with an uncomfortable, perpetual feeling that I had somehow done something wrong. I know I am not perfect, that sometimes I am moody and lose my temper. Perhaps, beneath it all, the demise of our friendship was all my fault. I never confided in her about myself or told anyone what was going on. I just let it fester inside me, this terrible secret I've kept about that night. Perhaps it affected things. Maybe if I told her now, she would understand, there was good reason for why I acted the way I did.

Leila moves to the lounge with a bottle of wine. 'You didn't text me, so I haven't ordered any food yet.' She smiles. 'We'll just have to drink instead.'

I take a seat on the edge of her sofa, wedged in the corner. I can smell cigarettes and it makes me crave one. There are piles of boxes on the table, old yearbooks, photographs, exercise books and letters.

'Is this what you wanted to show me?' I ask. I stare at the table and then at the bottle of wine in her hand. 'I can't, I'm driving.'

'Crash here then,' she says. 'I'm not going anywhere. Or just take a cab.' She shrugs. Leila slips to the end of the table, placing the bottle down, rummaging through a box. 'I thought it would be nice for us to sift through some stuff I had,' she says. 'A reminder of the good old days – carefree, without any responsibilities.'

I move closer.

'I spent the whole morning going through it,' she says. 'The thought of that hideous reunion just brought everything back.'

I count four boxes, laid out in a neat row, then I lean over the table.

'This is quite a stash,' I say. I pull out a framed photo, but then my chest tightens as I make out the faces: there's Leila with

Stephanie, Peggy and Melissa, seated on the grass, cross-legged.

I place the photo on the table, face-down. 'You haven't changed much. Still beautiful,' I say.

'Thanks,' she says, winding the corkscrew into a bottle. She prises it out, and the bottle pops. She pours me a glass, filling it to the top. 'Go ahead,' she says, grabbing a breadstick from a box on the side, biting each end of it. 'Take a look.' She wipes her mouth with the back of her hand and hands me a packet.

I sit down and open it. The first thing I see is a picture of Leila's cat, Smiggle, curled on a chair in her parents' living room. I have a copy of this photo at home. Leila developed a duplicate for me.

'I never did get over that cat,' she says. 'Do you remember him? I still think about him a lot. If I ever find out who did that to him, I swear . . .'

Leila moves to the kitchen, gets a packet of rice out of the cupboard and begins boiling water.

'I remember,' I say, my skin prickling. 'It was cruel how they killed him.'

I leaf through more photos, hoping – *praying* – not to find one of me. There are plenty of shots of boys I don't want to remember, sloped on the side of a ferry in Dover, staring out to sea. Must have been one of those school trips to Calais – just one thing on my list of disasters. I remember throwing up on the side of the boat, all over my Jesus sandals.

I stop suddenly.

There's a picture of Leila's parents: her mother, Sushmita, lying on the sofa with her feet propped onto a pillow, the folds of her sari hanging over the edge of the seat. Leila's dad – Kishore, I think his name was, stands over her, smiling. His hair is lightly oiled like a tossed salad. It was one of the few times I remember him smiling.

'I forgot how much I loved taking photographs,' she says. 'But Rahul hated it. Always complained.'

Rahul.

'Mainly because his skin was so bad at the time,' she laughs. 'Do you remember it? Pitted like a strawberry.'

I remember Rahul, although I would prefer not to. He was one of those pointless characters from childhood that made it onto stage only because of his pretty little sister whom he was secretly jealous of. He did everything he could to stop me seeing Leila. I could never understand his problem.

I skim through more photos until I find one of him.

There's one where he's leaning against a Fiesta, one leg crossed over the other. His arms are folded; head cocked to the side. The sun is shining, lighting up one side of his face. It's not easy to make out his *favourite-child* features, but I remember how twisted they were.

Next up, a photo of me, taken on the day I allowed Leila to apply some make-up. I stare at myself – unrecognisable – my heart sinking into my stomach. My hair is cut into a bob. My face appears spud-like, round and puffy. Cheeks circled like a clown with pink rouge. Lashes clumped with blue mascara.

'What is it?' Leila dawdles towards me. 'Why are you looking like that?'

'Nothing.' I shove the picture back in the pile and place it neatly on the table.

'*Come on*, show me.'

'No.'

It all comes back to me. The way Leila had convinced me to dress up, despite my begging – pleading – for her to stop. How she said it would be good for me to try on a bit of make-up.

Relax, Rita. It's just an experiment.

Leila sifts through the pile and finds the photo. It's like she already knows which one is likely to cause me distress. She throws her head back and laughs. 'Look how unhappy you are. I remember it so clearly.'

'I don't know why I ever let you do that,' I say. 'And how come you have a photo of it, anyway?'

'You agreed to have one taken, Rita.'

'I would *never* agree to that.'

'You did. You agreed to most things I suggested.'

She returns to the cooker, pouring rice into a boiling pan of water, shaking in flakes of salt.

'We were close in those days,' she says, stirring the pot. 'That's what we did. Stupid stuff – stuff that didn't mean anything.' She stares out of the kitchen window, and I see the side of her delicate profile. I notice, then, how vulnerable she is, yet how vicious she can be, too.

I clear away the photos, placing them back in the box, but one falls out of the packet and onto the floor. I bend down to pick it up. At first, I don't recognise what I'm seeing, but then it slips into focus.

December 2001.

It's a picture of the entire cast at the end of year school play: *Cat on a Hot Tin Roof*, the Christmas before we finished school forever.

I remember that moment, just after the curtains fell, when the cast came out on stage to take their final bow. I oversaw the stage lighting, and I remember how I softened it a little, allowing it to glow and float over the cast, pulling the lever to create a shimmering rainbow. Specks of multi-coloured light danced across the front. Leila's hairclips glistened. She was the lead actress, playing Maggie. The light simply loved her and followed her around.

The cast waved at Stellans, calling out to him to join them on stage. I saw him run out, as if doing so reluctantly, and only because it would look bad if he didn't. His tie rippled to the side of him, and he stood awkwardly beside Leila. They all bowed, smiling, but Leila's was the largest and brightest of them all, a real star. I remember how proud I felt.

But suddenly, in this photo, something is revealed – in a stolen moment, which I notice, but I'm not sure that anyone else at the time really did. A loving glance between student and teacher that goes on for a second too long. Captured by the click of the camera – a flash, and revealed by this still image in my hand. How did I miss it? Stellans has his head bent, and now I remember how she kissed him lovingly on the cheek. It was just a small peck, and ever so quick; it could easily have been something innocent. But the electricity between them is undeniable, their closeness is clear. In that split second, I now see something of the years they've shared.

I'm staring at the photo when Leila approaches.

I glance up, my mouth dry, searching for meaning in her eyes. Leila looks down at the photo and snatches it out of my hand. She sits down quietly on the sofa.

'It was a long time ago,' she says.

She places the photo down and reaches out to pour herself a large glass of wine.

'What do you mean?' I ask.

She stares down at the floor, then gulps down her wine.

'It shouldn't have happened. I see that now. But it did. Nothing I can do to change it.'

She leans back onto the sofa, folding her legs to the side, tucking her feet under her dress.

'Are you saying that you . . . and Mr Stellans. . . ?'

I see her nod, but she doesn't move. She sits there, ever so still.

'But *when* and for how *long*?' My mind is racing. I want to know everything. I want to know all the details.

'For about four years. It started three months after he joined Brentwood.'

'I never knew. How could I not know?' I whisper, more to myself than to her.

'It ended the summer we left school. He'd gone by that point, if you remember – he left after the school play in December. I couldn't tell you about it,' she takes another sip of wine, 'for obvious reasons.'

'I can't believe what I'm hearing,' I say.

'I know what you're thinking, but it wasn't like that between us. We were in love.'

I open another box of high school memorabilia and pull out a yearbook. My heart is racing. It's dated 2000, the end of Year 11. I begin leafing through the pages, determined to find a picture of Mr Stellans so I can rip it out and keep it for an investigation.

'It's better to cook rice fresh,' she says, as she watches me frantically thumbing the pages. 'The Indian I order from does a lovely chicken curry, but their rice always has this strange, gone-off butter smell . . . What do you fancy eating?'

I'm still turning pages. I settle on a double-page spread, staring down at a list of teachers I vaguely remember.

Mrs Valley – Art.
Mrs Smith – Religious Education
Miss Harris – Geography

'I fancy lamb,' says Leila. 'What I like about The Taj is that they throw green peas into the sauce. Have you ever tried that? Lamb curry with green peas. It's delicious.'

Mr Lavender – Chemistry
Mr Hingston – Biology
Mr Stellans . . .

My cheeks burn. There he is, suited with spiky hair. A boyish picture of eagerness, of alleged professionalism and innocence. He's standing by a window with the sun streaming in. Leila's footsteps near and I feel helpless.

'I don't need a lecture. It was a long time ago. What we had between us is nothing like that story in the papers.' Leila stares down at the open page in the yearbook. 'Are you listening, Rita?' She nudges me. 'It was different.'

'Leila, you have no idea what this means – how *serious* this is. Why didn't you ever tell me about it?'

She drops her head and slowly exhales.

'Do you want something stronger? *This wine.* Honestly, it's like drinking *Ribena.*'

I watch Leila return to the kitchen, her feet heavy, and I follow her.

'When was the last time you spoke to him?' I ask. 'Are you still in touch?' My head is rushing. The air is still. I hear the water boiling.

'We've spoken now and again,' she mumbles.

She moves to the window, staring outside onto the street below. 'I found him on Facebook, and we just kind of. . . connected. That's the power of social media.' She sniggers. 'I happen to like his books, and like I said, he's a talented writer.'

I move to Leila's side, the scent of her sweet, amber perfume sinking into me. 'But it's so much more than that,' I say. 'Don't you get it? He has been grooming girls.'

Her face falls and she brushes past me. 'Your reaction is exactly why we kept it quiet. We knew no one would ever understand it.'

'Understand? What is there to *understand*?' I try not to lose my temper, so I take a deep breath; I'm slow counting in my mind. 'This is child abuse. Don't you see? He *manipulated* you into thinking it was all innocent.'

Leila opens the freezer door and stands there for a while, her eyes closed, head dropped back. She rustles around for ice cubes, dropping a few into each glass.

'I'll order a selection of curries for us to choose from,' she says. 'I know how *particular* you can be. It would be good for you to try something different because if I remember correctly, you can be very fussy.'

I glance up at the clock, wanting to get out, wondering how it is that I'm becoming embroiled in a story I can barely believe is real. It's nine o'clock and it's growing dark. Outside the kitchen window, street lamps flicker as if tired. I open the latch and a cool breeze wafts in. I hear Leila on the phone in the hallway, placing the order for our takeaway, complaining that they ought to develop an app for easy ordering.

But now I've lost my appetite. All I want to do is to shake Leila, to make her see sense. Or Lawson – maybe I should call him. I just wouldn't know where to begin with a story like this.

'You need to come forward,' I say, determinedly, when Leila returns. 'A girl has accused him and if you testify too, it will help bring him to justice.'

'No way,' she snorts. 'It's not the same thing. That girl is hardly innocent, is she?'

'And what about you? Do you blame yourself too? Do you think you led him on?'

She moves to the sink, staring down into it.

'Leila . . .' My voice is softer. 'This is not your fault. Don't ever think that it is.'

I approach, draping my arm around her, pulling her close. We stay like that for several moments before the phone in my bag vibrates.

'Who is that?' Leila gently pulls away from me. 'Why so many messages? Your phone has been going off all evening.'

I tell Leila about the WhatsApp group, but her eyes are puffy, and by now, her speech is slurring. 'What are they talking about, this WhatsApp group?' I notice how she spits out her consonants.

'It's the latest on Stellans. It is not good.'

I tell her there are things she needs to talk about, that things are not as she remembers them to be. Childhood memories are like that – the world you recall and believe in is not always as it seems. But Leila grows defensive.

'I don't know why you keep going on about it, Rita. I never invited you here to judge me. I thought it would be nice for us to meet up, after all these years.'

'Leila, *please.*' I draw closer to her, my childhood friend who I've known for so long. 'He is accused of having an underaged affair. You need to get your head around it.'

Her shoulders fall, her arms grow limp.

She picks up a glass and pours herself some whiskey. She offers me one but I shake my head. We move to the sofa and she sits beside me, cloaked in silence. She's twirling her tumbler, rattling her ice around. She brings the glass to her lips and gulps some whiskey down. I notice her eyes are growing heavier, as she reaches, clumsily and haphazardly, for her cigarettes. She lights up, her hands trembling, blowing smoke up towards the ceiling.

'I knew what I was letting myself in for,' she says. 'I might have been fourteen, but I knew what I was doing. There was nothing that happened that I didn't agree to. It was my decision – in fact, it was my idea,' she laughs. 'He never even wanted a relationship.'

'That didn't seem to stop him though, did it?'

'I consented.'

'A child cannot make an informed decision.'

She scoffs, batting her eyelids. 'I don't know if you remember what I was like. I could be very *persuasive.*'

Leila says persuasive like it's something to be proud of. I reach out my hand, placing it onto hers.

'None of this was your fault. Do you hear me? None of it.' I surprise myself by how calm and assured I have become.

She brushes my hand away. 'Please don't patronise me. I'm not some sort of victim.'

I stand up, walking towards the window to get some air. My temples begin to throb, and I glance behind me at the table. That is the precise moment when the lights go off.

Leila jumps. 'What's happening? What's going on?

'Just a blackout,' I say. 'They said it would happen. It's been on the news. We need candles.'

She flicks her lighter and carries it like an Olympic torch, opening and closing the cupboard doors.

'Let me help you,' I say, moving closer.

'Please don't,' she snaps.

I step back, her words stinging. I watch her rip open a bag of tealights. The kitchen glows as she lights them. Flames dance like courtesans in the dark. There we are, two grown women, surrounded by boxes containing fragments of our younger selves.

Leila catches a glimpse of my phone lying on the counter. She leans forward and snatches it.

'I want to read some of the messages,' she says.

I turn away, thinking it best to give her some space, but after a few minutes, she tuts and starts laughing.

'They don't even know what they're talking about.' She replaces my phone on the table. 'I work in TV. I know *exactly* what the media is like. Sensationalising everything.' She pours herself another glass of whiskey.

'You can't be serious,' I say.

'I'm very *serious.*'

'You're drunk, Leila. Enough.'

'I need my Indian,' she slurs. 'Where's my fucking Indian? And who the hell are you to boss me around?'

I cover my eyes with my hands, unable to watch her stumbling about. She crashes into the back of a chair and laughs. 'Whoopsie!' she yells.

That's when it occurs to me that all this time I had feelings for her, when I thought that maybe, somewhere inside her, she might feel something – anything – for me, she was with *him*. It was all, and always, about him.

Leila pulls out another cigarette from her packet and she lights up, blowing smoke out of the window. She turns to me.

'You would never understand because you've never even kissed a boy, have you, Rita *Marsh*?' She laughs. 'Never even kissed a girl, eh? Well. Except for me.' She throws her head back, laughing harder, more sinisterly.

'Stop it,' I say.

'We were best friends once, right?' she says, sarcastically, her words blurring into one. 'Friends-that-shared-h-h-h-*e-v-e-r-y-t-h-i-n-g* . . .'

'It didn't always feel like that,' I say. Leila was getting into my head and when she got into my head, I could neither see nor hear anything else. 'I could never understand why, one minute, you'd act as though I was the most important person in your life, and then the next, you'd completely ignore me.' My head hangs. 'I see now why that is. All along you've been—'

'Because you were suffocating, do you understand that? Can you blame me for wanting to get away after *e-v-e-r-ything* you did?'

'Everything *I* did?'

'Don't act so innocent!' Another heavy spit of a consonant. 'You were definitely, most definitely. . . not that. Nope.' She begins wagging her finger.

I grab my phone, my bag, my jacket, ready to leave. When her back is turned, I also grab the yearbook, slipping it under my shirt. Leila grabs my arm, squeezing hard onto it.

'Lamb curry with green peas. You like a bit of Indian, *oui?*'

'Fuck off.'

I storm out of the front door and hear it slam behind me and I am stunned, really stunned at what just happened. What a fool I have been. Under the shelter, my body trembles. I'm overwhelmed with disbelief, but more than that, I'm overcome by a tremendous sense of sadness. I'm torn that after all these years,

I have discovered her secret. Someone somewhere is laughing at me – I feel it, the humiliation, my own stupidity.

I stare down at my phone. I see three notifications of new messages hurtling in.

That's when I see what Leila has done. She's written a message from my WhatsApp account in the Brentwood Reunion group.

IT'S ALL LIES!!!! NONE OF IT IS TRUE!!!!

The mob are out in full force:

The latest headlines are out, kiddo. That poor girl was GROOMED. What are you chatting about?

OMG! have you SEEN his books are selling out!

WHAAAAT??? NO WAY!

Did you read his last one about that boy gone missing? It's not half bad! LOL!!

Someone posts a message about the integrity of the girl accusing Stellans, just like it always is when women must defend themselves.

Not everyone can be trusted, y'know!

Yeah, some girls are literally ASKING for it

There are pictures of her drunk, flashing her bare breasts at parties. Another message appears concerning the Jeffrey Epstein story, still in the news. Grim details of his requests for massages and his sleazy girlfriend, trickling through. A trail of hashtags in quick succession, citing #metoo.

This is a time for women to speak out, one says.

There'll be a major shit storm, prophesies another.

But in that moment, all I can remember is the way the rain falls, how the breeze sweeps over my cheeks, how badly my chest hurts. I'm clutching onto the yearbook, wondering what there is in those pages that can somehow explain this. Why it was that our friendship, which I cherished, was not enough for her. How she could look me in the eye all those years knowing she was with an older man.

9

The next morning, I'm clanging dishes in the kitchen; I even burn the sausages cooking in the oven.

There's a fire in me that feels like it's scorching my skin, spreading all over my body as I struggle to breathe. I'm trying to figure out dates, times, key events. How and when it all started, this alleged *love affair*, which to everyone else, and certainly from where I'm standing, is nothing but sick and perverse.

I cannot fathom how I managed to get through school never suspecting a thing. I'm playing memory Tetris with timelines, slotting each brick impression – me walking to school, moments in class, sneaky chats in the girls' toilets – into others: her parents, her father, her brother, Rahul. I'm even wondering: did this have anything to do with Leila moving down from Scotland? Perhaps she was lonely. Perhaps she was vulnerable. I want to speak to Spike and Spider, but they won't speak to me now. I even think of Lawson because he is the only other person I know who'd understand.

I walk into my office and grab my phone to thumb him a text:

Need to talk. Urgent! Got some important information.

Within seconds, a return message:

Will send you a time and location for a meeting in the next 48 hours.

I peel apart the layers of a fresh bin bag, blood whooshing around my temples as I bend to empty the waste from the basket.

I see now that, somehow, their relationship was obvious. I just didn't notice it. Didn't see it at the time, but it explains a lot about Leila's mood swings. Her strange behaviour at school. Why, for example, she constantly talked about her period. I remember once seeing her circle her due date in red biro in her homework diary as if to mark when her essay was due. I realise now it was because she feared missing menstruating.

I lift the bin bag up, twisting it round, knotting it at the top. As I walk into the hallway towards the front door, I hear Margaret coughing in her room upstairs, but I do not run to her. I'm waiting for a girl to arrive from Ascot Care. She's going to help out for a few days, just to give me a bit of time to get my head straight.

Back indoors from emptying the rubbish, I jump as the front door slams behind me, but before I can run into the kitchen, the phone rings. I lean against the wall to answer it.

'Rita Marsh? This is Kasia. Kasia Sobczyk? You requested cover? I'm just calling to say, I know you were expecting me at 9 a.m. but I'm caught in traffic. I'll be at least another hour.'

'Thanks for letting me know, Kasia.'

I slam down the phone, and before I can control myself, I run into the kitchen and grab a photo of my parents. It's a shot of them seated on a bench in the garden during summer. I hurl it against the wall and watch as the frame smashes, shards of glass all over the floor. I stand there for a while, staring at the photo. My father stares up at me, condescending, ashamed of me. My mother, doing what she always does: observing silence as if it is part of her meditation practice. I bury my face in my hands and try to calm my breathing.

I need help. I know I do. I must stop trying to rescue everyone else and start dealing with my own issues. It was stupid to give up on therapy so soon after only one session. But it's not easy going back to confront your demons when you've spent your whole life being silenced.

I pour myself a glass of water from the jug filled with ice and sliced lemons intended for residents, and I watch the fleshy bits spin around the glass and settle at the bottom.

I stare down at my phone, scrolling through my contact numbers. I stop at Dr Geeta Goswami. I'm tempted to call her, but I don't.

Instead, I think of Leila, how precocious she was at school, how much she loved all the attention. Is that what Stellans saw in her? There she was, her skirt rolled up at the waist, socks deliberately trailing down her ankles, legs shaved and oiled. She refused to fasten the top button of her shirt, no matter how many times I told her to. I, of all people, had learnt a difficult lesson. I knew what a tease she could be. One minute, into you, another, ghosting you for days. Worse still were her mind games. And should you ever dare call her out, she could make you feel like *you* were the one with the problem.

Then I remember something more.

It's English and Leila is seated at the front of class. Next to her is Jason, the school clown. She's giggling in a way that draws his attention, and I see now, she's leading him on. I see her *leaning closer* to him, gliding her fingers over the edge of her exercise book. Jason shuffles restlessly in his seat, grinning. He dangles an idle arm just inches from her back. His hands are loose; uncertain how to behave. I notice his fingers, thin with dirty nails. Jason grows ever more animated. His skin so pale; a web of blue lines is visible. I prick my finger with the sharp tip of a pencil, wanting to plunge it into his neck, to tear out his veins.

Now, here I am, aged thirty-five, still thinking of Leila. Clearly, not over it. I take another sip of water, crunching the ice between my teeth, feeling the shock of pain as it hits the back of my throat.

I slam my glass down onto the table and move to the sink, breathing faster as I attempt to control myself. I turn on the tap, rinsing my hands in cold water, splashing it onto my face.

I grab my phone and tap out a message to Javid. I need to see him; I need to talk to someone about this situation.

Where are you? Want to meet up and chat about the gossip post reunion?

But before I press send, the doorbell rings. I have no choice but to muster up the strength to go and answer it. As I pull open the door, I see a young woman standing on the doorstep, her back to the sunlight.

'Rita Marsh?'

Her mousy brown bob shines as she turns her head to the side.

'I'm Kasia.' She smiles. I take a step back to let her in.

'Thanks for turning up at short notice,' I say, clenching my jaw, trying not to sound sarcastic.

Kasia breezes past me, and I open the door wider to let her in. She's clutching a brown leather bag and a phone charger. 'Right then. Feel free to run me through the rota and I'll get started.'

After I brief Kasia and talk her through the specifics about Margaret and Derek (how Margaret is miserable and needs cheering up, how Derek has taken to wandering around in only his underwear), I return to my bedroom and close the door. I walk over to my wardrobe and pull down a box, just behind the one full of school photos I was sifting through earlier. This is another box of mine, containing memories – a few random things I've collected over the years which I haven't looked at in ages. I lift the lid and inside, I find what I'm looking for. The pages are crumbled with curly handwriting on the front. I stare out of the window and something more returns. It's another memory of Leila and I, moving from the haze and into clear view. We're both fourteen and at school.

Leila was walking along the main corridor alone, brushing her fingers across the blue painted walls, across leaflets and flyers stuck to a corkboard. I watched her from the side, as she stopped outside the staffroom door, tucking a loose tendril of hair behind her ear, straightening her skirt. She coughed into her hand and raised her arm to knock on the door. It was unnecessarily loud, I see that now. It was like she was asserting her presence. I don't know why I never noticed it then. Within seconds, Mr Stellans appeared in the doorway, his blonde feathery hair windswept, like he'd just walked in from playing football. Leila flashed him a coy smile and Mr Stellans leaned an arm against the door frame, his head tilted, crossing one leg over the other.

'May I have the key to classroom eleven?' Leila giggled.

Stellans nodded, expressionless. The door closed gently behind him as he disappeared into the staffroom.

I watched Leila as she swayed, curling the ends of her hair around her fingers.

When the door opened again, she bolted upright and Mr Stellans dangled a bunch of keys above her head. I heard her laughing as he held them up higher. Thinking about it now, I see how his game was a perverse power trip.

Leila rose onto tiptoes, reaching out to grab the keys. He lowered his hand, and she snatched them off him. For a split second, they stood still, staring at one another.

I decided to follow Leila.

That day, the school corridor was bustling with Oxbridge students brought in to discuss the virtues of an elite education. It was dark and damp; clogged with the stale stench of wet coats and muddy PE kits. I remember trailing up the stairs, my hand sliding along the banister. I was about to open the door to classroom eleven, but I stopped outside, watching Leila through the glass. Her movements were slight, delicate. When I turned the handle, Leila jumped.

'God, Rita. You scared me.' She placed her hand against her chest to calm herself, then cleared her books away, stuffing them haphazardly into her bag.

'Sorry,' I mumbled. 'I didn't mean to creep up on you.'

'Well, you did!' she snapped.

She threw her bag over her shoulder, grabbing her blazer and coat from the back of her chair. 'What are you doing here, anyway? Was anyone else with you— behind you?' She looked straight through me, as if I wasn't there.

How stupid I was, to think she was there to catch up on homework during lunchtime. Now I can see that this must have been one of their secret arrangements.

'It's just me.'

She sighed; she appeared disappointed. 'Well . . .' She looked up, searching my face. 'What do you want? You're making me nervous.'

'Nothing.'

'Then what are you doing here?'

My mind scrambled as I searched for a plausible excuse, one that she wouldn't see straight through. I scanned the classroom, noticing a ruler on the ledge in the corner. I walked over to it and held it up. 'I came for this,' I said, tapping the ruler lightly against my hand.

Leila nodded. 'Well, I need to go. I've got so much homework to do, I can't keep up.'

But I held onto her arm as she turned. 'I can help you,' I said quickly. I cringe now, as I recall how desperate I sounded. 'You can come round to mine later. We can go through stuff together. I have time. Maybe we can hang out a bit.'

She shook her head, and I dropped her arm. 'It's Drama. I need to write a short script. Then a letter in German. You don't have a clue since those aren't even your subjects.'

I spotted her bag open; inside, a roll of clothes.

'There's too much going on at home. I can't concentrate,' she said. 'Besides, I need to do this alone.'

Leila was about to turn to leave. Before I could stop myself, I grabbed her arm once more.

'What now?' Her voice was shrill. 'What are you doing?'

'It's just . . . I never see you . . .' My hand brushed her arm as it fell. 'Every time I'm around you, you never want to be with me.'

She rolled her eyes. 'Rita, we're good mates, but I've told you before. Sometimes, you can be so *intense*. I can't breathe. And you act so weird . . . I needed space over the summer. It's one of the reasons why I didn't call you.'

You needed space over the summer to see him.

I clenched my fists.

'Can you understand what I'm saying?'

I wished the ground would open and swallow me whole.

She saw my eyes filling, so she reached out her hand, resting it onto my shoulder.

'Let's chat later, okay?' she said.

But before I could even blink, Leila rushed out of the classroom, the door left wide open behind her.

I was in a daze, and I stood there alone, the sounds of the other kids merging into one – their shouting, running and laughter. I felt like I was drowning, water filling my ears, entering my nostrils. I leaned onto the desk to steady myself, and then I left the classroom.

I took only a few steps, the echoes of children reverberating around the corridor, bouncing off the walls like tennis balls, when I noticed that the door to the literature room was open. It was a small, dusty enclosure with shelves running from floor to ceiling across the entire wall, where all our English textbooks and reading materials were kept. Usually, it was locked. As I approached, I heard voices:

'I know, but I couldn't this time . . .' It was a man's voice.

'I waited *ages* . . .' A girl's.

I pushed open the door and stepped inside. I saw Leila with Mr Stellans, leaning against the window ledge. At the time, it seemed so normal, so innocent – I thought nothing of it. But now I see their faces were close, their bodies only inches apart.

I coughed, startling them both. They pulled away from one another, quickly. Leila ran off before I had time to say anything.

'Did you want something, Rita?'

It was Mr Stellans, scowling at me. He was always scowling at me.

'Nothing, Sir.'

'Then disappear. Next lesson is about to start.' And with that, he nudged me out, locking the door, before storming off.

In my bedroom, I stare down at my hands, weak and shaking. Outside my window, I see a raven soar across the sky. If I disliked Stellans then, I truly hate him now. Men like that should surely pay for their deceptions.

10

I'm seated in my van, parked outside Dr Goswami's house.

I finally gave in and called her. Geeta said I needed to face my inner fears: those things responsible for propelling me to want to always rescue others. I should be willing, she said, to confront the past, which would allow me to appreciate the beauty and splendour of the full life in front of me now. I didn't tell her about my years of hunting. But I told her enough about my life in the care home and discontent with world affairs for her to pontificate.

Inside her room, which today smells like dried roses and cinnamon, I close my eyes and settle into my leather seat. Geeta pulls the back down so I can relax. She tells me to focus on my breathing, but I'm so tired, I feel like I might fall asleep.

'How did you feel after the last time you were here?'

She is wearing a frilly shirt and a new-age necklace with an amber star pendant. Her voice is low and velvety, thick like chocolate.

'I felt strangely sensitive, like you'd ripped off a plaster and with it the top layer of a scab that was healing,' I say.

She nods knowingly. 'I'm sorry you felt that,' she says, 'Though of course, it's perfectly normal.'

Geeta tells me we'll try something different this time. Something akin to hypnosis, except not full hypnosis – a technique merged with visualisation.

'I just want you to concentrate on your breathing and follow my voice. Do you think you can do that, Rita?' she asks. 'This is a much gentler and more subconscious process than having an active conversation.'

'I can do that,' I say, yawning, relieved I won't have to talk too much. I'm overcome by a sudden wave of tiredness. My eyelids feel heavy, and eventually they close. My mouth is strangely dry and, annoyingly, my nose is blocked.

'Focus on your toes, your soles, your ankles . . . and then your calves . . . Let's tense and relax them . . . slowly moving upwards . . .'

Next, she has me counting down from one hundred to zero. With each beat, I feel my body growing heavier, as if it's sinking beneath the surface of the sea.

By the time I get to thirty, I'm as good as gone.

I think I see an image of my mother biting her nails. Possibly see her smile when I hand her my report card. A warm feeling begins to fill me, like someone is pouring treacle into a hole at the top of my head. I cough a little to clear my throat. A memory of the New Year's Eve party, of inhaling cigarette smoke, comes to me next.

'What do you see, Rita?'

I'm sinking deeper, my spine vibrating, slowly dissolving. I see myself dancing at a party. Must be New Year's Eve, the year 2000. I'm in a house and the music is loud – too loud for it to be pleasing. The air is smoky and stale. There are people shouting at me to get out of the way.

'Not much,' I say. 'I think . . . I'm at a party.'

She whispers now, asking me to go back further still, to say out loud any impressions I see or feel.

'Don't worry if they don't make any sense,' she says. 'Just name them. Acknowledging them is progress. Progress, with small steps, is how we begin to identify our patterns of resistance.'

I feel my body drift, as if I'm floating on water: a river, then a sea. I want to stay there, enjoy the expanse of blue, the waves, the fresh air, the vast emptiness. But then, as if I've drifted out too far, the water grows dark. It feels thick and heavy against my skin. A charge beneath, like a tremor, creates a strong current, which carries me further still, further into a void of black – further than I'm willing to travel. I feel like I'm being carried into an oil slick. 'I don't like this,' I say. 'I don't feel comfortable. I feel heavy, like I'm about to sink any minute.' I hold onto the edge of my seat, dig my nails into the leather; I feel the rib-trim and stitching.

'You're safe, Rita. Imagine you're holding onto a ring and that you're floating. No harm will come to you. I'm here. I'm right beside you, guiding you . . . Now tell me, what do you see?'

'I'm at home. I'm in my bed . . .' I feel my throat constricting. My face flushing.

'Breathe, Rita. Remember to breathe.'

'I'm seven years old, I think. I'm in my bedroom . . .'

I see it then, before the picture is fully formed, I know what I will see, there. It's a dark outline in the night, standing above me in my room, slipping and sliding like a shadow on the wall, telling me to lower my blanket . . .

I wriggle in my seat, my T-shirt stuck to my back; I'm sweating. The denim from my jeans feels heavy and stiff, like cardboard against my legs.

'I don't like this.' My voice wobbles. I feel a blanket over me. 'I don't want to continue. I don't want to do this . . .'

'Rita, please trust me. You're safe. You're perfectly safe. I just want you to tell me what you see. A little further, be brave, Rita. Be a warrior. Just a little further . . .'

I feel an arm reach out, the heavy thud of it over my chest, grabbing the edge of the blanket, grabbing clumps of my hair. A cold rush of air washes over me and then . . . it goes blank. Simply, darkness . . .

Cold sweat drips down my face.

I open my eyes, my cheeks damp. I throw an arm over my eyes to shield me from the light, since the room feels so bright.

'You've done well,' says Geeta. 'You should be very proud of yourself.'

But I'm shaking, unable to speak, annoyed with myself for allowing that scene to rise from beneath the carefully controlled surface of my mind. I feel like I might be sick. I reach over the side of the seat, and I dry retch. Geeta rushes beside me with a bin. She places her hand onto my back, patting me down gently.

'Would you like some water?' she asks.

I shake my head, throwing my legs to the side of the chair to haul myself up. She steps back and another wave of tiredness washes over me. I feel strangely light-headed, like all my thoughts have been obliterated.

'I want to go,' I say. 'I know what is there, back in the past, now part of my memory. But I see no point dredging it all up. What is the *point* of doing that?'

Geeta stares at me, waiting for me to finish, a little surprised by my reaction, which she presumably thinks is all part of my healing.

'It's not you, it's me,' I say. 'I just don't see the point of all this. Why I should have to do the work, when there are men out there, getting away with it? I don't see them doing any work on themselves. Do you? I don't see them trying to heal their *sickness*.'

She sits silently, allowing me to continue. I can see it in her eyes, an inner triumph that she's discovered something – something deep, a wound, something torn and broken, that's interesting to work with.

'Was it someone you know?'

My body seizes. I shake my head.

'It was someone my father knew from back home,' I say. 'He was staying with us for a few months before getting a place of his own. He was a lodger. He worked long hours as a doctor, so he was hardly at home.'

Geeta lowers her voice. 'Did you speak to your parents about it?'

My stomach clenches. 'They knew. But I was told to keep quiet, because of what it might do, if word got out.'

'I see.' She shakes her head.

'He was well known.'

'Where is he now?'

'I don't know,' I say. 'I'll never know because both my parents died in a car crash. So that is the end of it.'

Geeta places a hand over her mouth, as if trying to stop further words from tumbling out.

I wipe my face with a tissue, the scent of lemon rousing me, and I stand, trying to restore my balance.

'You've done a great deal of work today, Rita. You should feel very proud of yourself.'

Pride is not what I feel, however. I feel anger, I feel rage. I want to tear through the furniture with a knife, stabbing at it again and again.

I gather my coat and bag, my body trembling. I want to burst into tears. As I leave the room, I can't help but question what I've done. Holding up a memory from the past does not change it. Neither does it avenge the crime committed. Revenge and the pursuit of justice is progress, because they're still out there, those men, trapping their innocent victims. I can spend my time wallowing in self-pity, or I can look forward into the future; do something about it.

Like the flick of a switch, all the haziness seems to disappear.

Geeta hands me her card, urging me to call her in a few days. 'Our work is not done here, Rita. This is just the beginning. Book another appointment when you're ready and we can continue.'

I stare down at her card, the gold letters of her name glinting in the light.

I tell her I'll call her in a few days when I have more energy. But I'm done talking to her. As I leave the clinic and the fresh air hits me, I think to myself that maybe this time it really *is* the end of therapy.

11

It's dusk. I'm in South Harrow Park with DCI Lawson. He turns, asking me what this meeting is all about.

'I have some information. Think it might be of interest to you,' I say.

He nods but continues to watch three boys in the distance kicking a football around. 'Go on,' he says. 'I'm all ears.'

'It concerns a case. One that's already live and in the media.'

Lawson raises an eyebrow.

'I see. Made up your mind about working with the police. Is this the start of a collaboration?'

'Not quite,' I say, brushing him off. 'But I do have something important.'

'Oh?'

'I know a girl. Another victim. She's been groomed by a man. He had an affair with her. It lasted four years, from when she was fourteen. He was her teacher. I suspect there are others still out there.'

Lawson turns to me. 'Already in the media, you say?'

I nod. 'Michael Stellans. The Ealing case.'

'The writer, Michael Stellans?'

'That's the one.'

Lawson scratches his head. I hear his phone vibrate in his shirt and he pulls it out from his breast pocket.

'Victim?'

'Leila Sharma. I know her. She was – is – my best friend. We met at school. Brentwood High. She's only just told me about him.'

He nods, reading – checking something, presumably. 'He was arrested but released,' says Lawson. 'Highly unfortunate.'

I sigh a little too loudly for my frustration to be subtle. 'But the girl came forward!'

'It's complicated,' he says. 'Historical cases always are. Some of the details in her story . . . didn't add up.'

'Like what?'

'Can't say.' Lawson pops his phone back into his pocket. 'Dates. Events. Tangible evidence. Things like that. But if your friend could step forward and make a statement, that might help move things along nicely.'

I stare down at the grass, resisting the temptation to tell Lawson how useless I think the police are.

'I can arrange for her to speak to someone else if she feels more comfortable,' says Lawson. 'DC Morgan is available.'

'Sarah?'

'Yes, Sarah. Lovely lady, Sarah. A good listener. Highly supportive.'

'What will Sarah do, exactly?'

'For starters, she'll speak to your friend. Take her statement. Then we'll go and arrest him. Start the process all over again.'

I feel my stomach flip. 'That doesn't work.'

'Oh?' Lawson kicks at something in the grass. 'Do enlighten me, Rita.'

'My friend, see, she won't admit she's been groomed. She might admit to having the affair. But I'm not sure she would want to make it formal, nor risk it going public.'

Lawson clears his throat. I'm trying to figure out what he's thinking.

'Rita . . .'

I flinch when he says my name.

'I think you and I need to clarify how we're working together.'

I swallow hard.

'Until we do,' he says, 'things could be, well, difficult.'

I turn to face him. 'I know I've messed things up. I know I owe you a clear decision. I've been thinking . . .' I feel my jaw grow stiff. 'I want to help,' I say. 'Really, I do. But I still need a bit of time to clear things up with Raven Justice.' I'm unsteady on my feet. Lawson glances at me and observes my shuffling. 'We need time to talk things through. If I'm working with you, I can't work with them, can I? Leaving the group can't happen overnight. It needs a conversation.'

'I see,' he says.

'In the meantime, we've got this live case on our hands, and we simply can't ignore it. This girl, she's blind to what's happened to her. I mean, she's in *denial*. She doesn't think he did anything wrong.'

Lawson sighs. 'Cases like this are never easy.'

'So, you'll speak to her?'

'If she's willing to come forward, sure. She might not want to, though. She might want to move on with her life. And if that's the case, that is *her* decision.'

My brain is in overdrive.

'So, you're saying you would just leave it at that? That's it? That's your official policing method?'

I know I'm pushing it. I can tell, by the way Lawson keeps fiddling with his car keys in his pocket, that he's about to lose his patience.

'Rita, listen to me.' He lowers his voice as if I'm a child to be reasoned with. 'You and I know the scale of the problem. We know what we're dealing with. But if it's an historical case, she would need to step forward and make a statement. Then we can go after him – go full procedure and build a strong case against him. That is the correct way to do things, don't you think? It's easier if another girl has already stepped forward.'

I shake my head. 'She won't do it.'

'Then what do you want me to do?'

'I'm asking you to look into it.'

'Based on your word? Look into what, exactly? This is absurd.'

'He's out there, writing books, for fuck's sake.' I'm losing ground with Lawson, I can see, but I'm so consumed with frustration at myself for having missed the signs, I have to try and make up for it. 'Look, I know what this sounds like—'

'It sounds like you're in danger of getting yourself embroiled in another mess, Rita.'

'What?'

'You're coming close to crossing the line again.' Lawson turns, growling at me. 'You don't seem to understand how this works. If you want to convict a criminal, you need evidence, a trial, and a court decision. Not a witch-hunt. But here you now are, telling me about a case that is not really a case because your friend can't admit that anything happened – asking me to intervene! Can you see how confused this appears?'

He scoffs.

'I'm telling you, he's guilty.' A final attempt to convince him.

'And I'm telling you, I believe you.' He unwraps a piece of gum and pops it into his mouth. 'I always have. But you need to follow a process.'

'This is so frustrating,' I say.

'Why can't *you* talk to her?' he says. 'Make sure she's comfortable. Persuade her to make a statement. If you do that, then yes, of course, we will pick it up from there.'

'I can't talk to her.'

Lawson rubs his head. His face is scarlet. 'I can't and won't protect you, Rita. Do you hear? If you meddle in this – even after I urge you not to get involved – I'm done with you. I'm under pressure too, for even considering the prospect of introducing a working arrangement with *you*. You know that not everyone, internally, is a fan of the idea. Your methods crossed a line, and after Zia, all sorts of questions are being asked.'

I bite my lip and taste blood.

'I've tried to reason with you, but I'm under the cosh. Leave this case well alone, or you're on your own. And another thing, please be clear about where we stand. Clock is ticking.'

I watch Lawson as he walks off, passing a row of marigolds, stepping onto the pavement. As I look up at the sky, at the hole-punched clouds, I cannot deny he is right. There is nothing I can do but to get Leila to speak up. If not for herself, for all the other girls.

The phone in my pocket buzzes and for a moment, my heart skips, thinking that it might be Leila. But it's Javid.

Hey! Sorry for the delay. Been so busy! Yes, let's catch up on the reunion. I have a bit of gossip. And you? What you been up to? Can't believe Leila turned up! LOL x

The next morning in Raven Court, I stare down at the Brent-wood High yearbook, opened flat onto page thirty, and tiled with teacher profiles. A photo of Mr Stellans stands out from the others. It's something to do with his expression, his grin. It appears sinister to me now.

I think about what Lawson said, and I want to slam the year-book closed. But his face is there, hardly changed over the years, similar to more recent pictures of him on the internet. Stellans appears boyishly thin. Under his eyes, glancing slightly to the left, there appear to be grey shadows. There is no way I can let him get away with this.

According to his biography, Michael Stellans first arrived at school in spring 1998. I was in Year 9, and I remember the day clearly.

*

The sun streamed through the classroom window, warming our faces, casting a pool of light onto the tables. As we shuffled inside, he was already there, standing at the front, behind his desk on which lay a big cardboard box. He looked about thirty and was wearing blue jeans, a white shirt, a black leather jacket that squeaked. He moved swiftly to the box, an air about him that reminded me of when my dad returned, fresh and carefree, from one of his trips to see his grandmother in the Gujarati village of Hodka, in India.

He was shabby, not bothering with his appearance, in the way that some men don't when they're resigned to spending the rest of their lives uncommitted. I can't deny that he had a certain confidence about him, however. He peered at us suspiciously as we took to our seats, the anticipation of the arrival of a new teacher rising amongst the pupils. Stellans looked like he was trying to figure out how long it might be before we became a nuisance to him.

Leila sat down at the desk just in front of Stellans, next to Jason. I opened my bag, took out my things. I opened a book to distract myself, but I heard Leila giggling. I scratched my pencil against the table, satisfied only when the lead snapped.

'Morning,' he said, smiling. He turned to face the blackboard and chalked his name onto it.

MR STELLANS (MICHAEL)

'That's me,' he said, pointing to the letters. 'But you get to call me Sir.' His voice was unusually deep. Somehow it didn't fit with the rest of him, his long, thin face and spiky blonde hair.

The class fell silent but there were a few sideway glances and sniggers. The grating and scraping sound of chairs irritated my teeth.

'As this is our first class together, I'd like to give you an opportunity to ask me any questions you might have. Sound good?' More silence. 'Who'd like to go first?'

No one said a word.

'Anything, from anyone? You lot don't look shy. C'mon.'

Leila turned her head, scanning the class behind her. Jason nudged her arm then leaned forward, whispering something to her.

Fritz raised his prawny arm. 'Sir, how old are you?'

'I'm thirty,' said Stellans.

'When's your birthday?' Sarah Peters.

'June first. Gemini.' He laughed.

In chimed Jason. 'Have you got a girlfriend, Sir?'

The class erupted with laughter.

Stellans hesitated. 'Unfortunately not,' he said. 'Believe me, I've tried.'

Before I could stop myself, my arm rose too.

'Why did you leave your last school?'

Stellans gave me a prickly look. Leila cocked her head when she heard my voice.

'Time for a new challenge, I guess. Besides, you all looked interesting.'

Leila stared ahead, her head barely moving. She raised her hand when no one was expecting it.

'Sir. Do you like Rumi?'

Stellans stopped for a moment, his face flashing with delight. I held my breath as he nodded. 'Very much,' he said, staring at Leila, 'and I love that question.' He dropped his head, his eyes still resting on her. 'You clearly have very refined taste.' Jason straightened up in his chair.

Mr Stellans said we'd be covering Yeats, Larkin, and Shakespeare's sonnets, starting with Sonnet 18. But that there would be plenty of opportunity for us to write our own poems, for those who received the poet's calling.

He asked one of the girls to hand out our set texts, and the class began.

I slam the yearbook shut and think of Spike and Spider, whether I could tip them off. See what they made of Stellans. They would be on it like a shot. But then I think of DCI Lawson, the ultimatum he gave me.

I can't get involved. I just can't.

Leila would have to be the one to step forward and report what happened to her. There is no way I could do it.

I grab my mobile and search for Leila's number. The smell of buttered toast wafts in from the kitchen where I prepared breakfast only forty minutes ago. I dial her number. I have no idea whether this is even a good idea after the last exchange in her flat, but I dial, regardless, walking to the hallway to pick up the mail from the doormat. I stop in front of the hallway mirror and stare hard at myself, determined to stay on the line as it rings, and not talk myself out of it. I hear the phone click as it connects. I hear it ring on the other end. Then it goes to voicemail:

Hi, it's Leila. Leave me a message and if it's not too boring, I'll call you back.

I hang up, my forehead pressed to the wall, my breathing heavy. *This is madness.*

I walk into the kitchen, aware I'm not alone. I'm keen to avoid Kasia before she thuds down the stairs with the vacuum cleaner in her hand. I pour myself a cup of leftover tea from the teapot and move towards the kitchen table, pulling out a notebook and pen from a nearby drawer. I sit down at the table, clicking my pen, staring down at the blank paper.

I click again. *I need to do something.*

I need to consider my options. I need a plan.

Upstairs, I hear the vacuum cleaner switch off. Kasia's footsteps trudge along the ceiling. She's moving towards the bathroom and in my mind's eye, I see her winding black cable.

Perhaps I can make Leila confess. After all, I know what she's like. I protected her. I always did. She must remember that time when we were kids, and a racist shop assistant accused her of stealing lipsticks – how I came to her defence.

Things are different, now. This is not about lipstick, nor racist shop assistants. This is about a paedophile roaming the streets. A man from the past whom we both trusted. A former teacher who thinks he ought to be excused for grooming girls simply because he enjoys the privilege of being *artistic*. I slam my pen down, not really thinking straight. I want to call Javid. I want to tell him everything.

I dial his number.

Javid answers, his mouth sounding dry, like he's only just got out of bed and doesn't remember why.

'Did I wake you, Javid? Why aren't you at work?'

'Jesus, Rita. What time is it?'

'It's ten o'clock in the morning. Are you okay to talk? I have a legal question for you.'

I hear him sigh, not the sigh of annoyance, more a sigh of weariness. I hear his head flop against the pillow.

'It's important,' I say.

'Fine. Talk. I'm awake now, but it's my day off. I wanted to have a lie-in. I know we need to meet up.'

'I need to know the legal standing of a young girl who has been groomed but who doesn't realise it. Can someone else go ahead and report it?'

'What?'

'I'm asking about a friend.'

'Rita, are you okay? What's this all about?' I hear the rustle of a blanket and I imagine that Javid is sitting upright in bed.

'I'm fine,' I say.

'Age?'

'Thirty-five. It's about an incident from the past.'

'Well . . . She's a grown woman so she needs to make a statement herself.'

My shoulders fall. 'Really? That's it?'

'It's the law. She can speak for herself. It's ambiguous if other people start speaking on her behalf. It means nothing and one must question the motivation . . .'

My mind begins to unravel like a spool of thread, with the end of it entirely missing.

'Rita. What is this about?'

'We'll talk later, I've got to go.'

'Rita wait—'

'Let's meet for dinner. We can chat then. When are you free?'

'Usual place at seven tomorrow?'

'Sounds perfect,' I say.

I hang up and retrieve my laptop. In the living room, I sit down and pull it out of its sleeve. I don't know what I'm doing – all I know is that I need to *do* something.

I Google Safe Streets then click onto the link. Earlier that morning I posted my dilemma concerning Stellans in the popular forum to see what other women made of it. I scroll to see the responses.

Posted by Dizzy-Lizzie: 08.10
This is difficult. Do you have any evidence? It was a long time ago, but you could still do something. If you want to report it, just go to the police. They should have trained officers who will be supportive in their questioning. But your friend must come forward herself for them to take it further. How close are you both? I think you should talk to her about it first. You need to be sure your friendship is strong enough to cope with the fallout. x

Posted by Sophia_Khan: 08.47
Would you like to see this man arrested and possibly
convicted?
This teacher needs to be reported. If he is convicted, he will go
on the sex offenders register. It's obviously a painful process. I
have been going through this for nearly a year and a half, and
in just over a week, I must stand in the witness box to be cross-
examined as my uncle is facing abuse charges. It's harrowing.
If you want to ask anything about the process, please feel free
to message me. xx

Posted by Nadine_23: 08.49
I'm sorry but what's more important? That your friend is
your friend, or we keep another sick pervert off the street??
He will just keep grooming and abusing kids. He needs to be
put away! I know what I would do. Here's the number for
Crimestoppers: 0800 555 111. N xx

Kasia thuds down the stairs. When the hoover knocks against
the door frame, it makes me sit up straight.

'I wasn't expecting you to still be at home,' she says. 'I've left
the breakfast dishes in the sink. Sorry, I just didn't get round to
it. Margaret and Derek seem comfortable. Would you mind if I
took my break?'

Kasia unfastens her apron and switches the kettle on before I
can answer. The low hissing sound seems to whistle right through
me.

'It's a lovely place, this. The grounds are so big . . .'

But I'm not listening to a word she's saying. I'm thinking of
Lawson. I'm thinking of Geeta, of my earlier session. I'm thinking
about why my head hurts. I don't hear the phone when it rings.

12

Javid and I meet in J. J. Moon's on Kingsbury Road. The street is bustling with shouty Indian street traders selling boxed mangoes and corn, drizzled in chilli and butter, from pop-up stands positioned on the kerb. I park my van in Aldi opposite the pub, which, on this warm Friday evening, is heaving with shoppers in pastel-coloured saris and flowing summer dresses.

Inside, I spot him standing at the bar wearing a white linen shirt and faded jeans. He's leaning against the counter, which is necklaced with red and white bunting, drinking whiskey and coke.

'God, you look awful,' he says.

I flinch and order a rum and coke before I tell him that he doesn't look so great himself. Javid chuckles as we move to a table.

'So, you saw Leila, then. How was it? Did something happen?' We take a seat and he stares at me expectantly, drumming his fingers on the table top ringed with beer stains. 'Must say, your call yesterday morning threw me.'

'Right,' I say, as I sip my rum and coke. 'Look, don't worry about it. I was just thinking about something and researching, hypothetically.'

'Something to do with Leila?'

I shake my head.

'Honestly, it's nothing,' I say. 'It's just that story about Stellans turning over in my mind, plus all that other stuff about Epstein in the news. It got me thinking about things.'

He stares down at the table, running his finger along the polished wood.

'His girlfriend has something to do with it, I'm certain of it.'

'Girlfriend?' he asks.

'Ghislaine Maxwell.' I shudder.

'He's a sick bastard, that Stellans. So many of them about. I never liked him; you know that, don't you? Do you remember before he arrived, there were a few rumours flying about him?'

'There were?'

'I'm sure of it. Like why he left the other school. The kids there said he was creepy.'

'I don't remember that.'

'Well, it all makes sense, now,' he says.

He leans back and sighs, staring up at the ceiling, then around him, at the tables littered with flyers.

'Why are you quiet?' asks Javid.

'I'm not.'

'You're in another world. You get like this sometimes and that's when I get worried,' he says. 'Rita keeps so many secrets, doesn't she?' He nudges my arm. 'You should let your friends in.'

I take another, larger, swig of rum and coke, rattling the ice in my tumbler as I place the glass down.

'So what happened then?' asks Javid.

'What do you mean?'

'Leila. You said she turned up.'

I shrug my shoulders. 'Well, I bumped into her on the road – just outside the school gate. We exchanged numbers, but that's about it. It was nice to see her. She looks great.'

'She didn't go in?'

'She wasn't keen.'

He notices my expression and takes a sip from his glass.

'What was that message about in the Brentwood Reunion group – the one about Stellans? Why deny the story about him?'

Javid catches me off guard. I had forgotten about that. I try to act natural.

'Leila and I happened to discuss the article and she had my phone. She sent those.'

Javid looks at me dumbfounded.

'That's a bit strange. Why would she do that? Does she not believe the accusations?'

'Clearly not,' I reply.

Javid shakes his head. 'Listen, just be careful, Rita. I'm here, if you want to talk, no pressure. I've always said that. I've been saying that since school, but you seem intent on being a weirdo. And now Leila reappears, just like that, and takes your phone.'

I reach out my hand and pat Javid on the arm.

'It was a reunion, remember? One that you organised. At reunions, we all regress to being teenagers.'

Javid smiles and then turns serious. 'But I know that story probably stirred up some stuff for you,' he says. 'You never talk about it, but I know it did.'

I purse my lips.

'Being at school, the reunion. Seeing everyone. Then the story about Stellans. I'm sorry. I didn't think. I should have been there for you,' he says.

'It's fine, honestly.' My voice is shrill. 'Really, I'm fine. And you've always been there when I needed you, getting me up on stage, forcing me out of my comfort zone.'

Javid chuckles. 'You should have seen your face.'

I want to laugh but thinking about it makes me cringe. 'So, what about you? How have you been?'

Javid raises his glass to his lips. I'm keen to divert his attention and he knows it.

'After you left the reunion, things got a bit mad,' Javid says.

'Oh?' I look up and notice the way his eyes sparkle.

'Me and Sanjay went for a drink . . .'

'Straight Sanjay, you mean?'

Javid laughs. 'Nothing is ever as it seems.'

I shake my head, partly relieved we've moved onto Javid's favourite topic of conversation – himself – but also aggrieved I might not receive any clarity on what I should do about Stellans.

'What happened to Matthew?' I ask. 'I thought he was *the one*.'

Javid stares down into his glass. 'Bit tricky that. I guess I'm not ready to settle down and get a dog.'

'I know how that feels.'

We drink only one more, since we're both driving, then we drift out of the bar, turning right to walk up Kingsbury Road. We pass Chaiwalla, the smell of cardamon and spicy rotis unfurling in the air, then we cross the side road and turn into Lezziz Charcoal Grill. The smell of shish makes me recall my conversation with Leila in the Pyramid. Something inside me feels uneasy.

'Hungry?' Javid glances at me longingly.

'I don't have much of an appetite, but don't let me stop you.'

We sit down at a cramped table, wedged into a corner. We're both checking our phones. Javid comments on the WhatsApp messages in the Brentwood High School group.

'They're still going on about it.'

'Now what?'

'Stellans.'

'Let's not,' I say, desperate to change the subject. Something about hearing his name is making me feel ill.

Javid comments on how pale I look and what terrible company I am this evening. I make up some excuse about not coping well in hot weather, my stomach still feeling sensitive.

'Why didn't you say?' he mumbles, biting into his pitta, which swiftly arrives with a bowl of olives. 'Honestly, Rita. You can be so funny, sometimes.'

'Funny ha, ha, or funny strange?'

'I think you know the answer to that,' he says.

I can't ask him anything legal in relation to Leila without arousing suspicion, so I decide to just drop it. As the evening progresses, Javid tells me more about the night he had with Sanjay, and I realise that something in my life is missing.

I'm better off without Leila, I know – and Javid is right to warn me not to get involved. But I can't help but feel empty and pretend that I haven't missed having her around. A depth charge of sadness festers in the deepest part of me.

'Don't be a stranger now, yeah?' says Javid when the bill arrives. 'And Rita, I hope for good news from you on the relationship front, as well. Go get yourself laid, at least. If not, let me treat you to another Chinese.' Javid laughs and I laugh too, but something inside me sinks.

By the time I return to Raven Court, all I want to do is go to bed and forget about what Javid said. I pray I don't see Kasia on the landing, that I'm not made to get involved in her small talk. But as I turn towards the stairs, I hear a banging on the front door. I swear under my breath. I've already made it clear that cold callers are not welcome – particularly at this time of night. But before I open the door, there's a voice calling from the other side. It catches me unaware, and I drop my keys.

'Rita, it's me.'

I hesitate, pressing my back against the wall.

'Rita . . . You there? It's me, Leila. I just saw you walk in. I know you're there.'

I open the door, and there she is. Leila is standing on my doorstep. She's wearing a summer dress with thin spaghetti straps, scattered with pink flowers. It is the kind that is so spare on top it's best not to wear a bra.

'I'm sorry. I did knock earlier, but the girl that works for you said you'd be back later. I was waiting for you.'

I turn in the direction of the stairs and see Kasia standing there. 'You both found each other, then.' She smiles. 'Everything is done

– they're comfortable, though Derek has been a bit quiet today, so if there's nothing else, I'll see you in the morning.'

Kasia brushes past me and Leila steps to one side.

'You'd better come in,' I say.

Leila walks into the hallway, running her fingers along the wall.

'It's been years since I've seen this place,' she says, heading towards the living room. 'It looks exactly as it did when we were growing up.'

Leila stares down at the carpet, pointing her toe and brushing it over the pile. 'There's so much space here. It's incredible.' She stretches her arms out and takes a sharp intake of breath.

My head is still pounding. All I keep thinking is that I don't need this. Not tonight. I feel nauseous.

'It feels like your parents are still here,' she says, turning to face me. 'It feels like they're in this room.' She hunches forward, crossing her arms, rubbing her hands up and down them. 'Gives me shivers just thinking about it.'

She notices the way I flinch, then she walks towards me, placing her hand onto my face.

'Look, about the other night. I feel terrible and I'm sorry. I don't know what came over me. I wanted to call to apologise, but then I figured that was not good enough. I was just shocked that's all.' She bites her lip. 'With everything going on, I probably drank too much.'

Upstairs, I hear a toilet flush.

'Forget about it,' I say.

Leila doesn't say anything for a while, but then she moves to the sofa and sits down. The room is so quiet, I can hear her breathing.

'You did the right thing. You said all the right things,' she says. 'It's me. I'm the one with the problem. All this stuff they're saying about Michael . . . I just can't believe it.' Her voice breaks.

I feel a sense of pain taking hold of me. 'I didn't want to hurt you,' I say, moving to sit down opposite her, although I did. In that moment, I did want to hurt her. I wanted her to feel rotten. After all, she had hurt me, cutting me out of her life then arguing with me for no apparent reason.

'I know,' she says. 'It's just that . . .'

'We're not children anymore, Leila.'

She falls silent.

'I'm sorry about your parents. I wasn't thinking. It must still be painful to talk about it.'

'It's fine,' I say quickly. She's changing the subject, which is just typical. 'Enough time has passed. You learn to move on, don't you? No point dwelling on it.'

She trails behind me as I walk into the kitchen, and I offer her a glass of orange juice. She holds it in one hand, rattling her car keys in the other.

'Do you have something stronger?' she asks.

I pause, but then nod, reluctantly fishing a bottle of vodka out from the cupboard.

'We can't afford to just ignore things,' I say. 'I apologise if I pushed you.' I'm unsure whether anything I say now will make a difference. 'I'm just sorry you had to find out about it like this.'

I drizzle a little vodka into her glass.

'It's just so hard to believe it's true,' she says, her voice shaking. 'I don't know *what* to believe anymore.'

She drains her glass, then suggests we open a bottle of wine and continue to talk about it in the kitchen. The blood rushes around my brain as I uncork it.

'There must be something in it – some truth,' I say. I lean my back against the counter, observing the shape of her. 'Men like that carry on for years, growing more confident the more they get away with it. I know it's not something you want to hear, but—'

'But that's just it, I never saw it like that. We were in love. He *loved* me.'

I stare into Leila's eyes, wild with fear. My throat scratches.

'But you were not the only one, were you? There were others.'

She shakes her head. 'He was never cruel nor unkind. He never hurt me or forced me. It was me, *me*. I tempted him. I *made* him cross the line.' She's breathing fast, vulnerable. She turns towards the kitchen table and pulls out a chair. 'I persuaded him. I made him do it.'

'He made you think that. Listen to me, Leila.' I take her hand from across the table and notice how limp and warm it is in mine. How her skin is soft and delicate, just like a child's. 'None of this is *your* fault. Do you hear me? You were a *child*. He should have known better.'

'My whole life has been built around those memories of him, of what we were together,' she says. 'There was some good to come out of it too. Look at me now. He encouraged me to go places. Look how I turned out.'

Leila rummages in her bag, hunting for her cigarettes. A click of the lighter and then she inhales. 'Do you mind if I smoke in here?' she asks, as an afterthought.

I open the back door and a cool breeze wafts in. I close my eyes and breathe in the evening air.

Leila runs her fingers through her hair, then stands, moving to the back door, staring out into the darkness.

She has her back to me, and I observe the slope of her shoulders, the way her hair tumbles down the arch of her back. 'There were others who saw good things in you too, but they didn't expect anything from you in return. He was your teacher. He crossed a line. Whether or not you can accept it, you were too young.'

I hear her sniffling, her shoulders juddering.

'Leila . . . are you alright?' I move towards her, placing my arm around her shoulders. She nestles her head into my neck and drops her weight onto me.

'He promised me I was the only one. That we were a *one-off*. It was not something he normally did.'

'He was manipulative. Men like that can make you believe anything.'

She puts out her cigarette, then picks up the stub. I take it from her and throw it into the bin.

'I need to talk to him,' she says, 'to hear his explanation.'

'Surely you should just go straight to the police.'

'I'm not going to do that,' Leila says. 'You don't understand.' She heads to the hallway, towards the front door. 'I don't want to re-visit it.'

'Leila . . .'

'Look, it's hard enough. So many years have passed between us. You don't know anything about my life.' Leila opens the door. 'You're not driving, surely?'

'No. I'll get a cab. Look, I'm sorry,' she says. 'I just want to get my head straight. I wanted to see you, to clear the air.'

She steps out onto the front doorstep and stares up at the stars in the sky. The two of us are lit up by the yellow light from the hallway. 'It was good to see you, Rita.'

'I don't agree with what you're doing,' I say. 'I think you're being naive. And furthermore, it's selfish. What about the other girls? What about them?'

She turns to leave and before I can stop her, she's getting into her car and switching on her engine.

'Leila, wait! Let me drive you,' I call. 'You can't go like that.'

She ignores me, however, and drives off. I swear under my breath as I close the door, finding my way, as I had originally intended, up the stairs to bed with a stonking headache.

13

05.00 Lawson:

?

05.30 Me:
Still thinking. Got a few things going on.

The next morning is Saturday and Kasia calls to say she's going to be late. That's the problem with agency staff: they've no sense of responsibility nor comprehension of how much work running a care home takes. I go up to see Derek myself. I notice something is amiss.

Derek is lying in bed, ever so still. The curtains are drawn, and the room is warm and stale. I place the tray down and approach him, to see if he's awake.

'Derek. It's me, Rita. How are you, love?' I reach out and tap his shoulder. His eyes are still closed. 'I've brought you some breakfast.'

Derek does not move. When I touch his face, he's cold. I check his pulse, then his heart. I move rapidly as the adrenalin rushes. I see there is no sound or movement from him. I know he's gone, and I lean against a chest of drawers. The last of the energy I have drains away. I slip to the floor, and sit still and silent for a while, trying to take it all in.

Margaret is coughing in the next room, and I tell myself I need to get up and snap out of it, to carry on as normal with the chores. Derek was ready to go. At least he enjoyed his final days. But the wind is knocked out of me. I run out of the room and into the bathroom, locking the door behind me. I lean over the sink and splash cold water onto my face to stop myself crying.

You think death is something you get used to, that it can't unsettle you when you've spent years in a quiet relationship of understanding with it. I've nursed the elderly through their illnesses, listened to their endless tales. I've spent nights warding off death's arrival whilst seated by a bedside, holding onto a frail hand. I've comforted folk in a quiet state of surrender when they're waiting – just waiting – to die. I've been there too, with a warm blanket, for whatever else they may require.

When the end finally comes, it's me who puts in the call to their family. Inevitably they begin to question whether a home was the right thing for their parents in the first place. So I think to myself, *what difference does one more dead body make?* But then it hits me hard. There's always one that reminds you of your own humanity; one that literally breaks your heart.

A strange and eerie peace descends. My ability to hear sounds in the distance becomes acute, like an animal detecting a frequency outside the realms of human hearing. To think how much Derek must have needed me, but I have never been fully present for him. I feel so guilty, knowing that I've attended to one problem, and in doing so, I've neglected the needs of others, right here on my doorstep.

I manage to make the necessary phone calls and arrangements, of course, but there's a whistling sound in my ears. My body is numb.

That night, whilst seated alone in front of the TV, flicking through channels, I stop on a news story about Jeffrey Epstein. More women are coming forward to recount tales of abuse, but I can't take it in. I'm strangely detached from my surroundings. It's as if I'm a prickly bit of Velcro suddenly ripped off from the felt.

I lean back onto the sofa, thinking about tomorrow; how I can't face cleaning Derek's room, how tragic it is that he has no family left to collect his belongings.

Just then, the house phone rings, but I have no energy to answer it, so I let it ring. It rings and rings, but then it stops. My mobile rings shortly afterwards. I answer it reluctantly.

'Rita. I'm sorry.'

It's Leila, her voice hoarse.

'I'm a mess, really, I am. I don't know what I'm doing. Listen . . .'

I sit on the sofa, my head held in my hands, but I don't say anything. I don't know what to say. My mouth has clammed up. I let her do the talking.

'I need to talk to Stellans and confront him about the stories.'

'Right.'

'You were not wrong when you said I need to do something about this.'

Leila says it's personal between them, but that before she is strong enough to talk to the police, she must confront him herself to question him about everything.

'He lied to me, Rita. I don't think I can ever live with that. Not after everything that happened between us. But it is a private thing between Michael and me and I need time to process it. I know you think I'm blinded by my feelings. That I can't be objective. But I can. I can see it now for what it really is.'

I'm building up the strength to say something, but my chest and temples ache.

'As long as you speak to the police afterwards,' I say. It's all I can think to say because from where I'm seated, this situation is still so unreal to me.

'I will. I promise.'

She's silent for some time. I can almost hear her thinking.

'There's just one thing I wanted to ask you,' says Leila.

I don't know where this is going and I'm not sure I like the sound of it. 'Go on . . .'

'I was wondering . . . if we could meet at yours. I'd just rather he didn't know where I live.'

My body tenses. 'Mine?'

'Hear me out—'

'Why can't you meet him in a public place?'

'It's not the same,' she says. 'We need privacy. I know it's a lot to ask, Rita. And I wouldn't normally. But you've been such a major strength of support – getting me to see sense. I know if I'm with you, I'll have a better chance of being objective.'

My hands are shaking – I'm so tired, so fed up, and yet I have no power to stop it. 'I would really rather not have to see his face again,' I say.

'*Please.* I can't think of anywhere else to have this conversation.'

'What about a hotel? Or in an outside space?' I ask. 'Anywhere but here.'

Silence. 'I just thought you'd understand.'

'Leila, that's not fair,' I say. 'Just meet him somewhere public.'

'But Raven Court *is* like a public place. It's safe and it's perfect. Rita, listen.' She sounds jittery. 'If I'm going to do this, I'd rather you were there and you're the only one I trust. I really need to do this.'

I hear her snivelling and something in her voice has changed. It's like when we were kids, and we'd be joking around, without a care in the world, but then suddenly she'd say something serious. The air empties from my lungs. I know exactly what she's doing: trying to make me feel guilty.

'Rita? Are you there?'

I'm weak. I'm vulnerable. In that moment, I succumb to her manipulation. The truth is, I need Leila just as much as she needs me.

I realise that maybe I can record Stellans. I can use this opportunity to gather evidence. If Leila won't come forward with a statement, or if she backs out of it at the last minute, I can use my phone to record him. I can leave it on the shelf to pick up their entire conversation. Stellans is bound to admit what he did. Then I can hand it over to Lawson and see what he makes of it.

'Rita, please don't ignore me.'

'Wait . . .'

But there is something else too.

After seventeen years, I have a reason to be part of Leila's life again. Despite my dread at seeing Stellans, it feels like something greater is at work, pulling Leila and me closer.

'This is a bad idea,' I say.

'It is?'

'But against my better judgement . . . okay. I'll do it.'

I can almost see her shoulders fall and my heart expands as her voice lifts.

'You know something, Rita? You are the best. Maybe I never told you that. But I want you to know now, you are the greatest. I don't know how I will ever thank you.'

I replace the phone, and a sense of warm acceptance washes over me. After all these years, a friend I have loved has told me, perhaps not in so many words, that she loves me, too.

14

It's five o'clock on Friday evening – it happens to be the thirteenth, a week after we agreed to meet Stellans. I hope it isn't a bad luck sign. The doorbell rings, and through the window, I see Leila admiring her own reflection. She's puckering her lips, and leans forward, ringing the doorbell once more. Her shoulders fall when I finally answer it.

'You took your time. Where were you, on the toilet?'

It's high school all over again and I laugh, rejoicing in the growing familiarity between us.

I notice her outfit, chiffon and shiny: a white vest and a red skirt that shows off her figure. She has painted her toenails red. They're peeping through a pair of gold sandals. It irritates me to think she's made such an effort to look good for Stellans, but she looks beautiful.

Stellans arrives at six. I do not see him standing on the doorstep, but I hear the bell ring twice. It is Leila who opens the door. I'm too busy opening a can of sweetcorn in the kitchen. I'm preparing a salad for Leila and me to eat, later. Since his arrival happens so quickly, and I'm so wound up by Stellans being here in the first place, I can't think straight. I'm not able to put my phone on the shelf in the front room without Leila seeing it. I figure I'll have to record from the hallway. I hope the sound quality will not be too terrible.

I bite my tongue, so furious with myself that I knock at the bottom of the can, emptying the sweetcorn into a bowl, spilling a few of the kernels.

Stellans' voice is low and muffled, more monotoned and taut

than I remember it. It grows louder as they move through the hallway, disappearing into the living room.

When the living-room door is closed, I creep into the hallway and place my phone onto the side table and switch on REC. Then I slip back into the kitchen, aggrieved that I'm having to behave like a burglar in my own house.

I hear Leila say she's so glad they agreed to do this. That it is good to see one another and to talk like grown-ups, after all these years. From the kitchen, I hear the two of them sit down on the sofa, and, unable to resist, I tiptoe into the hallway once again, craning my neck to listen in on their conversation. I hear Stellans asking how she is keeping. Leila gushes her replies, ever so politely.

'I'm okay. Life turned out the way I imagined it would. And you? How are things with you?'

'I get by,' he says, then he pauses. 'My life is not as interesting as yours, however, and well, as you can imagine . . . things are somewhat complicated now.'

They remain quiet for some time and for a second, I imagine they're kissing, tasting one another, after so many years apart. But Leila clears her throat. I hear her speak.

'I'm not the girl you once knew,' she says. 'A lot has changed.'

Stellans: 'I'm sure that's true. But we don't change as much as we think we do.'

I move closer, peeking through the crack in the door. I just about make out the back of his head, his thick, greasy, unkempt hair, hanging over his collar. He's wearing a checked shirt with short sleeves and Leila is seated on an armchair at right angles. She's staring at the floor, curling the ends of her hair with her fingers.

My phone vibrates and I panic. I rush to the hallway table and switch it off. When I return, I fix my eyes onto the two of them. I can't move. I can't believe what I'm seeing.

Stellans pats the seat beside him, and Leila stands, seating herself beside him on the sofa. She isn't looking him in the eye, but she's blushing. Then I see Stellans reaching out ever so slightly to place an arm around Leila's waist. She smiles, tilting her head to the side.

'What is this place?' Stellans again. 'I've never seen anything quite like it.'

After a while, I hear something – like he's standing, moving towards the back of the room. 'This is an antique. My grandmother had one just like it.'

I wish he would sit down and not pry into my things because I am very tempted to knock his teeth out.

'Is what they're saying true?' Leila. Finally, she's getting to the point of the meeting.

Silence.

His footsteps. 'Leila—'

'I need to know.'

'No. It is not true. None of it is true,' he says. 'That girl, Rani, is *obsessed*. She's had it in for me from the start.'

Rani. It is the first time I have heard her name. I note that it is Indian.

'Why would she say such things? Why would she make it up if it's not true?' Leila's voice is a little louder. I'm pleased – relieved – her line of questioning is building with positive momentum.

'I don't know. You know how kids are.'

'Kids?'

'Not you, Leila. You were different.'

I can barely breathe. The hallway feels so oppressive, so suffocating. I run to the kitchen to grab a bottle of water. Within seconds, I'm back again. I hold the cool glass to my cheek to help calm me down.

'I know what you must be thinking.' Stellans again.

'Do you? Do you really?'

'Yes, I do. Because I know you, Leila. I know everything about you. I watched you grow up, remember? Watched you grow into the woman you are now.'

My stomach turns. I hear Leila sobbing and something inside me burns.

'What was I supposed to think? I felt so disgusted. Please tell me her accusations aren't true, because otherwise . . . I should have you arrested.' It's Leila, her breathing shallow, her voice hovering thinly above them.

Stellans releases a long breath, and I hear him crash onto the sofa once more, the sound of the leather squeaking. 'You know what being in the public eye means. You know that world so well. You become an easy target. People make things up. As for kids, they can't help themselves, particularly those with a grudge.'

'But why something like that? It doesn't make any sense,' says Leila.

'I was teaching her at the time. She was extremely talented, a bit like you were – still are. But she was troubled – terribly troubled. Unstable, even.'

My throat constricts. He is *comparing* them.

'She reached out to me for extra tuition. But then it was clear that she had feelings for me. She grew obsessed – completely neurotic – writing me letters, following me around. I suggested, discreetly, of course, that she find herself a new teacher. It was harsh, but I tried to be reasonable. I tried to be understanding. I don't think she ever got over it.'

Silence.

'Leila, you can't possibly understand what I've been going through. All these years without you. I never forgot about us. There's so much I wanted to say. I just knew today wouldn't be enough . . . I want you to know, I wrote something . . .' I hear the rustle of paper.

'Well, I forgot you,' spits Leila. 'And I've heard enough. I don't want to hear any more about it.'

'Please, Leila. I never forgot you,' he whispers. 'Don't ever think I did. I don't think I ever will.'

Leila is breathing fast; I hear her breathy rasps. I feel her pain. Every part of my body tenses.

'You have no idea what I've been through,' says Leila.

'I'm sorry. Really, I am. I never wanted to disturb you. This is my problem to deal with. The last thing I wanted was to involve you.'

'But I *am* involved, don't you get it? People are not stupid, Michael. They will put two and two together and then point a finger at *me*.'

I hear Stellans stand, his voice trailing from somewhere in the direction of the window.

'You were so young. I did everything in my power not to hurt you. But I was utterly besotted and hopelessly in love with you.'

'So, this was all my fault, was it?'

'It wasn't anyone's fault,' he says. 'It just happened. I know it shouldn't have— I should never have indulged in any of it. I was wrong to take advantage. But there was no power in this world strong enough to resist your advances.'

Advances? What advances?

'What do you mean?' says Leila.

'You came to me, Leila. You offered a chance for me to be happy. I was just an ordinary man, and there you were. So beautiful. You were way out of my league.'

'What are you saying?'

'Of course, I was going to take my chances,' he says. 'What man wouldn't?'

'But that's not how I remember it,' says Leila 'We both had an equal part in it, didn't we? I know I came on strong, but . . .'

I can't believe what I'm hearing. Around me the air is fizzing. Before I'm able to stop myself, I barge into the living room.

They look up, alarmed at first, but then their faces relax.

'Hello, Rita. I remember you,' says Stellans. 'It's good to see you after all these years.' He stands and reaches out his hand, but I do not take it. My chest is heaving. I'm still holding the bottle tightly. I didn't even bring my phone.

'What are you doing?' I say. 'What the hell is going on here?'

Leila stands up, next to him.

'Excuse me?' Stellans glances at Leila, her head level with his shoulder. She's frozen, her arms dangling on either side of her, unsure what to do with herself.

'Rita, what are you doing?' she whispers.

'What am *I* doing? What are *you* doing!' I jab at the air with the bottle.

'I think there's been a misunderstanding.' Stellans has his hands up as if in a state of surrender. 'I'm very happy to talk about it.'

'I don't want to talk to you, you *pervert*.'

'Rita, please. We're just talking. Let us clear things up between us.' Leila's face is flushed, like she is embarrassed – by me. I throw my head back and laugh at them both.

'Well. Just look how that turned out.' I can barely spit the words out without shouting them. Leila grabs onto my elbow.

'What the hell is this?' Her face is close to mine, so close I can see a vein throbbing just above her eyebrow.

'Maybe you should ask your *boyfriend* the same question. I want you to leave,' I say sharply to Stellans. Then I turn to Leila. 'I've had enough, okay? This was a bad idea. I can't tolerate him being in my house.'

Leila tugs at my arm. 'Rita, please! For God's sake! Why can't you just leave it?'

'Can't you see what he's doing?' I'm shouting at him now. 'You are messing with her head. You're nothing but a criminal. Do you know that? A fucking criminal. Give me a good reason why I shouldn't call the police, and have you arrested myself!'

Stellans holds up his hands, taking a step back. 'Woah, listen . . .'
I see the blood draining from his face. 'This is a mistake. A *terrible* mistake. Please, let's just keep calm and discuss things, okay?'

Leila steps back. 'Rita, *please*. You are making this so much worse than it needs to be.'

I stare at her, my love, my friend, unable to decipher on which side she belongs.

'Listen to me,' I say, grabbing onto Leila's arm. I'm shaking her shoulder hard in a desperate attempt to shake some sense into her. 'Look me in the eye. Can you really not see what he's doing, how *manipulative* he is?'

Stellans is on his feet, but given the tension between Leila and me, he does not interfere.

Leila wrenches herself free, stepping back, scowling at me. She shakes her head, as if to say she can't believe it; I've lost my mind. Like there's something wrong with *me*. Like I've gone and ruined things, gone too far – as usual – just like I always did.

'That's enough!' Stellans – the audacity of him, daring to interrupt my truth-telling.

I turn to face him, hissing like a wild cat, ready to tear into him. He swallows hard.

'Rita,' he says, staring at the floor, as if the thought of me and who I am is scrambling around in his mind. 'Rita Patel. I remember you from my English class.'

'So?' There is something about his tone that sounds like a teacher talking down to a class of disobedient children.

'So, I think I *understand* – what this is about.'

I glance at Leila and then back at Stellans. Seeing his face trembling, I begin to laugh. It is terrible, but I can't control it. 'This has nothing to do with me, but of course, you would try that.'

Leila faces me.

'Stop it,' she says. 'Stop this right now. It's ridiculous.' She grabs her handbag. 'Don't get involved, okay? This really is none of your business,' she says. 'And you're right. This—' she swings her arms around her, 'was a *terrible* mistake.'

'Wait,' says Stellans, calling after her. 'Leila, *please*. I wanted to give you—'

'Get out of my way, Rita.' Leila hurries past me, staggering into the hallway like she's drunk. At the front door, she stares at Stellans one last time as he stands in the living-room doorway. I watch her as she storms out of the front door, her feet crunching into the gravel. Every part of me feels defeated. In her car, she turns the key in the ignition but then, for just a moment, she stops, staring at the road ahead. She drops her head onto the steering wheel, and her shoulders judder. Then she straightens. The wheels screech as she pulls away.

I'm standing there for a moment, trying to take it all in. Everything has happened so fast. My hands and lower lip tremble and I grow intensely aware that Stellans is still in my house.

I close the front door and walk back to the lounge. I place the bottle in my hand down onto the table.

Stellans looks up as I approach. He's scratching his head, wiping his hands onto his trousers. Clumsily, he rearranges his glasses.

'I had better leave too,' he says. He straightens his shirt. 'I appreciate you giving us the space to talk.' He bends to retrieve his coat from the sofa. 'I remember how bright you were,' he says. 'Always a hard worker, with good, solid grades . . .' He smiles, as he turns, the wrinkles in the corner of his eyes like speech marks, '. . . albeit with an overactive imagination.'

I look down. Before I can stop myself, I grab the bottle, and in one swoop, I bring it down, crashing it over his head. There is a second, just a second, when he is stunned. His eyes wide, shining like crystals.

The bottom half of the bottle is smashed. Blood has spotted my T-shirt. Stellans tumbles down, his glasses falling from his face.

His right cheek smacks against the floor, his back twists. All this happens so fast, and yet I see it vividly in slow motion.

I stand back, my breathing fast and shallow struggling to process the strange angle of Stellans' contorted limbs. My ears ring.

Standing over him is both surreal and yet so real. It grows more real as the seconds and minutes pass, as the truth becomes undeniable. Here is the crumpled, beating flesh of him, this former teacher of ours, lying on the floor in my very own living room. The sight of him shocks me into a lucid state of floating, stillness and end-of-world quiet. I see the rise and fall of his stomach, but the rest of him is still. I'm peering down at him, as the weight of this truth, like a thunderous cloud, reveals itself so clearly.

What have I become? I have never done anything like this in my life, never raised a hand, no matter how bad things have been, no matter how tempted I've been during hunting. My thoughts terrify and horrify me because I know something inside me has snapped. I've arrived at a point where there is no turning back. I know this for sure, because more than remorse, more than shame and regret, or something instinctual inside me impelled to seek help, moved by compassion and empathy to provide this injured man some assistance, I want him to feel, really *feel*, the consequences of his actions.

15

19.32 Javid:
Hey. I'm passing by yours. U in?

19.33 Me:
Now's not a good time, Javid.

19.34 Javid:
Oh? Why is that? What are you doing?

19.36 Me:
Busy with one of the residents.

19.36 Javid:
Later?

19.39 Me:
Maybe.

Ten minutes have passed but Stellans is still lying there. I am standing over him, taking in the outline of his body, amid the silence and the strange whistling in my ears. Time is suspended, a swing-ball from a Newton's Cradle stuck in mid-air. I am still trying to comprehend what is happening.

I lean forward, relieved to see Stellans' chest still moving. I need to think; I need a proper plan.

I roll up his coat, crumpled beside him and stuff it into a cupboard in the hallway, underneath blankets, cushions and old magazines. Then I locate his phone and switch it off. I'll need to figure out what to do with it.

I walk into the garden, crossing the lawn a fair distance through the dark until I reach the crooked outhouse; a shabby, old building standing erect, despite itself. It's hardly used but it's still strong, despite a rotten timber roof. Its blacked-out, barricaded windows mean it's self-contained. The doubly thick and insulated walls mean it's soundproofed and warm. I unlock the door, which creaks like an old ghost as it opens. Inside, the dusty air fills my lungs. I rummage quickly through my garden things and I locate my toolbox, sliding open the lid. I lift out my hammer and a box of nails, to help secure doors and windows – should I need to – and as I close the box, I nick my finger on the edge. I suck hard on it, biting it between my teeth. I search the wooden shelves, my hand slapping against tins and bottles covered in dried-up insects and cobwebs. Eventually, I find what I'm looking for: a fresh roll of duct tape, so new, it's still covered in film – it even has the B&Q store label on it.

I run out of the outhouse, carrying a canvas bag of my things, the door slamming behind me, a layer of paint dusting the ground like icing sugar. The outhouse, which I haven't used properly for at least a year, is secluded to the point where you could easily lock someone in there and no one on the outside, not even someone curious like Kasia, would ever know what was going on inside.

I run across the green so fast, I almost trip over the broken stones along the path. I'm breathless, panting, the bag in my hand. A strange feeling of mania and delirium fills me like helium. I'm overcome by a sense of power because, finally, I am in control. None of this was intentional, but perhaps it was meant to happen.

Once inside, I place my bag down and stand over Stellans. I take a roll of duct tape and search for the corner, picking it back with my fingernails. I wind it firmly, securely, around his ankles. The violent swoosh-like sound pierces my ears as I tear through the plastic with my teeth. I'm careful not to catch the thick hairs on his legs because otherwise I know it will burn like hell when I remove it.

I wheel in one of the three electric emergency stretchers I have waiting. The belts at the bottom on either side are perfect to secure Stellans. Of course, I must tie him up. In a state of shock, he might become violent when he wakes up. I lift him onto the stretcher. His body is floppy and heavy, but the task is straight-forward enough. I've had so much practice over the years that I know how to do it in a way that does not strain my shoulders. I lower the bed, nudging him onto it. His body is soft and limp like a wet rubber suit and I strap him in securely, first his wrists and then his ankles. I strap his torso also, to stop him from twisting and turning too much. I raise the bed, my feet pressing down onto the button at the bottom, near the wheel. I roll him out towards the outhouse, into the warm evening.

As I reach the door of the outhouse, I stop to catch my breath. I pull the keys from my pocket, but to the side of me, I notice that Stellans is coming round.

He groans under the duct tape, short grunts and then a long *mmm* sound, jerking his head from side to side as he regains con-sciousness. His limbs jolt, his fingers twitch. He is momentarily suspended by the incomprehension of where he is – things still a little hazy, probably muddled. The bruise on the side of his head is so large it looks like he's been slapped with a plate of blueberries. His torso thrusts and I frantically search for the key to the door. As it finally dawns on him that he's tied up, as the last memory of him falling appears fully, a slow panic seems to envelop him. He shakes his arms and wrists, his legs, his ankles. I know it's no use, he's firmly strapped in, but that doesn't stop him. My heart beats like strings playing crazed pizzicato.

The door opens, but to keep Stellans hidden, I wheel him in much deeper – deeper towards the back where there's a dark room with a locked door. It's a room I've not used much since my own parents' passing. They used it to store files, old equipment, and other rubbish. I never had any use for it because I regularly recycle. I unlock the door and nudge it open with my shoulder. Inside, it's musty, with damp seeping into the wood from when it last rained down heavily. The light flickers and hums as I switch it on. I scan the room, considering what to kick out of the way to make room for the stretcher. I want Stellans to feel comfortable, but I've no intention of keeping him here for long.

I had forgotten how much I cleaned up the place after my parents died. Medicines, fabric sheets, cotton pads; precautionary equipment such as leather belts and knives are neatly boxed and piled. I watch Stellans, his eyes wide and round. He's thrusting his head and torso, faster and faster, from side to side, moaning and groaning, making strange guttural sounds. He's trying to escape but I know his attempts are futile. When he glances up, his eyes are wild and white, searching mine. It's as if we're in some sort of reversal of roles and I'm now the adult, he's now the child; a sense of poetic justice emanates. He looks at me for some sort of explanation and I notice a tear trickling down the corner of one eye.

I wheel him into the corner.

'You had a nasty fall,' I say. 'I'm sorry I hit you. Please understand it wasn't intentional.'

I inch the stretcher closer to the wall in the corner of the room, then press down the lever with my foot, locking the wheels. Stellans stares up at me, his eyes scanning the air as if chasing the flight of an invisible horsefly. I move to the ledge, pouring Ketamine into a cup from a dusty brown bottle, ripping open the wrapping of a tube of cotton pads.

'You're probably in a lot of pain. It's best you take this. Just to help you through the worst of it.'

I dab his forehead with the cotton pad, but it doesn't seem to help. Stellans begins screaming, the sound trapped inside his throat since his lips are taped. He shakes frantically to try and release himself. I have no choice but to tighten the fastenings around his wrists and ankles. I move the buckle to a tighter hole, making sure the leather straps are secure. In a box behind me, I hunt for some rope and find some coiled in a tote bag. With a garden knife, I cut off a length of roughly four metres, then I slice through it again to make four pieces. I wind each bit around his limbs. When he's still and secure, I rip off the duct tape from his mouth so he can speak. His mouth opens, round and large, and I administer him with the drug before he can resist it. I know his instinct will be to swallow it. Stellans coughs and splutters. After that, he begins screaming.

'Where am I? What are you doing? This is insane. Let me go. I said, let me go!'

I am fully prepared for him.

'Stop screaming,' I say. 'No one can hear you. I won't harm you; I promise. I just want to talk to you.'

I plead for him to keep his voice down, to stay calm. But he continues his verbal assault. In the end, I have no choice but to splash a little water from the tap onto him. He falls silent, his eyelids heavy, his face and body surrendering under the influence of the Ketamine. He mumbles something to himself, but he only has the energy to do so faintly. I think of Leila, how, were she to walk through the door, I would begin to explain this.

'The PIN to your phone,' I say. 'I need it.'

I hear him mumble inaudibly.

'It's just a precaution. I'll give you your phone back; I promise.'

'1-7 . . . 0-3 . . . 8-4.'

Something inside me prickles. That combination of numbers is familiar. It's Leila's birthday.

I feel sick.

I watch him, this pathetic figure of my childhood, thaw like ice under the influence of medication. He will be out for precisely three hours and I'm grateful for the time to think. Three hours is enough time for me to clean up after him, to remove his blood from the carpet. My plan is to then have a conversation with him, to extract an explanation, and to let him go after that. That is what I tell myself.

But I can see Stellans drifting in and out of consciousness. I see his wallet, slipping out of his trousers. I take it for safekeeping, stuffing it into my pocket. I leave Stellans there, melting onto the crisp white sheets, and I lock up everything behind me.

With all that work, I've broken into a sweat. Back in the house, I switch Stellans' phone back on, then punch in the code, watching the home page light up. I see he has five missed calls and a text:

SO sorry about earlier. Please call me. LS x

I grab my laptop and check Twitter and Facebook to see if Leila has posted anything about the events of her day. But there's nothing. I see on Javid's timeline that he's out at Jerry's Bar for the night. There's a selfie of him grinning, a tumbler of whiskey in his hand. I check my own phone, wondering if Leila has at least texted me. The screen is blank.

I feel numb. I am barely able to concentrate. I collapse onto the sofa, the room around me fizzing. I deliberate what to do next. I know I must dispose of his phone. Keeping it is careless. Stellans could report me to the police after I release him. Make up all sorts of horrible stories. I could be arrested. But if I get rid of his phone, I could at least deny he was here, pretend none of this ever happened. It would be his word against mine.

In that instant, I'm up, grabbing the keys to my van. Within twenty minutes, I'm at the end of the road, on a side road opposite the bridge that stretches over the Grand Union Canal.

Stellans' phone pings once more, as another text arrives:

I'm so worried about you. Where are you? Please call me. LS
x x x

I stare out of the window, watching cars drive by and I dial Stellans' voicemail:

Michael, it's me, Leila. If you're listening to this message, please call me. I'm sorry about what happened. It wasn't my idea to confront you the way we did. I know it wasn't right to do that. God, I'm so sorry. We need to talk alone. Please forgive me. And Rita too. It's not her fault, either. She tried to do a good thing, but she has issues. I don't know if you remember what she was like at school. She doesn't mean any harm; she just can't help it. Anyway, please call me. I can explain everything.

My body shakes, the fury rising inside me.

Michael. Me again. Please call me.

Michael, it's Leila. Please. I'm on my mobile, waiting.

Michael, I'm really worried about you. I can't stop thinking about you.

Michael, please. Call me back. Where are you?

I get out of my van and smash the phone with my foot, then gather the pieces and pop them into an old plastic sandwich bag I find in the driver's door. I run across the busy main road, looking left then right. Once at the bridge, I empty the pieces into the canal.

*

It's midnight when I wake up. I'm back at Raven Court. The room is dark, and a horror movie is playing on TV. There's a scene of a woman standing over a coffin, a young boy beside her. I must have fallen asleep after I came home. I think I drank half of a bottle of whiskey.

The air is heavy and cloyed with the smell of sweet and sour food. There's a full moon in the sky that leaves a silvery pool of light on the carpet, next to the dried blood stain. I know I need to clean that thoroughly – to remove every smear of red from each and every fibre.

I hear bats circling outside the window. I get up, and head out into the garden.

Stellans presses his eyelids closed as I switch on the light. I stare down at the splodge of vomit on the edge of the bed that must have trickled out from under the duct tape. I speak to him in the calmest and most measured voice I can manage.

'I don't want to hurt you,' I say. 'I just want to talk. None of this was intentional. I lost my temper, that's all. I'm very sorry.'

His shoulders loosen, and I know he's listening. He looks like he might be reasonable, I think I can get through to him.

'If you promise not to scream or to shout, I will take off the duct tape. Do you think you can do that?'

He nods.

I rub my hands together and attempt to peel off the duct tape. 'Sorry about this,' I say, 'it's ever so stubborn.' Like an efficient wax, I rip it off. He winces, his eyes glassy and red, tears streaming.

'I'm so sorry,' I say.

Stellans gasps for air, as if, all this time, I have denied him oxygen. 'What will you do to me?' he says.

I stare down at him, disarmed by his question.

'Nothing. I just want to talk to you. I'm sure you know why you're here.'

'I don't understand, honestly, I don't. What is this all about?'

I'm surprised by how naive he is, how he can possibly question what I mean. But I'm also unprepared for how desperate he sounds.

'I want your confession,' I say. 'I want you to admit your wrongdoing. After that, I'll let you go, I promise. It will be good for you to do this.'

He narrows his eyes and breathes heavily, as if what I've just proposed is out of the ordinary. 'But this is between Leila and me,' he says. 'It's none of your business. Does she know what you're asking?'

'You've broken the law and committed a crime. That makes it the business of all moral civilians.'

He shakes his head. 'It's out of the question. I can't do it.'

'Can't do it, or won't do it?'

He presses his eyes closed, as if it is *me* that is the problem here, *me* that is being unreasonable. It is his blatant disregard of the truth that riles me the most. You would think a man tied up and laid out on a stretcher would have the decency to be honest.

'I want you to confess what you did to Leila and to the other girl in the newspaper, and all the other girls you've messed about with who are too afraid to step forward.' I was thinking of Epstein and Weinstein in the news, how I would not be willing to wait so many years to resolve this situation.

'But it's not fair. It doesn't make any sense,' he says. 'How can I confess to something like that? I am not a criminal.'

'What you did was criminal. Don't you understand that? You had sex with a *child* when she was too young to consent. How can you possibly justify your actions?'

He shakes his head. 'Please. Don't say it like that. Don't make me out to be a bad person. I did something wrong; I admit it. But I never harmed her – ever. She consented. Just ask her.'

I know then that this is not going to be easy. Stellans needs time to come round, to comprehend the gravity of the situation.

'Take your time if that's how you want to play it. I'm willing to wait if that's what it takes.'

'What is this about, Rita? Is this about Leila or is this about something else?'

I flinch. For a moment, I do not move. It is just like him to play stupid mind games. He doesn't understand how much anger I have festering inside me, nor what he is dealing with.

'What are you trying to prove when Leila herself is fine?' he says. 'It's in the past. Why can't we leave it alone?'

'You're not in a good position right now, certainly not one that allows you to negotiate.'

'You can't make me do anything I don't want to. Do you hear?' Stellans is shouting, swearing. He begins calling me terrible names.

I have no choice but to replace the duct tape over his mouth. Against my better judgement I leave him there, because I know this isn't going to be sorted out easily, at least not for now.

I figure I'll just let him sleep; give him a chance to rethink his position and try to reason with him again in the morning. Truth be told, I need to gather my own thoughts concerning how I can keep this situation under control. I know I'm thrashing about in water, way out of my depth. But I hold on and continue because I know that I have in my possession the only thing to help set Leila free. The thing that conserves our friendship, and that will finally make her see things clearly.

16

The next morning, I drive to the shops in my van, pulling up outside Stanley's, the charcuterie with a skewered slab of pork hanging up in the window. Here, nestled amongst quaint coffee shops and posh boutiques, where nothing is priced up and labelled properly, the parking is free for thirty minutes.

I sit in my van for a while, slumped motionless behind the wheel, just staring out of the windscreen. My phone vibrates:

Maybe we need to gather evidence against him. Anyone know anything??

Nah! It's been so long. Leave it to the journalists!

Yeah, I agree. No point getting involved. He'll get his just deserts! Trust me.

I finished his latest book. Did I tell you?? It was a bit rubbish!!! LOL xx

If only they knew the truth, the reality of events outside the Brentwood High WhatsApp group.

I marvel at the fact that I managed to wake up early and exchange pleasantries with Kasia like normal, even though things are now so far from being normal. I told Kasia she's doing a great job. Suggested she finish up at lunch, take a few days off. She didn't answer as I left the house. She probably can't understand why I'm being so nice, or maybe she needs the work and doesn't appreciate a shift cancellation. But what does she expect? Only yesterday I complained that her toast was too dark – almost burnt.

From my van, I watch as people idle in and out of the automatic shop doors. A woman walks along the pavement pushing a pram. A toddler in pink runs beside her, grabbing onto the stretchy hem of her shirt. I feel myself begin to smile.

Later, when I arrive home, heaving several bags of shopping through the front door, I glance up at the post office clock in the hallway, surprised to learn that it's just gone two in the afternoon. I haven't even got lunch on the go for Margaret, and I remember that Kasia is not here either. I slip into autopilot, just like I've done for the past seventeen years. Just like last night, when I hit Stellans.

In the kitchen, I rustle up a tray of food: a plain soft chicken sandwich, a glass of orange juice. This tray is for Margaret. But I prepare the same for Stellans, too. On his tray, I lay out the notepaper I've bought on a serviette, placing a gold fountain pen next to it. The pen once belonged to a former resident, Elizabeth Gosling, and I'm pretty sure that, since she's buried beneath the ground, she won't mind me using it.

That's when it occurs to me: having Stellans locked up on my property feels dangerously normal. Anyone watching this scene play out in a movie would think there's something psychologically wrong with me. It is extraordinary to think how things have escalated in less than twenty-four hours. How seamlessly I have transitioned to become another person, whom ordinarily I would fear. But someone has to do this. The switch in personality is inevitable. If you commit a crime as serious as the one Stellans has, you cannot expect forgiveness – that's what I keep telling myself. The system is powerless to hold you to account because it cannot cope with the scale of the problem. Even Lawson said so. That's why I'm here, and people like me. To put back the right into this country.

I walk towards the outhouse carrying Stellans' tray. My hand is shaking, but I try desperately to keep my own memories at bay. They slither up behind me like a snake, hissing with greater venom. I see a flash of a door creaking open, then there's me, a little girl . . . that man whom I called 'uncle' . . . He's drawing closer to me, and I catch a whiff of him, stinking of beer, the gristle of his beard against my cheek. His bulging eyes stare down at me, and even in the dark, I can disappear into the black holes of his pupils. His warm breath brushes the tips of my ears as he tilts his face, whispering, *my clever girl, Rita. My fair English princess.* I'm wearing nothing but a T-shirt and he tells me to roll over . . .

I'm breathless. I struggle to breathe.

Stellans must sense me approaching because, as I move closer to the door, I hear the buckles on his bed rattling.

The stench of his urine stings my nose as I enter. I see his face is bobbled in sweat, droplets trickling down his neck and mottling the pillow. I bite my lip trying not to look too closely at the broken sight of him. I confess I feel ashamed. I don't want to keep him tied up like that any longer than I must. But I've come this far, and I know I must carry on.

'Not long now,' I say. I try to comfort and reassure him. 'All I need is a written confession and then I'll untie you. I'll drop you off wherever you want to go.'

He stares at me, his eyes wild and searching, crawling all over my face.

'Don't look at me like that,' I say. I place the tray of food down onto the side table.

'This is your own fault, do you hear? I am not a bad person. I am not ordinarily violent. I've never done this before – ever. I've spent the last five years meeting men like you, but I never once hit them.'

I gently remove the duct tape and Stellans gasps like a drowning man who's coming up for air one last time; the prospect of inevitable death settling in.

'Rita, *please* . . . This is completely insane!'

'Don't make this about me,' I say, pacing up and down the floor. I can't even look at him. 'This is about *you. You* are in no position to argue.'

'I swear – you *must* believe me! I didn't do anything to harm her. This is all a *big* mistake.'

I scoff, every bone in my body urging me to walk out. 'If you say so.'

I move to the back of his head, pressing down the red button on the control panel so that his back is positioned upright. He's mumbling, but the humming sound of the headrest drowns him out. I pick up a bottle of water, twisting off the cap, squeezing water into his mouth. He gargles, then he chokes a little. I stop to give him time to settle, all the while acutely aware of the sound of my own heartbeat.

'This is not just about Leila, this is about Rani too. *Plus* all the other girls you've been messing about with. You obviously have a problem, do you know that? I think it's high time you take responsibility for it. Write it out of your system.'

He stares up at the ceiling as I squeeze more water from the bottle.

'Are you hungry? You must be hungry,' I say. I know he hasn't eaten for hours and letting him starve would be stupid and irresponsible. I don't want Stellans dead. I need his confession. That's all I want.

He licks his lips, then winces, presumably because his face stings. '*Please.* Let me go . . . I beg you, don't do this.'

I stare down at his trousers, the material darkening around his crotch in a shape that resembles the outline of Belarus on a map.

'Look, I'm so sorry. I should have given you time to go. I'll make sure I give you an allowance to use the toilet.'

I shake my head. In that moment, I feel truly terrible. 'Again, I'm sorry,' I say. 'I'll bring in a commode.'

'What will you do with me?' he says. Stellans keeps asking me this question, repeatedly. His constant whining grinds me down. Hearing him say my name, again and again, does not feel right. It gives me a strange sensation, like nausea. 'Just stay quiet, okay? Please don't make this more difficult.'

I fetch more rope from the tote bag on the side and tie it around his torso several times, from his waist all the way up to his neck, knotting it tightly at the back of the headrest where I am sure he can't reach it. I check he can still breathe, that the rope isn't pressing too hard onto his blood vessels. Stellans jerks, and screams inside his own mouth, which he is careful not to open after my last instruction.

I release one arm, unwinding the rope and then loosening the strap and buckles from his wrist carefully. He's secure, I am sure of it – he can't do much with that one arm free. I roll a table towards him and lift it to a height level with his chest.

'Don't do anything stupid,' I say. 'Because if you do, it will make things worse. I've tied you up because, well, things have gone far enough, haven't they? We can't trust each other.' Listening to my own voice, I sound short-winded.

Stellans presses his free hand against his cheek and nods as if to reassure me.

'Eat,' I say, placing the tray of food on the table. 'You need to keep your strength up.'

He stares down at the chicken sandwich and swallows hard. Then he promptly picks it up, moving it closer to his mouth. I step back, my eyes fixed on him and everything he's doing. His movements are stiff and awkward. I sit down in the corner of the room, atop a wooden stool that wobbles ever so slightly.

When he's finished, Stellans drops his head against the headrest, as if the task of eating has taken too much out of him. He lets out a long, nasal exhale and I see his shoulders relax.

'Even if I gave you a confession, it is unlawful,' he says. 'You've tied me up against my will – I can hardly move my chest. Why would anyone believe it?'

'Drink,' I say, not wishing to engage in a conversation, but I'm struck by how considered his voice is, as if he's trying to make sense of things. He has a point; a good point, that suggests I haven't thought this through. Stellans is smarter and more manipulative than he appears.

He lifts his head, picking up his bottle of water, his free hand trembling. The bottle is half-full and he finishes it off. When he's done, he drops his hand, and the empty bottle falls into his lap.

'I don't want to die here . . .' he mutters.

'I didn't mean for any of this to happen,' I say. It's important to me that he understands that. 'You won't die here; I promise you that.'

'This is not the way to resolve things, Rita,' he whispers. 'There is another way.' I hold up my hand to stop him from continuing.

'I want you to confess that you had an affair with Leila when she was only fourteen.'

He shakes his head.

'And whilst you're at it, you can admit to having an affair with Rani – plus anyone else underage you've been messing about with. Admit you have a problem and say you're willing to seek help for it.'

'But who is it for?' he asks.

I stare at him.

'It is for Leila, and it's for me. Consider it penance for ruining her childhood – making her do things before she was ready. I'll also keep it handy for the police.'

'I cannot admit to something I didn't do. There were no others apart from Leila, I swear! And Leila herself would never support this.'

I think I see him scoff just then – the *audacity* of him – and I have a good mind to hit him.

'I can't believe I never saw the signs at the time,' I mumble. 'How could I not have known? It was obvious. And Leila was my best friend. She was supposed to tell me everything.'

'Is that what this is all about? Is that what hurts you the most? Because if that is the issue, then Rita, I'm sorry. I take full responsibility for it. What I did was unforgivable. The blame rests with me. Not with Leila. I agree – I see it now – she was innocent.'

His voice is so assured, so responsible, I'm almost tempted to give in.

'You were a child. There were things we could not tell you,' he says.

'Leila was a child, too. But that didn't stop you.'

'Rita, please. I'm in no position to argue. You got me, okay? I was wrong and I'm sorry. Heaven knows I regret it. But this is all history. Let me go and let's forget it.'

'I can't do that.'

'Rita, listen to me. I can't write a confession. I can't confess to something for which I am not entirely guilty. This is not justice. Do you understand? That is not how it works.'

Up until this point, I have not considered the prospect of hurting Stellans – not really, anyway. But seeing him there, hearing the drone of his constant denial, his stubborn refusal to admit the depravity of his behaviour, and to see it for what it really is, fills me with rage. There is no telling how long this duel will play out, but I am willing to see it to the end. This man might be tied up and defenceless, but he is proving difficult to break.

I'm faced with a terrible dilemma.

If I let him go, even after he confesses, he will probably go straight to the police. A little bit of digging, and that's me arrested. With this, and everything else with Zia, I would most likely be jailed. On the other hand, if I let Stellans stay, still refusing to give in, he could end up a permanent resident. I would be a prisoner, too. Stuck here, having to look after him. I think of Javid, and what he would say if he could see me now. This situation is a mess. It is only a matter of time before Stellans is reported missing.

I remove everything from the tray and stuff the dirty serviettes into a plastic bag. I unscrew the lid of the fountain pen and tap onto the table with my finger. He looks down and then up at me. I place the pen gently into his hand.

'All you need to do is to write the—'

'Rita, listen to me. You've got this all wrong. Let's discuss it like adults and come to some sort of sensible arrangement—'

'I know exactly what I'm asking. And I know exactly what I am doing. None of this is unreasonable,' I say quickly.

He clamps his eyes shut and begins to shake his body, pulling at the rope with his free hand. He drops the pen, jerking, moving his head forwards and backwards. Blue ink bleeds into the sheets. I panic, thinking that perhaps I have not tied him up securely, but then I feel calmer when I see that there's no way his torso can free itself.

But still, he continues to struggle. Before I even realise what is happening, he's screaming. His shoulders judder – it takes me by surprise. I step back, my eyes darting about the room. I just want him to stop. I don't know what to say or do. In a panic, I pick up a wooden block from the corner of the room, lifting it over his head – not intending to hit him, just to scare him.

'I will do it, I mean it. I will do it!' I stare down at his crown, at the patch of dried blood from where I hit him with the bottle. My arms tremble. *What am I doing?*

His eyes widen. 'Is it not enough that you're holding me hostage? What more do you want? I can give you money. Do you want money? I have money if that's what you want.'

'You can keep your money,' I say. 'Just write the confession. That's all I want.'

'There must be something else you need. Something you need to buy.'

And there it is again, that condescending *teacher's* tone. Assumptive of its own authority.

'I've seen how you live. You must be struggling.'

I'm still holding the wooden block in my hand, and I grip it tighter, my knuckles turning white. I want him to shut his mouth. I want him to stay quiet.

Just then, my phone buzzes.

'No one can hear you, so please don't scream,' I say as I pull out my phone from my back pocket and peer down at the screen.

My phone is connected to the CCTV in Raven Court, and there is something suspicious.

On the screen, I can just about make out the outline of a woman approaching the front door to Raven Court. It's not easy to see her face, but as the camera adjusts into focus, the long hair, swept back into a ponytail, is unmistakable. The doorbell rings, and sure enough, my phone begins buzzing again. I throw the wooden block into the corner and glance at Stellans, watching his body prick with something like hope, as if someone will discover him and this dark chapter will close.

'This is not over,' I say. 'I mean it. You need to confess.'

His head drops, thudding against the pillow.

'Saved by the bell,' I say.

17

Leila is standing on the front doorstep, her eyes bloodshot and puffy, her hair wet and streaking over her face like an oil slick. For a second, we stare at one another, each of us waiting for the other to speak. Eventually, she shatters the glass of silence between us.

'Can I come in?'

I open the door, shuffling to the side to let her pass. She drops her head, walking into the hallway like nothing happened. I close the door after her, and a wave of adrenalin hits me, knowing that, if I pull this off, I could ensure that these two events, Stellans being locked up and Leila's arrival, never meet.

In the front room, Leila drops her bag onto the sofa and settles on the edge. I sit down in the armchair directly opposite, watching her rub her temples.

'What happened when I left?' she asks.

'What do you mean?'

'I've been trying to call Michael, but he's not answering.'

'Why would you call him? Why would you care after everything he's done?' I try to keep calm. I try to be reasonable.

'Don't start,' she says. 'I don't need a lecture from you, okay?'

'As far as I'm concerned, it's quite simple. Stellans is a paedophile, and he needs to be locked up. You need to question why you're defending him. You need to think long and hard about that.'

'We had an affair,' she says, rising to her feet, traipsing across the living-room carpet. She stands by the window, peering out into the afternoon sky, then turns, staring at me. 'It was not right, and I admit it, I was too young to engage in it. I have tried and *tried* to question it all. But no matter what I do, no matter how many times I go over it in my head, I can't put it down to *abuse.*'

She walks over to me.

'You can understand that, can't you? You can understand what I'm saying? I was a *willing* agent, do you hear me? I am not damaged, I turned out just fine. Look at me, Rita!'

She takes my hands, hers clammy in mine, and gently squeezes them.

I can't bear to look into her eyes, deep and dark, for fear of losing myself in them, for fear of confessing what I've done. If anyone could get to me, it would be her.

I pull my hands away and move to the window. I can feel her staring at the back of me. Her eyes boring into my skin. I try to settle my heartbeat. 'You know you're not alright. Far from it.'

'I have a job, I earn money. My life turned out just fine.' She takes a seat on the sofa.

'Seeing him the other night has changed things for you, hasn't it? Because you said to me you had finally realised what he did to you. But now . . .' I turn to face her. 'That is what being groomed *does* to you. It leaves you confused, in denial, even.'

She's silent.

'It is an act of *coercion,*' I say, 'intended to trick you into thinking that you are a willing celebrant of the twisted arrangement, that you are somehow in *control* of it. Hell, that you even instigated it. But all along, it's really your abuser in power, pulling at the strings, controlling, and *coercing* you into doing unspeakable things.'

I hear coughing upstairs. I don't know if I'm imagining it, but I hear Margaret calling after me and I stare up at the corner of the ceiling and see a red light flashing.

Leila is taken aback and clambers to her feet. 'What's happening? Is everything alright?'

But it's too late. I'm already darting up the stairs, two steps at a time. I leave Leila on the ground floor, see her in my mind still standing in the living room, beside the fireplace, resting her elbow on the mantelpiece. 'Everything is fine!' I call.

I'm breathing hard, feeling the heave of my lungs. I'm standing over Margaret and I see that her face is shrunken like a dried-out raisin.

'What is it, Margaret, what's wrong?'

I'm staring at Margaret, but I'm not able to take her in. I sit down beside her on her bed, my mind racing, and I reach out to touch her forehead. She's warm against my fingertips, her eyes murky and searching mine. 'Talk to me, Margaret. You called me, didn't you? Is everything okay?'

'I'm hearing noises,' she says, closing her eyes, shaking her head. 'I'm seeing terrible things.'

'It's just your imagination,' I say, holding her hand. 'You know that Rita Marsh is here, that everything you ever need is taken care of.'

She slips her hand out of mine and turns her face away.

'I want to go,' she says. 'It's my time. They're calling for me.'

I step back, watching the rise and fall of her chest, as she draws out longer, wispier, ribbons of breath.

'Who do you see, Margaret?'

'It's Bill . . . I see him calling for me. There's a little girl next to him, he's holding her hand. It's my daughter,' she says.

It takes me aback hearing Margaret talk like that. I stand there for a while, honoured and humbled that she chose to disclose the secret of her life to me, visions of an afterlife I've never seen. When I see her dozing off again, I close the door behind me, the air thick and hot, eerie, and suffocating.

Leila looks up as I enter the living room. The sight of her hits me then. She's like a strange light that flashes and dances in the air, like a mysterious djinn, here to deceive me.

'I don't think I can go through this all over again,' she says. Her hand rests on the mantelpiece, as if to balance her.

I take a seat on the sofa, staring down at the carpet. I see the patch I've scrubbed hard at, the faint stain of blood, which in a certain light could easily pass as red wine. It annoys me that it's still visible. 'I'm just trying to be a good friend by telling you the truth. If you can't accept it or see it for what it really is, there's nothing I can do about it. But it isn't just *you* involved in all this.'

'Michael has already explained that,' she says, 'and I believe him, or at least I thought I did. I don't know – I don't know *what* to think.' She covers her face with her hands. 'This is all so confusing. What happened after I left?' she says.

I pinch the skin on the back of my hand. 'What do you mean what happened after you left? Nothing happened. Everything was normal. Stellans gathered his things and I said, jolly good riddance.'

I hear coughing from upstairs once again and my ears prick.

Leila stares up at the ceiling. She kicks off the sandals from her feet and moves to take a seat in the armchair opposite me.

'You are a good person, do you know that? I have so much admiration for what you do, and I'm sorry to drag you into all this. It's just . . . I don't know where Michael is. Something doesn't seem right about it.'

'Who *cares* where he is?'

'Look Rita, your behaviour was out of order yesterday. I know you care. I appreciate you trying to help me, but you can't speak on my behalf. I was so embarrassed.'

And there it is again, just like it was at school. Me, trying to protect her – I have done nothing but defend her, and there she is, making *me* look like I'm the one in the wrong. Leila has this way of making you feel inadequate, as if everything that goes wrong in life is all your fault. To think of the times, when we were young, when she went truanting, and I covered for her, lying to her mum when she called me asking where her daughter was. It didn't matter that I didn't know because Leila didn't *ask* me or *tell* me about it in advance. I made something up, I always did. I covered her back. But of course, anything I said to her mum always made it worse . . .

I stand and move to the window, staring out into the empty road, at the grass and trees and then at the BMW parking up. Javid is getting out of his car. I turn to Leila, my face flushed, heart pounding.

'Leila, listen—'

She cuts in. 'We're not fourteen anymore, Rita. You don't need to protect me.'

'Okay, fine,' I say, every part of me seizing, but also wanting to shake some sense into her. 'Then go and sort it out yourself, why don't you? I never asked to be involved in the first place.'

She is silent. Stunned, even.

'Do you remember Javid?' I say.

'Who?'

'Javid from school. That skinny Pakistani boy I hung out with sometimes. The one that wrote for the school paper.'

She shakes her head. 'What has that got to do with anything?'

The doorbell rings and I swear under my breath. The last thing I need is for more risk to present itself. Stellans could be discovered. If nothing else, the noise is bound to disturb Margaret. 'Let me refresh your memory,' I say.

Leila sits upright, slipping her feet into her sandals. I hear her heels sliding into the plastic soles. 'I didn't know you were expecting anyone. Jesus, Rita. There's always something going on in here.'

'I'll try and get rid of him,' I say, rushing into the hallway, 'but this is not over, do you hear? We need to address this.'

As if things are not complicated enough, I don't understand why Javid must turn up. I swing open the front door and pat down my hair, to appear as if everything is normal.

Javid flashes a smile, his teeth sparkling. 'Hello, gorgeous. What you up to? Don't mind me. Just passing through! It's what happens when you try and brush me off with a text. Leaves me no choice but to check up on you.'

I stand there stiffly, facing him as he peers at me from the doorstep.

'Can I come in? Or would you rather another six months of silence between us? C'mon, what's going on? What are you hiding in there?'

I open the door, and Javid breezes past me. I catch the whiff of his cologne as I follow him into the living room, watching as he looks left and right. I hold my breath as he sets eyes on Leila, and suddenly, he squeals, 'No way!' I stand in the doorway as he reaches out his arms to embrace her.

'I remember you – wow. What a blast from the past! You haven't changed much.'

Leila blushes. 'I remember you too,' she says. 'Good to see you.'

They hug, and I feel strangely out of place, like an intruder.

I listen as the two of them exchange pleasantries, and I crash onto the sofa, observing a vase of dried flowers on the windowsill.

Javid waves his finger at me as he turns. He's laughing. 'So, you met up, after the reunion. Had you both been in touch before, or is this the first time after school, after so many years?'

'The first time after so many years,' I mumble.

I rearrange myself in my seat. It now feels strangely uncomfortable. I'm thinking of Stellans, tied up in the back of the outhouse and I ask myself how it ever came to be like this.

Leila tells Javid the story of how we met at the reunion and exchanged numbers; how we've been chatting ever since, even though Leila couldn't face seeing anyone else from school. I'm relieved she thinks of something to say. The last thing I need is for

Javid to suspect anything. He clenches his jaw, following my line of vision, and stares down at the carpet.

'Rita didn't mention you both talking – but I'm sure she was about to tell me,' he says, smiling mischievously. 'As for the reunion, you didn't miss much.' He leans against the fireplace, stretching his back, as if to make a point about how well things have turned out for him. He stares down at Leila curled up on the sofa. 'Presumably you heard about it, and everything else?'

Leila stares absently into the distance, turning something over in her mind.

She appears to have a different conversation going on inside her. I stand up, offering to make everyone some tea.

Leila nods. 'Tea sounds good,' she says, but then she follows me into the kitchen, Javid trailing behind her. They both take a seat at the table.

'If I'm honest, I don't remember you so well,' says Leila, turning to Javid as I boil the kettle.

I figure her comments take Javid by surprise, although I'm too busy boiling the kettle. 'But then those school days were such a haze,' she says.

'You were always so busy,' I say, pulling out three mugs from the cupboard and slamming them down onto the counter. I'm trying not to sound sarcastic, but I am struggling, really struggling, to hold it back. 'Hardly in touch with playground politics when you had so many *other* things to think about.'

'Well, I don't know about you, but I'm glad those days are over. What a waste of time,' says Javid. 'Still, I've kept in touch with Rita all these years and a few other less interesting people. How about you, Leila? Is there anyone you're in touch with?'

Leila shrugs. 'No, not really. Not even Rita, until now.'

I bite my lip and my mouth salivates.

'But here we now are. Friends again,' she says. Leila looks at me. 'I'm grateful for it.' I feel my face flush.

'That's nice,' says Javid. 'I'm glad something good came out of the reunion. I was clearing out some old school things the other day, and I remember, you were in that school play, weren't you? I was running the school paper at the time. It was quite a big story. I found all my old school articles.'

I glance at Javid, and then at Leila. I have no idea where this is heading.

'Yeah, well. That was a long time ago,' Leila says, brushing her shoulder as if there's a bit of dandruff on it.

'You do like a bit of drama though, don't you, Leila?' I simply can't stop myself.

She looks down at her watch and laughs, determined not to rise to my snide remark. 'Oh dear. I'm late for an appointment,' she says. 'I am so sorry, Rita. I've completely lost track of time. I need to get going.'

'But I've only just boiled the kettle!'

'It was lovely catching up. Perhaps I'll call you later and we can chat on the phone?' Her eyes search mine. They're pleading, so I nod. From the corner of my eye, I see Javid is watching us.

Javid leans his elbows onto the table, leafing through the morning papers, peering at a page of horoscopes. I usher Leila into the hallway so as not to cause a spectacle.

'Just look at the mess caused by Stellans being here. I never wanted him over, remember? This was all *your* idea.' I'm whispering, trying to make sure Javid doesn't hear us. But I feel him listening, his eyes crawling at the back of my neck. I resent the fact that I must lie. What this predicament, now spiralling out of control, is forcing me to do; pulling me in, deeper and deeper with no rope to hold on to.

Leila runs a hand down her thigh to straighten her skirt. 'Fine,' she says. 'I should never have got you involved. I'm sorry about that. But you don't need to throw it back in my face every five minutes.'

'Leila—'

'Just leave it. Let's speak to each other in a few days.'

A few days? I am not even sure what might happen in a few days.

'Leila, wait—'

I move towards her, but she holds her bag up to her chest, making her way towards the front door. She stops just short of turning the handle then faces me once more.

'Maybe it's best that I talk to Stellans directly,' she says.

I don't reply. I'm stubborn, resolute in my view of what the *right thing* to do is. The *right thing* to do is to report him, that paedophile, to come clean about what happened. My only crime is that I hit him, tied him up. I didn't harm him otherwise. But even I can see that it's not possible to come clean anymore – not given the circumstances. Some might be sympathetic to my holding him hostage since, strictly speaking, he is a criminal. But others, like the police, people like Lawson, would come down hard – especially after Zia.

I watch Leila close the front door, and I move into the living room, following the outline of her through the window. She gets into her car and drives off into the distance. This is the second time in two days that I've watched her leave.

Javid slips up beside me. 'What's going on, secret agent Rita? This doesn't look like a normal reunion to me. Come on, spill the beans, or I will tickle it out of you.'

'What are you talking about?' I brush past him, walking towards the kitchen. 'I'm in the middle of making your tea, so please be quiet, unless you want to make yourself useful and help me do some washing.'

'I've re-read the article about Stellans,' he says quickly, changing the subject. 'And I've done some digging. Sifting through old stuff from school jogged my memory, and I must say, it's something of a strange coincidence, isn't it?'

'What is?' I ask. 'Now who's playing secret detective?'

'Her sudden reappearance is extremely strange.'

By now, I'm in the kitchen, re-filling the kettle, pretending there's too much limescale on the bottom. I keep myself occupied by peering into it, scraping at it with a fork.

'You mean the Stellans article?' I turn on the tap, emptying the water. I splash water in the sink, just to make some noise, *anything* to distract him. 'I don't think she knows much about it. She's too wrapped up in her own life to pay him any attention.'

If only that were true.

'Well. I read it again, just to refresh my memory.'

'And? So, there's another pervert at school, left to teach children with no consequences. What's new about that? Most likely, he was not the only one in Brentwood.'

'Ooof! Rita, this is not a joke, and that is a bit dark, even for you, don't you think? Do you know of any other teacher messing about with children?'

I shake my head.

'I went to that school, too – and I have a right to know.'

'You know Javid, you should have been a writer, because for sure you have an overactive imagination. There's nothing like that with Leila.'

He stands by the window, wedging his hands in his pockets.

'It's just that I remember stuff,' he says. 'I remember all the stories about Leila and Stellans. There were rumours, weren't there? She must have mentioned it, given everything going on. Was she involved with him? Does she know something?'

I slam my hand down onto the counter, harder than I mean to.

'Just stop, okay? Find something else to occupy your thoughts. Trust me, this is going nowhere.'

Javid is stunned, like he's just been stung by a bee.

'Alright, alright. Calm down. What's wrong with you? Jeez.'

I wonder whether I should cook Javid a meal. I know what he's like. Food is the only thing that would distract him and keep him quiet. 'Shall I cook something?' I ask.

'No. I've lost my appetite.'

I re-boil the kettle.

'This is so fucked up, don't you think? We all went to that school. It affects every one of us who knew Stellans. I'm seriously worried about you, Rita. I know what you were like back then. Leila messed you up and I don't want to see you get hurt again.'

My stomach turns as I remember how one time, I cried on Javid's shoulder for two hours; how he sat there and listened to me rambling on about my confused feelings for Leila.

'You and her, it's not good news,' Javid says. 'It's like mixing avocado with treacle.'

'What?'

'Maybe I am hungry,' he says.

'It was a long time ago.' I turn to him, ruffling his hair. 'I know you care about me. We've been friends for such a long time, haven't we? You're the brother I never had – do you know that? Believe me when I say I will always be grateful. Now: what do you want to eat? You're like a child that constantly needs feeding.'

'She broke your heart.'

'She did nothing of the kind.'

Javid stands behind me, resting his hand on my shoulder.

'Look, I've got to go. Even your cooking can't interfere with my plans. But this is not over, right? I'm telling you to steer clear of her because if you don't I'll end up having to pick up the pieces. And I can't do that . . . I can't watch you go through that all over again.'

Javid is right. Javid is always right. But I can't tell him how inopportune his advice is right now. I want to tell him everything – the only true friend I ever had. He never made me feel like shit or made me do things to pay him back for just *being* there when I needed him.

'I'll pop round in a few days,' he says. 'You can fix me lunch then, to make up for your non-existent tea-making.'

'Sure.'

I stare down at his shoes, black and shiny, as he heads towards the door. I hear it close behind him and, after a while, in the distance, the sound of his car engine revving.

The sky pales; evening awaits. Things have moved so fast with Stellans, I can't keep up with it all. The air is warm and muggy. All I want to do is to take a bath, to submerge myself under the water, to not have to think about what is really going on.

That night, after a long soak, I toss and turn in bed, making plans in my head about what I'm going to do next. But the voice in my head is speaking to me again. It tells me, in no uncertain terms, to keep hold of Stellans. To be patient. *Good things happen to those who wait; eventually he will break.* That voice is me – my instinct and intuition that allows me to see clearly. It's confirmation that what I'm doing is right. I can't possibly expect anyone else to understand. How could they understand when they do not have the insight? I am prepared to keep Stellans, prepared to wait for his confession. This is my contribution to the universal laws of justice, and it is very much required.

18

Brentwood High WhatsApp group, 9.09 a.m.

Have you seen the latest on Stellans?

Apparently, the girl said it went on for 2 years!

Yeah, I read it started when she was twelve and he was, like, 47.

IT MAKES ME SICK!! THEY SHOULD ARREST HIM!!

*I don't know why the police are so useless. They should
fucking kill him!*

In the outhouse, I stare down at Stellans, at the flakes of blood,
dry and crispy, clotting his crown.

'I've been thinking about everything you said,' he says. He
swallows, his voice breaking.

It appears he's had time to think – lucky him. What a privilege
for this man to be able to do nothing else but to think of himself. I, on the other hand, have not stopped thinking about others
all night. *I* have been worried about Leila, her family, what they
would do if this ever came out. *I've* been thinking about Margaret,
her slow demise, the strange things she says as she nears the end of
her life. I've been thinking of all the girls Stellans touched in plain
sight, the pupils, teachers, parents he deceived. Only *then* do I
think of myself. Why I was never heard. Why, after speaking to
my mother on that terrible night, finally drawing up the courage
to tell her about what happened to me – in my bedroom, in our
very own house – she silenced me, took sides with Dad.

'I've got this all wrong,' he says. 'I see that, now. I've committed a terrible crime. I struggled to see that until you opened my eyes. I'll go to the police, I promise. I'll testify to the authorities. Let them decide my punishment. I take it willingly. But I beg you, Rita. *Please*, just let me go from here.'

I move to the side of him, staring at the side of his face. By now, Stellans is so smeared in his own filth, he is barely recognisable. I've tied him up tightly, there's no way he can move. But one arm is free, that's all that matters. He ought to be grateful.

'I don't trust you,' I say. 'I never did to be honest. I certainly trust you less since I've read all those stories.'

His eyes bulge, as if the mere suggestion that he is not to be trusted is incomprehensible to him. 'You *can* trust me, you really can! You're right. I'm wrong. What I did was . . . *unforgivable.*'

I stand there for a second, not sure how to react, so I sit down on a chair to gather my thoughts. 'Leila doesn't seem to think so and that's the problem. You brainwashed her, do you know that? You need to reverse your grooming and convince her otherwise. Let her see you for the wicked man you really are.'

'Come on, Rita.'

God. *Come on*, he says, like we are somehow friends.

'You're unrepentant. That's a problem for me. It's a very big problem.'

'No, no! It's not like that at all. I was wrong. If I could take it back, I would. You're right, Rita. You're *so* right. I've made such a mess of things . . .'

His voice is starting to grate. I feel the slow creep of a headache. 'Stop feeling sorry for yourself and just write the bloody confession, will you? I want this to be over and done with as much as you do.'

I hand him the pad of paper and a fountain pen. 'Hurry,' I say. 'This is already going on for longer than I expected.'

Stellans reaches out for the pen, gripping it unsteadily between his fingers. 'Did you have this all planned?' he whimpers. I hear the nib scratching against the paper. 'When Leila called me and asked to meet me at Raven Court, was this all part of the plan?'

'Don't be ridiculous,' I say. 'I'm not the criminal here. You are, remember? None of this was premeditated. But here we are.'

'Does she even know about this?'

He stares at me, his face twitching. He knows he is pushing things, yet he continues asking me questions.

'Why should she know? You think you're so important to her that she wants to be caught up in your life again? Of course she doesn't know!'

For a second, I consider what Leila would do if she *did* find out. After all these years, I could not be certain of her loyalty. I know that she could never call into question my motivation. She knows, or at least she must know, based on our previous conversation, that I care only for her feelings.

'And what would she do if she found out? You're both friends, aren't you? Best friends at school, you were. Do you think she would still want to know you if she thought you were capable of *this*? Have anything to do with you again after it?'

His voice is sneering.

'She's in no fit state to think clearly about anything, so keep her out of it.'

'Why would you keep this a secret, though? Why would you do something she would never agree with?'

I stand up, walking towards him. I slam my hand against the edge of the bed and Stellans jumps. 'Shut up, okay? You're talking too much, and I really don't like it. Leila is not herself. She is not thinking straight.'

'And you *are*? You think this – *this* – is the behaviour of someone stable? Just look at how bad this is. Look how this appears. End it now and I promise, I'll say no more of it.'

'Be quiet,' I say. 'And hurry up if you want time on the toilet.'

'Is this even about Leila or is this about *you*? Are you wanting to exact revenge for something I accidentally did to you at school?'

'I said, shut up.'

'Gaslighting. That's what they call it now, isn't it? The new modern-day crime. Did I do that to you? Did I undermine you in some way? Because if I did, I am truly sorry.'

'Don't make this about *me*. This has nothing to do with *me*. This is about *you* and *your* crimes.' I step back. *Why does he keep doing this?*

'But don't you see? That's how it comes across. Listen to me, Rita. Even if I wrote a confession, no one would believe it. Why would they believe *you*? It's *your* word against *mine* – and given the circumstances we find ourselves in, you would hardly be in a strong position.'

My knees feel weak.

'I remember what you were like at school, the awkward teenager, always sidelined, ignored. Looking back, it must have been terribly difficult for you. I only wish I had helped you more.'

'What are you talking about?'

'I failed you and I'm sorry. Something has disturbed you – the discovery of my relationship with Leila perhaps, which is, of course, understandable. But there is something else too. Rita, let me help you.'

'I know what you're doing. I know what this is. You're trying to unravel me. But it's not working, you scumbag. And I should warn you, it's best not to provoke me.'

I turn to sit down because in that moment, it all feels like too much. Memories of school begin surfacing, skittering on the water's surface like drops of oil. I see myself, all those years ago, running after Leila in the playground. Flashes of us seated together in the classroom. That night, and that moment when we touched one another, exploring each other for the first time. The way she ran her finger down my spine. To this day, I've never felt anything close to what I felt then. For a second, I begin to question what I'm doing, whether I should risk it all and let Stellans go.

'I'm sorry. Really, I am. I don't want to make things worse than they are. I will do what you say. If it's a confession you want and you really feel it would help Leila, I will gladly give it.'

'Thank you,' I mumble, relieved that, after everything, he is finally listening.

'But how can I be sure you will release me?'

Sigh. I stare at a spider scuttling across the floor, meeting the edge of the wall. 'Believe me when I say I don't want to keep you here any longer than I need to. I never wanted this.' My voice breaks so I cough, covering my mouth with my hand.

'I'll do what you say. But I need time to write.'

'Go ahead. I'd be delighted to give you time.'

I close my eyes, listening to the scrawl of the pen against the paper. I almost fall asleep waiting for him to finish it. After around thirty minutes, he nods, handing me back the sheet, as if he's proud of himself for being so productive.

My shirt is soaked in sweat, and my skin feels itchy. I stare down at his scribbly writing, smudged with dirt, smeared in blood, and try to make sense of it.

What does a man do when he fears for his life? He can do nothing but write of those fears, and list truths in a fashion that might keep him alive. There is no question Rita Marsh is mad. I do not fear to tell the truth about her. She has not been right ever since she was a child. She has forced me to write a confession, and this is what I write now.

I am being held against my will, my legs bound, my torso tied. I have not eaten properly for what feels like days, nor drunk more than a few sips of water. She said she will allow me to sit on a commode – and that, she considers a privilege. But I am still waiting. I have not seen daylight since she tied me up and even the paper I write on is blurry and bright, hurting my eyes. I only pray that someone finds me, that I do not die here.

When I first met Leila, it was a moment of revelation. A flicker of something inside me that revived me after so many years, wandering. She defied age, something about her possessing a power to reconcile all differences – age, cultures, artistic preoccupations. She stitched together those pieces inside me that were thread-loose for years. I know this sounds insane – she was a child, but you must believe me, whoever is reading this. I saw in her something that perhaps no other person did.

I was attracted to her, I was intoxicated by her, consumed by everything about her. It was not a perversion; it was a pure and truthful adoration. But I confess, I let it take over me. I know it was wrong. I know, I should never have acted on it. I crossed a line. I should never have crossed it. But it was never for the reason the world assumes it to be, some depraved desire and dark fantasy that a grown woman couldn't possibly satisfy in me. It is not as if I've not thought about it over the years, why I did it – what dark force possessed me to indulge in such a relationship. Each day, my shame grows, eating away at me, gnawing at my bones.

You must understand that once there are feelings, it is difficult to reverse. Whoever is reading this, I promise you that I am not a pervert. In the eyes of the law, I am a criminal, yes, I am surely that and I admit it. Perhaps, because of that, I am not a good person. But I am not a bad person, either. I am a criminal only because I loved a child in a way that I never should have done. I sought help. I've been trying to transcend my own transgressions to become a better person. But the love itself was truthful, and she loved me too. Just ask her of her own feelings and she will clearly tell you. They were deep and real and ever so beautiful.

I stare at his confession, trying – and failing – to hide my growing irritation.

'That's it? That's all you wrote in the time I gave you?'

He grinds his teeth, and an angry vein surfaces like a throbbing under-skin worm on the side of his face.

'Why do you keep provoking me? Why do you keep doing that?'

My heart beats so hard, I feel as if my ribs might crack. Sounds on the outside, faint and distant and muffled, like the rustle of leaves in the slight breeze, the creaking of the garden gate, appear so much louder than they really are. Those sounds crash about inside me, like cars skittering and skidding at high speed. For a moment, I don't know who I am anymore. This has got way out of control. I don't know how to claw it back.

I scrunch the paper into a golf ball and aim it at him. 'It's not good enough,' I say.

Stellans flinches as the paper hits his head. He screws up his face.

'For the life of me, I don't know what you want.'

'You know what I want.'

'Honestly, I don't,' he croaks. 'Is this even about Leila? Or is this about something else? Perhaps, you and her . . .'

'I want key details. A complete chronology of events. When it started – and *how* exactly. Also, what happened next. I want to know how it ended. I want it all written down. Don't miss anything out or I'll—' I wipe my brow with the back of my hand. 'Am I making myself clear?'

He nods.

'But what if I can't remember everything?'

'What?'

'There are huge gaps in my memory. You can understand that, can't you? You can understand, from everything you've been through yourself, that sometimes, we can't process things or remember everything in the correct order. Time scrambles events, particularly if they are painful. Memories are amorphous things. Remembering is like catching sailfish. For God's sake, Rita. I know you understand because you're *smart.*'

He is animated, talking to me like I'm still his student.

'And what will you do with a confession? What good will it *possibly* do? Please, whatever I did, I am sorry. Just let me go!'

But there are too many things missing from his confession to let him go. I move closer to him.

'Last chance,' I say. 'Is there anything else you have to say for yourself?'

From the corner of my eye, I see a sharpened knife lying on the ledge, the blade glinting in the sunlight. A silver light tinged with blue splays onto the stone wall.

'I don't know what you mean. I know you think I'm guilty of more. But you must know that is simply not true!'

'I knew you were up to something,' I say. 'As I look back, I think I caught you, but *you* made me think *I* was going crazy.'

I did remember. I remembered it all.

On his face, a death stare. 'I tried to *help* you, Rita. Can't you see that? I know it is not as you remember it. Sometimes, our minds confuse things, it is perfectly understandable. Adolescence is intense. But I swear, I tried to help you. You were so alone, so vulnerable. I remember you talked to Mrs Smith a lot about things.'

My face flushes as I remember that too. Me, pouring out my heart about feeling so defeated and worthless. A moment, just a flash, of something intimate and private.

'I tried to reach out to you. All the teachers at Brentwood did. It was after your mother came in to see us. We tried to extend a trustful hand, after such —'

'My mother?'

'She came to talk to some of the teachers. Said you were having problems. Rita, you were . . .'

My head rushes, time expanding, contracting; past and present converging to a single point. I can't understand why she never told me that. I step back, unsteady on my feet. The sensation of my body floating and lightly skimming the air, drifting then falling . . .

But Stellans does not stop talking. I begin to lose all sense of where I am, why I am here. How we got here, even. Before I know it, before I can even stop myself, I grab the knife from the ledge. I'm standing over him.

'Woah, woah, Rita! What are you doing?'

I don't know what I'm doing. I can't stop myself.

'You're lying,' I say.

I tower over him, standing on tiptoe; I'm holding the knife just below his navel.

'Rita, *please*. This is crazy!'

'Why are you lying?' I know I can't stab him. There's no way I'll do it. I want simply to threaten him.

'Rita, I beg you. I will do it! I will write anything else you want, I swear. If you don't like what I wrote, I will change it.' He breathes faster, harder. 'Please . . . put the knife . . . down.'

For a moment, I freeze. My hand shakes as I grip the knife more forcefully.

Stellans is coughing – wheezing like he might be sick.

My hand burns, I'm gripping the knife too hard. Finally, I throw it to the ground, rubbing my hands together to relieve them.

'You don't deserve any more of my attention,' I say. 'Do you understand? I should let you waste away until there's nothing left but bones.'

After that, I leave him there alone.

19

I do not realise, at first, that the memories bubbling up from my subconscious mind are because I'm spending so much time with Stellans.

I see myself seated on a coach, just back from a school ice-skating trip, thinking about the terrible evening I've had. I must be sixteen, I think, pushed firmly against the wall separating adolescence and adulthood.

I disembark from the coach, the sky dark, the pavements wet, and walk along the street to where Dad is parked. I catch him smoking beside his car, outside the church a few yards from the school gate. He looks up guiltily.

'You are early,' he says.

'Don't let Mum catch you doing that,' I reply.

'It was good?' He throws down his cigarette, stamping on the stub with his foot. He's wearing his worn corduroy jacket with a scarf wrapped round him. I notice several cigarette butts on the pavement beside him.

I shake my head.

'You did not enjoy it?' he asks.

I shrug my shoulders and we walk towards his Fiesta.

'I don't know,' he sighs. 'I never had any trips like this. You people do not understand how lucky you are. In my school in India, it was homework and a slap with a chappal if you did not complete it.'

But lucky is not how I would describe it.

When we get home, Mum asks me whether I've had a good time. I shrug, walking heavily up the stairs to my room. I take a shower, changing into my night shirt, and lie on my bed, staring up at the ceiling. I hear a murmur of voices downstairs.

Wrapping my duvet around me, I open my bedroom door and stand in the hallway upstairs. Mum and Dad are talking.

Mum: 'She doesn't have any friends, that's the problem. She's lost inside her own head. I've been trying to get through to her for months, but she doesn't respond. I blame that night . . . when something happened. We should have done something about it – it goes over and over in my mind. It makes me so angry.'

Dad: 'Time is passed now. She must learn to get on with her life. She has a good home. We have a steady income. Do you know how hard we've worked to give her what she has now? If we say anything it will spoil her life. I am not in agreement that we need to keep talking about it.'

Silence. A clang of dishes.

Mum: 'Sometimes I wonder to myself whether us being so wrapped up in the business is not helping.'

'Maybe she can talk to someone,' he says. 'Get it out of her body and system.'

'Maybe a counsellor,' says Mum. 'That is a good idea. But it's all so incredibly expensive.'

'We have twenty-two residents living in Raven Court. There are many people here to listen to her talk.'

'Don't be ridiculous. She needs somebody to talk to who is a *professional* – or at least a friend, her own age. Someone who understands what she might be going through . . . with all those delayed changes.'

I note that my mum says *'delayed changes'* like it's some sort of terminal illness. All this time she's ignored me, I put it down to indifference. But she noticed. I see now that she noticed.

'Maybe she needs a boyfriend,' says Dad, 'maybe she has one and she keeps it secret, and it is not working very well.'

My mother snorts. More dishes clanging. 'You don't know

your daughter much, do you? A boyfriend is probably the last thing she wants.'

A week passes, and that's when I see it on the six o'clock news bulletin. It's Stellans, a picture of him on TV, seated comfortably in an armchair beside a log fire, flanked by wooden beams. It's one of those writerly shots staged in an old country manor. He looks suitably shabby, true to stereotype, as if that said something of his creativity and artistic temperament. I turn the volume up. The newsreader is wearing a stiff mustard-coloured jacket, her voice is as soft and cool as a prison cell:

> *Michael Stellans, a former secondary school teacher and now an author, is reported to be missing. He was last seen on the morning of Friday the thirteenth of September by his literary agent, David Kingsley.*
> *Michael Stellans was recently accused of having an affair with an underaged pupil, an accusation which he has since denied. We are urging anyone with any information regarding his whereabouts to please come forward.*

My throat constricts, my windpipe narrowing. The Chinese food in my stomach just sits there, turning. Somehow, seeing this story play out on TV makes it distant and, strangely, less real. I flick through the other TV channels, but I see nothing more about him. Just more nonsense on Brexit. A documentary on start-up businesses.

I grab my phone, flicking through my messages. The WhatsApp mob is out in full force, riled by this recent development:

> *OMG!! Can you believe it????*

Nah, this can't really be happening.

The thing is, we will all be contacted – I mean, anyone linked to him!

What does this paedo have to do with us?? I've got sweet FA to do with him!

I'm so transfixed by those messages; the letters start crawling. I could go to prison, my identity outed as the hunter that caused a young man to commit suicide. Just then, my mobile rings. I panic – praying this isn't the police; I've nowhere to hide, but I know I must answer it. I put my plate down on the side table and swipe to answer it.

But it's not the police. It's Leila. Her voice is nasal, an octave higher than usual.

She's breathing fast and heavily. I can tell she's been crying.

'What is it? What's the matter?' It's a stupid question, since I know precisely what's going on; I know more than she does.

'It's Michael. He's missing. Have you heard? It's all over the news.'

I slide onto the floor, just by the sofa, and sit cross-legged. I'm not sure what to say or do.

'I did hear something,' I say. 'Knowing Stellans, this is probably just a hoax. He's probably hiding out somewhere until the story blows over.'

'But he's not taking any of my calls and he's never done that before. It's just so *unlike* him,' she says.

I flinch. 'I thought you said you only spoke occasionally?' The sinews in my neck tighten.

'Rita, now's not the time. What matters is that Michael is missing. If this gets out, it will be terrible. Don't you get it? You and I saw him on the day they say he disappeared!'

It's like a foot is pressing down onto my chest. The way that Leila lies does not sit comfortably.

I feel my phone vibrate and take a look at the screen.

21.05 Javid
Have you seen the news about Stellans? Terrible! Call me
when you get a chance.

I press my phone back to my ear. 'Do you think anyone knows that he came to see us?'

'No,' she says.

'Are you *sure*?'

'I think so.'

'Maybe this is a sign that he's guilty,' I say. 'Don't you get it? Why would he go missing if he was innocent?'

'But that doesn't make any sense!'

'It makes a lot of sense from where I'm sitting.'

I wonder whether Leila is coming round, whether this might be the moment she finally gets it.

'I need a bit of time to process it,' she says, her voice faint. 'It's all too much. I'll call you back.'

She hangs up, but I'm still there, the phone in my hand, staring at the screen.

I scramble to my feet, storm through the kitchen and out the back door. I unlock the door to the outhouse. Stellans' eyes are as wide as the moon, as I switch on the light, the milky whites of them dazzling. I rip the duct tape from his mouth and Stellans gasps. The adrenalin in my body rushes with such speed and ferocity, I feel unsteady on my feet. I try to contain myself by leaning one arm onto the metal bars on the side of his bed.

'This has gone on for long enough. You need to write this confession. After that, I'll release you.'

Tears stream down either side of his face, drops falling onto the crisp cotton sheet. Stellans is shaking, his sheets soaked in sweat. He's helpless, defeated. He tries to lift his head.

'I won't hurt you,' I say. 'Trust me when I say I want this to be over.'

He clenches his eyes closed, and he coughs and splutters.

'None of this was meant to happen. I lost my temper, that's all. I lost it when I heard you talking to Leila.'

Stellans drops his head and releases a long exhale. His lips tremble.

'I'll untie you enough so that you can write. But just one thing. I want you to name Leila, do you hear me? I want you to *name* her in that confession.'

Silently, he nods.

'And Rani too whilst you're at it – and all the others.' For a second, I feel a sense of triumph that in the end, we arrived at a good understanding. This is over – finally it's over. No matter what happens now, with Stellans' confession, the truth will be revealed.

20

The next day, I run errands, clean the home, and go about the minutiae of life, putting off the inevitable until I must return to the outhouse – to my prisoner. I stare down at Stellans, the outline of his long, svelte body, his pale hands and spidery fingers. Perhaps, had the circumstances been different, I ought to thank him for enlightening me concerning the effort my mother made, talking to my teachers. Something dark and shadowy, like an unknown force hidden inside me all these years, begins to inch forward. It's like a hooded figure, creeping up from behind me, drenched in black, ready to throw a blanket over my head and to drag my head and neck back.

'Where is it?' I ask.

I can forgive my mother; my father is more difficult.

Stellans looks up at me, snarling.

'Fuck you, Rita Marsh. I've decided: I'm not doing it.'

His lips move in rapid motion, but I've already ceased listening. I'm staring down at the pad, folded, and closed, and I open it, hurriedly scanning the blank pages.

'But we had a deal,' I say. 'Why are you making this difficult?'

'*You* had a deal. I don't have to *do* anything. Kill me if you want. Let's see if you can do it.'

I'm trembling, frantically leafing through the pages, staring down at him. 'Don't you want this over and done with? You said you would confess everything. You said you would do it!'

'Finally, I've figured you out. This has nothing to do with what I did. This is some sort of bargaining tool so that you can get the better of Leila.'

'You're making a big mistake,' I say.

'Maybe you want to blackmail her.'

I move towards Stellans, my face drawing closer to his. He spits at me, a splatter of his stale filthy mouth all over me. 'For fuck's sake!' I scream. 'What are you doing?' I close my eyes and I turn away. I grab hold of the knife on the ledge to protect myself. 'You are wrong. So wrong. You're making this so much worse than it needs to be.'

'There's something not right about you, do you know that? You need help. Get the hell away from me!' He shakes so violently, trying to escape, I hear the jars and bottles of antiseptic and white spirit rattling on the side ledge.

'Are you surprised it's come to this?' I say, checking the leather straps are still secure, just in case he has any funny ideas. 'I would have released you ages ago if you'd just done what I asked of you. But, oh no. You must make it difficult.'

'Bring Leila here and we can discuss it sensibly. You're right, I should take responsibility for what I did. I'll talk to Leila, okay? I'll apologise directly. But this stuff about a confession is simply bullshit.'

He falls still, and silent.

'You and I have history,' he says, after a moment.

'Shut up,' I say. 'Don't bring me into this. I don't want to be associated with you and I don't need your counselling.'

'But your mother—'

'She's dead. No point bringing her into it, either.'

For a second, he's stunned, but then he begins laughing. I catch a glimpse of his teeth coated in yellow. But as I move closer, I see tears rolling down the sides of his face.

'Not a day goes by when I haven't thought about it.' His voice breaks. 'Am I a monster? Did I damage her in some way? And then there's you.' He turns his face. 'All I did, all I ever wanted, was to help you . . . but I see now, my offer back then was simply inadequate.'

I'm not listening. I can't listen.

'Your mother . . . she told us not to ask questions. Said it would be too painful. So we didn't. But we should have. The policy in schools now is much stricter. Looking back, the fact that we didn't enquire is a terrible failing on our part. We should have done better. I know that now. It was simply not good enough.'

'What are you talking about?' I'm breathless, losing patience.

'She urged us to give you space . . . said that you were unsettled.'

'Unsettled? That's all? Nothing *else*? No specific details?'

'But regardless of that, Rita, I know you well enough to know that you don't want this. I *know* you; I know you better than you think. You shared things with me when you were young because you trusted me.'

'I shared nothing with you, what are you talking about? We barely spoke. You were always telling me off, remember?'

'We all knew – figured out – what had happened. Once, we talked about it – I am certain. I asked you why you were always so sullen.'

A flash of something hits me then, and I remember a conversation we may have had. Stellans asked me to stay behind after class. I just can't remember what we spoke about.

'It's all too common. Some things are painful to spell out. I understand. But this – this is not you. This is not how to deal with things. Leila and I were different. I *beg* you, Rita. Do the right thing.'

In that moment, I see myself as a child, walking through a dark corridor, surrounded by voices, children's voices, eclipsed with shame and loneliness.

'Rita . . .' Stellans is struggling and jerking again. 'You can't do this. I will die. Do you understand? I will die here!'

He squeezes his eyes closed, his eyeballs sliding around under his eyelids, like he might be searching for an explanation, perhaps, of how it has come to this.

'I need some air,' he says. 'I'm struggling to breathe. *Please.* I need to move my limbs.'

But there's no way I can take the risk. He struggles on, regardless.

'What are you asking for exactly? What is it you want?'

'I need to walk outside. Just for a few minutes. After that, we can talk.'

I glance outside the window. I see the sun emerging from behind the clouds with an intensity so acute, the sky seems to swell. I am not prepared for his request. I cannot properly process it.

'I'll open a window,' I say, reaching for the handle. I grab the bar, but I struggle to open it.

'*Please.* Just for five minutes. I can't breathe, lying here.'

I look down at him, grief-stricken. 'I never wanted this. I am a good person. I never told lies. I resent being reduced to this. I told you, didn't I, that I'll let you go if you write a confession. But now you're making this so much more difficult than it needs to be. You need to understand that if I do this, if I let you go outside, this really is the last chance.'

He nods. 'I'll give you the confession if you allow me some fresh air.'

It's a request I find difficult to refuse as it's not too unreasonable. So, I replace the duct tape over his mouth because the last thing I want is for him to keep talking. I untie the rope and straps around his ankles, heaving him up. He is floppy, like a rag doll, and – as a precaution, since all this is against my better judgement – I grab a knife, bringing the sharp edge of the blade close to him, pointing the tip at his temple.

'Don't do anything stupid,' I say.

He licks his lips and nods, sweat dripping down in small beads from his rumpled brow.

I am sure this is a mistake. Every bone in my body tells me it is a mistake. But I help him onto his feet regardless, allowing him this chance to prove to me he is a better person. I help him to balance. He struggles to stand as I tie his wrists in front of him. He leans on me, but I move my body away from his. I can't bear to touch him, so I stand behind him. I stretch out my arms, placing my hands onto his shoulders to steady him, but doing so at a safe distance. Eventually he finds his balance and begins walking, taking a few steps forward, small shuffles with his knees locked straight and back hunched. I stop him from going any further as I place a blindfold over his eyes. I open the door, and Stellans inches into the garden. He's hobbling, inhaling the air deep into his lungs as if every inch of his life depends on it.

'Thank you,' he says. 'Thank you very much.'

'Keep walking.'

I watch his feet drag forward into the scraggly grass. He holds his hands in the air so I can see them, his head tilted towards the sky. He is breathing heavily, moving between the weeds, creeping along the stone path. In the distance, the windows of Raven Court are blackened by a film of dust. For a moment, the building appears as if it were not mine. I realise then just how empty, abandoned, and unloved it is. It seems to have aged, as if it needs a reminder of why it exists.

Stellans moves his face to the light and the clouds creep over the sun, as a raven cuts across the sky. The two of us are shadows, slipping and shifting against a backdrop of stone.

I see images in my mind, like cream curdling on the surface of spoilt milk. Sensations and smells I have not experienced and cannot remember experiencing since I was a child. My head is pounding, but this is not a usual headache. This is something else. That's when it happens. I throw up – I throw up so violently, it feels as if I've brought up the walls of my stomach. The burn of the bile singes the back of my throat and I wipe my face with my palm. I realise – it takes only a minute – that Stellans' blindfold is off, and he is running.

In a shot, I'm up, watching him run, his tied wrists bobbing in front of him. He struggles to heave himself forward, but he overestimates how much energy he has. He takes only a few steps before he stumbles, falling in a way that suggests he is a broken man. I watch as his face thuds onto the dewy grass, flat on his stomach, and I lunge forward, pressing my left knee into his back. I hold him down under my weight as my hand grips onto the back of his neck, the knife still in my hand pressed into him. He screams, his chesty voice gravelly. I press his head firmly into the soil.

'Why did you have to do that?' I whisper in his ear – not wanting to make any noise in case Margaret hears. But my voice sounds alien even to me. I wheeze, barely able to control my breathing. 'You've let me down. You're a liar. I despise liars!' I spit.

He shakes his head, but he just won't stop screaming, spluttering into the grass.

'Get up onto your knees, and don't try anything or I'll knock you out, do you hear me?'

Stellans rises to his knees, struggling to find his balance, all the while jerking uncontrollably. I dig the knife a bit deeper into his back and he instantly quietens. All I keep thinking is, I should have known he would do this. Why did I ever trust him? I need to get him inside as quickly as possible.

Back inside the outhouse, he stares down at the bed. He turns and sits down, lying down onto his back, all the resistance and fight in him drained; finally, he's surrendered.

'You will write this confession,' I say. 'Do you hear me? You will write it exactly as I say.'

He nods quickly. 'Whatever you want. I will do whatever you want.'

But I'm not thinking straight, because having to dictate a confession to him means I will have to piece together parts of a story I can neither remember nor understand.

I tie a rope around his torso, securing it behind the bedrest, down below, almost at the bottom of the bed, which there is no way he could stretch his arm to reach.

'I am going to give you until this evening to draft something,' I say. 'And if it's not ready by the time I get back, there will be consequences. Got it? This is it.'

He nods.

I stand up, walking towards him, placing a pad of paper and a pen beside him.

I untie one hand, just loose enough so he can move his fingers – just like before, although now, I feel I need to be extra careful. I secure the straps around his ankles.

Stellans stares down at the paper and swallows hard. In his eyes, there is still a faint line of resistance, I can tell.

'This really is your last chance,' I say. 'What happens now is up to you.'

I lock the door behind me and make my way back to the main building.

21

Later that night, I go for a drive. I figure I need to clear my head, to build myself up for what must inevitably come next. I've given Stellans many chances to co-operate, but now I'm forced to confront the prospect that he might never write a confession. I will be required to employ stronger measures. Failing that, I must release him. None of these options sits comfortably with me. I drive around aimlessly within a three-mile radius, past the park, the tube station, the halal butchers. I soon figure that driving is of little use. I return home, trying to convince myself that I need more time, that the answer will surely find me. The only thing that matters is that I stay focused.

At Raven Court, I park up. Glancing out of the driver's window, I see Leila standing on the front doorstep. Her hair's scraped back into a bun. She's wearing a white skirt with a lace trim that flares against her shins.

I step out of my van, grabbing two bottles of whiskey that I forgot to take out earlier. The door clunks behind me.

Leila turns, glancing down at my bag and then at hers. She smiles stiffly.

As I draw nearer, I see her face is damp and flushed. Her eyes are swollen and red.

'I'm glad you're prepared,' she says. 'I need a drink. This situation is just . . .'

I hesitate, trying to figure out whether this is a good idea. Any minute now, the police could show up and the two of us together would appear suspicious. I glance at the pavement, at her red painted toenails glistening in her sandals. Finally, I nod. I figure, what harm could it do? I pull the keys out of my pocket and turn to unlock the front door to Raven Court.

We walk into the hallway, a sudden rush of warmth enveloping me from having Leila close. She walks ahead of me like she's dazed, knocking her elbow into the wall. She enters the living room as I make my way into the kitchen. I place my shopping bag down with hers, onto the counter. I pull a tray from a stack in the corner, preparing a bowl of ice and dishes of crisps and olives, grabbing two glasses and several toothpicks. When I enter the living room, I place my tray down on the coffee table. Leila slopes towards me and pours herself a large glass of whiskey.

'Easy,' I say. 'Aren't you driving home?'

She shrugs her shoulders. 'I'll get a cab.' She takes a long, slow sip. 'I just don't know where he is.'

'I'm pretty sure Stellans is fine,' I say, still aggrieved from my encounter with him, earlier. I pick up an ice cube and pop it into my mouth, enjoying the cold, sharp shock of pain as it hits the back of my teeth. Tonight, I want to forget about Stellans. I desperately need one night's peace and quiet without having to worry about him.

Flopping onto the sofa, Leila kicks off her sandals and cracks her toes. I notice she isn't wearing a bra. Something inside me flickers.

'I've been calling and calling – worried *sick*. Do you know,' she sits bolt upright, the hem of her skirt rising, 'I've had to tell them what's going on.'

'Tell who?'

'Work. It's written in my contract. They told me I need to keep a low profile. The last thing they need is a scandal involving a potential presenter.'

'But you're not a presenter,' I say.

'Yeah, but I'm working up to it.'

I smile, moving towards her on the sofa, enjoying the sight of her melting under the influence of alcohol. I notice her hair tumbling out of her bun and my breath catches. Her skin glistens, golden, like she's slathered in oil. 'Just have a drink and forget about it,' I say. 'If there's one good thing to come out of this, it's that you and I are together.'

For a moment, she smiles, a smile just for me, lighting me up on the inside, making me forget about everything. I realise then that I need to express how I feel. I am a grown woman of thirty-five and it's time I started living.

We clink glasses, then gulp, wincing as the whiskey burns the back of our throats. We slam down our glasses on the table and burst out laughing.

We are an unlikely pair, Leila and I, but we have something. A rare and unusual friendship. From the very first moment we met, she knew I was dependable, a doorway into herself, into the deepest part of her.

'Why does everyone let me down?' she whispers as she unfolds, unravelling her hair from her bun.

'They always do,' I say. 'That's the problem.' I'm thinking of my parents. I'm thinking of Stellans.

Stellans.

'But not you. You never did that,' she says.

'No, but—'

'You never took advantage of me either.' She smiles.

Leila shuffles towards me, resting her head on my shoulder and my heart races. We've been here before, but this time, I convince myself, it's different. I close my eyes, wanting this moment to last.

'I just wish he would have told me, that's all. Because now it looks so suspicious.'

Stellans again.

'We were probably the last two people to see him, Rita. Can you imagine?'

I consider whether I should put her out of her misery and just tell her how it is: that I have him tied up in the outhouse and I did it for her, to make sure she received justice.

'If he wasn't guilty, it wouldn't be an issue, would it?' I say, stroking her hair, silky and soft between my fingers. 'But he has guilty written all over his face.'

She nuzzles into my neck. 'All this . . . is so unexpected,' she says.

I close my eyes, allowing her words to sink in. I know she's right, that from now on, we must stick together, but still, he lingers, threatening to ruin the moment.

'If anyone asks, say nothing. The only thing people need to know is that you and I are friends. We're reunited, after all these years, and that's wonderful. Everything else is irrelevant.'

She hesitates, then pulls away from me, staring at me like a child pining for candy. 'You mean, don't tell anyone he was here?'

'Precisely.' I pull her tighter towards me. 'Come here.'

'I don't know, Rita. That feels wrong.' She makes herself comfortable on my shoulder. 'He doesn't deserve that. What if he's in danger?'

'He deserves worse,' I mutter.

I lean back, reaching out my arm and she turns, comfortable on my shoulder. I scrawl my name into her back with my fingertip. The alcohol makes me sink deeper and Leila laughs. I watch as she combs her fingers through her hair. I watch it rippling down the arch of her back. I pull her close to me and my fingers walk up her arms, circling the ball of her left shoulder. Leila closes her eyes and shudders; she giggles like a teenager.

'This takes me back, a little.' She smiles, then clambers to her feet, stretching, turning on the stereo. With a glass in her hand, she rattles the ice, knocking back her drink in one. I watch her, breasts pointing towards me, hips swaying and gyrating to the music. My mouth is open, my tongue dry; a demon rises in a flash of wickedness in my eyes.

'I love this song,' she says, resting the glass against her throat, sliding it down towards her top button.

'It's so hot in this place,' she says. 'Don't you ever turn on the air conditioning? How do those old people cope?'

Residents. I had forgotten about Margaret, whom I haven't checked on since lunch.

'They're fine. They sleep a lot.' I can hardly take my eyes off her. 'I only have one left now. I suppose, in some way, I've been winding the business down.'

She stares at me blankly.

'What will you do?'

'Run a coffee shop.'

Leila bursts out laughing. 'After this place? Come on, get up,' she says, placing her glass down on the table. She reaches out. 'Loosen up, will you? It will do you some good.' She grabs my hands, hers cold and wet from the icy glass and she pulls me up, throwing her head back and laughing harder.

'What are you doing?'

'Maybe we don't need any men,' she says. 'No good ever came from them, and right now, we need a distraction.'

'You're drunk,' I say, half enjoying the sight of her unwinding, the other half fearful of what might happen next. 'But I don't disagree. It's why I decided long ago to go with how I really feel.' I move closer to her, pulling her towards me, feeling the warmth of her against my body. 'But not everyone is special,' I say. I rest my hands on her hips, trying and failing to sway in time to the music. My feet are clumsy, heavy on the floor. The room is spinning, spinning around. 'None of them have been you, Leila.'

'Rita . . .'

I move closer, then closer still, bringing my face to hers as she closes her eyes and throws back her head. I hold onto her back and she lets herself fall. She pushes out her chest and I feel the weight of her drop into my arms.

'What am I doing?' she says. She hoists herself up again.

I feel her breath feather my cheek, the oaky smell of her whiskey. I cup her face and tilt it towards the light. I lower my hands onto her shoulders.

My lips meet hers and I press down hard, hungrily, like an animal, tasting her – wanting to devour her.

There is a delayed reaction, but she opens her eyes. She skewers me a look between my brows, and gasps. She shoves me off her, then slaps my face and chest. She straightens her hair, her eyes wide as marbles, and she staggers away from me as if remembering who I am, annoyed at herself for forgetting, if even for a moment.

'What just happened? Why did you do that?' She stands there, her head cocked to the side, a hand pressed against her cheek.

'I'm sorry,' I say quickly. 'I thought it's what you wanted? It's what I wanted. I wanted it all along.'

'What are you talking about?' she spits, wiping her mouth.

She scans the room, swaying, staggering – holding out her hands as if trying to steady herself. She moves to the sofa and takes a seat. 'I don't know what you're talking about,' she says. 'You've taken advantage of me.'

I panic as I realise what I've done and yet I can hardly deny that I'm glad – relieved even – that I just went for it, on some level knowing there would be consequences. 'Calm down, it's nothing,' I say. 'It's obviously a misunderstanding. Just forget about it, okay?'

She swallows hard, pressing her palm against her head. 'Don't tell me to calm down. You've got this all wrong,' she says. 'You do *know* that, right?'

'You're overreacting.'

'I'm not like that, do you understand? I'm not like *that.*'

'So what's *this*?' I ask, waving my hands about. 'Why come here in the first place?' I have no idea why I am shouting.

She jerks back like I've just slapped her in the face.

'Why are you playing with me?' I say.

She laughs a cruel laugh, high-pitched and piercing. 'Can't you see? You're overbearing, Rita. Incapable of drawing a line. We're friends – yes, we are friends, despite everything you are. But you always go too far. You always *spoil* things.'

I move to the side to switch off the stereo, and pour myself another whiskey.

'There's something wrong with you, do you know that?' She sounds just like Stellans, parroting what he says, a sure sign of the invisible influence he still has on her. She doesn't stop. She goes on and on. It's as if water levels have been rising for some time, and now, the banks have burst. 'A man is missing, and you do *that*! How could you? What is *wrong* with you? He could be dead!'

'What is wrong with *me*?' I scream. 'I'm not the child whore, messing around with men as old as their own fathers.'

She stands there, shocked still, her chest rising and falling. The room is electric. Finally, she gathers her bag, eyes swirling with the current of whiskey coursing through her body.

'Wait—' I lean forward. 'I'm sorry. I didn't mean that.'

'Fuck off, Rita.'

She slips her feet into her sandals, staggering out into the hallway. 'You are a bitch, do you know that? I don't need to explain myself to you. You're nothing to me, do you hear? Our *friendship* means nothing.'

Her words are like a knife, plunging into me. I place a hand over my chest as if to stop myself bleeding.

'You don't mean that – you're just angry.'

'I mean it, Rita,' she calls.

I run ahead of her and slam my hand against the front door.

'Get out of my way.' She slaps my arm, but I grab hold of her shoulders, bringing my face close to hers.

'Rita, stop it! Get away from me!' She slaps my chest, my face, my head. Her fingernails scratch into my flesh.

I cover my face and I fall back, my scalp and cheeks stinging. Before I can stop her, she bolts out of the door, running down the road into the darkness. I collapse onto the sofa, panting, my head rushing, staring into the bottom of my whiskey glass. I feel the scratches on my face stinging and bleeding.

What have I done?

What have I become?

I gulp down the last of my drink, convincing myself that it's okay. I stopped myself before it got out of hand: I didn't hurt her. I didn't hurt *him*. I stopped myself because I know the difference between right and wrong. I know where the line is.

But just then the doorbell rings and I'm unable to move.

I think to myself that if it's Leila, I will apologise, take some time to explain myself because the last thing I need now is yet another complication.

The bell rings once more. It's followed by a fist banging on the door.

I pull out my phone and click onto the app that's linked to the CCTV camera, and I see, through the grainy picture, an inevitable ending. I think, this is it. This is the moment the police want, where everything tumbles down, when they dig and find dirt, reducing me to nothing but a common criminal. I have no choice but to face it.

22

'Hello, *Rita*.'

Lawson is standing on my doorstep, wearing a beige trench coat and smiling wryly.

'It's been a while, hasn't it? May I come in? Rita is still the name you're using in public, I take it?'

Staggering, I reluctantly open the door, then wider still, staring down at his feet. He's wearing brown leather shoes, scuffed along the sides. I can't seem to take my eyes off his socks, berry red with skulls and crossbones. I could have sworn they are trying to communicate something to me. He carries a scent with him, like petrol, combined with the air of a man who feels more at ease in the outdoors.

Lawson steps into the hallway. Thankfully he is alone. But him coming to see me at home can only mean trouble.

'Nice place you've got here, Rita. *Raven* Court.' He chuckles. 'Who would have thought it, eh? Not at all what I expected.'

He steps further into the hallway, glancing on either side of him, nodding at the patterned walls, the tasteless framed prints.

'Sincere apologies for not calling beforehand, but you know how it is. I didn't want to impose on you. You needed time to think. But things move on now, don't they? And well, here we are.'

He makes his way into the living room and stands in front of the fireplace, lifting a framed photo of my mum and dad. It is an evening shot of them standing beside the pier in Blackpool, with a rollercoaster in the background, blinking with coloured lights.

'What do you want?' I ask.

I sit down on the sofa, irritated that he's touching – examining – my things, without necessity, without my *permission*. I do everything in my power to resist giving him the impression I've been drinking, but Lawson sees the dirty glasses on the table, the half-empty bottle of whiskey.

'I do hope I'm not interrupting,' he says, rolling his eyes. 'You've a few scratches on your face. Are you alright?'

'I had a friend round. She's gone now.'

'I see. A friend with a cat, I take it?'

'Funny.' I grab a tissue and pat down my cheek. I'm not bleeding too badly. Just a few drops. Could be worse.

Lawson watches me, perplexed, digging his hands into his pockets. He lifts himself onto his toes, and glances out of the window. 'So, how have you been, Rita? Had time to consider things? Must say, I've missed seeing you out and about. But I suppose you've been busy.'

'You could say that,' I mumble.

'*You could say that,*' he mocks, pulling out a small notepad from his coat, flipping over the leather cover, leafing through the pages.

I lower my head into my hands, heavy and spinning. 'Look. I've had a bit to drink. Can we make this quick? It's possible I might vomit. I would hate for you to see it.'

'Oh? Well, I can be quick, sure. Let's start with where we stand. Are we working together or not?'

I feel my chest burn. In that moment, I know, under the influence of alcohol, I'm about to say something I cannot stop, something that will be difficult to reverse. 'I've been thinking a lot, about my life, longer-term . . .'

'Oh?'

'I don't think I can carry on with hunting in any shape or form.'

'Well now . . .' Lawson looks down. 'That certainly is a turn-around. Highly disappointing, and highly convenient.'

'What is that supposed to mean?'

My mind is scrambling, my reasoning sluggish, but I know that anything I say now will be of vital importance. I'm struggling, really struggling, to concentrate.

'Where is he?' asks Lawson.

'I don't know what you're talking about,' I snap, a little too quickly. I'm sounding defensive.

'Oh, I think you do,' says Lawson, smiling. 'It's him, isn't it? Michael Stellans. The man you came to see me about only a few weeks ago concerning that business with your friend.' Lawson licks his thumb, leafing through his notebook again. 'Fourth of September, it was,' he says. 'I remember it so well. And look where we are. Goodness me. Monday twenty-third. Now, that poor man is nowhere to be found.'

'I don't know anything about that, but I heard the story on the news.' I stare at the whiskey bottle, and it occurs to me that I could easily knock him out with it too. There is enough space in the outhouse for the two of them.

'What's going on, Rita?' His voice has changed. It's hard and serious and ready for revenge. 'I can't help you if you're not straight with me. Not that I have any reason to help you, given that we're not working together. Shame, that.'

I'm trembling.

Lawson peers at me inquisitively. 'Where are the other two you're usually with? Tattoo collar and the ginger beard?'

'I haven't seen them since Zia's death.'

Lawson looks down. 'I see. Well now. The end of rock and roll. The end of an era.' I see him thinking and the way his face hangs, the way his brow furrows, is simply terrifying. He has no idea how much power he has, though I'm well aware how exposed I am.

'Let me explain,' I say, holding up my hand. 'It is true I came to see you. It was after attending a reunion and meeting up with an old friend called Leila. We were both horrified by the story, and—'

'Leila, the girl you mentioned before, who you thought had been groomed by Michael?'

I don't know what to say. I have no choice but to say *yes*.

'Then what?' he asks.

'Then what? What do you mean, then what?' I jump to my feet, my head rushing. I grow increasingly animated. 'I came to *you*, didn't I? And *you* didn't help me. He's probably not missing. He's probably run away because he's been found out.'

Lawson tilts his head back and rolls his eyes. 'Rita, surely you must see how suspicious this all appears. You come to see me about a man – and days later, that man is missing. All this, only a few weeks after Zia. I told you then, as I'm telling you now, there is a *procedure* to follow in regard to Michael Stellans. It exists for a reason. A man is missing, a man considered *innocent* until there is enough evidence to prove he's guilty. We must investigate it. Something serious could have happened to him.'

'Sure . . . because there is nothing better you could be doing with your limited resources, is there?' I clench my jaw, determined not to let him get the better of me.

Lawson is breathing heavily, and then snorts.

'I don't disagree. Allocating vital resources to clean up after a sting gone wrong is double the work if you ask me. But some people like to take control of things themselves, don't they?' He turns, scanning the living room. 'Wasting resources is hardly good for tax-paying folks, however. They don't like that. So I'm delighted you're giving up hunting. It's a good and healthy decision, if you ask me. Though I'm naturally disappointed we won't be working together.' Lawson sighs. 'What will you do next?'

'I'm thinking about it. I could downsize my business. Run a café someplace.' This conversation is going on for far too long and is beginning to feel painful. The more I talk about my plans, the more they feel silly. 'Look, you can't pin Zia on me. That would be unfair. I tried to do a good thing and it didn't work out, so now, I'm getting on with my own life.'

'Well, I'll need to report back internally and see what the others say.' Lawson purses his lips. 'Luckily for you, they now have other things to contend with. Most likely, some will be relieved. Mind if I look around, Rita? Lovely place you've got here, must say. I'd love a tour.'

I drop my shoulders and glance at the shelf where I've left my box of cigarettes. I'm trying not to dwell on the slow panic rising inside me. I know what I've done is potentially reckless, severing ties with the police at a time when I need them on my side. But with all that alcohol swimming inside me, I feel both resigned and yet invincible.

I'm about to light up my cigarette when I hear a loud thud against the ceiling just above my head. Lawson and I shoot one another a look. Before I can think what to do next, I drop my cigarette and run to the stairs as fast as I can.

I burst through the door to Margaret's room, Lawson behind me, the swoosh of his jacket brushing against my knee. He's standing to my left, short of breath, wondering what the hell just happened to make us move so unexpectedly.

I scan the bedroom, but Margaret is not there – she's not in her bed. I move towards the window, to the other side of the bed, and there she is. She's fallen off the edge, a sheet pulled down with her, lying pale and unresponsive. I kneel to touch her, but she feels cold, just lying there with her eyes half-open. Her arm is stretched out, her torso twisted. I feel for her pulse, kneading my fingers all over her wrists, but I know it's too late.

Lawson leans against the wall, his head bowed.

'Now's hardly a good time for a tour around Raven Court,' I say.

23

My eyes are crusted with sleep. Around me, the room feels like it has swollen overnight and is sinking. There's a bad smell in the air, like burnt steak. I remember Lawson and I cringe as it all comes back to me. I lie back onto the carpet and stare up. It feels like the ceiling is falling. That's when it hits me like a wave: Leila does not love me. The truth is, she never did. Of course, deep down, I've always known that she didn't have feelings for me. And yet, there's always been a part of me that indulged in the fantasy that, maybe one day, she would. My body feels vast and empty like a deserted island. With Margaret gone too, there's a terrible ache to my sadness.

I manage to muster enough strength to roll onto my side and I walk to the back door, making my way towards the outhouse. With all that alcohol in my system, my sensitivity is heightened, my bearings upended, but my thinking is sharp. I hear the birds singing, their notes as if emanating from inside me. The breeze feels cool against my cheeks, and I notice how the sky is tinged with grey since the sun has not yet emerged from behind the clouds.

I unlock the door, half-expecting Stellans to be standing on the other side, waiting for me. But it's just my imagination playing tricks on me. He must have heard me, though, because as I enter, he starts groaning.

I barely recognise him; his face is a mess. There are shadows smudging his eyes, prickling wires of blonde hair sprouting all over his cheeks. His neck is covered in grey filth, staining the collars of his shirt. I rip the duct tape from his mouth and Stellans gasps, his eyes darting about the place like a wild bat.

'I'm late. Sorry about that.' I glance at my watch, noticing it's midday. I reach for a bottle from the ledge and flick open the top, squeezing water into his mouth. I get my timing wrong – I must still be drunk, because at that precise moment, Stellans wants to talk to me.

'I've done it. I've written the confession,' he says. His voice is faint and weak as if it took every ounce of strength for him to be able to complete this bit of writing. He begins coughing, spluttering. He struggles to swallow. I quickly move forward, untying his left arm, propping him up, slapping his back. I don't want him to die. Not like this, not now.

'Where is it?'

I scan the floor and there I see the pad, his dirt and dried blood smudging the pages like the drawings of an infant. I bend, but then realise I cannot trust him enough to take my eyes off him for even a second, so I tie up his arms again.

I bend down, once more. 'That's good, very good,' I say. 'I'm glad you came to your senses. Makes things much easier from here, onwards.' I gather the pad and loose pages. His writing is barely legible, the lines erratic and child-like. There are other pages too. Early drafts of his confession, which he discarded before giving me a chance to read them; versions that he was not happy with.

'What now?' he croaks.

I glance around me, bracing myself for having to make good on my promise.

'I need time to read it, and then prepare,' I say. 'But I've given you my word. It's all over.'

'You know I'll never tell a soul about what happened,' he says, desperately, as if to convince me before I change my mind, as if my word is simply a tease. 'You do know that, don't you? I swear, Rita, I won't breathe a word.'

I stare at him, trying to figure out whether I believe him, wondering how long until I will be able to forget all about him. This could be a game, where as soon as I let him go, he will run to the police and then they will come after me and will not be lenient. But I'm no longer afraid of Stellans, no longer afraid of what he does. He does not have power over me. I am fully in charge.

I stare down at the pages, at a version of the drivel I read earlier, only now with a clear admission of his guilt.

I had an affair with a girl underage. I fully admit it was a crime. Leila. Rani. I could not stop myself from doing it twice.

'Do what you want,' I say. 'I did what I had to do. I'll take whatever comes next because as far as I'm concerned, I've got what I wanted. Finally, it's clear what you've done – what you are. Names, dates, and places. You did well.'

He's silent. It's as if he's trying to work out what to say. But he leaves it, which is just as well. After all that's happened between us, I'm in no mood to discuss anything.

24

That night, the night of his release, the moon hangs in the sky like a full glass of milk. In the back of my van, curled up like a foetus, Stellans is silent. His knees are pressed tightly against his chest; arms crossed over his stomach. The tension is unsettling. Hangs in the air like a giant spiderweb ready to blanket me.

After a while, Stellans jerks forward. He's grunting, snorting. But he looks fine to me, there's no sign he's fallen ill, which is a relief considering how long I had to keep him hostage.

Stellans' face is sunken like his cheeks have melted into his cheekbones, but it's his eyes that stand out the most. I feel them skewer the back of my neck, telling me there's still plenty of poison left inside him.

It is dark, too dark to see clearly. With number plates smeared with mud, I drive to Leechpool Woods in Horsham through smaller roads. I believe there are few or no cameras, here. The trees stand back from the main road, tall like soldiers, the area so shadowy and dense, you wouldn't want to be left there alone.

I pull over onto a remote side road, flanked by green. Horsham, as an area, is an odd choice to release a man after you've held him hostage for twelve nights. But it's the only town I know where I'm certain I won't arouse suspicion. It's so middle to upper class that surely, it won't be a natural consideration to think there's something unusual going on. The area is accessible too, with a car park nestled deep inside the woods that, according to a Google search, is open all hours to the public. At times like these, I can't tell you how important it is to remain practical.

The doors of my van swing and squeak on their hinges. I turn, see that there's nothing behind me, and I look back to Stellans, curled up in the boot. His eyes, in a permanent state of ice-fixed startlement, pierce right through me.

'It's okay,' I say. 'I'm not going to hurt you. I'm letting you go. You ought to be grateful. I never wanted *any* of this. Don't ever forget that. I am not a bad person. Things just got out of hand, alright? It's time to put it behind us.'

I'm overcome by a feeling of finality; that after all these years, I can leave behind a part of my life and begin a new journey. No more lies. No more double lives. No more broken parts of me.

Stellans blinks, rolling his eyes to the back of his head. He closes his lids then drops his face. I'm fumbling around the boot in search of a blanket, which I figure he can take with him.

But Stellans does not move, nor does he make a sound. I hear the snap of a twig behind me. It makes me jump. My heart beats so fast I know I must hurry up.

'It's time,' I say, but I don't think he hears me, so I clear my throat, I make my voice louder. 'We're here, it's time to get out.' The fluttering in my stomach rises. 'This is what you wanted, isn't it? I kept my word, even though you're a criminal.'

I tap him on the shoulder, but he doesn't respond. So I shake him hard, and he groans as I bend over him. I bundle him out of the boot in the dark, wondering if his floppiness is some sort of act. Whether he's trying to distract me, disarm me. It wouldn't be the first time. There's a thud as he knocks his head on the side of the door, and I let go of him because I cannot hold onto him any longer. I have no strength to carry him; he is suddenly so heavy. I'm surprised how weak he is, how tired I suddenly feel, what it has taken out of me to finally arrive at this moment.

His body slips out of my arms, collapsing into a heap on the grass. He groans, cradling his knees and begins sobbing. In the deepest part of me, something breaks hearing him cry like that. I feel ashamed – terribly ashamed of how I've treated this man.

But I can't let him get to me. I can't allow myself to lose it. I must remain calm. I must remain strong. We've come to the end of a journey, he and I. Our souls forever karmically bound.

'Rita . . .'

I can barely hear him; his words are ever so faint, formed with short, wispy, breaths.

'Please . . .'

I bend down to lift him up with all the strength I can muster. I throw his arm over my shoulder, propping him up as he slips in and out of strange mental states. His head slopes to one side, as if almost hanging off his neck. It is clear he cannot walk. Neither can he stand up straight. His body leans awkwardly into mine, his bony elbow jabbing into my hip.

'What is going on with you? Why are you like this? Are you unwell?'

He doesn't answer, so I tighten my fingers around him, feeling his ribs, his elbow and wrist. By now, I have no choice but to carry the full weight of him, dragging him deeper into the forest.

I take him as far as I can go, all the while fumbling around for a torch. It's in my pocket; I'm shining a light onto the ground. The golden orb dances only a few steps ahead of us.

'I'll do everything I can to make you feel comfortable. But I must leave you here, do you understand? I don't want to do it, but I must. None of this would have happened if you'd just *listened*.'

We reach a suitable spot, as far as we can go together. It's beneath a giant oak tree with its branches stretched in the night sky as if in praise of the heavens. Its trunk is so thick, it commands an almost holy presence. I touch the ground, damp and cold, soil consecrated, and I drop him there, beside the tree. His back knocks against the base of the trunk when I ease him down onto the earth, his body wilted.

My principal thought in that moment is, I have gone too far. I know I have gone too far. But there is no way I can reverse

things, nor take any of it back and change it. I know that whatever happens next is my own fault. But I tell myself, too, that we
cannot regret the choices we make when our moral axis points so
strongly in favour of our motivation; when that motivation is the
betterment of others, of society at large, of young children. This
situation feels terribly unjust, because all along, I tried to do the
right thing. It eats at me, all this, like a hand grabbing the fleshy
walls of my stomach, slowly squeezing it. I watch Stellans fall,
and I simply walk away, walking towards whatever is my fate
from this moment on.

I take only two steps forward, when I hear him call my name.

I turn towards him, wanting to get out of here but also needing
to listen to whatever last words he wishes to say. I kneel, hoping,
really hoping, for a few words of explanation. Why he did it. Why
Leila. Why Rani. Why he felt taking young girls was necessary
in the first place, when there are so many grown women in the
world, ripe and ready for a different kind of friendship. I'm hoping he will say something finite, to justify my actions. Even to
reassure me that after I've gone, he'll just leave things and not go
to the police.

But he does not speak. Stellans has no strength left inside him,
not proper strength, or power, at least. His voice is simply a whisper, dried like a leaf, and hoarse.

'Water . . .'

'Excuse me?'

'Water . . .'

My cheeks burn to the bone. I do not want to run any more
errands for him, but here we are, our final moments, tomorrow
a great unknown. I walk towards my van, to retrieve a bottle
of water from the back, but just as I open the doors, I hear
him moan.

I return with the bottle of water and kneel down beside him,
unscrewing the plastic bottle.

234

'There is something I need to tell you ...'

'What is it?'

'A letter,' he mumbles.

I sit upright, unable to comprehend what I'm hearing, but his words are clear. I hand him the bottle.

'*Letter*, is that what you said? What letter are you talking about?' All this time, when I asked that he complete the *simple* task of writing a confession, he resisted, never once divulging anything about a letter. Yet now, it seems, his memory returns.

'Is it a letter ... for Leila?'

He simply nods, but very slightly.

'Where is it?'

A long breath rushes out of his lungs making a faint *haaaaahhh* sound.

'Coat,' he says, his voice broken.

I had stuffed his coat into the cupboard, I remember that. It was shortly after I struck him with the bottle.

I nod reluctantly, the sight of this dying man beginning to take hold of me. I find myself choking up, a sort of delayed reaction to everything I've done. But still, I convince myself this is an elaborate hoax, that somehow, he will survive it.

'I'll make sure she gets it,' I say, although I will need to read it first. 'I'll make sure I alert the police to your whereabouts. Just stay right here and I'll make a few calls.'

His face is damp. His eyes are streaming. But his face has changed. It's vacant, as if somewhere inside himself, he is departing.

I get up to leave, not wanting to engage further with him, trying to get out of there as quickly as I can, but then I hear footsteps. Before I've even reached the van, Stellans lunges forward, grabbing hold of my neck, locking me tight into a headlock. My body lifts, my shoulders pull back. My legs are dangling, kicking the air, and I'm writhing, twisting, clawing my nails into his arm, which now feels so strong, so powerful around my neck, he could easily be a different person. The blood rushes to my face, I can't breathe, I can't breathe, the sight before me is grainy . . . I think to myself, you bastard, you had me fooled. There I was, feeling sorry for you. And then, as the picture before me fades, as the voice in my head feels further away, I think, this is it. After everything I've been through, it ends like this . . . But then, somewhere inside me, I think, hang on a minute – no way! No way is he getting away with it. Why the fuck should I be the one to die and he be the one still standing? That's not how it works. That is not justice.

With all the strength I have, I elbow him in the ribs, hard. Stellans lets go and I fall to my knees. He staggers back a few steps, whilst I have my hands around my neck, trying to steady my breathing. But he pounces, yanks my hair, and I almost scream out. He's pulling it so hard, I'm sure he's removed a clump and my scalp is bleeding. We roll, we twist, the earth and mud slapping against our faces, bark and twigs gashing our skin, but I can't scream because it will attract too much attention. I'm screaming inside. I can't believe this is happening.

His weight is on me, his hands around my throat, strangling me. I need to think fast and I stretch my arm out, reaching for a rock wedged into the earth and I try, I try, to push it free. I stretch my fingers, straining, shaking, to ease it just a little towards me. He's still strangling me, and red dots appear in front of my eyes. My face burns . . . but I grab it. I grab hold of the rock.

In one blow, I hit him, and Stellans falls back. It's a blow reminiscent of that last blow with the bottle, the rock as weighty as the glass bottle in my hand, the move as swift and as smooth. He groans, and immediately I see the blood. In the dark it rushes like black ink all over his face, running down onto his neck and shoulders.

He falls on his back, still groaning, and I panic, unsure what to do. I'm panting hard. I feel my neck, hot and stinging, afraid he has damaged me in some way. I grab the bottle of water and pour it over my head and then I crawl over to Stellans and pour water over him too.

I'm breathing hard and fast.

Stellans appears to have fallen unconscious. I'm sitting over him, trying to work out what just happened. But after a minute or two, he starts coming round.

'Why did you do that? I let you go, you fucking arsehole, I let you go!'

He groans, rolling onto his side, his hands pressed against his head. I don't know whether I trust him, whether this is another dramatic performance to make a fool of me again. But there's something about the energy around him that tells me this is real. In the dark, the air pulses with a new kind of strangeness. Something is different.

I hear him whimpering, I hear his pain. I'm standing over him, staring down at the outline of his body, trembling.

He struggles to say something. I'm just relieved he's still alive. I lean over, my knees pressing into bits of bark and mud, drawing closer to him so I can hear.

'I can't see, Rita.'

'It's dark,' I say, the adrenalin crashing through my body. I know there's something seriously wrong, that he might not survive this. But he tried to kill me. I had to defend myself.

'I hit you hard and you deserved it. What were you thinking? Why did you do that? I let you go.'

'Ambulance . . .' he whispers. But it is out of the question. There is no way I can call an ambulance. Neither am I sure I can trust anything he says.

I cannot believe how complicated this entire situation now is. I need to get out of here. When he's discovered, I'm certain he will start talking.

'I won't . . . make it,' he says. There is a terrible strain and pain in his voice.

I start to rise, brushing my knees and thighs. I do not want to think about it.

'If you don't move, you won't lose too much blood. So don't move. You have a head injury.'

He is mumbling something, his voice rising.

'You can't escape, Rita,' he says, with all the breath and sound he has left. It's spiteful, malevolent.

I bite my tongue, trying to keep calm, determined not to let him disturb me. *He is alive, I have not killed him. He is alive . . .*

He mumbles something again, but by now, I've heard enough.

I climb into my van, starting up the engine. My mind is blank, I can't think straight. I do not think, in that moment, of calling the police, even though I know that there is a strong possibility he might die here. I convince myself that the woods are well frequented by dog-walkers and those taking their early morning exercise. I am certain, or at least I hope, that someone will find him.

I hear him groaning behind me, and then a grunt – and silence.

I stop, listening for any more noise, but I hear nothing.

Then I get out fast, as fast as I can, my foot pressing down hard on the gas. I drive back along the main road and I switch on the radio to distract me. I catch a glimpse of my eyes in the rear-view mirror, the whites of them dazzling, alive in the moonlight.

I try not to think of what's just happened, that strange silence. I think of Leila instead, feel myself slipping to thoughts of DCI Lawson. I'm glad I'm not working with the police. To ever work with them now is simply out of the question.

But those images of Stellans persist; they're haunting. Images of him sprawled out, clutching his head, the blood of him soaking into his clothing. There is no way he could survive it. Deep down, I know that.

I hear his voice still, consider fragments of his earlier, inadequate, confession. I can't help but think how stupid he is. *Does he not realise? He made things worse. So much worse. And after I had released him . . .*

25

It's morning and the adrenalin still courses through my veins. As I walk towards the outhouse, I feel the air fresh and cool against my skin. Inside, I enter the back room where Stellans last slept. The imprint of him is still visible in the creases of his sheets, phlegm and vomit staining the linen along with blood from where the straps around his wrists and ankles cut into him. It's a brutal reminder of what took place last night. If only he had not tried to kill me, I would not have had to defend myself. I had no choice but to hit him. That's what I keep telling myself.

I move to the side of the bed and press my foot down to unlock the wheels. My arms feel at once heavy and light as I roll the bed out along the stony path leading to the main building.

Inside Raven Court, I wipe down the frame with a cloth soaked in bleach, and wash the bedsheets at ninety degrees. I carry out my tasks with a clear and level head, completing the operation in just under four hours; all the while, that image of Stellans in the woods is still vivid, and haunting.

I curse under my breath over how long it all takes, but as I pull the warm sheets from the tumble dryer, my phone starts ringing. There's a cramp in my foot and my back begins to throb, but I hobble towards the living room regardless, hissing and spitting all the way to pick up my mobile. I'm half-expecting it to be the police, a part of me resigned to the fact they will eventually come for me.

But it's not the police, it's Leila. My stomach flips, her voice a strange interruption to my internal monologue.

'Rita, listen . . .'

I'm listening, breathing hard. My chest feels tight. I consider whether I should listen to anything she has to say, or hang up.

'I need to talk to you. It's about the other night.'

The other night . . .

'We've known each other for too long,' she says, 'and although what you did was totally out of order, and I'm still furious and I would rather not talk to you because of it, there's something you need to know . . .'

It's her voice, rasping – frenzied – that keeps me still.

'What is it? What's happened?'

'The police have been round, Rita. They're asking me questions.'

It's like the wind has been knocked out of me. 'What questions?'

'A man. DCI Lawson, and a woman, DC Green. Two of them in my flat, asking me so many things.'

'How do you think they found you?'

'They searched Michael's house. My name was in an address book they found in his study. They're working through it. Working through everything.'

'I see.'

'But that's not all,' says Leila. 'DCI Lawson says they've spoken to a few people at Brentford High. He knows all about the reunion, he looked up Mrs Smith's Facebook memorial page. She died. Did you know that?'

I did not know that.

'I think from there, DCI Lawson began sniffing around, contacting ex-students, seeing whether anyone would talk. Someone must have said something because he asked me about the rumours at school all those years ago. He asked whether there was any . . . *truth* to them.'

The word *truth* catches in my throat and my head rushes. Images of last night whirl like dervishes.

'What did you say to him?' I ask.

'I didn't know *what* to say, did I? It was the way he asked me about it. As if he already knew something. They're treating Michael's disappearance as suspicious. So obviously, DC Green asked whether I've been in touch with him.'

'And? What did you say?'

'I panicked!' says Leila. 'I didn't know what to say!' Her voice trembles. 'I just told them both that we exchanged a few notes here and there over the years, but nothing else, not since that story of the other girl broke.'

I'm silent, thinking fast, breathing slow.

'It feels like a mistake,' she says. 'I should have told them the truth. But what was I supposed to do? I was *terrified*.'

Leila is defensive, mistaking my silence as delivering a verdict of poor judgement. I can tell she's moving away from the phone because her voice trails; all the while, my mind is scrambling.

'I'm so scared,' she says. 'We need to align our stories. Don't you see? We could both be in serious trouble.'

I want to say no, I'd rather not meet right now. You hurt me. You lied to me, using me as if I were a reliable car when all you wanted was a different, more socially acceptable model. *Do you know, I left your boyfriend in the woods last night, having nearly killed him? But you should be aware that this man you adore so much tried to kill me. He would have succeeded had I not stopped him!*

But I say none of those things.

'That was all? That's the only thing you said?'

'That's all,' she says.

'Fine,' I say. 'You'd better come over, then.'

I don't know what else to say. I don't want to be alone. 'I've got a few things on, but I can see to them quickly.'

She's silent for a second, and I wonder what she's thinking.

'Me coming over doesn't mean there's anything going on between us,' says Leila. 'It's important you know that. What you did . . . it was totally out of order. If it wasn't for this situation, I don't think I would ever want to see you again.'

'I get it,' I say, quietly.

'Do you? Do you *really*?'

I hang up the phone, a part of me fearful, a greater part of me excited and wanting to feel her close.

This is the moment when I realise my life will change. That if I am ever to move on, to get out of Raven Court, it will be because of this moment, right now. All this time, I've dreamed of doing something of my own. Not to be wrapped up in the plans of others – like my parents. Now is my chance to make things happen, to lead a simple life. With Leila and I together, I consider the prospect of being with her as I always wanted. She might not have feelings for me, that much is clear, but the events of our lives are bigger than simply our desires. We are connected, whether she likes it or not; we are bound forever.

I tidy up, running around the house in a frenzied daze – delighting in the possibility of making future plans, partly clouded by this disaster looming. I throw cushions onto the sofa in a way that doesn't appear too contrived, run a dishcloth over dusty surfaces, the cabinets and fireplace. I don't bother with the carpet because I have no time to vacuum, but the blood of Stellans is still there, ever so faint. I grab a bucket, filling it to the top with soapy water. I scrub and scrub, in a desperate attempt to remove the last trace of it.

I work myself into a sweat, then I go upstairs into the bathroom to splash cold water onto my face. I move to the bedroom, staring down at my double bed, concluding that even though my room is ugly and filled with furnishings that most people would call outdated, the room is certainly big enough for a guest. I wonder what Leila will think if I offer her my room. The idea of her staying here, in Raven Court, where I can keep the curtains tightly drawn so no one will ever see her or know she is with me, begins to excite me.

I send her a text:

I'm sorry about what I did, really, I am. I am so ashamed and don't know how you could ever forgive me. But this is serious. I think you should stay over for a night or two, if you can. It will be safer. Who knows what might happen? We need to stick together, like you said. There is no alternative!

A few minutes later, she replies:

Ok. But remember what I said.

I shake my head, grabbing onto fistfuls of hair. I stare at my complexion in the long mirror bedside the window. My face appears sallow, my shoulders hunched. The woman staring back at me is conniving – dark and light, all at once. But I cannot deny that her spirit is broken too; shattered into a thousand pieces, confused about which side of life, of good and bad, she belongs to. I throw my head back, staring up at the ceiling, and I laugh. I laugh so hard, I sound increasingly sinister. I don't recognise who I am anymore. Something in me, like a shadow, rises and begins to take over. That's when I know, regardless of what I call myself, whichever name I live by, from here onwards, I can reinvent myself. I am powerful. I am changeable – like a chameleon, forever transforming to suit any given situation. A single name could never do me justice.

Leila turns up a few hours later with a weekend bag.

'Alright?' I say. I'm mesmerised by the sight of her standing on my front doorstep. She's carrying a small box containing a few work files. The light freckles through her hair and my heart quickens.

'I'm just staying for a few days,' she mumbles, 'given the special circumstances.'

She brushes past me, smelling of roses, her flowery skirt swooshing at her knees. I open the door wider, a hand resting on the phone in the back pocket of my jeans. I'm just checking it's still there – just in case it rings.

'This box is heavy,' she says, standing in the hallway.

I notice the gold chain around her ankle, the swing of its charms, glinting in the light – shells, a seahorse, a broken heart. I notice how golden she appears, too, as if she's lit up from the inside like a lantern.

'Why bring files?' I ask. My eyes roam over the lines of her – but I move them away quickly when she catches me staring.

'I'm still working,' she says, her voice firm, matter of fact. She places her hands onto her hips and stares up at the ceiling.

'With everything going on, how can you concentrate?'

She scoffs, like I've said something stupid and straightens up. 'Some of us still need to make a living, Rita. Not all of us . . .' She mutters something under her breath and begins digging around in her bag for her cigarettes.

I carry her bag inside. It's the least I can do. I feel glad – relieved, in fact – that Raven Court is so private.

The front door closes behind me. I stand in the hallway beside Leila as she inspects her bag. I want so badly for this to be the beginning of something new. Where we can both start afresh, renew our friendship. Leila might not love me, but under the circumstances, perhaps she will learn to in time. What matters now is that she's here and that she needs me close. Whether she likes it or not, I was her first call. I was always her first call.

'What is it?' Leila says. 'Why are you staring at me? Do I have something on my face?'

'I was just going to ask . . . Would you like some tea?'

'I suppose so,' she mumbles, rolling her eyes.

I walk into the kitchen, my limbs loose and carefree. I keep thinking of ways I can help Leila. She needs me by her side.

I switch the kettle on, pleased with myself that the place is so clean. For once, the air is light and dust-free.

Leila walks into the kitchen, taking a seat at the table.

'You do know that this is only for one or two nights. That's what we said. I don't want you getting any funny ideas.'

'Yes, I do know. You don't have to worry,' I say.

'I *do*. After the other night . . .'

I don't know how long this will continue, her trying to scold me. 'I feel terrible. I just want to forget it.' I make the teas, then join her at the kitchen table, taking a seat opposite her.

She blows over her mug and takes a sip. Restless, she stands up and moves into the living room. She says she wants to sit somewhere comfortable. I trail behind her but note she doesn't sit down. She places her cup on the table, pacing the floor, unsure what to do with herself.

It's clear that Leila needs me around. She is nervous, and maybe even incapable of looking after herself.

I sit down on the sofa, watching her as she stares out of the window, just like I remember she did at school, on the off chance that Stellans might walk across the playground.

'What I did was unacceptable,' I say. 'I'm ashamed and I'm sorry.'

She shakes her head and looks down. After a while, she mumbles, 'It really is quite remote here, isn't it?'

'It's accessible.'

'It's so secluded,' she says. 'All those trees with their branches overhanging.'

It's true they needed cutting back, but getting jobs like that done around here, because of the size of the place, costs a small fortune.

'The main road is only a few minutes away,' I say.

'But that's what I mean. It's a patch of wilderness slap bang in the middle of suburbia, like it's been dropped here from someplace else.'

I'm not sure where this conversation is heading.

'That's why Mum and Dad liked this plot,' I say. 'They couldn't make up their minds whether they wanted to be part of the city or not.'

'And where do they go?'

'They?'

'You know . . . the ones that pass over.'

'They get picked up by their loved ones and then they go to the morgue . . . like the rest of us will in time.'

Leila stands abruptly and shivers. 'I had better unpack,' she says. 'I need to lie down. I'm so tired.'

I watch her from the sofa as she lugs her bag up the stairs. I want to see how far she gets before she calls me over to help her. But she doesn't call me. She climbs the stairs, one by one, determined to do things on her own, as if she's making a statement about not needing me around. She grabs the banister for support, and I hear her puffing and panting. But then I hear a knock – the corner of her bag hitting her shin, presumably. She's unsteady on her feet. She cries out as she collapses. Finally, I bolt out of my seat to help her.

She's seated in the middle of the stairs, licking a finger. I lift the bag with ease, watching as she smears a drop of the blood into her skin. Just for a moment, my hand brushes against hers.

'Bloody bag.'

I smile to myself. 'I'll get you a plaster.'

I dump her things in my bedroom and rub my hands on my jeans. It is only right to give her my own room because she could be here for a while. After the way I behaved, it is the least I could do. This room is the most comfortable in the house and I know she will be safe here. I've already made the bed nice and cosy. Fresh sheets, something floral.

After a few minutes, Leila creeps in, taking a seat on the edge of the bed, tracing her toe along the grains of the carpet.

'It hasn't changed. Don't you find it weird still being in the same bedroom after all these years?'

I know what she's implying. That I haven't moved on, that my life is somehow *constrained* as a result. As if moving out of a parental home is some sort of demonstration of self-worth and independence.

'This is a big property and it's all mine. I can use any room I want. I chose this bedroom because it's the best one and, well, because I like it.' I move towards her, taking a seat beside her. 'And now it's yours, for as long as you need it. Like I said, I want to make it up to you. I am deeply ashamed of my behaviour.'

She sighs. 'I don't want to talk about it – not now at least. Besides, I won't be here long. I'm just staying until things calm down.' She turns quickly, as if she's only just remembered something. 'We need to get our stories straight, Rita. Let's not get distracted.'

'Mmm.'

'What does *mmm* mean?' she says.

'It's just that I know the police and what they're like. He's a paedophile and given the accusations against him, they will hardly take his disappearance seriously. I hate to say it, but chances are, he has run away because he's guilty. Just get some rest and then we can go over it.'

She bites her lip and stares down.

I leave her alone in my bedroom and close the door behind me. I think it best to give her some space, so I sit downstairs in the living room, just wanting some peace and quiet. But by around four o'clock in the afternoon, Leila creeps down the stairs, just as I'm dozing off in front of the TV. She says she wants to take a bath because she's finding it difficult to relax.

'Is there anyone else in the house?' she asks, seating herself down on the sofa, wearing a pair of my socks. 'It is so quiet.'

'There's no one living here but us,' I say.

She closes her eyes, pressing her back against the sofa. 'That makes me feel a bit more at ease,' she says. 'I just had this strange feeling . . .'

'Ignore it,' I say. 'It's just your mind playing tricks.'

'But wait . . . How do you make any money if there are no residents?'

'I have enough saved over the years. I can afford to re-evaluate for six months and make new plans.'

'That's exciting,' she says. 'Café and a quiet life?' She laughs.

'Most likely.'

We stare blankly at the TV, but after a few minutes, she wants to go upstairs again.

I watch her as she climbs the stairs, gripping the banister for support. I hear her enter the bedroom and I follow shortly behind her on tiptoe. I stand in the hallway, drinking in the sight of her through the crack in the door.

I watch Leila gather her things, her subtle, graceful movements. She's like a swan, courting attention, but beneath the surface, frantically treading water. She lifts her underwear from her suitcase, rolling up the towel I left out for her on the back of the chair. She glides to the bathroom. I feel compelled to follow her.

I hear a click as she locks the bathroom door and then I move, standing outside it, watching her undress through a small hole which I made in the wood when I was younger. Back then, I used a small nail and pushed it through the timber, covering it up with a strip of dried paint so no one would notice the damage.

I need to make sure Leila is not harming herself. Who knows what damage this episode with Stellans might do?

In the bathroom, I see Leila standing in front of the mirror, staring at herself. She's examining her body, pale and hunched. She's frail – she looks too thin, like most of her energy is spent. She takes off her clothes and sits down on the toilet. She's scrolling through her phone. Her eyes move rapidly. After a wipe and a flush, she gets up and runs a bath, bending over the tub, revealing the rickety arch of her spine. She ripples her hand in the water, throwing in some salt. Then she pours in bubble bath from the bottle resting on the ledge. Eventually, when the bath is filled, she climbs in, sinking her body into the water. I hear it rippling; watch her press down her fingers against the foam, playing with the bubbles. A dripping hand trails along the edge. Leaning back, steam rising, she closes her eyes.

All this time, I'm holding my breath. My head is light, and I can barely stand up straight. I creep into my bedroom and open her suitcase. I run my hands over her clothes, which she has stuffed in with very little care. Her underwear is lacy, stringy knickers with bows. B-cup padded bras with a pearl sewn in the middle. There are piles of vests with spaghetti straps, a few T-shirts, three cardigans and flowery skirts. More clothes than she needs for just a couple of days. Everything is so colourful. I'm overwhelmed with a sense of sadness just then. I feel pathetic, pining – still pining – to be close to a woman who will always remain elusive.

I return to the bathroom and knock on the door. 'Just checking whether everything is alright in there?'

'I'm fine,' she calls weakly. Through the hole in the door, I see that she's wiping her face and eyes with a flannel. 'I won't be long.'

For a moment, I stand there, listening to her run the water again. 'There's no hurry. I'm just checking in on you,' I say.

Downstairs in the kitchen, I pour myself a glass of whiskey because I need to calm myself down. Seeing her in the bath like that is unsettling. It's been years since I've ever allowed myself to be touched, since I've seen naked flesh like that. The last time being once or twice – legless after a night in a bar – with men who helped confirm the very reason why I despise them. The phone in my back pocket vibrates:

20.01 Javid:
He's still missing. It's so weird! How can a man just disappear
like that?

I know then that this situation, of Leila staying with me in Raven Court whilst Stellans is considered missing, will inevitably grow complicated. The consequences of my actions are clear, as are my choices. I can do nothing and wait to be arrested or do something active and evade the law. Either way, I need to manage the situation as best I can, to think properly and to plan how I respond.

The scent of strawberry shampoo unfurls around me, and I hear the bathroom fan purring. I climb up the stairs and walk into my bedroom. Leila is lying on the bed in a cotton nightie, her damp hair streaking across the pillow.

I sit down on the edge, taking her hand in mine and she turns to me, whispering.

'Where is he, Rita? I don't believe he would run away like that. What if something terrible has happened?'

I shake my head, holding on to her hand more tightly.

'Nothing has happened. Most likely he's gone into hiding until the story dies down.'

'But what if he has . . . killed himself?' Her eyes dart around the room. 'Men do that, don't they? You hear about it all the time – when they are falsely accused of being . . .'

'It's hardly false, though, is it?'

She stabs me in the eye with a look she gives off when she's having one of her mood swings. I'm convinced she will grab my throat. I touch my neck, still sore from when Stellans attacked me. Leila climbs off the bed and quietly walks into the bathroom, locking the door behind her.

I go after her, standing outside. All I can think about is how she might do something stupid to herself.

After a few minutes, I bang on the door with my fists. 'Leila, let me in. I'm sorry. Let's just talk about it.'

'Go away,' she calls.

I step back, leaning my back against the wall, sliding down until I'm nothing but a crumpled heap. There's nothing I can do but wait for Leila to talk to me.

26

We appear to have agreed, in the week that passes, during the awkward slips of silence between us, amongst all the comfort cooking and eating, the constant run of bubble baths, foot rubs in furry socks, and Netflix and ice cream movie nights, that it's probably best not to talk about Stellans. I consider this a perfectly acceptable arrangement since the last thing I want is to think about him. Leila doesn't appear to be moving out anytime soon – neither do I want her to. If anything, we've discussed what we might say, should someone we know pop round and ask us how long we've been living together. Two friends from childhood, we'd say, reunited and living together to cut down on costs. It's all perfectly normal. It takes no time at all for my thoughts to move on to finding something more comfortable for just the two of us.

I've been scrolling through Rightmove for three days: *Find your happy*, it says. *Search properties for sale and to rent.* I've been working my way around the country, looking at different out-of-the-way locations. Finally, I type: 'Isle of Arran, Ayrshire' into the search bar, tick the 'in Scotland' box. I set a range of prices from £250,000 up to £400,000. Then I think differently, go back to click 'to rent' instead. I apply a random budget: £2,500 per month. Three houses appear. One of them immediately grabs my attention.

Silverburn Farm is a spacious and beautifully presented detached villa with many traditional farmhouse features. Located in a much sought-after elevated area in Whiting Bay, this property sits above the village with views over the Clyde and the Ayrshire coast.

It feels fateful for Leila to be returning to Scotland, having moved down to London all those years ago. I think to myself, this could be it. An opportunity to leave London does not come by that often. I could take time out, plan my next move. That coffee shop I've always dreamt of, the prospect that Leila mocked, feels like it could be real. How many of us live in London without ever seeing the rest of the country? I can't remember when I've felt so excited about my existence and yet so terrified, all at once. With Leila staying over, I've been able to imagine a different kind of life. But that sight of Stellans haunts me still. Not knowing what happened to him after that night in the woods is troubling. I want to believe he's alright. That somehow, he returned to his former life. No body has been found after all. But I also know that blow to his head was fatal. Not many would be able to survive it.

I type a message to the estate agent to request a virtual viewing and hit SEND.

I'm hoping Leila will be well enough to keep me company. I've spent most of the week clearing Raven Court so I can prepare to sell it.

For days, I clear away boxes, roll things into bubble wrap; sticky-tape and label. I tick off chores and ruthlessly discard old items: chairs, commodes, railed beds, broken dressers; anything I can no longer stand the sight of. By the end of it, the rooms in Raven Court are so empty and clean that every breath of mine is echoey. The walls are bare, making them seem wider and longer. The house is swollen like a pregnant belly but with nothing left inside it.

Behind me, there are cardboard boxes stacked up against the wall like Lego bricks. Black refuse sacks snaking along the hall with no space to walk between them. Only this morning, I tripped up several times, stubbing my big toe whilst carrying the laundry basket. I've spent four afternoons this week sifting and sorting through faded boxes containing old things that belonged to me in a former life: misfit crockery, tasteless ornaments, frayed tea towels.

The smell of baking bread warms the air with the subtle notes of yeast and something else – something bitter, like vinegar – coating the back of my throat.

Leila drifts into the kitchen like a ghost, unwashed and wearing a shabby T-shirt and jeans. Her hair is unbrushed and her voice is weak. Every one of her movements is subtle. I want to prepare something decent for her to eat and I'm about to stand up, to throw on an apron, but Leila parks herself at the kitchen table, rocking backwards and forwards. Her cheeks are blotchy, and she opens her mouth as if she wants to say something but struggles to find the words. I peer at her and she begins to shake, tears rolling down her cheeks, pooling into the grooves of her sunken collar bones.

'I think I need a little something,' she says.

'You know I can't do that.'

She begins moaning.

'What's the matter? I ask.

She's not listening, however. It makes me cross when she doesn't listen. The fact remains, Stellans is still missing but still, she keeps making everything about her.

'Shall I get you something to eat, Leila? That will make you feel better, surely? Anything you like. Just tell me.'

But she just sits there in silence, watching dust motes floating in the air. I move closer to her, noticing a fresh bruise on the side of her face.

I admit, there have been accidents. Leila has been walking around the house, bumping into things. Under her T-shirt, there are bruises, like beetroot stains, all over her thighs and upper arms. Once, in the middle of the night, I woke up to find her standing at the top of the stairs, staring down the stairwell like she was about to throw herself down. Since she's been here, I've seen just how bad her lifestyle has been. One night I found her rustling through the medicine cabinet. 'I just need something to help me relax,' she says. 'Please. I don't have my own stuff.'

The house phone rings but I do not run to answer it. Leila seems uninterested.

'Shall I get that?' I say.

I've heard Leila on the phone, speaking to her producer. He's called a few times, enquiring when she might return to work. I suspect this is him calling now, to check up on her.

She shakes her head. 'It doesn't matter anymore. It's like you said.'

Seeing how she's come undone so quickly, I advised her to reconsider her career options. No good will ever come from her being in television, not with all that pressure.

The phone stops ringing, and I lean over the table to hold her hand.

'We need to talk,' I say. 'We need to discuss our future.'

Leila glances down.

'Can you just give me something to take the edge off the pain?' she asks. 'Only, it would really help.'

I stand next to her, placing my hand underneath her chin and lift her face up to the light. 'Look at me,' I say. But her lips tremble, her eyes fill. 'This is too much. You know it's too much. I know you like a lift now and again, but this is altogether something different.'

I decide it's best to give her plenty of space, to help her develop a new sense of awareness. But as I turn to leave, Leila gets up too, grabbing a cookery book from the top shelf. She hurls it at me from across the room, narrowly missing my face.

'Alright, I get the message,' I say.

I grab a needle from the box on the shelf and return to her, to try to administer the medicine. I can't take any chances, so I give her a shot of Zenophyl, the same dose I give to the residents who complain they can't sleep. It's what she wants. She had asked for it. The sharp point of the needle pricks her skin and she smiles, almost delighting in the plunge of the syringe. Her eyes glaze over and her shoulders fall. It's not enough to get her addicted, just enough to help her relax, to help ease her tantrums.

I watch as Leila sways, staggering into her chair, resting her head onto the table. Eventually, she closes her eyes, her breathing slows, then flows in longer waves; her body relaxes. She reaches out her hand, just as she begins drifting, and I slip mine into hers, feeling the warmth of her butter-like skin.

'Please don't leave me,' she says.

I can't tell you how wonderful it is to hear her say that.

I carry Leila up to the bedroom and place her gently on the bed, removing her jeans. I pull back the covers, tucking her in. Before I turn, I decide it's only right that I climb into bed with her. I feel the cotton brush against me, feel the warmth of her heartbeat. I drink in the stale scent of her hair, the oily texture of her skin. I brush her cheek with my fingertip. Her deep breaths turn into snores, as she sleeps on her side. I watch her, unable to keep myself from watching her, as she falls, deeper and deeper, as the sky darkens, and my breath merges and becomes one with hers.

We wake up the next morning, our limbs entwined. Leila's back is pressed to my chest, her hair against my lips, my breath warming the folds of her ears. The scent of her unfurls around me, soothing me, relaxing my shoulders. We do not stay like that for long, however, because there's a knock on the front door, and it is thunderous.

'Who the hell is that?' Leila jumps out of bed, frantically grabbing her jeans. She struggles to balance as she pulls up each leg.

I run to the window, peering down onto the street. The road is only just visible through the shimmering trees. A flash of blue light splinters my eyes, cutting through the leaves. I make out a woman in uniform, seated in a police car. She switches the engine off and throws open the door.

It's then I know, this is it. The real test of a story comes only from how well you repeat it.

'It's the police. Just keep calm. Do exactly as I say.'

I watch the woman through the window, straightening her skirt, making her way up the front path. I turn to face Leila, quickly, as I hear the crunch of footsteps in the gravel. Voices billow from the front doorstep. They're knocking on the door again.

'Stick to the story, okay? If we stick to the story, and make sure it's consistent, we'll be fine.'

Leila stands before me, her eyes wide and puffy, her cheeks pink. I move towards her, cupping her face, brushing a strand of hair away from her eyes.

She looks down, biting her lip. Her brow is lined with sweat.

'Listen to me,' I say. 'Nothing bad is going to happen.' I remind her what we agreed, that we would avoid divulging that Stellans came round that night. It would raise too many suspicions. It is the last thing we want. She agreed, but I've been concerned ever since. Leila does not fill me with confidence that she would stick to this. 'Do you remember what we agreed to say? You realise why it's important, don't you?'

She nods and I kiss her forehead, tasting the saltiness of her skin on the tip of my tongue.

'I need you to focus. I need you to be strong. Do you think you can do that?'

We make our way downstairs, and I watch Leila overtake me with a sudden burst of energy. She pats her hair down, combs it back with her fingers. She tiptoes into the kitchen, whilst I make my way towards the front door. I know that what happens next is critical. This is the moment we've both been dreading.

'Hello, Rita.'

It's DCI Lawson, standing on my doorstep. The sight of him takes me back to the last conversation we had. I know he's searching for something to pin on me.

Today, he appears especially well groomed: clean-shaven, eyes bright, like he knows something that I don't and it confirms what he suspected all along. His energy is spring-like, and I haven't seen this in him before. It's something akin to excitement.

A woman stands beside him, her black shoes crunching into the gravel as she shuffles the weight between her feet. Compared to him, she looks inexperienced, with a face that resembles a teenager's. But from the way she clenches her jaw, I can tell she's keen to assert her authority. This woman means business. Looks like Lawson found himself a new partner.

'This is DC Green,' says Lawson, glaring at me. The woman nods, firmly.

'Hope we're not disturbing you,' she says. 'This won't take long.'

I step back, unsure how this new dynamic will work. Does Green know about previous conversations I've had with Lawson?

'Is everything alright?' I ask.

'Just routine,' says Lawson, with a grin. 'We're working through the area. We have a few questions, *official* procedure. May we come in?'

I have no choice but to let them in. Leila is still in the kitchen; I hear the bubble and boil of the kettle. My mind scrambles as I realise it's the first time I need to explain her presence to an outsider, just like we rehearsed. Eight days have passed since that awful night. It is imperative I create an impression that everything is normal.

Lawson and Green take a seat in the living room. I watch as Green crosses her legs, scratching at her sheer tights. There's an awkwardness to her movements that tells me she's not as confident as she seems.

'You may be aware that we're investigating the disappearance of Michael Stellans. We're obviously exploring all avenues and your name came up,' she says.

'Oh?' Leila walks into the living room and takes a seat. I immediately feel my chest tightening. 'Remember me? I'm Leila. I'm Rita's friend. I've already spoken to you both, but I can answer any questions you have. Nice to see you again.'

Lawson nods. He seems a little surprised. 'Nice to see you again too,' he says. He turns to me, his eyes searching mine, but I turn away.

'I want to help,' says Leila.

I marvel at the way Leila suddenly appears lifted, compared to earlier on.

Lawson and Green glance at one another then away, as if they've agreed, in the silence between them, that it's best to change tactic. I see now that Lawson may have told Green about my previous involvement with Raven Justice. With Leila here, I can only hope that they don't mention it. It would take some explaining to Leila. But I would not be surprised if Lawson did that out of spite, because I've resolved not to work with him.

'I appreciate this situation is somewhat complex and . . . unusual.' Lawson clears his throat. 'There's nothing more we need to ask you, Leila. But since this is the first time we're here in a more official capacity, I've a few questions for Rita.' He smiles with a mischievous glint in his eyes.

'Just wondered whether you've seen Mr Stellans, Rita?' asks DCI Lawson. 'He was a teacher at Brentford High. And you were one of his students.'

'Yes, I remember him,' I say. 'Not someone you easily forget.'

'That right? Have you seen him at all since school, kept in touch at all?'

I shake my head.

'Do they know where he is?' asks Leila, thankfully, sounding a little more sympathetic, a little more normal.

'I'm afraid not,' chips in Green. 'We're exploring various lines of enquiry, both in London and in Germany.'

'Germany?' says Leila.

My ears prick.

'So he's not passed by, visited you at all? And you've had no contact with Michael Stellans since school?' asks Lawson. He points his question at me like a gun.

'Can't say I have,' I mumble.

He nods. 'I see. Interesting.'

'Why would you be searching for him in Germany?' I ask.

Green watches Lawson scribbling something on his notepad. She appears aggrieved that her boss has taken over.

'He appears to have made a few visits. So we're just looking into it,' says Lawson.

'Have you heard any information that might be relevant?' asks Green. 'Any information about Mr Stellans from, perhaps, *another* source of yours?'

What is most disappointing, more than their unrelenting questions, is not knowing how much information they have on me. I know DCI Lawson, I know what he's like, but I have no idea why he's behaving like this.

'I'm sorry,' I say. 'I would certainly not hesitate to work with or inform the police if I had any information that might prove useful. I try to be a responsible citizen. But these days, I like to live a quiet life. Keep myself focused on my business.' I smile at Lawson. 'I'm sure you can appreciate that, can't you?'

'Relieved to hear it,' he says. 'Society needs good and responsible citizens. Provided you stay that way, there will be no trouble.'

He smiles and from the look in his eye, I wonder whether we've put Zia behind us.

There is still Stellans to deal with, however.

Leila looks down, like she's thinking about something.

DC Green stands up, walking to the French doors at the rear end of the living room. She stares outside at the back. 'This is an enormous property, isn't it? Very impressive. Just you living here on your own, is it?'

I nod. 'It belonged to my parents. They left the care home to me.'

Lawson scrapes his teeth against his bottom lip, then scribbles something down like this is somehow new information. I grow aware of how much his presence, and hers, is beginning to bother me.

'Big responsibility,' says Green. 'I imagine it keeps you busy.'

'Unless you like to keep yourself busy with other things,' chimes in Lawson. 'You strike me as a woman particularly well-suited to multiple occupations.'

'Actually, I'm thinking of selling up. The care-home business was really a dream my parents had.'

'Interesting,' says Green.

Lawson nods, like he understands.

'She is busy, is our Rita,' says Leila. 'She's always running around.' She laughs nervously. 'She is incapable of a quiet life. Full of ideas!'

We all look around the room, awkwardly.

Eventually, DC Green breaks it up.

'Sorry to hear of your loss,' she says, shuffling the weight on her feet.

'Loss?' I say.

'Your parents,' says Lawson.

'And also, I hear you lost one of your residents recently,' says Green. 'We're aware of Raven Court and its reputation in Harrow. Just how vital your service is . . . a shame to wind things up.'

'How many are living here now?' asks Lawson.

Leila fiddles with her hair, shaking her foot, then we both scramble up, following them to the back.

'No one lives here but me. Leila is just visiting. Aren't you, Leila?'

Leila nods.

Green peers at the boxes. 'Are you moving? You've obviously been packing. Going anywhere soon?'

'We're thinking of getting away, yes.' I say. 'There's no law against it, is there? It makes sense given the circumstances. Like I said: I prefer a quiet life and it's high time I lived it.'

Lawson glances at Leila and then at me. 'Well, I imagine it can't come quick enough given how much you've been juggling things. Only, it would be good to have your contact details. For any further conversations we might need.'

I bite my lip.

'Tea?' asks Leila. 'I've just boiled the kettle.'

'No, thank you,' says Green. 'We can't stay too long.'

'You've been extremely helpful,' says Lawson. 'Very helpful, indeed. If there's anything else we need to ask you – perhaps leverage your *expertise* in some way, we'll be in touch.'

'Please do give us a call,' says Green. 'And good luck with . . . well, whatever comes next.' She hands me a card with just her name and number, embossed in shiny black ink.

I take the card and turn it over in my palm. On the back, a smiley face. It says, 'Call me.'

'What happens next?' asks Leila, trailing behind Lawson and Green as they make their way down the hallway.

'Well, we're doing the normal due diligence, working our way through the local CCTV footage, going through phone records,' says Green. 'Not many cameras around here. But our efforts will no doubt throw up a lot of information concerning Michael Stellans' final movements. It might take some time. We're light on resources, as you know.' She glances at me. 'We're doing the most we can, considering the circumstances.'

'And did you check his house again – for anything you missed the first time? Did you find anything?' says Leila. I'm aware her voice is rushed, almost desperate. 'Was he in Germany a lot?'

Lawson nods. 'It has allowed us to open new lines of enquiry, yes, and we are beginning to explore that as well. I'm afraid I can't discuss the details of Germany with you – did he mention anything to you?'

Leila shakes her head, dumbfounded.

'Well, we may have further questions for you too, Leila, since I know you knew Michael well.'

I lean against the wall, wrapping my fingers around the box of cigarettes inside my pocket.

'Well, we won't take up any more of your time. Thank you.' Lawson nods.

Green is smiling, her lips warm and friendly, though her eyes say something different.

Leila sees them out the door, and I hear Lawson whisper something to Green before the door closes.

When Leila returns, she is animated, pacing up and down the living room.

'That was weird. What's all that about Germany? And why did we deny he was here – *why*?' she splutters. 'It makes us look more suspicious because eventually, they will find out!'

She flops onto the sofa, her head pressed against her hand. 'It makes no sense, Rita. We should have come clean and let them know he came here. We've got nothing to do with Michael's disappearance. Why not just be honest about it?'

She is not wrong. But she's not right, either. I explain, in no uncertain terms, that I know all about their 'procedures'. There are no CCTV cameras close enough to place Stellans here, and I never once called him. He never called me, either. There's no way I appear on his records. And who cares about Germany? Stellans had many secrets. The fact that Leila *did* call him, endlessly, is just another matter to deal with. She would have to admit to the affair, and that was not necessarily a bad thing. But she would have to keep quiet about meeting him here. This much we agreed. As for my own CCTV footage, that was long gone. The remnants of it in a giant steel container in Ealing Recycling Centre.

'But his phone can be traced here, can't it? The network signal could be located from the night of our . . . confrontation.'

I'm silent, trying to think straight. I try not to make it look obvious to Leila that I'd already thought of that, too. I smashed Stellans' phone, throwing bits of it into the Grand Union Canal, which, of course, I don't tell her about. 'They won't touch me,' I say, finally. 'Besides, if they can trace it here, they can trace it leaving again, so they'll know we had nothing to do with this.'

'How can you be so sure? Is there something you're not telling me? I felt you were behaving strangely.'

I move to the sofa and sit down. Leila shuffles beside me. 'I know because I have a strong feeling. Besides, I know someone who can help advise us,' I say.

'Who?'

'Do you remember Javid?'

She leans back, her eyes crawling over the ceiling. 'Rita, what's going on? We need to talk about this. Can we trust him?'

'I'd trust him with my life.'

'Then why are we waiting? We need to get him on the phone and talk to him!'

'We don't need to do that yet,' I say. 'He's there, but only if we need him. We're fine for now. Trust me, we're fine.'

She's crying. 'Can't you see? This is a mess. It's getting so complicated. I'm so scared, Rita.'

I draw closer to her, wrapping an arm around her shoulder.

'The trouble with you, Leila, is that you're always tense and far too dramatic. Do you need something to help you relax?' I ask. 'Because if you do, I can offer you something . . .'

27

Nine days have passed since that night in the woods; Leila beside me all this time. In the air, there's a dank, musty smell of rotting wood. The last of the blue sky gives way to grey, the rain outside my window is pelting. After the surprise of the police visit only yesterday, I spend three hours sat at the kitchen table, reflecting on Stellans, on what might have happened to him.

Now, it's day ten, slipping like a shadow against the wall, but still: we hear nothing.

Upstairs, Leila sleeps. It's a slumber induced by a further injection she begged me to administer at the back of her knees. My hands feel numb as I scroll through Rightmove. Since yesterday, there's a growing urgency to my search.

I long for the perfect hideaway to rent on the Isle of Arran, and I've made good progress, shortlisting six properties, enduring four virtual tours with Graeham, the restless estate agent, who fumbles around with his iPhone, moving about each room in a grey suit, carrying a camera lopsided. I've fallen in love with Silverburn Farm, boasting the freedom of lush, open fields, with sheep grazing freely without stress or anxiety. As I know well, your first love is always the strongest and this property has views overlooking the shoreline of the Ayrshire coast: perfect for a future café. I can check the legalities, necessary permissions, and business rates when I get there. All I need to do is to make a final in-person inspection to check that the property is, in real life, everything I've seen virtually. After that, I will transfer a deposit and pack up this place for good. I have never done anything as big as this, nor taken such a risk, relinquishing the only life I've ever known with an unhinged woman as my accomplice.

There's a knock on the front door. Something about the weight and rhythm of it feels familiar. I get up and peer at the CCTV app on my phone – it's Javid, peering into the peephole.

When I open the front door, he recoils, his dark eyes glaring at me, almost accusatory. His head hangs heavy, his coat is bobbled with rain. We do not say anything to one another, but I open the door wider, and he brushes past me and stands in the hallway.

The wind whistles through the crack in the door but we stand there for a while, staring at one another. Then, as if he's heard me deliver some terrible news, he rushes into my arms, and holds me close to him. It takes me by surprise.

'I'm so worried about you,' he says. 'Why didn't you call me and let me know you needed help?'

He pulls me even closer to him. He does it with such force, it somehow tells me how much I mean to him. But it scares me too, since I have no idea what he's talking about. We stand there for a few minutes, then he pulls away, holding me at arm's length.

'What's going on?' he says.

'What do you mean?'

'Leila called me.'

I feel as if I've been punched in the stomach.

I grab Javid's arm and lead him into the living room, all the while unable to meet his eyes. We both sit down on the sofa, somewhat sombre.

'It's complicated,' I say. 'I wanted to talk to you, to get some advice as a lawyer. Is that what Leila mentioned?'

I'm fishing, desperately fishing. I need to know what Leila said.

He stands, running his hand through his hair. 'It was strange, Rita. Firstly, I didn't know who it was on the phone. Nor how she got my number. Then, she kept talking – rambling – about the fact that Stellans is missing, that maybe *you* need advice. *Please call Rita. Convince her.* She kept repeating the same thing, over and over again. *She won't listen to me.* She sounded like a drunk woman.'

I lean back in my seat, a part of me relieved that Leila said nothing more, but growing nervous too, because I know now, I must tell Javid more than I am prepared to.

'Okay,' I say. 'Let me explain.'

Even if I want to, I can't hold it back from him. I tell Javid about Stellans coming round to see Leila – how it was at her insistence. Javid listens, then swears under his breath. He crashes onto the sofa with his head dropped into his hands.

'It would have been better to come clean. Because now, it's far worse since you're withholding vital information.' Javid peels off his jacket, pulling his arms out of the sleeves, folding it neatly onto his lap. 'You know me, this is my world. I can be objective, open-minded. And I know you. I knew you were hiding something. I knew it! You should have just told me at the outset.'

'I'm sorry,' I say.

Javid stares at me, then reaches out his arm and places it around my shoulders. I shuffle closer to him.

'The police came to me too, asking all sorts of questions,' he says.

'They did? What did you say?'

'Not much. There's nothing to say. *I* haven't seen him, have I? I'm not the one withholding information that could be important in a missing person investigation.'

'I never wanted to get you involved.'

'Rita.' Javid's voice is soft and breathy, and for a moment, I want to blurt out everything – to even go as far back as the hunting. But a flash of the woods that night holds me back.

'From now on, I need you to be straight with me,' he says. 'I need to know everything if you want me to help you.' He frowns. 'Do you understand how difficult this could get for you? None of this looks great.'

His voice has changed; it's at least a couple of notes lower than his usual tone, addressing me like I might be his client.

He stands, taking a few steps towards the window, shaking his head. 'I knew Stellans had been here. I just *knew* there was something you were hiding.' He stares out through the glass, his eyes settling on something in the distance, then he turns quickly to face me. 'Why did he come over? Was it to see Leila? I bet it was. Those two were close at school – there were so many rumours. What disappoints me is that I didn't hear it from you, earlier. All that time I asked you what was going on – and you simply fobbed me off, saying it's nothing.'

'I'm sorry.'

He sighs. 'This isn't nothing, Rita. Still, what matters is how we manage things moving forward.'

I stand, pacing up and down, a palm pressed to my forehead.

'Did she have an affair with him?' he asks, suddenly.

My face drops.

'God! I knew it!'

I feel overwhelmed. This is it. *It's all over.* An ornate tower of complex brickwork, obliterated. I know what Javid is like. I know how he likes to dig. My heart is beating so fast, I think I might faint. He'll want to know everything . . . and then I won't be able to stop myself.

'I have nothing to do with Stellans. Yes, he was here. What happened was personal between them. I barely said a word to him. That paedophile is nothing to do with me,' I say. 'This is Leila's business. She needed help, so I was here for her.'

Javid scratches his head, then looks around the room as if he is wanting a cigarette. 'The police are looking into everything – granted, they're a bit slow. But it's only a matter of time before they establish he was here. They will want to know exactly what happened – what was said, and between whom. So, Leila is knee-deep in shit. She will have to figure out what to do next.'

I laugh nervously.

'You give the police more credit than they're due, Javid. They can't *prove* he was here. I doubt they will even work it out.'

'His *phone*, Rita.'

'I'm not sure he had one.'

'Everyone has a phone.'

'Not Stellans. He was one of those old-fashioned artistic types.' I am talking about Stellans in the past tense, and it occurs to me how ludicrous it is to be talking about his phone. Stellans is dead, I just know it.

'Then CCTV.'

'But there's none in the vicinity. I chucked out the CCTV from in here.'

Javid shakes his head. 'What? That alone is suspicious. Why would you do something like that?'

'It's part of . . . house clearing.'

'For Christ's sake, Rita.'

'Okay, look.' I clench my eyes closed and draw a sharp intake of breath. 'Hear me out.'

Javid glares at me. 'Speak – and make it fast. Because I'm running out of patience.'

'He *was* here – yes, he was here. But I was simply hosting for Leila. She wanted to see him because, after that story about Stellans, she felt they had things to discuss, things deeply private. I think you can understand.'

Javid shakes his head, pressing his eyes closed. 'I don't want to picture it.'

I stand beside him, tugging at his sleeve. 'She needed to talk to him, okay? It was important. She was worried there might be stories that come out about *her*. It was a *constructive* conversation, that's what it was supposed to be. It makes me sick – because everything you thought about Stellans is true. He is a paedophile and a pervert – yes. But Leila is a friend and, in that moment, she needed my help. She was my priority.'

His eyes are warm, soft, full of concern. It's remarkable, considering the lies I have told.

'The police should know, Rita.'

'They are incompetent!' I reply. 'I've heard you say so yourself several times over the years.'

'Everyone knew something was odd.' Javid rubs his brow. 'Just goes to show how important it is to trust your instincts.'

I nod, unable to disagree.

'But what I don't understand is why you got involved in the first place. Why – when it was between the two of them? Why not just tell the police he was here? If there's nothing concerning going on, why not be straight about it?'

I collapse onto the sofa. Finally, the million-dollar question surfaces.

'Because it was *Leila*, I suppose. That's why I was involved. And if they knew Stellans was here, given that he's now missing, they would throw all sorts of accusations around.'

Javid paces the living room, as if searching his mind for some reminder of what I might be talking about. He stops, dropping onto the armchair opposite me, biting his tongue.

My mouth is dry. I feel my eyes well. 'I don't need the police prying into my business, Javid.'

'It's a mess,' he says. 'But I get that you wanted to help Leila.'

My eyes fill up and a tear drops onto the back of my hand.

'But this is so serious,' he says. 'You could face jail for withholding information.'

My body tenses. I wonder where I should start. 'I didn't know he was going to go missing straight afterwards, did I?'

He stares down at the carpet, and it is his silence that feels the most judgmental. I know a verbal onslaught is coming. He's building up to it. I can feel it.

'Javid.' My voice rises and falls, echoes fluttering around the

271

room. 'Leila was out of her mind with worry. I had no choice but to step in. Regardless of what we might think, their lives were wrapped up in one another, so it's normal that she needed me.' I smile. 'She *needs* me. After all that stuff at school, she needs *me,* can you believe it?' The thought of it makes me laugh.

His face pinches. 'Is that what this is about? The fact that she needs you. Where is Leila now?' He looks up. 'Is she here?' He glances left then right, as if taking in the sight of the room for the very first time. 'And why is it so empty in here?'

'She didn't tell you she was here when she called you?'

'No. She omitted that important detail.'

'Well, I'm leaving,' I say. 'That's why I'm packing.'

Javid stares at me, dumbfounded. 'What are you talking about? Are you out of your mind? You can't just *leave.* Not with a missing person investigation under way – in which you might well have been the last to see the missing person!'

'I've done nothing wrong.'

Javid blinks several times. 'And where will you go, hmm? On a nice cruise across the Mediterranean?'

My voice breaks. 'I'm thinking . . . Scotland.'

Javid stands, stepping towards me – towering over me.

'Scotland?'

'Isle of Arran.'

'You're being ridiculous, do you know that? If you run away,' says Javid, 'it will look suspicious. The police will think you're hiding something.'

'What is that about the police?'

We both glance up as Leila steps into the front room wearing an old nightie. It's open at the front and she's carrying a wet towel. Javid looks away, and I rush towards her, taking the towel from her, taking my own fleece off to wrap around her shoulders. She swats me away like I'm a terrible nuisance.

'Are you alright?' asks Javid. Javid throws me a look. 'Is she alright?' He glances back at Leila. 'What is going on here with the both of you?'

Leila plants herself on the sofa, and I am unable to take my eyes off her. 'We've been through this before,' I laugh, my voice shaking. 'Everything is fine. Leila gets like this sometimes, usually when her medication wears off.'

Javid shoots me an alarmed look.

I walk into the kitchen to find Leila a fresh pair of leggings and a T-shirt from the laundry basket. When I return, she's in the hallway facing the wall, her back arched and palms slapping against the wall. Javid is beside her. I'm not sure if Leila is sleepwalking or if the medicine is playing tricks, but she is unsteady on her feet. I reach out my arm, placing my hand firmly on her shoulder, but she staggers back into the living room, knocking into the table with her knee. A glass falls from the top – Javid lunges forward to catch it. He places it back onto the table, then grabs Leila with both arms as she falls, limp, into them.

'I've got you,' he says. 'Come here.'

I watch, motionless, as Javid edges Leila towards the sofa, placing her down gently as if she is a delicate ornament. She yawns, rolling onto her side to lie down. I move towards her, noticing how stale she smells, like sweaty plimsolls. Javid kneels beside her, and Leila falls onto her back, staring up at me, her hands twitching like those of a child.

'It's me, Rita,' I say, moving closer. 'I'm not going to hurt you.' I need her to pay attention, to listen carefully to what I'm saying.

Javid is nervous. 'Is she out of it? She looks like she's out of it. Has she been drinking?'

I turn to Javid. 'She's fine. She's stable. In good condition. I've been looking after her.'

Leila begins laughing. She's hysterical, tears streaming down her face.

'What's happening?' I say. 'Why are you laughing like that?'

She wipes away her tears with the back of her hand, then stretches out her arms and legs, staring at her toes. She curls and uncurls them. 'I feel tired all the time. But you like it that way, don't you, Rita?' She laughs again but this time, her laugh is weaker. She turns to Javid and nods sleepily. 'Rita likes to treat me like I'm one of her residents.'

'I told you. The medication I'm administering is necessary. You've been out of your mind lately. And you asked for a dose this morning. You wanted it,' I say.

'I did?'

I'm annoyed with Leila for being so ungrateful. Javid grabs my shoulder. 'What are you doing? What is she talking about?'

'Can you blame me?' spits Leila, her arms sprawled out over the side of the sofa. 'I love you, Rita. You do know that, don't you? You are a kind person, and I'm grateful you're taking care of me. But sometimes . . .'

I turn to Javid.

'It's just something to calm her down. She needs it,' I say.

'This is fucked up, do you know that? You need to sort your-selves out. I have to go – will you be alright on your own? I want to help you, really I do, but I need to make some calls to check a couple of things if I'm to get involved.'

I hear the front door slam as he leaves.

I watch Leila drifting off again. 'Water,' she whispers. 'I feel thirsty.'

For a second, an image of Stellans flashes through my mind. I walk to the kitchen to fetch Leila a glass of water.

With my mind strangely detached from everything going on, that familiar ringing in my ears begins. I stand by the sink, turning the tap. I begin slow counting.

I don't know how long I stand there, staring down into the water swooshing and circling into the mouth of the drain. I guess it's longer than I had intended, trying to calm myself.

I am a good person, aren't I? So what if I lied to the police? I can get out of it. I crossed a line, sure, but my reasons are justifiable. Besides, they don't know anything else. It was Stellans who attacked *me*. He has not been found dead, not officially, so maybe he is still out there.

The muffled sound of cardboard distracts me, and I jolt back into the present moment.

I find Leila on her knees in the hallway, rummaging in an open box I packed earlier. She's rifling through papers, pulling out envelopes. One catches her eye, and she stares down at the front of it, cocking her head, her face strangely contorting. She looks up as I approach.

'What is this?' She picks it up.

'What do you mean? It's nothing.'

She stares at the envelope again. 'But it has my name on it.'

'It does?'

She waves the envelope around. 'What is *this*?' Her voice is louder, more hysterical.

'You don't want to read that,' I say. 'It's not for you.' I lunge forward but she's too quick. She jumps to her feet, snatching her hand away. She's holding the envelope behind her back. I swallow hard.

Leila brings her arms to the front of her and stares down at the envelope. 'That handwriting. I *know* that handwriting.'

'There's no point,' I say. 'It will just upset you if you read it.'

I don't want her to read the letter, not like that. I was just looking after it, obviously, and had every intention of giving it to her later. It's Stellans' confession I want her to read first – scraps of writing, but still valid. That's what Javid needs to read, too. He can build a case out of that, and then the world will understand what really happened.

But before I can stop her, Leila runs up the stairs with an energy and speed that seems to have erupted from nowhere. She enters the bathroom and slams the door shut before I can stop her. I hear the lock turn just as I arrive.

'Leila! Leila! Open the door!'

I'm shouting and shouting for her not to open the letter. I'm banging my fists on the door, pleading that it will do her no good. But it's too late. There is no power in the world that can stop it.

Through the door, I hear paper ruffling and unfolding, the sounds of her gasping.

The toilet lid slams down; I hear her weight drop onto the top.

I lean against the wall, resisting the urge to peep, my knees shaking under the weight of me. My back slides down the wall. I listen as she reads it out loud, her voice creeping beneath the gap in the door.

10 September 2019

Dear Leila,

I'm seated beside a window in the bar of the Bridge Hotel. It's where you and I once met in Northolt, one crisp November night. I'm drinking a double scotch – I've probably had one too many. I wouldn't say I'm drunk, a little shaky perhaps.

I'm writing you a letter because I want you to know: no matter what you read about me in the press, there was never any doubt that I loved you. I want to make sure you receive this, should there be things we're unable to say to one another in person when we meet at Raven Court.

I was a broken man when you left me all those years ago, but more than broken, I was disappointed. After everything I did for you, I felt you had used me, discarded me, when all I ever wanted was for you to begin university and to be happy. That weekend when we broke up, you told me I suddenly appeared old and that you were wrong to have never noticed this before. Worse still, you accused me of holding you back – like I never advocated for you, when all I ever wanted was for you to fulfil your potential. In a stroke, you wrote me off, shattering dreams I had of us spending the rest of our lives together. I can't help but feel that, perhaps, you held me responsible for some of the struggles you experienced with your grades at school, even though I tried to help you maintain your academic focus. When you ended our relationship, it felt like you were punishing me. Regardless, it took me a long time to get over you. It left me questioning my own self-worth and identity. Don't think I've not thought about my own failings over the years, however. I realise now it must have been very difficult for you to keep our relationship secret. Also, to cope with the pressures of dating an older man, which you handled with such maturity.

But I do want you to know, I never intended for us to meet the way we did. And whilst I know it was hard for you, I sometimes questioned whether you'd ever stopped to think of the risks I took to be with you. I'm not sure whether you have any real understanding of the price I paid for our relationship.

I lost my job. I was summoned into the headteacher's office and told my position was untenable given a rumour that surfaced after the school play we did together. For a while, I struggled to pay my bills. Luckily, no charges were pressed that year – and there was no real investigation. Later, I found another position. Of course, it was never a contest in who had more, or less, to lose. We both took enormous risks to be with one another, and we did so because we wanted to.

I don't know if you want to know anything about what happened to me after we broke up. We've spoken so little about that time.

After that final year in Brentwood High, I had a breakdown. It took me many years to get over it. I seemed to have a delayed reaction to the trauma of it. One night, I was sitting in the cinema watching Mystic River, and I heard a 'pop' go off inside my head. A tidal wave of blackness burst forth and in just a few seconds, my whole world – my identity, my reality – was obliterated; I didn't know who I was anymore.

I've been okay since then, just getting by, just getting on with it. But around three months ago, just before you called, I decided I needed professional help. I'm writing this letter because, really, I'm told it's a good idea by my therapist. I hope it comforts you a little to know I'm receiving some sort of treatment after all these years.

It's been three months since my first session with Dr Keller. He tells me I'm making good progress. It unnerved me at first, this idea of therapy and rehabilitation. I questioned whether talking and writing could really provide a cure, transforming an innate instinct. Dr Keller runs a clinic in Berlin which is very unusual in its focus, and the only one in Europe designed for men like me. Germany is more progressive than the UK in that regard. They seem to acknowledge that some men are different, with special feelings.

I haven't been able to tell Dr Keller everything. One can never be too sure how far you can trust a doctor to keep your secrets. But I do trust that by the time I have my next appointment and start a programme of rehabilitation, I'll be able to process things.

I realise now that what we had was a moment in time, never to be repeated. I am grateful for the little time we spent together, and for a chance to reunite with you after all these years. I do not expect you to make room for me in your life. I know that you feel differently and have moved on. Perhaps I was a fool to think that a woman like you would ever want to be with a man like me in the first place. I just wanted to *share my thoughts – you can make of them what you will. Should my words fail me when we meet, at least you'll have this letter to read.*

Let my words comfort you in times of loneliness, serving as a reminder of our love. The kind of love that endures and took us both by surprise. Know also that there is no other man capable of loving you as I did. Ours was the 'real deal'. Should we ever look back and feel sorrow for anything that happened between us, let it only be for the circumstances that came between us.

Michael

After a while, Leila unlocks the door and I glance up as it opens. She stands over me like an angry phantom. Her face is scarlet, her eyes wild and disbelieving. It's as if she doesn't know who I am anymore, nor why I am there. I'm an unwanted presence in her life, regardless of how many days I spent caring for her.

'Why didn't you give this to me?' She waves the letter in my face. Her voice is cold and venomous.

'I knew it would upset you,' I say, scrambling to my feet. 'There was no point in you reading it.'

'But it was addressed to *me*, not you. It was not *your* decision to make.'

'Listen.' I raise my hand and cover my face just in case she slaps me, which seems highly likely. 'You came to *me*, and you wanted *my* support. So *I* did what I had to do. I was trying to protect you. None of this was intentional. I honestly forgot about it. That night is a blur. You can understand that, can't you?'

'You mean that night when Michael was here?'

I nod. 'After you left, he gave me the letter and told me to give it to you. I must have left it in my pocket. I'm sorry, okay? I had always intended to pass it on.'

She shakes her head. 'I don't believe you,' she says. She grabs fistfuls of her hair, tugging hard at it. 'I don't trust you anymore. I don't believe *anything* you say.'

'Leila, *please.* I'm sorry —'

She steps back, holding her hands up, waving the letter in the air like a flag.

'I was wrong,' I say. 'I admit that. I shouldn't have made assumptions. But please don't be mad at me. I don't think I can handle it.'

I am consumed by heat, as if my body is in an oven with a fan whirring on full speed.

Leila presses her face to the wall and thuds her head against it. I move towards her, placing my hand on her shoulder.

'Leila.'

She falls to the ground, pulling her knees close to her chest, wrapping her arms around her legs. She lowers her forehead, rocking back and forth.

I kneel beside her, holding her. 'I'm here to help you,' I say.

I know then that I have no choice but to administer something more to help calm her down. I slip down into the kitchen and then return with an injection. Leila willingly holds out her arm, as if she's ready for me. She's resigned to my way of thinking. She barely flinches as I dab her arm with a ball of cotton wool, cold with disinfectant.

I move quickly before she grows limp, lifting her up into my arms and dragging her into the bathroom. I undress her, our flesh touching, and help her into one of my freshly washed Bugs Bunny T-shirts. She leans on me as I help her walk, shuffling, into the bedroom.

As I lay her onto the bed, watching her body sink into the sheets, I hear the springs in the mattress. Her mouth falls open and her jaw relaxes. I want to climb into bed with her, to lie with her for a while, to keep her company, but as she slips into a dream state, the house phone rings.

'I'll get it,' I say, running to the other side of the bed, grabbing onto the handset. I hear Leila moan, turning onto her side.

The line crackles as I place the receiver to my ear. There is no mistaking the voice on the other end. I know exactly who it is.

28

The next morning, I'm standing beside the living-room window, waiting for Rahul to arrive. It's incomprehensible to me that he should appear now – after so much time.

I move to the sofa. I try to steady my breathing and I begin counting.

The energy in the room hisses like an angry cat. The walls feel like they're inching closer to me.

At eleven o'clock, a grey VW Golf pulls up outside. When the engine stops, a tall, lanky man steps out of the car, the door clunking behind him. He's taller than I remember him. His skin appears darker, too, possibly owing to a late summer vacation. He wears faded jeans, a black polo neck, brilliant white trainers. He looks around him, perplexed, as everyone always is, by how such a secluded residence could exist within the leafy suburbs of Harrow-on-the Hill.

Childhood memories surface: a flash and then a slow unfurl. I see Rahul bursting into Leila's bedroom when Leila and I are mid-conversation. I see another scene of him, lumbering near the school gates, his face slapped with the drudge of having to walk his sister home from school. I remember one evening, when Rahul answered the front door after I'd spent five minutes ring-ing the doorbell. I remember his malicious grin, the acerbic tone in his voice as he relayed, with great pleasure, a message from his sister. *Leila says she's busy and doesn't want to see anyone, so why don't you just go home, Rita? You know you're not welcome here.*

I remember how he laughed at me, how he bared his teeth. He slammed the door shut in my face, and my stomach sank. The ground felt unsteady beneath my feet as I had no choice but to walk away.

Now here he is. Rahul is approaching the front door of Raven Court. He's lost none of the swagger of his youth, that confidence of knowing he was – probably still is – the preferred child. I slip towards the front door, wanting to open it before he presses the bell, but I stand there anchored at the foot of the stairwell, unable to move.

I hear Leila upstairs, dragging her feet. I hear the thud of her box of files and the ceiling shakes. Everything is quiet, and I imagine her seated on the edge of the bed, running her fingers over Stellans' letter, her hands shaking, her hatred aimed like a knife in my direction.

I wipe my palms onto my thighs and open the front door. Rahul stands before me, forcing a smile.

'You haven't changed a bit,' he says. I can't figure out whether that's a good or a bad thing. He stares at me for too long, and that familiar condescending look in his eyes returns, typical of our childhood relationship.

'Is she ready to go?'

I nod, pursing my lips. 'Come in,' I say. 'I'll go and get her for you.'

Rahul stands stiffly in the hallway, leaning against the wall, then walks into the front room. I close the front door behind him, and he looks around him, screwing his face up at the sight of the boxes lining the walls. He turns as I stand in the doorway.

'You're moving?'

'Selling up.' I lean my shoulder against the edge of the frame.

He nods and looks down at his trainers. 'Where are you going?'

It's strange how we've slipped into familiarity, in advance of any pleasantries exchanged.

'Maybe north, until I figure out what to do.'

He raises an eyebrow, then glances at the stairs. Leila descends like she's injured, clutching her box of office files, the weekend bag on her shoulder weighing her down.

Rahul's face darkens as she nears.

'Jesus,' he says. 'Look at the bloody state of you.'

Leila is wearing a pink shirt that's creased. It hangs over her jeans, and her hair is still wet from the shower, scraped back, and secured by an oversized clip. There are dark circles under her eyes and her skin is blotchy. I know it's simply a side effect from her medication; it will clear up in a few days. But I can see she doesn't look well and that it's bound to appear suspicious.

She drops her bag on the floor, then eases into the living room. Leila gropes the edge of the furniture until she reaches the armchair. Taking a seat, she slips on her shoes, scattered by the side of the sofa just next to her.

'Let's get you out of here,' says Rahul, cutting me a look. His tone is accusatory as if I'm some sort of criminal.

I glance at Leila, but she refuses to meet my eye. We haven't spoken since she found Stellans' letter, and I wonder whether she'll say goodbye.

'You can come back whenever you want to,' I say. 'You know where I am.'

But Leila ignores me. I'm fighting, with all the energy I have, to stop the tears from falling.

'Has she been taking something?' asks Rahul.

Leila picks at the skin on her fingers.

'Just a few tablets – sleeping pills, and a little something to help her relax. She insisted on taking them herself.'

He tuts under his breath. 'We'll be in touch,' he says.

He turns to Leila, towering over her. 'As ever, you're incredibly selfish. You have no idea how worried Mum's been.'

I watch Rahul open the front door as Leila staggers into the hallway. She takes a deep breath and closes her eyes as an autumn breeze wafts in, her hair billowing. For a second, I want to hold her, to tell her how sorry I am for everything I've done. But it seems too late for that now.

I watch the two of them walk down the front path together, Leila a step behind Rahul. Rahul picks up speed, Leila falls behind him as she struggles with the bag on her shoulder. He glances back at the property, then throws everything into the boot of his car. Leila is sat at the front, her head pressed against the window, her skin pale and taut.

I bite my tongue, trying to hold back the tears as Rahul returns for the box of files on the doorstep. I taste metal as he closes the front door, determined not to cry until they've gone. It disorientates me, watching the car start, seeing Rahul pull away from the kerb as if for the last time. He accelerates down the road and my stomach somersaults. I throw myself onto the sofa, my head dropped into my hands.

29

Time cannot be measured in a state of loss, but time has surely passed – another week, in fact. It ebbs and flows, sometimes it plays a constant, dreary note. With my head hung low, as if pressed permanently to a concrete floor, I think of her. I find myself constantly thinking of her. But it's no good. She's gone. I can wish her back, but that does not change things. Impressions of her are still strewn on the cold wooden floors of Raven Court. Now those moments we shared are like cheap Polaroids which I don't remember taking. I question it now, question whether it really happened. Stellans. Leila. Those years of hunting – why on earth I did it. Memories are amorphous things, never to be relied upon.

I think of Leila, when she and I were teens.

It was just after Mum and Dad bought Raven Court and we were here, in this very bathroom, standing where I stand now. Leila had this idea that we should take a bath together, that as girls, we should celebrate our bodies and not hide anything. Besides, she had spots on her back she could not get rid of. She wanted me to cleanse those parts she could not reach. *I never get a chance to take a bath at home*, she said. *And I can hardly ask my mum to help me. There's never any peace and quiet, never any hot water at home when I want it.* She slipped off her blazer, unbuttoning her shirt, pulling down her skirt, with some difficulty.

'Come on. We're friends, aren't we?'

She ran the hot water, filling up the tub. I watched her slip into the water and then I removed my own clothes, folding hers and mine, piling them together onto the side. She laughed as I stepped into the water behind her, felt my ankles warm; the foam felt like cotton balls. Leila leaned back, her head resting against my chest, I felt the full weight of her press down onto me.

'So this is how it is,' she says.

I remember how she sighed, how water spilt over the edge. She didn't care about causing a mess. She knew it would not be down to her to clear it up. I was just happy to be there.

The steam rose and curled around us as the water lapped quietly, our bodies weightless. I gently brushed hair from her brow, gathering it slowly in my palms, twisting it into a wet turban that dripped onto her shoulders. I took a sponge and washed her back. Afterwards, we lay like that for a while, surrendering to the water, nothing said, nor needing to be said, between two young girls who pledged their friendship to the very end.

Tonight, I throw on my leather jacket and grab the keys to my van. I don't know where I'm going exactly, only that I need to drive around. I am at once alert yet lacking any clear direction. Lost and defeated, in desperate search of hope. I slump behind the wheel, pulling out sharply from the kerb, accelerating so hard that a flock of ravens let out a terrible scratchy caw. With gruff notes formed at the back of their throats, their bodies plump and covered in thick, shaggy feathers, they sound like cross teachers berating a child. I watch them surf updraught, soaring higher into the skies, circling just above me as I drive. One glides through the air, drops a stick from its beak, another swoops to catch it. This symphony of nature plays out like a strange dance before a trick mirror.

I drive towards Kenton, a town squashed with seamless grey semis. Pulse-line roofs beat against the sky to my left, English pubs, and fried chicken huts flash past me on my right. I'm weaving in and out of traffic, overtaking, then dominating the road. I press my foot down harder and veer towards a roundabout that has a miniature Stonehenge monument standing phallic in the middle.

After a while, skipping in and out of autopilot, semi-conscious of where I am, I notice I've landed on a country road with dewy green fields on either side of me. I pass a sign that says *Welcome to Bhaktivedanta Manor, Hare Krishna Temple. International Society for Krishna Consciousness.* The air smells fresh and holy and as I wind down my window, I spot a herd of cows and bulls, huddled peacefully together over a pitcher of feed, their nostrils wide, occasionally touching. I drive past the fields, up onto the tarmac lane, hearing their moo sounds murmuring in the distance. For some reason, I'm approaching the temple gates. I think to myself how nice it must be to live like a cow, with no worry nor strife. What it must mean to live a simple life.

The Tudor manor stands resplendent against the sun, cob-webbed with black wooden lines. I watch Hindu devotees in coloured saris and woollen shawls swoosh by. Men draped in orange dhotis, garlanded with mala beads, approach the temple doors. Men and women, girls and boys, Indian and English, bend to remove their socks and sandals. They wedge them into boxed shelves nailed wonkily to the wall and I hear the ding-a-ling of prayer bells. I lower my window some more, inhaling the air and I want to join them, to join with my Indian self, instead of suppressing it because of my dad. A waft of masala incense drifts by.

But when I consider it again, I think better of it. Life is com-plicated enough. The last thing I need is to open up another box when all these years, I've tried hard just to feel comfortable. There comes a point in every person's life, when you must simply accept yourself as you are, without the constant need for approval. I've spent the past five years being everything other than myself. Dif-ferent names. Different ages. I can't run anymore.

I reverse out of the parking lot, my head strange and light. All I can think of is how I must hold it together, not let myself grow confused – if not for my sake, for the sake of others, for the sake of the children. I pull up at Raven Court, the sky dark and heavy, the air feeling violent. There is a rage in me that begins to grow and swell, one I haven't felt since the time I was in school. I think of Rahul as I emerge from my van. I think of the audacity of him; how he could dare scuttle back into our lives like a stag beetle, fresh from the rotten wood of his existence, only to pronounce judgement on a situation about which he has little understanding. I think of Stellans, how I killed a man. I feel such shame, such disgust with myself.

That night, I dream of Stellans. See his body floating in a pond which I know is not far from the woods where I left him. He's floating with his face up, chin just above the water; cheeks smeared with the oily slime of green algae. He shoots open his eyes and then he grins, his mouth full of twigs and damp, curly leaves. He's laughing at me, laughing, laughing.

You can't escape, Rita . . .

I dart upright in bed, unable to breathe, the sweat dripping down from my forehead. My T-shirt is soaked right through and stuck to my back. I switch on the lamp next to me and I tell myself, again and again, that it's just a bad dream. Stellans' body has not been found, which means he got away and is hiding somewhere. I was careful to clear everything up after him. There is no evidence to suggest any criminal activity.

Three more days pass and the rain falls hard. I keep my phone close, hoping Leila might change her mind and call me. I just want to know she's okay, that she understands why I held Stellans' letter back. That morning, in a moment of madness, I call her whilst drinking, first thing as soon as I get up. I'm polishing off a half-bottle of red wine, a Diablo Dark Red with vanilla notes brushing the back of my throat and flushing my face. After that, I move on to a bottle of sweet rum. I'm drinking like a teen who is unsure how to drink, awkward and terribly self-conscious. With my head foggy, I dial her number. It goes to voicemail but, fearful that I am now so intoxicated, so unravelled that I am incapable of sounding rational, I hang up.

I thumb Leila a text, every part of me certain I will regret it. I press SEND, anyway.

PLEASE Leila. This is to@rture. Let's not do this!! It's MEE. ME. Not enyone else but UR friend, Rita Marsh. Do you even know me? Please call mee. I miss you so murch. You have no idea what I would do for U!! xxx

After it's sent, I sit on my bed staring at her contact entry in my phone, at the little round circle with her filtered face up close. I feel like I've done something irreversible. I've crossed a line, sabotaged any hope of ever hearing from her again, but all I really want is to know whether she has begun the process of healing, and what that feels like. Of course, she does not answer. Silence is her preferred language, now.

Still drunk, I manage to muster enough motivation to brush my hair, now so embarrassingly overgrown, black roots sprout through the blonde like cress. In my bedroom, I stare at myself in the dusty mirror, unsteady on my feet, unable to recognise the woman I have become.

Rita Marsh, that's my name, isn't it? It's who I am. But now, I understand that names reveal nothing about our true selves. They are simply words, vibrations, sounds engineered to give things meaning. What is a name, but a convenient label given to us by our parents?

I hear the brass flap on the letter box snap downstairs, and I jump a little in my skin. I place my hairbrush on the dressing table and descend in my shorts and T-shirt. The cold air pricks my skin. A postcard has arrived, its edges poking out from the holes in the steel basket. I bring back the lid of the letter box so I can read it. Some of the letters are blurry.

On the front, I make out it says: MANY GREETINGS FROM SCOTLAND, set against a collage of shots of the rugged Highlands. On the back, a few lines of small, neat handwriting:

Thanks for taking care of Leila. She's okay, we've kept her safe in a place where she can recover and receive proper treatment. She's not up to visitors (in case that's what you're wondering). She might be in touch when she's out, don't know, hard to tell. That's up to her. Please don't get in touch with her directly, and please stop calling. She's fragile and needs time. I'm not passing on any of your messages. Rahul.

I return to my bedroom, setting the postcard down on my bed-side cabinet, propped up against a box of tissues. It tortures me to think that Leila wants nothing more to do with me, that she's been badmouthing me to Rahul. I sit down on the edge of the bed and open the bottom drawer of my cabinet. I fumble around haphazardly, pulling out a packet of photos. There's one of Leila seated on the steps of the school playground in Brentwood High. The sun shining to the side of her. As I squint, I notice something which I never noticed before. It's a blurry face staring down at her from a classroom window on the upper floor. I place the photo down, struggling to swallow.

For the rest of the week, even the smallest, lightest chores, like doing the laundry or preparing myself a meal, prove difficult. Thoughts of moving return to me. If Leila is not coming with me, I can still go ahead, although all motivation to implement plans is gone. The prospect of moving alone, to the Isle of Arran, no longer holds the same appeal. Also, I know that I would be a fool to move now, with everything I've done.

When you've skirted the periphery of moral boundaries for

so long, when you've committed a crime as terrible as the one I have committed, a state of unbelonging is inevitable. In that state, good and evil merge as one. You think they are different because that's what society teaches you when you're growing up. It's drummed into you. But the wise woman who has lived with multiple names and faces knows that it's more like a spinning sphere. A sphere that grows and grows until, eventually, it engulfs you – until you become one with it. It occurs to me that perhaps it's not so bad being me, nor being different. I'm part of a select group of people – an elite, living on the periphery of society, willing to fight for what they believe in. Some might call it a privilege.

Later that night, after I sleep all afternoon, then finally get up to have a shower and wash my hair, resolving to make plans to get on with my life, no matter how hard it might be, I settle down in front of the television. Flicking through the channel menu, something on BBC news catches my eye. It's a flash of woods. I'm shocked still, unable to take my eyes off the screen:

Body found in Leechpool Woods, Horsham, at 3.20 p.m.

A policeman is talking into the camera holding up an empty dog leash. The camera pans over to the dog, we see a wider shot of it sniffing at the ground. Panoramic, there's a scene of the woods, then a zoom-in on a patch of soil just beside a giant oak tree.

I hold my breath, placing my ice-cream tub down beside me, my heart thumping. I lean forward, squinting at the screen, unsure whether I'm seeing things accurately. On the table in front of me, my phone vibrates.

I'm staring up at the TV, then back at my phone, listening to the newscaster rattle off details of the body that a local child has found. I can't help but think it's ironic that a child found Stellans.

Have you heard??!! They're saying that the man they found is Stellans!

I see no evidence of Stellans being named on screen.

CNN have also picked it up. It's on every news station.

TBH I never really liked the guy, especially after the story about that girl came out. I never wanted him dead, though.

Are they SURE it's him??

Who else could it be? It matches the description!

I throw my phone onto the sofa, and switch to CNN. I increase the volume, numbers ascending. The police are not saying much, only that they are launching an urgent investigation. But then, there it is. A ticker line crawling like an ant along the bottom.

Body suspected to be writer Michael Stellans

In that moment, time stands still. The room around me is so quiet, I feel the thud-thud-thud of my own pulse beating. I glance at my phone. I want so badly to dial Javid's number, but I hold myself back.

I run upstairs. In my bedroom, I'm pulling down a suitcase to pack my clothes. I grab whatever I can find that's clean: three pairs of jeans, socks, underwear, several T-shirts. My phone rings and I stop dead in my tracks. The police – it must be the police. *This is it. It's over for me.* But when I swipe to answer it – it's like he's read my mind – it's Javid.

'Rita. Thank God.'

I am silent, unable to speak, but I'm breathing heavily and so is he.

'Speak to no one,' he says. 'You need to listen to me – take my legal advice. It's likely the police will pay you a visit. Worse still, they'll name you as their main suspect. You were the last to see him, and they will figure that out. We've got to get this story straight, Rita. I'll do everything I can to make sure it doesn't escalate, but you've *got* to listen to me. You've got to do as I say.'

'What's going to happen, Javid?' I say, as my voice breaks.

'We need to get your story straight *before* you make a statement. You need to go to them before they get to you. Don't say or do anything without me present, do you understand? That's important. And for God's sake, don't watch the news. It won't help. Remember, you did nothing wrong. It was just a meeting. Like you said, it was totally innocent. We've got to separate those two instances.'

I hang up the phone. I'm slipping into a void of darkness. I want so desperately to disclose the full story because now, I'm struggling to breathe: the heavy burden of it is killing me. How can I lie? How can I do that to Javid?

My phone vibrates once more, and I rush downstairs to see what further developments there are.

I flick to Sky News, and there it is, grainy black-and-white images of a body being carried out of the woods. The title at the bottom reads:

Anyone with information please call: 0800 108 108

I turn up the volume a little more. The silver-haired news announcer confirms that a body has been found with clothes soaked in blood. He says a murder investigation has opened, and that, according to the police, anyone with any information should come forward.

WhatsApp messages are firing in so fast I cannot keep up with them:

OMG it is so upsetting!

Man, there are some barbaric ppl out there!

I'm about to switch off my phone, unable to read any more, but a final flurry of messages catches my eye and I run down them:

Do you think it was a revenge for something? Maybe there is more to it than what they're saying. Scum like that deserve what's coming!

Yeah, I don't blame them TBH, but the whole thing is so sick!

Remember that girl that came forward to accuse Stellans? Can you believe she's retracted her statement!

I cannot believe Rani has retracted her statement. It's like it always is for girls who are victims, shadowed by the events – the motives, the lives, of perpetrators.

I TOLD YOU it was dodgy in the first place!!

Yeah, tell me about it. Some girls just love to cause trouble, don't they? Poor Stellans, he may have been innocent.

My body is still, suspended in time, as I try to process the reality of what's unfolding. The horror of Stellans' body now found. The injustice that Rani must live with. The realisation that I am a murderer.

The air, and all the energy I have, slowly escapes me. The TV screen grows blurry as my eyes fill. The phone in my hand vibrates once more. I peer down at the screen and my breath catches.

21.30 Leila Sharma
I'm going to the police.

30

Leila agrees to meet me by the river Thames, one last time. It's reassuringly in the opposite direction to where we both live. I'm evading Lawson, who has been calling, leaving messages. Leila prefers somewhere neutral. She knows we must talk, before we part ways. As I leave Raven Court, I notice it's a beautiful day. I offer to buy Leila lunch. But she declines, communicating curtly by text. Hers in single syllables, mine with added flourishes. I tell her I perfectly understand; maybe it's naive of me to think we can ever return to the way things were.

But I'm not stupid. I know the score. A deep part of me is aware, just as a fly trapped in a spider's web is aware, that at any given moment, the spider will pounce, and it will be eaten. Moments like these are decisive, where outcomes are so obvious, so inevitable, there's little point in resisting.

At Harrow-on-the-Hill station, I pass traders manning stalls: flowers, fruit, and fancy vegetables. I grab a bunch of roses which I think Leila will like and once I've paid for them, I make my way down the stairs onto the platform, heading towards central London.

The tube arrives almost instantly and after an hour, switching lines, I find myself climbing the stairs at Southwark Station. Stepping out onto the pavement, I turn left, walking down towards the latticed lines of Blackfriars Bridge, stretched out like a stray arm over the river Thames.

I'm almost at the river now, and I feel a strange sense of finality, of things coming full circle. Southwark is where all my problems began several weeks ago. My heart quivers as I pass pubs, hotels, fish-tank buildings with blue-tinted windows. When the river air hits me, that stale, stinking smell of sweaty socks, the sight of Leila hits me too. She's in the distance, seated on a wooden bench. Her head and shoulders like a small silhouette stamped against the horizon.

She drops her head forward, like she's scrolling through her phone. As I move closer, I see her hair is shorter, the blunt ends of it resting past her shoulders. The sun streaming to the side of her looks just like the photo I have in my drawer. It feels wrong to offer the roses I'm carrying to her now. They appear like a token gesture, hopelessly inadequate after everything I've done, when what we need is a deeper conversation. I arrive at the edge of the river, placing the flowers down, just under the iron rail. For a second, I think of Zia.

Leila lifts her head, sensing I'm there. With her gaze fixed forward, overlooking the grimy water, I sit down beside her and for a while we say nothing.

'It's good to see you,' I say, after a while. 'I'm glad you're on your feet again.'

She snorts. 'He's dead, Rita, are you happy? It's what you wanted.'

I swallow, the full weight of the situation sinking like an anchor in my stomach. 'It's not what I wanted,' I say. 'I didn't want that.'

Leila looks down at her hands, clutching onto the strap of her bag.

'I can't stay long,' she says, quietly. 'I've left Rahul, I'm taking control of myself.'

'Good for you,' I say.

I cross my legs and lean back into the bench. I gaze out onto the horizon and breathe in the cool air, listen to the squawking seagulls circling overhead.

'I mean it when I say I'm going to the police. Today is about getting our stories straight – you know that, right?' She turns to face me. 'You were right. Not about everything. But you were right about the fact that I should not allow my life to be ruined by him, or anyone else for that matter.'

A weight appears to lift from my shoulders hearing her talk like that – finally, after all this time.

'I can't even say his name,' says Leila. 'He's dead now, can you believe it? I can hardly take it in.'

'I'm keen to co-operate,' I say. 'I know it's the right thing to do.'

She nods. 'So I'll tell them my side of things, the history between Michael and me. If I tell them about that, the rest is perfectly understandable: why we met up, the intention behind it, and, of course, your involvement.' She straightens up, her voice harder. 'But you *did* lose your temper that night, Rita. It's just like you always do. And that's a problem. I need to tell them about that, and it's bound to look suspicious . . . You'll have to justify that yourself.'

It takes me back hearing that tone in her voice. One minute determined, another, accusatory. 'What do you mean? I know you're still mad about the letter, but this is not the way to punish me.'

'It was not *your* letter, was it? Given what's happened, I feel terrible not to have read it sooner.'

'He practically confesses he's a paedophile in that letter.'

'Leave it, Rita. He's dead. Did you not see it all over the news?'

I bite my tongue. 'Are you looking to give me a *motive* for his murder so that I fall under suspicion? Is that what you're doing? Because all I ever wanted was to help you, Leila. Do you know that? Ever since we were young, I was always there for you.'

'You tried to control me,' she snaps. 'You're no different to the men in my life. My father, Rahul . . . Even Michael. You've no idea how much damage—'

'And the letter? Will you share that with the police? Only I made a copy, of course. And by the sounds of it, it's just as well that I did.'

Leila flinches, and I immediately regret what I've said.

She turns, shooting me a look, and I see how vulnerable she is.

'I want us to go to the police,' she says. 'I want us both to explain that we saw him that night – all of it.'

I consider her statement. 'Then what? What happens after that, and to us?'

'I don't ever want to see you again,' she whispers.

My head rushes. I try desperately to keep calm. After everything that's happened, I can't afford to lose it now. 'You need to understand something,' I say.

'I'm done trying to understand,' she replies. 'I'm done listening to your sorry excuses. You are strange and spiteful; I should never have trusted you.'

'You and I, we're not so different.'

I feel it coming, after all these years. I feel the truth in me rising, yearning for release, to tell someone. The water ripples, a breeze brushes against my face. I pull my jacket tightly around me.

'There's something I haven't told you. It's something difficult to talk about, but which might help explain something . . . why I am the way that I am.'

She stares at me.

'I've had a lot of time to think about it,' I say. 'I even tried therapy. I should tell you. I owe you an explanation.'

'What is it? What are you talking about?'

Leila shuffles closer to me. 'You're scaring me.'

'It was a long time ago, but . . . something happened to me, too. So, I get it. Really, I do.'

I have her attention now. She listens as I tell her what happened to me. She's staring at the cracks in the concrete.

'It's difficult to talk about it, so I kept it locked inside, all these years. But I see now, I'm not okay. Despite putting on a good show. Despite overcompensating. Now I need to let it go . . . because it's been responsible for causing a lot of problems.'

Leila leans back, her voice a whisper. 'Why did you never tell me?' she says.

I shrug.

'The hardest part is knowing – and believing – you're telling the truth, even when the ones you love, your parents, don't want you to.'

I can't talk about what he did, I can't go into the details. All I tell her is that after that night, everything changed.

'I tried so hard to make sense of it,' I say. 'But the details of that night are unclear. What I do remember is trying to convince Mum and Dad to report him to the police. But Dad said it was a private family matter, not something to advertise in a broadsheet.'

Leila shakes her head and lets out a long exhale. '*God* . . . I had no idea.'

'I guess that's why I never wanted Stellans to get away with it,' I say.

She stands, staring out over the river, biting the nails on her right hand.

'Look, Rita. I know it's difficult, and I feel terrible for not being there for you, and I'm sorry, *really*, I am. But somehow . . . I can't deal with this right now. I know that sounds terrible, but it's too much. It's overwhelming.'

I listen to her talking, but her words float over me, passing by like feathers in the wind. I don't want her sympathy. I don't even want her understanding. I just want, in that moment, to shake off this secret, and a little empathy and compassion from the woman I've confided in. Leila continues, however.

'A man is *dead*, and you and I are suspects, not officially, but soon to be. I know this is hard – inconsiderate, even. But I need you to stay focused.'

I stand, shaking my legs. I light up a cigarette. She watches me smoke, fumbles around in her handbag and pulls out a packet of Camel Lights.

I consider what would happen if I continue – if I take it a step further and tell her about Stellans in the outhouse, just to punish her. But now it occurs to me that she'll think divulging my secret is simply a primer to help justify my actions. Most likely she will take *his* side, and not even let me finish explaining.

'I'm not like you,' she says. She takes me by surprise. 'I can't just bury things.'

'What does that mean, exactly?'

'We can't walk away. We need to face this and own it together. We've done nothing wrong, even though we were the last to see him.'

'But it's not that simple,' I say, stamping out my cigarette butt on the pavement. 'It's more complicated than that.'

'What are you talking about now?' She sounds annoyed – inconvenienced, even. I wonder when it was that things started to go wrong, how our friendship ended up like this.

I search her eyes, knowing that this is likely to be the last time they will look on me with some trace, however faint, of affection. I know I must tell her – I must tell her the truth now. But the words are lodged in my chest, clogging my throat.

'What *is* it, Rita? Why is it not that simple?'

I take in the full sight of her, the outline of her slender frame against the backdrop of London, every part of me feeling like a part of her. Her words, my words, this terrible story, now merged into one. But I can't speak. No matter how hard I try, I just can't do it.

She shakes her head and waves her arms about. 'You know what? I'm done with this, do you hear? I'm sorry about what you went through – really, I am. And I'm sorry about your parents letting you down. But right now, we have a *situation* to deal with and I feel like you're just trying to avoid things.'

'I'm not the one avoiding things.'

She scowls at me. 'I knew this was a mistake, you always have some sort of game to play – an *agenda*. You think you know better than me, don't you? Treating me like I'm stupid. Tell the police whatever you want. I'm leaving, Rita, do you hear me? I'm going to tell them *everything*.'

She leaves, but no part of me can follow her, so I watch her go, crossing the road, turning the corner and disappearing into the distance. I feel anchored to the floor, unable to move my feet. Reality morphs into a state of fantasy. I struggle to separate what is outside and what is inside of me. Beside the river, in the open air with pedestrians walking past, I feel myself sinking. I gaze out across the water, with its foamy lines and curling ripples, and I know this is surely the end. We make our own choices based on the cards we're dealt, and the choice I have made leads only to a dead end. I must do what I ought to have done all along. I must face up to the consequences of my actions.

That night, I walk along the river, a little tipsy. I've been drinking dark rum in Riverside Bar, just along the bank of the Thames. The air is crisp and dark; the cold chills and bites my fingers. I'm standing, staggering, beside the wooden O of Shakespeare's Globe, this place on the edge of London's South Bank feels all too familiar.

There's a heaviness in my body, pressing my weight down onto the floor. My steps drag, like this is the last walk I'll ever take. A part of me is reluctant to go on, another part aware it must continue.

I snuggle up in my puffy jacket, my head slow and sloshing. My face is hidden, but this time, there's no mistaking it. It's me. Not the other woman, who goes by other names, in search of men committing their heinous crimes. But me, Rita Marsh; with nothing to show for the good fight she gave in honour of her convictions.

I hear the water, waves licking against the stony barrier and iron gates, though for a second, I consider whether those sounds are inside my head. I've drunk way too much alcohol; all I want to do now is to forget. Approaching the edge, I climb up, staring down into the murky darkness. I'm holding onto the rail, onto the line that separates what is above from below, what is real from the unreal, and I lean forward. The cold bar presses against my stomach.

A breeze blows and I feel it cut into my cheek. I feel myself unsteady, up high, as I look on either side of me. People walking, talking, enjoying light conversation. Lovers linking arms, a woman roller-skating in headphones. People enjoying the evening air, before the harsh reality of winter draws closer. I stare out front, far into the horizon.

It seems like only yesterday I was here as Holly, but look at me now. I wonder what Zia's last thoughts were when he climbed the wall, overlooking the water's edge. Perhaps he is watching me, laughing at my predicament, wanting to thank me for the roses I left for him. He's ready to pull me down into the water, until it fills my lungs and nostrils, until it clogs my throat, that taste of river water and alcohol slowly choking me. He tells me how ironic it is that after everything I accused him of, we've ended up in precisely the same place; the two of us, hunter and perpetrator, Asian brother and sister, not so different, after all.

I grip onto the railing more tightly, then lift myself up on to my toes. There is nothing I want now. After all's said and done, I struggle to see how I can ever be happy. Nothing I do will ever right itself or be normal. In that moment, there is nothing but the end.

The wind is strong, and my hoodie slips down around my neck. I imagine I'll black out on the way down, that it would be better if I hit my head so as not to experience the sudden shock of the cold. I tiptoe higher, lifting my weight, feeling my calves strain. I drop my head back, opening my mouth wide, wanting to inhale and to taste the air one last time. The air is fresh, my nostrils flare. I take in a long, deep breath and wobble. I grab onto the edge more tightly until my knuckles are white. My head spins as I struggle to balance.

But then, behind me, I hear someone.

Panting. Short, sharp breaths, a long exhale.

'Are you alright, love?'

A man stands behind me, he can barely speak. He is breathless. I don't even know who he is.

'You don't want to do that. Whatever it is, it's not worth that.'

I relax my grip of the railing. I struggle to find the words to answer him; neither do I want to talk. I do not turn around; I just want him to go, to leave me the fuck alone.

'We can just sit on the edge and talk if you like.'

I want to tell him: I'm done talking. I've nothing more to say. What words are left when I tried to save the children, but I ended up failing them, and myself, instead? The only woman I love – have ever loved – does not love me. She cannot forgive me. I left a man in the woods to die, and now the police are coming to find me . . .

My ankles are weak, too weak to carry the weight of me and I feel myself growing giddy, and I reach out my hands on either side of me, trying to balance. I even laugh, since it occurs to me, I can be like a raven, soaring in the night sky, with nothing left to stop me, lifting higher and higher, true to my street name . . .

I hear a gasp. 'Easy, love,' he says, urgently.

I lower my hands, steadying myself with only a finger resting on the railing. I balance myself on the concrete edge. I'm clutching tighter onto the metal.

'I've got you, take my hand. No need to be afraid. I've got you, love.'

I feel him move closer, this kind, gentle man, speaking to me in a warm, authentic voice. He's pleading for me not to jump like he really cares, urging me to instead *trust* him. I feel the warmth of his thick fingers reach out for me, grabbing onto my hands. I feel his gentle tug and pull, easing me down off the edge, helping me to land safely on the pavement. As my feet touch down, I see, through watery eyes, a flash of London: the landscape inky, and a busy crowd, going about its business, faces blurred. There's a flash of lights, orange, white and blue, merging into one. In the distance, I hear seagulls.

Here we are, two strangers standing silently on the edge of the Thames in London, a city that thrives and is alive: a city that swells with secrets. Murder is the headline this city loves most, not my story, a story of a hunt and a trail that leads to no satisfying conclusion. The real story of how and why a woman begins hunting the worst kind of criminal in the first place.

The man, Mark, places an arm around me. A pocket of time expands and contracts, filling me with the events of my life. I see myself as a little girl in happier times and I so desperately want to reach out to her, to hold her. My shoulders drop and the tears begin to fall, but Mark simply moves closer, wrapping his arms around me with everything he has. He reassures me that sometimes the nights are black, but he says he's here, and available to talk whenever I feel like it. I sink into him; sink into his woollen jacket, soft against my cheek, smelling of boot polish, metal and of fish and chips. In that moment, we are one and I lose all sense of who I am. It hardly matters anymore. The two of us stand under the dark sky. The two of us are alone.

31

The next morning, I find myself back in Raven Court, walking around in a daze. I recognise the rooms around me – the living room, the kitchen, the hallway – but I remain disassociated from where I belong.

The place is quiet; thoughts don't stay in my head for very long. They seem to evaporate, as quickly as they come. I'm a hollowed version of myself, empty and broken, unsure; sure only that I can't continue as I am. I am different: raw, wounded, hunched under the pressure of everything that's gone on, though a deeper part of me is ready, just as I was always ready, to take responsibility for what I've done.

In my bedroom, I take down the box of photographs I've kept from school, the one containing the yearbook and several other remnants of childhood. I stare down at the girl I once was, a younger, fresher girl with short hair and a face full of hope. I want so desperately to talk to her, to appeal to the highest aspect of her and for her to listen to me. I want to dare her to choose something different, to convince her that she really can *be* something.

And then I do what I should have done all along.

I dial Javid's number, holding my breath as it rings. When he answers, I break, telling him that I need to talk to him, urgently.

'Rita, what is it?'

I tell him there are things he doesn't know; that he ought to prepare himself for the worst of it.

'What do you mean?'

I tell him I hope he'll still consider me his best friend, that when I'm done telling him my story, I hope – I pray – that nothing will have changed between us. He deserves to know the truth, regardless of his own opinion. He deserves to hear it from me, not DCI Lawson.

I swallow hard; I swallow hard to keep everything down. I can't go on as I am, I say. Did I ever tell him that his was the most meaningful friendship of my life? Javid is silent, then says, his voice panicked, that I'm scaring him.

I blurt out the words quickly, before I change my mind; before he has a chance to stop me, between the salt on my lips. The quick-fire juddering of my chest is so fast, I can barely utter a coherent sentence.

'Don't move. I'm coming over. Just stay where you are.'

He says he'll get in his car right now, that he can be over in ten minutes.

But I tell him to stay where he is. I tell him to sit down.

Then, in no uncertain terms, I give him my confession.

32

I killed a man. In trying to save the one I love, I've become a criminal myself. I struggle to comprehend how I, an innocent woman with good intentions, driven to free other innocent women and children, have ended up here.

My phone pings, and I stare down at the screen:

18.35 Clive_609
I like your profile.
You look gorgeous in your school uniform.
Much older than 12.

I'm seated in the first-class lounge at King's Cross Station, waiting for a train to take me to a safe house that Javid has arranged. My shoulders are hunched like a woman broken-boned, hair dyed dark and frizzing from the rain. My luggage lies beside my feet. Around me, cups and saucers clanging, the venomous hiss of a coffee machine. The screen above me flashes train times. A stream of ding-dong service announcements chimes in. I glance down at my phone, waiting for Javid's cue. I know, as sure as the crunch of handcuffs locked, that since confessing everything to him forty-eight hours ago, I must do exactly what he tells me to, to prepare my testimony.

18.40 Clive_609
Where are you, baby? You can't get rid of me that easily?
LOL x

I exit the Playground chatroom – I don't even know why I entered it in the first place. Perhaps it was a final moment to reconnect with the past, to bid farewell to what my life once was, because now I know, more deeply than I did before, there is no way of ever turning back.

It's ironic that those who hunt eventually get hunted down; falling prey to the transgression for which they hold others to account. I would be lying if I said it hadn't all been so addictive: the thrill of the confrontation, another one of those men, because mostly it's men, handed over to the police. But I never imagined this kind of poetic justice.

Train now on Platform 1 is the 19.06 London North Eastern Railway train, calling at all stations to Lincoln: Stevenage, Peterborough, Grantham, Newark Northgate and Lincoln.

Flicking my phone onto silent, I grab the handle of my suitcase and wheel it beside me as a cold breeze from the station foyer sweeps over my face. I make my way to the entrance and a cacophony of commuter sounds rushes towards me like lost children running to reunite with their mothers. Around me, trains arrive, trains depart. The low rumbling sounds of wheels grate against the steel tracks.

I slot my ticket into the machine and the barriers fling open. As I stumble through, I scan the station for a sign – any sign, indicating Platform 1.

18.45 Javid
I see you…. Leila will be here any minute.

There he is, just opposite Pret a Manger. I run towards the platform, past the attendant waving his hands at the driver, as if to announce that this train, at least, must depart on time. Carriages streak by in the corner of my eye, and for a second, I consider whether it is easier *not* to have to go through with it. I could end it now; throw myself off the platform in front of an oncoming train. It's not how I pictured the end, but at least it would be final. But I've been in that dark place before, and now I must move on, to focus on what really matters: preparing my testimony.

Javid stands up when he catches sight of me, his face worn, dark shadows beneath his eyes. He tries so hard to smile, to look hopeful, but I feel the full weight of his despair. He glances over at the train, as if he has already read my mind. He shakes his head and stares at the ground.

I remember what Javid was like at school, the only loyal friend I ever had; the one who stood by me for years and years afterwards. Now, here we both are, all grown up with many moments passed between us; both of us burdened with the weight of hindsight. I cannot shrug off the feeling that this is all a mistake, that I still have a chance to correct it.

Javid runs his fingers through his hair as I approach, scanning the crowds as if to be sure that no one is following us.

'Leila must be running late. I hope she turns up; we need her to verify she'll support your version of the story.'

My voice trembles. 'Do you think she'll come? Do you think she would do that?'

He glances around him. 'No idea. She's still in shock, as you can imagine. When I talked to her, she gave the impression she might. What you need to think about now is *you*. Not her. Focus on getting your story straight so you can go to the police before they come to you.'

'Did she say she would be here? We need to work together, you said so yourself. Did you make that clear to her?'

Javid looks down, like my questions are painful for him to hear.

'I did. But she needs time to process things, Rita. You can understand that, can't you? She hasn't gone to the police, yet. But she will.'

Javid clenches his jaw and I throw myself into his arms. That familiar scent of him, citrus and cinnamon, is a strong affirmation of who I am.

He pulls back. 'I'm so sorry. You know that, don't you? I'm just so sorry I can't represent you. I feel terrible, but I can't do it.'

I look down at my feet, my scuffed trainers, and I nod.

'You've confessed to me, and I can't mislead the court, nor put something forward which suggests you're innocent. Fiona Carter is great, she's one of the best I know. Tell her what she needs to know and that will help reduce the sentence . . .'

Another service announcement chimes in: *The 19.06 London North Eastern Railway train now waiting on Platform 1, calling at all stations to Lincoln, is ready to depart.*

'She'll do everything she can, I know she will. Stick to the plan. She'll meet you in the safe house and then you can take it from there.'

I swallow to keep the tears down, but my body is weak and my shoulders tremble.

Javid holds me at arm's length. 'You're doing the right thing, Rita. Coming clean means we have a better chance of lowering the sentence. I'm just so sorry I can't represent you.'

I nod, my throat constricting. 'It's okay, Javid. You've done enough. I could never ask that of you. Just the fact that you're here, as my friend, is enough.'

I lean against the brick wall, palms flat against the stone, trying to breathe easy. I need to get on the train, but Leila isn't here. Javid stands beside me, my luggage at my feet. My mind rushes: the station sounds and my own thoughts merge into one.

Javid looks around him. 'I don't know where she is. Look, we can't wait. You'll have to get onto the train.'

I hear Javid urging me to stick to the facts, to say only what needs to be said. Of course, there will be press attention, it is inevitable, he says. But I need to be careful about how I present myself, since we can't trust the police to paint me in a good light.

I'm not really listening, however. All I keep thinking is, how can this be the end when there are still thousands of predators out there, getting away with their crimes?

I grab my bag, heaving it off the platform. Beep-beep-beep, and in an instant, the doors close. I wait for a few moments before I look back through the window.

I wave to Javid, because to give him any more would mean I'd surely break down. What hurts me most is having to say goodbye to Javid like this. There are only a few people we meet in our lives, rare and precious friends, who are willing to stay with us to the end, no matter what the end looks like, no matter what we tell them.

I know Javid would never turn me in, but I know he is an idealist too. He struggles to understand the fight some women have inside them, the reason why we do this.

A station attendant approaches the door and pulls Javid away. I scan the platform for any sight of Leila, but it's clear she's not there. I blow Javid a kiss, a heartfelt kiss, my eyes welling, my chest full. 'I'm sorry,' I mouth back. 'I'm so sorry.'

I turn and walk down the aisle, as the train pulls away from the platform. I grab onto the railings, staring down the narrow carriage. Before me, rows of damp heads and hatted crowns. My hand brushes over the velvet tops of the seats as I falter down. The vibration of the train's engine tremors under my feet. My eyes are firmly fixed to the floor, I avoid the upward glances of passengers on either side of me. Though the carriage is barely full, it feels crowded.

I peel off my rucksack and take a seat near the window, the faint smell of coffee unfurling around me. I stare outside, sights skittering past; dusk streams over the buildings as the train gathers speed.

After a while, the sky darkens, streaking over the meadows, the rickety sound of the train over the tracks like a lullaby, coaxing me still. I breathe in deeply and close my eyes. A faint scent of calendula washes over me, a mist of indigo.

I am tired, so very tired. Tired of running; tired of this life. I just want to sleep and never wake up, for all the problems in the world to disappear.

Further down the carriage, I catch a glimpse of a shadow – a dark hunched figure in a coat, hovering. The sight of it moving, then shape-shifting through the small window of the connecting carriage.

Back gardens flash past to the side of me, and every now and then, the flash of a barren tree, scraggly branches hanging over a garden fence, slices through the scenery.

Leaning forward, I unbutton my coat, convinced I'm so tired I must now be imagining things. I slip my arms out to make myself more comfortable. I slide my phone out of my jeans – and I see a flurry of messages.

19.15 Javid
I promise you, Fiona Carter is the best.

19.16 Javid
I love you, Rita but you've GOT to face up to this. Never forget how strong you are. I know you can do it!

I call Javid. It rings once before he answers.

'Tell me again what you said to Leila,' I ask. 'I just want to know exactly what—'

I hear him sigh.

'I never compromised your confidentiality, Rita. I'd never do that. But she's figured it out. I didn't have to say much.'

My heart thumps inside my chest.

'Rita, you can understand why she wouldn't want to turn up, can't you? It was a big ask. You need to forget about her and concentrate on yourself. That's the only way through it.'

On the other end of the line, I hear Javid walking, the sound of commuters in transit.

I breathe heavily, concealing the phone under my hand so no one can hear me. 'But I need her for certain parts of the story to verify what Stellans did to her – so that the police will understand my motivation.'

'They know that already. It doesn't change things. Stellans is dead, Rita. It didn't ever have to get that far.'

'I did it for her. It was only ever for her, for the children. This was never about me.'

Javid hesitates. 'And before her? What about Raven Justice? Rita, for God's sake. What you did is unpardonable. In the eyes of the law, it does not make you a hero. You killed Stellans. You did that all by yourself. No one asked you to. I know you were defending yourself, but before that, a man committed suicide.'

I glance around me; a man in the seat a few rows down turns his head to look outside.

'She has her own lawyer,' says Javid, 'so I don't know what she'll say. Her primary motivation will be to protect herself, to present her side of things. I suggest you do the same.'

My body seizes. I'm trying to think and to take it all in, but my head is rushing, firing a million thoughts at once. There, towards the end of the carriage, I see it again: the shadow of a figure approaching in a long black coat, collar pulled high. My phone slides out of my hand and crashes onto the floor. I bend down, scrambling under the table, trying to retrieve it.

I keep my head down, holding the phone close to my ear.

'Javid, I think I'm being followed.'

He is quiet.

'What?'

'I'm serious.'

'Don't be ridiculous. No one knows where you're going. You're being paranoid.'

'I'm telling you, there is someone here!'

Javid hesitates. 'Rita, it's impossible.'

'Javid, please. You have to believe me.'

He sighs. 'Get off at the next stop. I'll come for you. I'll drive you to the safe house myself if I have to, but you've got to be there tonight. Do you understand? We can't wait any longer. We need to get to the police before they come to you, and by now, they'll be looking for you.'

I raise my head, but I can't see anyone there. I scramble out of my seat, struggling to balance; the train is moving fast, the rickety sound of the tracks beneath the floor is disorientating. I topple against the headrests as I shuffle down the carriage, my hips swaying, my hands slapping against velvet tops.

'Rita . . . are you still there? I know you're afraid. It's going to be okay. You can do this.'

The figure behind me, I am sure, is gathering speed. It's as if it catches sight of me and is ready to capture me. I'm running now, running down to the end of the carriage, certain that the figure behind me is chasing after me – that it is not my imagination. It is real.

There is a terrible crash – a tray of sandwiches knocked, commuters shouting and swearing at my back.

'Stupid woman! What the fuck are you doing? Watch yourself!'

But I do not watch myself. I do not stop.

'Rita, are you there? Rita, talk to me!'

The phone is still in my hand. But I'm at the end. There is nowhere else to run.

'Javid, someone is here, someone knows something, and they're after me,' I cry. I'm wondering if I'm going mad.

I hear Javid panting, the sounds of the station behind him; a crackle of interference on the line between us.

'What are you *talking* about?' Javid is shouting. 'Pull the lever and stop the train! Tell them you're sick and get off.'

In the corner beside the exit, I see it there, the lever – a shiny, red lever – and all I need to do is to pull it, to make it end, but the figure behind me is quick and lunges forward.

My head slams against the side, a blow, a shock. I feel nothing at first as I crash into the fire extinguisher, but then I stumble; there's pain – shooting pain – in my abdomen. I fall onto my side, but it is too late. After all this time, I cannot run. I cannot hide.

There are screams, haunting screams, a sound of an altercation between some of the passengers.

'Someone get him! There's a robber on the train! Stop him! Get him down, get him down, he's stabbed her! Jesus Christ! He's stabbed that woman!'

He's stabbed me.

I do not realise this person has stabbed me until I hear them say it.

I place my hand onto my stomach and feel the warmth of it.

I see a kaleidoscope of lights, flashing – whirling and swirling around me.

'Rita, talk to me! What's happening? Rita, are you there?'

Javid's voice is distant, but I still hear the low whisper and rhythm of him speaking.

Beneath me, the judder and grate of the train's wheels against the tracks pulls me in. A whistling sound, a long interrupted high note, punctures the air as the train slows and grinds to a halt. Voices fade in and out, fluttering like butterflies above.

A male passenger shouts. 'I've got him, I've got him!'

But I'm detaching from myself, like a witness to it all – no longer caught up in the drama.

A woman is clutching my hand. *'Madam, I've got you. There's nothing to worry about. I've got you. You've been stabbed, but we're getting help.'*

Gasps and cries. Footsteps running; bodies crashing into the side and into tables.

I hear another woman scream. 'Leave me the fuck alone. I know her, okay? I know her! She's a fucking bitch!'

My mind is playing tricks because this state appears real. That voice; I know that voice. It's Leila.

The male passenger again. He says he's got her. '*Can everyone help to pin her down?* It's a woman! She's stabbed that woman over there!'

'She deserved it. She ruined my life. Her name is Rita Marsh, and she is a liar and a murderer. She killed a man. I had nothing to do with it!'

Leila.

A man with long black hair and tattoos all around his neck joins me now – I am sure of this. I feel him. A grainy presence. He kneels beside me, the thick, calloused palm of his skin with all its rough bumps and ridges against my cheek. He holds my head. But perhaps now, I really am dreaming, fading, slipping in and out of the other worlds that the residents at Raven Court always told me existed.

Sounds around me converge; every impression begins to coalesce. There's a mist, then a single point of light, but this point, the point of it all, begins to disappear.

Then a flicker of blue, a rush of sirens.

'Police! Make room, please. Everyone, stay calm. Police coming through . . .'

Is that DCI Lawson?

I feel myself rising, skimming against water, travelling through air. I open my eyes and for a moment, everyone is there. A collage of faces of everyone I've ever met, and children, so many children, playing hopscotch and skipping ropes.

I'm flying, soaring with wings outstretched, the shimmer of my feathers catching the light – searing into the night. I experience, if only for just this moment, a sensation of freedom; transcendence from right and wrong and the liberty to be loved and to be who I truly am.

Rita Marsh. It's who I am now, it's who I always was.

Madam, you're okay. You're going to be okay. The ambulance is here.

In the end, whatever comes next, I could never be anyone else.

TEN MONTHS LATER

33

Life is never black or white, neat and tidy, *compartmentalised*. Life is complicated. More than complicated, life is nuanced. We can never know how things will turn out; all we can do is learn from our actions.

I've had enough time to think, and as I look back, of course there are things I regret. I regret I did not die that afternoon on the train. That somehow, I woke up in a miserable blue room in Northwick Park Hospital with paint peeling off the walls, tubes sticking out of my nose and mouth. That I recovered and ended up in here, in HMP Bronzefield Prison, where the walls are phlegm green and the place smells of fags, and farts, and disinfectant.

Bronzefield was purpose-built for law-breaking women like me, somewhere on the outskirts of Ashford in Surrey. To think this town, once voted 'best place to live', is just over twenty miles from Harrow-on-the-Hill. It's criminal to think that's even allowed, to lock people up so close to their own homes, near busy markets bursting with life, fresh produce, the beautiful expanse of coastlines washing beaches carpeted with glistening sand. It's an additional layer of punishment on top of an already hefty sentence.

Eight months have passed since I was sent down, amid the furore, the outcries, the endless press attention. I can still hear the sound of the demonstrations, when permitted, real and virtual, of people shouting, screaming, holding up placards, chanting, *Justice for Raven Justice! Free Rita Marsh!* Spike and Spider were at the front, leading the coalition, dropping their grudges the minute they heard that one of their own needed help. I was touched by that – touched by their show of support. As I walked up the steep steps into court, everyone finally knew my name – it's not something I will easily forget. The long line of sombre, straitjacketed police, trying hard not to grow agitated, was a little less surprising.

Javid always said my case would attract attention, that it would be smoother if I told the truth, told them how it all started. First, with catching paedophiles, next with self-defence, a wound from a broken heart, the stab of childhood friendship. I thought it would be easier if I gave them my confession. I even thought that maybe, with Coronavirus ravaging the streets, the authorities of this great nation might have better things to deal with. But as it turns out, they wanted to make an example of me, hold me up to the other hunters, to the general public, as a way of demonstrating how *not* to do things. At my hearing, Judge Nelson, speaking through his facemask, took pleasure in reminding me that the police uphold UK law for good reason. *There's been too much deviation from it for me to let you off lightly . . .*

I received ten years for manslaughter. Fiona says it's not as bad as it seems. I'll only serve seven. They took two years off my sentence for helping the police out as Raven Justice, which the public don't know anything about. But, if it all goes well, and I'm good, I'll be released from prison in late 2024, after serving five years.

But there are other things I regret too, about being inside. I regret not being able to say goodbye to Leila, to offer some explanation of what happened concerning Stellans. Though I dropped charges against her for stabbing me, it didn't seem to help. She let me know, via her lawyer, that she wants nothing to do with me. *Ever.*

I also regret not having a proper conversation with my parents now that I see the value in talking. There's a counsellor in here and I've been giving it a go, exploring this notion of therapy, socially distanced, talking a bit about my childhood experiences.

Today, I have a visitor. They won't tell me who it is. I'm to wait until the warden calls my name so that I can be escorted into the waiting room. I haven't had a visitor for a month. The last one was Javid. He brought with him self-help books and *Women's Digest* so I can read Geeta's Corner. He's checked in on Raven Court after I closed its doors; says I ought to feel reassured there's been no break-ins, vandalism, graffiti on the side walls, as we prepare for sale.

It's cooler in the waiting room than in my cell. This afternoon, a few of the other inmates I know are in here. There's Annabel, inside for fraud and corporate theft, whose husband comes to visit. And then there's Keisha, inside for armed robbery, meeting her girlfriend. As I wait, drumming my fingers on the wooden table, cheeks hot behind this facemask, I see a beige trench coat, the sight of sensible, grey shoes.

'Hello, Rita. That is the name you're using in here, I take it?'

His voice is muffled, speaking behind his facemask, but the tone is unmistakable.

I do not look up. I have nothing to say, nothing to be ashamed of, though I fear, more than anything, additional complications.

'Very funny,' I say.

'How are you keeping?' Lawson says. 'Hope they're treating you well. Terrible this turn of events in the world. Who could have imagined?'

'I'm well, thanks for asking,' I mumble.

Lawson leans back in his chair, crossing his legs, placing his hands behind his head. 'You'll be out in no time,' he says. 'Back to being the Rita we all love and despise.' He chuckles. 'But so much wiser than when you first arrived. Now that is surely something.'

I snort, clutching a pebble in my pocket. It's one I found on the beach, the one time they let me out on good behaviour. They allowed us a trip to the sea, would you believe; an immersion in the raw, natural elements, designed to clear our minds and to rewild us. They see it as good for the rehabilitation of offenders. With everything going on in the world, there is greater sympathy for inmates.

We sit there for a while, Lawson and I. Lawson makes small talk, cracking a few jokes. Mostly, I'm bored. Much to the irritation of the other visitors, I remove my facemask to smoke – but when the warden gives me a stormy glare, I put my cigarette away.

Soon, the hour is over, and the room empties. Lawson stands, nodding discreetly to the warden. The warden nods, then leaves us to it. That's when I know that something is up – that there's more to this meeting.

Lawson takes out a file from his briefcase and pushes it towards me from across the table.

'Thought you might find this interesting.'

I glance up at his face, take in the sight of his eyes more acutely, warmer, gentler than I remember them. A new wife making his stomach so much rounder with cakes. 'What is it?'

'Take a look,' he says, taking a seat once again. 'You've nothing else decent to read in here.'

I turn over the cover.

On top is a brown envelope. I open it up and see a picture of Leila, a close shot of her face. She's smiling, but she looks older, and her hair is different, cut short, tucked behind her ears.

I slam the file closed and push it back to Lawson. 'I don't want to know.'

He leans back in his chair. 'Just thought you'd like a reminder of what she looks like. She pays a price, too. Just as you do now. A victim – and that afternoon on the train, she turned into a criminal. You were kind to her, of course,' says Lawson. 'She got away with stabbing you. Got away with lying to the police about that night, too. Her destiny is different, it seems. Oh, by the way, did you know she's moving into teaching?'

I bite my tongue.

'English Literature.'

My stomach pinches, and I feel an ache, close to the wound now stitched and healed. I don't want to hear any more – and pull up my facemask. I don't know why he's here, winding me up like this, but I can hardly leave.

'Must get to you, the injustice, the irony of it.'

'Not really. She was never the problem,' I say. 'What she does now is up to her. There are bigger issues in the world to deal with.'

'She got off because she doesn't have baggage, I suppose that makes it easier to move on, but you—'

'What about me?' I ask.

He leans forward. 'You're more than one woman. Made for different things. Deep down, I know you're a good person, Rita. I've always known that. You're a bit of a loose cannon, but . . . I could do with a good woman onside, one who knows a few things.'

I stare down at the file.

'Keep looking,' he says.

I open the file and place the brown envelope to one side. I begin turning over the next page, and see a line-up of different women, all dolled-up and glamorous, like they might be about to film a make-up tutorial for YouTube.

'Sophisticated, aren't they? And notice . . . all women.'

'I had noticed.' That's Lawson for you. Still so highly observant.

'It's not what you think.'

'Enlighten me,' I say.

'They run the biggest child trafficking racket in Europe, out of London,' says Lawson. 'Luring then grooming children online – but not just online. Many of the kids they've groomed disappear in broad daylight. They target mainly gaming platforms, in groups, where they know kids will bring in their friends, because they are innocent and don't know any different. This group is another level, Rita. I'm not talking common paedophiles

– although, as we both know, they're bad enough. These women are running a trafficking *business*. They take their time, they're clever, *sophisticated*. They plan and then prey on the vulnerable in the virtual and real world. They'll plan for at least a year or more, playing the long game, building up trust online, forming a *deeper* relationship. And then . . .'

I swallow hard, unable to move in my seat. 'Why are you telling me this?'

'Lockdown has moved kids online in greater numbers. There's no getting away from it. It's a new world out there, and these criminals are taking advantage. How about it, Rita? Want to help? I could do with a woman on the right side of the law. One who knows her way around the internet.'

I bite my lip. I tell myself again and again: I don't want to get involved. *I don't want to do this.*

But then I leaf over the next few pages, and there they are: pictures of the children. Boys, girls, toddlers, teens. There's even a newborn baby, swaddled in a cellular blanket.

'They also have a special target,' says Lawson. 'The children of immigrants. See, they're particularly vulnerable. Children are disappearing from the street, bundled into cars; immigrant children snatched from their families on their way to being housed. Children unaccompanied because they've lost their loved ones.' Lawson twitches.

I feel sick, so sick.

'If you're interested, I'll have it arranged.' He leans back in his chair. 'We'll give you some privileges, naturally.'

I turn my face away.

'Cigarettes, gourmet food, a job with real *purpose* – one that gives you a reason to live. And of course, there's plenty of outdoor exercise: the beach, markets, that kind of thing . . .'

I hold my breath. I face him. 'We discussed this before, remember? I'm not interested. What makes you think I will change my mind now? I get mad, don't you get it? I can't control my anger.'

'You're inside. You've plenty of time to reflect on it. Besides, there's not much else you can do when you're already locked up. When you're out, of course, we'll explore what comes next. We've got a few years to experiment.'

I shake my head. 'I don't know.'

'We can explore anger management. Look, I respect you, Rita. I don't want to change who you are. All I ask is that you work with us, not against us. Channel your energy, your frustration, so that this time, you can make a positive difference. Let's do it properly. Organised. Legitimate. In collaboration, not in conflict, with the police.'

I run my fingers along the edge of the file. I want another cigarette. As if by instinct, Lawson reaches into his coat and throws me a packet.

'This is the future,' says Lawson, 'and you know it. You've *always* known it. Police and vigilantes, working together – within the law.'

I run my fingers over the photos, the faces, delicate faces, of the children.

'These coalitions mean well, but they exert a dangerous kind of influence. We can't hide from the fact that the problem is huge, and it's getting worse. The police need to do a better job, granted. But we're doing our best. Collaboration, Rita. It's the only way I see it working. Just say the word.'

That night, whilst lying in my single bed, sheets cold and crisp, pillow thin like a slice of bread, I dream of my parents. They're seated in the lush grounds of Raven Court, drinking rosé, talking about the care home, how it's doing well – far better than they imagined – how in time, it will require stronger management. Mum and Dad keep drinking, oblivious to my presence in the kitchen, watching them. Dad says opportunities like this don't come often. The priority is to make as much money in the UK as possible.

The image fades. I see an image of a playground: swings, a slide, a roundabout spinning fast with Disney characters whizzing past. Parked prams and three-wheeler bikes, scattered. The green, full of children flying kites, throwing and kicking balls. I turn, and just then, I see a man and a woman skirting the edge of the field. They're watching the children, leaning into one another, whispering.

I dart out of my bed in a cold sweat, rushing to the sink, and I throw up. I splash cold water onto my face, patting my cheeks down with a towel, staring into a mirror of warped metal at the woman I am now. I sit down on the edge of the bed and open the file that Lawson insisted I take away with me, leafing through the pages, until I get to the back. I notice something I didn't see before. A green folder.

I open it up. A photo. I recognise that face.

I'm staring at a photo of a child with dark hair, piercing blue eyes. I know that face so well. It's my face. The photo is one from Greenwood Primary School, one of those official photos. I'm wearing a chequered dress, summer uniform, set against a backdrop of grey curtains. I've got goofy teeth, two teeth at the bottom missing. Freckles, before they eventually faded. I must be around seven or thereabouts, before anything bad happened. I've a big smile, full of hope, a head filled with so many dreams about what I'll be when I grow up.

I know Lawson's game. He wants me to remember who I really am, to ignite that raging fire and motivation. I don't know how on earth Lawson ever got hold of this photo.

In that moment, I realise, the world is different. But in many ways, the world is the same. I can be whoever I want to be because my essence does not change.

I am Nisha, I am Amadi, I am Krystiyan, I am Jane. In my face, every girl and boy you could ever meet, every child broken and in pain.

I'll get them in the end. I always do. I'll hunt them down, one by one, because I know how to.

I know who they are. I've always known who they are. I know where they live. I can reinvent myself again when I get out and find them when they least expect it.

Five years *is* a long time, but I don't need to wait five years.

This is the revenge of Rita Marsh.

You have been warned.

ACKNOWLEDGEMENTS

I created Rita Marsh and her fictional world to help channel my anger and outrage concerning a societal issue that disturbs me the most. It's taken a unique group of people to help me midwife this novel into the world.

Thank you to my wonderful husband, David (Raju) Chauvet, who never once questioned why I spent so much time scribbling. A writer can only write professionally if there is rock-solid support in place. From David, I also receive unconditional love. To my children, Yelisse and Dharmil Chauvet, thank you for accepting your mother's need to spend long periods in solitude, honouring the writer's call. I will never be able to make up for lost time, but always remember how much I love you. To my wonderful mother and father, Gauri and Ramjee Patel, my two elder sisters, Sangeeta and Meena Patel, and my nephew Dylan Patel, who encouraged me all the way, never once doubting whether this book would come. To my agent, Nelle Andrew, who pushed me to do better and to be better. Her early editorial insight – and, dear God, boot camping – has been instrumental in making Rita as strong and powerful as she is. To the incredible team at Faber, Louisa Joyner, Sara Helen Binney, Hannah Marshall, Hannah Turner, Phoebe Williams: you rock! Thank you for your incredible support and for believing in Rita as much as I do. To Chris Norman, Founder & CEO of GOOD, my business partner and dear friend, thank you, in general, for never telling me to slow down or that I can't do it all. I am tremendously grateful to you for entrusting me with the legacy of your life's work, whilst respecting that I must also complete mine.

Thank you to all those who read early drafts of Rita and offered constructive feedback to help elevate the words: Jonathan Barnes, a teacher and writer whose words, '*This* is the one,' were precisely the confirmation I needed, at a time I needed it most. Jane Mackelworth, Don Hunter, Jean Hyland (from City Lit's Advanced Writing Masterclass Group). Rebecca Lewis, Tracey Weller, Emma Lowther, Megan Preston Elliott, Rosemary Amadi, alongside our mentor, Ayisha Malik (from LWA's 2021 CFG group).

Finally, to the team at Spread the Word, organising the London Writers Awards, particularly Ruth Harrison and Bobby Nayyar: thank you for offering me a much-needed early career platform. Your work promoting equity, diversity and inclusion in publishing is truly phenomenal and is as essential now as it ever was.